DON'T OPEN THE DOOR

AN UNPUTDOWNABLE GRIPPING PSYCHOLOGICAL THRILLER WITH A BREATHTAKING TWIST

COLE BAXTER

ILLUSTRATED BY
NATASHA SNOW

EDITED BY
ELIZABETH A LANCE

CONTENTS

Mailing List   v

Chapter 1   1
Chapter 2   13
Chapter 3   23
Chapter 4   31
Chapter 5   43
Chapter 6   51
Chapter 7   59
Chapter 8   67
Chapter 9   75
Chapter 10   85
Chapter 11   95
Chapter 12   103
Chapter 13   111
Chapter 14   119
Chapter 15   129
Chapter 16   137
Chapter 17   145
Chapter 18   153
Chapter 19   163
Chapter 20   173
Chapter 21   181
Chapter 22   189
Chapter 23   201
Chapter 24   209
Chapter 25   215
Chapter 26   225
Chapter 27   235
Chapter 28   245
Chapter 29   253
Chapter 30   263
Chapter 31   271
Chapter 32   279
Chapter 33   287
Chapter 34   295
Chapter 35   303
Chapter 36   311

Chapter 37	323
Chapter 38	331
Chapter 39	339
Epilogue	347

THE PERFECT SURROGATE

Chapter 1	357
Chapter 2	363
About Cole Baxter	371
Also by Cole Baxter	373

To get updates about new releases, please follow me on Amazon! You can also follow me on Bookbub! Or join my reader Facebook group! Sign up for my VIP Reader Club and find out about my latest releases, giveaways, and more.

CHAPTER 1

Marc stood over the body of a monster he'd just killed, needing to make sure it was actually dead. He was panting like crazy, like he'd just run a marathon.

Aside from the sound his respiratory system was making, there was a distinct dripping noise. Small droplets of blood traveled down his bloodied hand, down his blood-drenched blade, and fell to the ground. The melodic sounds they made were almost soothing, almost beautiful.

Also, the sound was definitely in the dichotomy of the carnage that happened inside this abandoned house. Or was it?

Marc had no idea it took such a great effort to hack another man to death. He'd killed many times before; however, that was with a gun. The knife was a completely different story.

It felt more personal in a way, not to mention exhausting. His knife kept hitting bones, sticking into all the obstacles, and he had to use great strength to pull it out, to finish the job the way he wanted to.

Nevertheless, it was exhilarating to do it the old-fashioned way. Marc felt alive like never before. He was aware of his surroundings; all of the smells, sounds, and small flutterings in the air, like never before. With this small action, he felt transformed; reborn.

In other words, he liked it this way much better and couldn't wait to get *hold of a better knife for the next time. Because there would definitely be a next time. He needed to feel this again, this rush, and soon.*

"Samson?"

His wife's voice snapped him back to reality. He was so engrossed in writing about his protagonist that he'd completely spaced out and forgotten where he was.

Samson was sitting in his office, like always, writing on his computer, like always. He was not in a dark, stinky, rotting crack-house following his favorite monster. And according to the New York Times bestsellers list, America's favorite monster as well.

It was important to be reminded of such stuff every once in a while. Of his whereabouts, not that Americans had a strange taste in literature. He almost chuckled at his bad joke.

Samson looked at the number of words he has just written. *Not bad.* Still, he was irked at the interruption. Marc was about to experience the surprise of his life when a true monster entered the game. It amused him to write about hunters becoming the hunted.

"Samson?" Teresa repeated impatiently.

With a sigh, he stood and followed the sound of her voice. She was in the bedroom, and he leaned against the door frame, taking in her frantic behavior. "Yeah?" He had to clear his throat. It had been a while since he'd uttered a word. It wasn't because they were in a fight or something – far from it – it was just because he had been writing all morning while she did this.

"Have you seen my blue sweatshirt?" she looked up long enough to ask before returning to her task. Their bed looked like she had dumped the entire content of their closet onto it.

There was a good chance she had actually done that. It certainly wouldn't be the first time. What was the question again? Sweatshirt. "No, I haven't."

"Could you check the laundry basket?"

It would not be prudent of him to point out how she was closer to the bathroom than he was, so he only said, "Sure."

Teresa looked stressed enough, like she always did as she packed for a trip. Being a real estate broker, she traveled for seminars a couple of times a year. That didn't mean it got easier over time.

She had the urge to pack the entire house just in case, never knowing what she might need while she was away.

He had tried explaining to her multiple times she didn't need any of those things, but it was in vain. She was simply stuck in her ways, feeling more comfortable like that, in peace, as though in control, and he had learned to let it be. Because he loved her, craziness and all.

"It's not in here," he reported dutifully. "Maybe it's in the laundry room."

He already knew she would send him there next and started walking on his own.

Usually, Samson would accompany her on these trips to act as a voice of reason, but this time, he had to stay home and write. His deadline was approaching, and that made him nervous since he was nowhere near finished. Like all writers, he had good and bad days. Lately, he felt like all of them were bad.

To make matters worse, Teresa wasn't traveling for business, she was going to visit her parents, and Samson was genuinely sorry he would miss that. He wasn't one of those people who hated their in-laws. Mike and Jenny were great people, and they treated him like a son, which he appreciated greatly, being an orphan and all.

At the same time, it would be nice to have the house to himself.

Oh, the fun I'll have. It would be true Netflix and chill in its literal meaning. He would watch all the movies he wanted and chill all by himself. He chuckled at his own joke.

"Is it there?" Teresa yelled from the bedroom.

For a moment, he'd forgotten what he was doing. He was sent on an important mission of finding one of his wife's sweatshirts that she liked to wear around the house. It was too old and mangy to serve any other purpose.

"It's not," he yelled back, returning upstairs. He could hear her curse.

Why would she need that old thing in the first place? He dared

not ask. Eight years of marriage taught him it was better to stay ignorant regarding certain things. He returned to his previous position by
the door, not daring to enter while she packed.

"Take one of mine," he offered.

"They're too big on me," she stressed in return, folding a third or
fourth pair of almost identical-looking jeans and putting them in the
suitcase.

She was on the petite side, and he was tall and lean, but he didn't
see a problem. It wasn't like she was going on a business trip and
needed to look her sharpest. She was visiting her mom and dad, and
he was sure they didn't care what she looked like as long as she was
healthy and happy.

At the same time, Samson knew Teresa cared what she looked
like and needed to have appropriate outfits for all scenarios, which
apparently included an old sweatshirt, and that was why he
remained quiet and let her deal with this on her own.

She eventually found several substitutes, but he could see that
she wasn't completely satisfied with any of them. So logically, she
decided to pack them all.

Samson could only stare at his wife and shake his head when she
wasn't looking.

Deciding to let her be until she needed him again, Samson
returned to his office and started editing the section he'd written that
morning. It didn't take him long to once again completely forget
about everything else and practically become Marc on his killing
spree anew.

A couple of hours later – or mere minutes, Samson couldn't tell
for sure – his wife demanded his attention once again. She always
interrupted him while he wrote, and that bothered him at times. It
felt like she had no concept of the importance of what he was doing.
To her, his writing was merely a hobby. The fact they were living
quite well thanks to his hobby because millions of people bought his
books never seemed to cross her mind.

"Samson, it's time for you to drive me to the airport," she yelled from someplace in the house. It was good they had such great acoustics.

Most of the time.

"Coming," he replied, making sure he saved his manuscript. It was tragic how many times he'd forgotten and learned to be more mindful the hard way.

This time, he wasn't annoyed by the interruption. He was fairly satisfied with the section he'd managed to write. Besides, he was the one who insisted on driving instead of her taking a taxi. It would be good to spend some extra time with her before his week-long solitude.

"Hurry up," she prompted. "I don't want to miss my flight."

It was rather ironic that she would blame him for her tardiness and not herself since she had an almost a chronic inability to pack like a normal person. Samson felt like he would sprain all his muscles while picking up the oversized suitcase she'd chosen for the trip. Of course, she had another, slightly smaller bag that she carried.

"Are you one hundred percent sure you packed everything?" he asked her as he dragged the huge, heavy, suitcase downstairs. The thing was heavy like a motherfucker, and he envisioned taking a week to nurse himself back to health.

Cut the crap, you're not that old.

Joking aside, if he didn't know his wife, he would suspect she was smuggling a hacked-up dead body in that thing. Stuffed with some rocks, was implied.

Seeing her worried expression, he realized too late what a mistake he'd made. *You stupid idiot.*

"I'm sure there are perfectly stocked stores in Pasadena, too, if you forgot something," he added in reassurance.

"You're right," she said offering a small smile as he sighed with relief.

Dodged that bullet. Teresa would most definitely miss her flight if she tried to open this monstrosity to make sure she had all the things with her that she would not need.

They were at the front door when Teresa dumped everything in her arms onto the floor and rushed back inside, running up the stairs.

"Where are you going?" he asked, although he already knew the answer. She'd forgotten something.

He tried so hard not to laugh every time he saw her running. Even he, who was supposed to be a writer, would have difficulty explaining what was happening with her legs in those moments. For some reason, from behind, it looked like she was making circles. It was strange that she didn't take flight at some point. Not to mention it was a miracle she wasn't constantly kicking herself in the ass. It was funny as hell yet endearing. She looked like a little girl in those moments and not a grown woman.

Teresa reappeared half a minute later, carrying her toothbrush.

"You could have just bought another one," he couldn't help teasing.

"Not like this one," she replied instantly, raising her nose ever so slightly. It was obvious that simply going to the store had never crossed her mind.

Teresa always had trouble admitting when she was wrong. Some would call that prideful, but Samson considered that one of his wife's many charms. Charms, by his definition, were all the quirks of a person, good or bad. Besides, her charms made teasing her that much more enjoyable.

"Ready?" he asked, preparing to lock the door. He really felt like he'd strained a muscle dragging the suitcase to the car. *I'm getting old*.

"Yes, and please hurry," she prompted. "I don't want to have to run across the airport to catch my flight."

He tried picturing that. There was no way she could run with the bags she had, but the image almost made him smile. Checking the time, he reassured her that something like that wouldn't happen. Even if they got stuck in traffic, she would still have plenty of time to spare at the airport, just the way she liked it.

Fifteen minutes later, he was cursing himself to hell and back for having that unfortunate thought because they were stuck in traffic.

Damn it.

"I really wish you'd taken a different way."

Samson gave his wife a look, because as far as he was concerned, the only direct route from their place to the airport was the airline, and the last time he checked, their car hadn't come with a pair of propellers to turn it into a helicopter. This was the only route.

He didn't feel like arguing, so he remained quiet. They sat in silence for the next couple of minutes. Teresa didn't care for listening to music, so he indulged her.

"Oh, come on. Move, you idiot," Samson burst out all of a sudden, startling his wife a little as he honked at the driver in front of him who was too busy texting to realize that the line had moved forward.

The line of cars in front of them looked like it went on forever. Although Teresa didn't say a word, he knew she blamed him as though she expected him to have some kind of a superpower to would help them avoid it. Her behavior irked him to no end.

It didn't take long for another moron to raise his blood pressure even further. "What the fuck are you doing?" Samson raged, using his horn profusely as another asshole tried to cut in front of him.

"Samson, calm down," Teresa snapped.

"Did you see what he did?" he yelled. "I could have hit him!" It would have been his fault for the crash and not that dipshit's, and he would be responsible for the damages.

"But you didn't," Teresa pointed out, as though that made all the difference in the world.

He couldn't believe that she was this calm about this whole situation. That was because she wasn't driving. If she were in the driver's seat and had almost hit that car, she'd be livid, too.

Samson wanted to get out of the car, drag the other man from his – preferably through a cracked window – and beat him to a pulp. Maybe that would instill some manners into him, and he would think twice next time before trying to cut in line.

"You're doing it again," Teresa's voice broke him from his reverie. "Calm down."

He was prepared to snap at her again and demand to know what she meant by that, but his jaw was clenched so tightly that he wasn't able to. He was also squeezing the wheel so hard his hands ached, so it was pretty self-explanatory what she meant.

It took everything in him to calm down enough to loosen his grip and relax his jaw. He was really losing it. The blind rage he experienced lately scared the shit out of him; not that he would ever admit it.

He was a man. It was perfectly normal to get angry. It was all the testosterone in him, causing havoc.

Just keep telling yourself that, asshole.

"Honestly, Samson, you really should get over yourself already," Teresa's words put an end to his inner monologue.

"Excuse me?" he inquired, turning to look at her. He knew Teresa became frustrated with his condition quite often, but she had never talked to him like this before. She certainly had never used that tone of voice before.

"Years and years have passed since you were in the war. You need to move on. It's not healthy."

Samson could only gape in return. He didn't know that PTSD had an expiration date and felt like thanking her for that piece of information.

It can *have an expiration date if treated properly,* he thought, then chastised himself immediately. He didn't need his conscience teaming up with his wife against him.

"I'm trying," he replied in a much calmer manner than he felt.

"I know, but it's all in your head. If you could just adjust your attitude, I know you can move past it," she encouraged. Teresa's tone was now much softer, so Samson nodded.

"I know."

Miraculously, the caravan of cars, trucks, and buses began to move forward again, sparing him from further discussion about his screwed-up head. After all that, he'd still managed to get his wife to the airport on time.

Teresa liked to be there a bit earlier, and she never expected him to linger with her, which he appreciated. If there was one thing he hated in this world, it was waiting for anything, anywhere.

The idea of having nothing to do but wait for his turn drove him insane, which said a lot about his personality when he thought about it. He was sure that his version of hell would be an endless line of people waiting for nothing, and never reaching their turn.

He banished that thought because it made his heart start to beat a little faster. That was some scary shit. He had to remember that for his next book.

Samson parked in front of the building. "Here you go, ma'am," he announced in a strange accent, trying to imitate a chauffeur from one of her favorite movies.

"Thank you kindly," she played along.

"That will be two passionate kisses and one big hug," he deadpanned.

She adjusted her glasses, somewhat lost in thought. "I don't know if I have that much with me."

"That's okay. I'm sure we can come to some kind of an arrangement." He waggled his eyebrows, and she chuckled before they kissed.

"Please do something about this hair of yours while I'm away," she said as they parted.

"Why? I thought you liked it shaggy."

It *had* gotten longer than usual, but he kind of liked it.

"It *does* make you look younger."

"Just what I've been going for."

"Behave, while I'm away, okay?" she warned in a teasing tone.

He laughed at the inside joke. To anyone else, it might sound like she was warning him not to cheat on her, and that was by design. In reality, she was warning him not to make a mess out of the house because he was known for making extreme messes when left to his own devices. Not even the military had managed to cure him of that.

"Yes, ma'am," he replied dutifully, earning himself another kiss.

Afterward, he helped her with her suitcases.

"Hug Mom for me, okay?"

"Of course."

"Love you."

"Love you, too."

Samson waved goodbye as she went inside. She was strong for such a petite woman, he had to give her that.

He hopped back into the car. Freedom awaited him, and he had no clue what to do with it. He loved his wife and their marriage.

Many of Samson's friends complained constantly about their wives and children, but he could say with utmost honesty that these eight years with Teresa were the happiest times of his life. Their marriage wasn't a fairy tale; they had problems just like all other couples, but at the end of the day, this was it for him, what he aspired to achieve.

Before he'd met her, he had been in the war, patrolling deserts and fighting for his life. Killing insurgents was the only thing he knew how to do, and he was good at it. There was no room for love or happiness in those days. Samson had been constantly surrounded by death and destruction. He'd lost a lot of friends in that damn war.

So maybe he wasn't the most reliable to judge such things. Who cared, as long as he was living his dream and was happy? And he was, despite the horrors he still carried with him.

Thank God he had Teresa. She was the best thing that had ever happened to him, period. She evened him out.

He only wished she would be a little more understanding of his condition. He knew she loved him, and he knew she worried about him greatly, but at times she acted a bit callous.

She was impatient for him to get better. He was, too.

If he was being completely honest, he *had* gotten a lot better. He was a mess when he was discharged, but he'd learned to adapt to normal life over time and lost a lot of the triggers that plagued him.

An occasional nightmare or angry outburst could not be avoided, especially not while he was stuck in traffic with a bunch of idiots. All the same, it was getting pretty manageable, or so he believed. Teresa disagreed, of course.

He was triggered far less often than before. After the war, he was so trigger-happy that he got rid of his firearms, frightened he would end up harming someone, including himself.

Now when he got stuck in the traffic, he played his favorite music and sang loudly, and that helped a little.

"Move it, you asshole," he boomed, honking. The music helped, but no one was perfect. Especially since there were idiots out there who understood nothing but a foot in their asses.

Samson drove home. Despite teasing his wife that he was going to throw a big party and invite the entire neighborhood, they both knew he would spend a quiet week at home, working and watching TV.

Maybe grab a beer with his best friend, Malcolm.

There was work to be done, and if anything helped with his PTSD, it was writing his novels. Through them, he managed to channel all the emotions, thoughts, and frustrations he wouldn't know how to deal with otherwise. The fact that his publishing house and readers loved them to the point that he could make a living out of writing was a big bonus and a true blessing.

Come on Marc, let's play.

CHAPTER 2

S amson went to work very dutifully, with discipline and full attention. He was slightly concerned that he wouldn't be able to meet the deadline his editor, Hunter, had set for him, so he didn't want to waste time. Although he was sad that he'd missed the chance to spend time with his in-laws, it was more important to stay home and write.

Ah, the glamorous life of an author. He spent time alone in a stuffy room, describing life and all the intricate circumstances, twists, and turns he wasn't getting to experience. *The irony.*

When he reached his word quota for the day, Samson decided it was time to eat. Standing up, he stretched, and that was followed by a lot of cracking noises. He loved what he did, but sitting down all the time was seriously fucking him up.

He'd been in constant movement, engaged, and mobile all his life, so all of this sitting-down crap was not for him. Alas, he was doomed to that until some genius invented a device that could convert his thoughts to paper without intermediaries.

In the kitchen, he opened the fridge and made a mental note that he would have to go shopping tomorrow. He couldn't live solely on pizza for a week, although he was tempted to give it a try.

Not feeling particularly hungry, he made himself a quick sandwich and ate standing at the counter. That was one of the things he learned while being a soldier: *Sleep wherever you can, for as long you can, and eat whatever you can, wherever you are.*

Those habits hadn't left him, although he struggled with the sleeping part. The nightmares had lessened, but they were still as brutal and soul-wrecking as the moment they first began. Usually, he dreamt about people he was forced to kill and people who were killed in return.

Samson had terrible nightmares about his time in Afghanistan. It was hard to watch his friends die in battle, blown to pieces by the makeshift bombs the terrorists liked to leave for them all over the abandoned cities.

He knew there were millions of ways to die on this earth but only a few were as torturous, monstrous, and sadistic as being blown to pieces.

The lucky ones would die instantly, but the rest... the rest could continue being for quite some time. And he intentionally chose that word – *being*, not living – because a pile of meat left behind wasn't capable of anything else.

Forcefully, he cleared those images from his head. For him, lingering on them felt like inviting the nightmares to be more frequent. Samson needed something to do because the worst thing for him was to sit around and think about the past. That never ended well.

He didn't feel like returning to work, figuring he'd earned some downtime. He knew his mind wasn't a well of words that could dry out, but he didn't want to take a chance. Especially not so close to his deadline.

Checking the time, he realized he had plenty of time before his workout session.

What to do?

Looking about as he finished the last bite of his sandwich, he knew exactly what he *should* be doing, and it wasn't Netflix and chill. He would leave that for tonight.

His tornado of a wife had left quite a mess in her wake, and since she'd warned him to keep a clean house, he decided to tidy it up a little.

He started with the dishes, both because he loved her and was just a tad bit scared of her, especially when she was pissed off. She was tiny but feisty. Samson smiled. He already missed her. This house felt especially empty without her.

He washed and dried the dishes by hand, not daring to use the dishwasher without supervision. There were a lot of things that could go wrong, hundreds of ways he could screw up, and he wasn't taking any chances.

Afterward, he folded all the discarded clothes neatly and returned them to the closet. He didn't bother to dust or vacuum, reserving that for the last day before his wife returned. Until then, he had no problem breathing his own skin cells. He'd inhaled a lot worse while serving.

With that settled, he was pleased to see it was time for him to go to the gym. Grabbing his gym bag, he hopped in the car. It was kind of ironic that he had to use a car to go exercise, but the gym he liked was a long way from home, and if he jogged there, that would be his exercise for the day, and he preferred something more rounding than a running session.

Samson had never cared much about working out, but one of the requirements when he was a soldier was to be fit, and he continued doing it because he wanted to stay healthy. He always felt much better afterward, although during the training, especially when dealing with large weights, there were times he felt like a sadistic bastard for punishing his body in the first place.

There was another reason he was so keen on exercising as much as possible: It was a great way to deal with his anger.

"Hey, Samson," a girl at the reception greeted him.

"Hey, Sam," he greeted back.

"Hey, Samson," another woman said in passing.

"Hey, Tina." She was one of the regulars that preferred to do her workouts in the afternoons just like he did.

"I read that book you recommended," Samantha said, offering him a locker key.

"What'd you think?" he asked, accepting it.

"It was amazing."

"Glad you liked it." He'd recognized early on that she was a fellow lover of the dark fantasy genre.

"Hey, Samson," greeted another girl whose name he couldn't recall.

"Hey."

After exchanging a few more pleasantries with the receptionist, he started walking toward the locker room to change. On his way there, his trainer, Pete, met him.

"Hey, Samson," he said in an overexcited way, in a high-pitched voice, mimicking the girls who'd greeted him. Pete was convinced that Samson could have any girl he wanted.

Happily married, he brushed it off easily, but it felt good on some level to hear it, anyway. He was pushing forty, and his deployments had left serious marks, physically and mentally.

So, it was good to know he still had it.

"Hey, Pete," he greeted in the same manner he had all the rest.

"Ready to party?"

"Sure."

Nodding, Pete went to prepare everything for them as Samson changed.

Although Samson would never act on anything, he had received a couple of invitations for drinks from regulars. He never told Teresa. He was faithful to his wife, but he was also no idiot. Some things did not need to be said.

He had turned all of them down, politely but firmly, making sure they understood he would never cheat on his wife. Perhaps it was a bit ironic considering his former occupation, but Samson refused to cross certain lines.

Kill a bunch of people is a-ok, but cheating is a big no-no.

Changing, he went to find his favorite trainer. And it was no surprise to find Pete flirting with some woman. He was young and single, so it was allowed. He told Samson he had this job specifically because he could do two things he loved most: Train and hook up.

That didn't mean the kid was unprofessional. He abandoned his latest conquest the instant he spotted Samson, then grinned like a motherfucker. "Let's get down to business."

And he meant it.

Half an hour later, Samson had lost all the previous thoughts inside his head. There was only the here and now for him. The pushing, the pulling, the endless counting, and of course, the endless pain.

"Come on, old man, give me one more," Pete encouraged in his usual manner.

Samson gritted his teeth, mustering all his remaining strength, and pushed his limit ... or what he believed was his limit. It always surprised him when he did more than was expected or required. Pete always knew he could, and that made him a great trainer, even at his young age.

"Perfect." Pete accepted the weights from Samson as he tried to sit up straight. The last couple of pushes had almost killed him.

But you did them anyway.

His trainer threw a water bottle to him. Samson's hands shook so badly, he barely managed to catch it.

"This was brutal," he commented as he tried to catch his breath.

"You did great. I'm proud of you."

Samson greedily drank the entire bottle of water although his trainer cautioned him to pace himself. He couldn't.

"Ready for another set?" Pete asked him a minute later.

"You're a funny guy," Samson grumbled, which made the other man laugh out loud.

"You told me not to go easy on you," Pete pointed out between the cackles.

He had, and that was a clear sign he'd suffered brain damage in Afghanistan.

"I didn't think you would actually try to kill me," Samson deadpanned. That was saying a lot, coming from a retired soldier.

"Come on, it's time to do legs."

"Great." Samson followed behind him. Leg cramps would make him forget about the upper-body inferno he felt.

Another half an hour later, the torture known as exercise with a personal trainer finally ended. Pete was funny like that. He always insisted they stopped after an hour, saying how the body would simply get overtrained otherwise and how it wouldn't produce desired results. Samson's complaints that he only wanted to stay in good shape, not end up pumped like the Hulk fell on deaf ears. Pete had his own ideas, and that was that. Samson rolled with it.

A normal person would go straight to bed after that, but as was obvious, Samson wasn't a normal person. Besides, this was his first night of freedom, and he wanted to celebrate it in some way.

He honestly couldn't remember the last time he and Teresa had been apart. And he took that as a good sign that neither felt like running away from the other.

Time to party, he thought with slight amusement. His definition of a party had definitely changed over the years.

Returning home, he flopped onto the couch, deciding to relax for a bit. He had showered at the gym, and his hair still felt a little damp. *Maybe I* do *need a haircut.*

He fished his phone from his pocket and dialed Malcolm.

"Hey, Sam, what's up?"

He was the only one who called him that, and Samson never minded.

"Hey, Malcolm. Teresa went to see her parents, so I'm home alone."

"Home alone, you say? I hope you're behaving," the other man jibed.

"It's disturbing how much you sound like her," Samson lobbed in return. What it said about him – that his best friend and his wife shared so many similar traits – he wasn't prepared to analyze. Ever.

"Thank you for saying that, asshole."

"Want to grab a beer at the bar?" Samson offered.

Malcolm liked to visit a very specific bar since because it had flat screens on every wall on which all kinds of games were played nonstop. Malcolm was almost an addict when it came to sports. And it wasn't limited to football: If it was played with a ball, chances were that Malcolm knew everything about it and loved it, not to mention knew all the players and their stats. He was like a savant.

"I can't. We're having a family night and playing board games. Wanna join?"

"Nah, I'll pass."

Malcolm chuckled. "Can't say I blame you. We tend to get a bit competitive."

That was putting it mildly.

"Some other night, then."

"Sure," his best friend agreed before disconnecting.

Samson took a deep breath and exhaled loudly. The house felt empty. He missed Teresa milling about, telling him about her day. The daily things that happened to her simply because she dealt with people were insane. And people were crazy. He should know.

Maybe I should write a book about her adventures, he mused, but for that, she needed to be here, telling him all the stories.

Was it weird that he missed her so intensely?

Maybe he wasn't *missing* her per se, maybe he was just feeling the absence of noise. He fired up the TV. It was tuned to a golf channel, but he didn't bother to change the channel. The announcer droned on in an extremely monotone voice.

Teresa could talk for hours without getting tired, and he loved hearing her speak.

And the funny thing was he'd never had problems writing while she was doing that, mulling around, popping in to see how he was doing every once in a while, and having a quick chat. He liked those small breaks with her. Even when she was watching TV – and loudly – he could continue describing the world hiding inside his head without a problem.

He wondered if his ability to work despite the noise around him came from the fact that he had been in a war where he was compelled to do his thing in far worse circumstances, under pressure, and surrounded by danger.

What was TV noise compared to that?

As it turned out, the silence made him uneasy. He turned off the TV to prove himself wrong. He wasn't.

At times like this, when he was confronted with himself, warts and all, he was slightly saddened that he and Teresa had never had children. Teresa never wanted any, was enjoying her life too much as it was, and he was okay with that. Samson never felt like he was missing something in his life, at any rate. They shared a great life; why ruin it?

There was enough suffering, pain, poverty, destruction, and disease in this world. Why condemn an innocent child to all that? Was that too cynical? Hypocritical? Samson couldn't be sure. And where did that attitude come from, anyway? His childhood wasn't bad. He'd had a great mother who loved him and would have done anything for him. And she had. She was a single mom and had struggled greatly to raise him. They had been poor but happy.

Samson had nothing but respect for his deceased mother; however, there were times he felt like he was the reason she had struggled so greatly. Who knew what her life would have looked like without him in the picture? Better? He was sure of that.

They had barely managed to make ends meet, even though she had worked two jobs, sometimes three. It was expensive being poor; he understood that now.

Samson had enlisted as soon as he was eligible, to help the weight on her shoulders. Sadly, not even that had saved her from an early grave. She died while he was overseas. He didn't even have a chance to go to the funeral and say his goodbyes. That was why he still visited her grave almost every week. *I love you, Mom*; he sent a prayer to the heavens. *I hope you're happy.*

Realizing he was throwing himself into all the dark parts of his soul, Samson decided to stop his train of thought. Stop with the thinking, period. Nothing good came of it, anyway.

I just miss Teresa, he tried to reassure himself.

This was a moment when his brothers-in-arms would call him a wuss, or a whipped man. Samson never gave a fuck. He loved his wife and was never ashamed to admit it.

He texted Teresa to call him the second she landed because otherwise, he would worry about her.

With that settled and his mind once again locked tight, Samson grabbed the remote.

"Let's get this party started," he said to the empty house.

He browsed through a list of horror/action movies, looking for something new to watch.

There was no surprise he liked that genre. It was the focus of his writing as well.

I wonder if they'll ever make a movie out of one of my books, he thought. He was excited by that prospect. Not that anyone was offering, but it would be special.

Teresa hated horror movies, and she had never read his books. She found them too scary and gruesome, so with her away, this was the perfect opportunity for him to sit around and indulge since he wasn't one of those people who would torment their partners on movie nights simply because it was his turn to choose the movie. He made sure they watched something they would both enjoy.

But now, the TV was all his. That got him excited, like a little kid.

When he found something he liked, he set everything up and ordered a pizza. While he waited, he went to the kitchen and made a shitload of popcorn. He even found some stashed Twizzlers and grinned because Teresa hadn't found them and eaten them.

Samson was going for the full experience. Once his pizza arrived, he placed everything on the coffee table in the living room. The final touch was the bottle of cold beer he grabbed from the fridge before he parked his ass on the couch and started the movie.

This is the life, he thought, taking a sip of his drink and a mouthful of popcorn. It was pretty salty, just the way he liked it. He settled for a gruesome action flick.

Samson was sure this spot would become the center of his universe for the week, and that was okay. The movie he chose, *The*

Dark Road, did not disappoint despite the cheesy title. Maybe cheesy titles were part of the charm.

Samson remembered a time when he liked a different kind of action film: He used to love watching war movies. But after living through such things, he preferred to watch something else. Watching actors playing war did something unpleasant to him. In a way, it pissed him off to remember how it looked. No matter how realistic they tried to make those movies, the reality was much worse.

That was why he avoided them. Who wanted to have all those negative feelings while trying to relax? Certainly not him. It was imperative to avoid any kind of triggers on his journey to full recovery.

Malcolm told him how one of their buddies from the war, Trent, cracked under the pressure and started going to therapy. Samson believed he wasn't so far gone to need to seek help from a stranger. He was dealing with it on his own and making money while he did.

Besides, he liked dealing with things on his own. After doing it all his life, Samson didn't know any different way to live; to be. That didn't mean he judged people who sought help. He felt everyone should choose their paths.

Then the main character on the screen just lost his head – literally – and Samson grimaced, taking a sip of his beer.

"Wouldn't want to be you, buddy," he said while saluting with his bottle.

Was talking to himself a bad sign? He brushed it off. Everything was fine unless someone talked back to him.

Not that he cared much either way. As far as he was concerned, watching horror movies and enjoying extremely greasy pizza that he washed down with domestic beer was pure heaven, insane or not.

CHAPTER 3

"The flight was okay, except that the woman who sat next to me stank of stale cheese for some reason, and I had to breathe through my mouth the entire time," Teresa complained to him once she called to check in.

Samson sympathized. "Luckily, it was a short flight. Imagine going across the Atlantic with her," he teased.

"Don't say something so horrific; I already feel sick to my stomach," she whined disgustedly, and Samson couldn't help grinning.

Sometimes, their sense of humor differed.

"How are Mike and Jenny?" Samson changed the subject, feeling like his wife was traumatized enough without his weirdness.

"Sad that you didn't come with me."

Samson was sad about that as well, but unfortunately, work came first. *Maybe one day, when I sell my movie rights, I won't have to work this hard.*

"Next time," he promised.

"Oh, and Lara came home, too, so we're going for coffee tomorrow."

Lara was her high school friend. Samson had heard a great deal about her over the years but had never gotten to meet her.

"That's nice."

"What are you doing?" she asked in return.

"Watching some movies."

"Horror movies?"

"Is there any other kind?"

He could hear her rolling her eyes, and it amused him to no end. They talked for a bit longer before disconnecting.

It was only ten o'clock at night and Samson had already watched one movie, eaten practically an entire pizza, and was ready to continue.

He debated whether to grab another beer even if he wasn't finished with the current one. It was probably better to pace himself. He had work to do in the morning, and he had learned the hard way that he couldn't write jack shit hungover. The same could be said for drunk.

But at the moment, he didn't want to think about the fact that Teresa was on vacation, not him.

He refocused on the task at hand: choosing another movie. "Let's see," he mumbled to himself. "What am I in the mood for?"

He wanted something special this time around. Pure carnage wasn't going to cut it. He wanted an amazing story, too. Samson wanted to be wowed, and if that made him a snob, then so be it. *Sky-high piles of dead bodies but with meaning,* he joked.

Samson had always been fascinated with death. Even before he started writing about it, even before he went to war and experienced it all around him. So, it made perfect sense that he chose to watch another movie filled with it.

As the movie started, he grabbed the bowl of popcorn to finish it off. *This is going to be good*, he thought, since the first shot was of a man getting strangled with a homemade catch pool.

Cool. It was fair to say he was hooked and couldn't wait to see what would happen next.

Ever since he started writing, he'd developed this strange talent. After watching something for a short time, he could predict what would happen next with pretty good accuracy. At first, he was quite impressed with himself, but eventually, he got bored. There was no point in watching something if he already knew how it would unravel.

These first couple of scenes took him completely by surprise and saw that as a sign that it would last until the end of the movie.

Gloomy music began to play as a heroine tried to get her bearings. He hoped she wouldn't die right away. Sadly, everything suggested she would be killed in the next couple of seconds.

Samson was really into it, anticipating it. How would it happen? Where would the killer come from? Subconsciously, he stopped breathing and leaned forward.

Will he kill her, or won't he?

All of a sudden, there was a frantic knock on his front door and Samson jumped, spilling some of the popcorn.

"Fuck." His heart went into overdrive. His first instinct was to run to the bedroom and grab a gun from the safe that he no longer owned.

You are not in any danger, he tried to reassure himself, as he attempted to clean up the mess.

The knock persisted.

"Fuck," he grumbled again. His senses were not what they used to be. *I'm getting old,* he thought, setting the bowl of popcorn on the table.

The knocking continued as he recovered. It even became more frantic, though he didn't believe something like that was possible. Someone was seriously trying to get his attention.

Mission accomplished.

Then, the doorbell rang as well.

"Coming!" he yelled, getting up with a grunt.

There goes movie night, he grumbled, having enough presence of mind to put the movie on pause before dealing with this inconvenience.

He was surprised at how late it had gotten and wondered who could be at the door. He wasn't expecting any late-night visitors.

Maybe it's Malcolm, he thought as he walked toward the door. Maybe his wife, Anita, finally got sick of his inability to play board games like a normal human being and kicked him out. He chuckled at the joke even though he didn't want something like that to happen. Malcolm and Anita were a solid couple. At times, he believed they were better at this marriage thing than he and Teresa were.

Then again, Malcolm wouldn't be violating his doorbell like this. Or would he? He was known to try to mess with Samson whenever he could.

Samson looked through the peephole first. *Old habits die hard.* Even in at home, he was forever assessing and looking for threats. He was taken aback by what he saw. Two young girls stood on his doorstep.

"Oh my God," one said, patting her arms as though she was freezing. The other one, who was doing all the knocking, was trying to reassure her everything would be all right. They looked pretty young, no more than twenty, even with all the makeup they had on.

Samson opened the door without further delay. The look of relief on their faces was confusing.

"Hello, sir," they greeted almost in unison.

"Hello, how may I help you?" he asked politely since he was sure he'd never seen either of the girls before. None of his friends had children this old, and besides, he was good with faces. He had to be, to distinguish friends from foes.

"We're so sorry to bother you, sir," the one closest to him, a brunette, started to speak. "Could we maybe use your phone?"

"We lost ours," added the other, a blonde. Not the natural kind, but perfectly dyed.

They looked pretty freaked out, and they were freezing their asses off. Samson couldn't help wondering what had happened, since his house wasn't on the main road. Nobody came here unless they lived here. This was the suburbs, and he gave the neighborhood a quick sweep, trying to assess any threats. The neighborhood was quiet; dormant.

These girls were not from around here, or he would know their faces. He remembered everyone he'd crossed paths with, which was a blessing and a curse. On one hand, it gave him an endless supply of characters for his novels. He could still remember what all of his teachers looked like – the ones from the middle school, too – and all the prom dates and cashiers at the stores. On the other hand, he could remember, with painful detail, the face of every man and woman he'd killed. They haunted his dreams and plagued him in nightmares.

"Sir, could you please help us?" the brunette prompted while he mulled over all that crap.

Usually, he didn't like to get involved, but these girls looked like they truly needed help, and he would kick himself if he didn't at least try. If Teresa was here, they would be already inside with tea in their hands.

That sprang him into action and Samson remembered his manners. "Of course. You can come in if you want or I can get the phone for you if you prefer to stay outside."

He gave them options. He was a stranger, after all, so he wasn't about to assume anything. There were a lot of weirdos in this world and women, especially young ones like them, needed to be careful.

Which was sad, but the world they lived in was full of predators.

"I'd like to come inside," the blonde said. "I'm freezing."

The other nodded in agreement.

"Sure, come on in," Samson said, stepping to the side.

"Thank you very much," said the brunette, with an expression as if he'd just offered food to starved men, which only further piqued his curiosity.

What the hell happened? And why didn't they have their phones with them? He was under the impression that the younger generation was practically glued to their phones.

Samson didn't like to assume. He was much more comfortable dealing with facts, but he could sense something bad happened.

As he closed the door, the girls looked around, unsure about where to go next or what to do.

Samson solved the puzzle for them.

"Just walk through there," he said, pointing toward the kitchen, realizing too late that his cell phone was in the living room.

He offered for them to sit wherever they wanted. The brunette chose to sit on a barstool at the kitchen's small breakfast counter, and the other girl followed suit. Samson went to the living room to fetch his phone.

"Here you go." He placed it on the counter next to them. Neither moved to accept it. He noticed they were shaking.

"Do you want me to turn up the heat?" he offered.

"No, thank you," muttered the brunette. "You have a very lovely home."

"Thank you."

Samson tried to be polite and mindful of the strange situation but he wasn't blind. They were attractive girls, and their clothes further accentuated that.

The brunette was tall. Not like him, but close, and she had a mane of long, curly hair that looked a little damp. Was it raining? He hadn't noticed. *Maybe it rained then stopped.*

He turned back to the brunette. Her features were almost aristocratic, which went great with her piercing brown eyes. Looking at her brought to mind those regal portraits of queens of the olden age.

The other one was slightly younger and the complete opposite apart from also being beautiful. She was a petite blonde, curvy, with radiant blue eyes. In short, she was a complete knockout and looked like the type of girl Samson had always chased when he was younger. *Much, much younger,* he corrected.

Samson cleared his throat, needing to clear his head although he wasn't quite sure how one action would help with the other. Come to think of it, Teresa was a petite blonde when they first met, but nowadays, she preferred to keep her hair natural-looking. She had a very nice light-brown color that always looked a bit sun-kissed.

"Call whoever you need to call," he offered, pointing at his phone.

"Thank you very much, sir," the brunette said, picking it up.

"You totally just saved our lives," the other one said with relief, clearly grateful they were here and safe.

"Lissa," the other warned, as though irritated that the other girl had spoken out of turn. Her next words confirmed as much. "This kind man doesn't need to hear about our drama," she said before looking at him. "We'll just use your phone then be out of your hair," she promised.

Was she afraid he would kick them out?

Samson heard what the blonde girl said and couldn't pretend he didn't. If they were in some kind of trouble, he wanted to hear about it.

"What did you mean by that?" he asked the blonde, ignoring everything else said by the other girl.

The girls looked at one another as though unsure of what to do next.

"You can trust me. If anything happened, I just want to help," he reassured.

Those were the magic words.

"It has been one crazy night," the blonde said with a sigh.

"You wouldn't believe us even if we told you everything," the brunette added with a wave of her hand. She was trying to pretend like nothing happened.

That only made him want to hear the story more. His interest was piqued. The writer in him was dying to know what forced them to appear on his doorstep in the middle of the night looking for help. The soldier in him wanted to learn if there was a threat that he wasn't aware of. The threat, he would have to deal with. The protector in him just wanted these girls safe and sound, out of harm's way.

That was why he said, "Try me."

CHAPTER 4

"I'm Candi, by the way," the brunette introduced, "and this is my sister, Lissa."

Sisters? He wouldn't have guessed that in a million years. They looked nothing alike. But genes could be like that sometimes. They liked to mix and match as they pleased.

"Samson Chase," he offered in return.

They shook hands.

Was it his imagination, or had Candi's hand lingered for a few seconds?

"So, what happened to you girls?" he asked in all seriousness.

"A double date from hell," Lissa whined, making a disgusted face.

Was that all? Something told him it wasn't. If a boring date was the problem, they wouldn't have ended up in his house in the suburbs. "What went wrong?" he prompted.

"We met a couple of cute college guys online," Candi started to explain.

Always a wise choice, Samson grumbled to himself. Perhaps he was too old, but he didn't understand this online dating crap. *You can't hold hands with a screen. You can't touch or kiss it, either.* Besides, so many things could go wrong when dealing with someone online. Didn't these girls understand the potential danger they faced?

Watching them still shivering slightly in the middle of his kitchen, Samson realized that they probably *did* know, especially now.

They should have been more careful.

Samson tried to be sympathetic. They were young, and young people made mistakes. How else would they learn?

"And?" he asked. He didn't want to appear pushy if they didn't want to talk about it, but if they were harmed in any way, they should tell him. He could help. He wanted that. Regardless, he would let them speak in their own time, and at their own pace.

"They came and picked us up," Candi replied with a half shrug.

It was on the tip of his tongue to ask for their names, but he refrained from interrupting.

"They looked super cool and well-dressed," Lissa added, as though that was important.

"I was supposed to be on a date with Dylan, and Lissa, with Chad."

"But we switched," Lissa added with a sheepish smile.

He didn't need to know all those details but remained silent nevertheless.

"Anyway," Candi interjected as though fearing her younger sister would say something even more embarrassing. "We drove around for a while and had some fun."

Was alcohol involved? He couldn't smell any.

What about drugs? Samson didn't ask. He wasn't their father.

"Then Chad, my date," she continued, "mentioned that they were taking us to some private party."

Samson didn't like where this was going.

Lissa scoffed, taking over. "He drove us here, in the middle of nowhere."

Samson resented that. He thought this neighborhood was great. Nice-looking houses, friendly people, and a lot of trees. He also realized those things wouldn't interest a young girl.

"And then he parked the car in some dark parking lot."

Samson believed he knew the spot she was describing. It was quite a walk from there to here, he realized.

"I see," he said simply. Samson didn't need to hear any more to know what happened and wasn't that surprised it had come to that. Based on what they'd told him, they met with the guys expecting to party.

He didn't blame them … not that he was trying to defend those idiots. The average young man thought about sex practically nonstop, but that didn't mean they should do things like that.

Boys should be taught from an early age to have more respect for girls. Samson believed it was wrong and shortsighted that only girls were taught to be careful, and that, on the other side, no one dealt with boys.

"They treated us like sluts," Lissa practically cried out, snapping him from his reverie. She looked hurt and offended.

Samson panicked a bit, hoping that she wouldn't start crying. He didn't know how to deal with that.

"Boys are idiots at that age," he blurted out, trying to comfort her.

"I think men are idiots, period," Candi grumbled in return before she straightened up and offered a small smile. "However, there are some exceptions."

Was she referring to him? "What happened then?"

"They tried, you know, to make us give them head," Candi explained as though she were talking about the weather, and Samson tried not to react to her choice of words.

"Which we didn't do, of course," Lissa said haughtily, flipping her hair. He was glad to hear that. It was good that they had standards.

"I mean," Lissa continued, unaware of his musings, "the least they have done was buy us dinner first and pay for a hotel."

That settled that. "Right," Samson replied, not knowing what else to say.

They are so young, he reminded himself. He was a stranger. And this conversation was extremely inappropriate. That did not stop him from asking, "How did they react to that?"

Candi smiled humorously. "In a usual douchebag way. Chad went ballistic."

Had the guys harmed them in any way? He couldn't see any visible marks, but that meant nothing. Even if they had just scared them, it was unacceptable.

"Especially after you told him there was no way you would do it, even if his dick was the last one in the world," Lissa pointed out.

Candi shrugged. "I'm not sorry for saying that."

"You shouldn't be. They were dicks," Samson blurted out before realizing what he'd said. He'd relaxed too much, and that wasn't good. He wasn't their friend.

"Exactly," Lissa agreed with a grin. "And I'm sure they are limp dicks." She laughed at her joke.

Did young girls talk like this nowadays? He was not a prude – hell, he swore like a sailor – and Teresa, too, was known for saying something extremely dirty in the right situation, but this felt different.

It made Samson feel ancient.

"Did they hurt you?" he demanded.

They shook their heads. That was a relief because otherwise, Samson would hunt them down and deal with them swiftly. He was a true believer in reaping what you sow. If these boys walked around tormenting girls, then it was only fair – just – that he do the same to them. Maybe that would teach them some manners.

Samson balled his hands into fists. The hunt would be exciting, as all the rest had been. He could already see it happening. They would beg for mercy, cry for him to stop, and swear they didn't mean it, and Samson would be deaf to their pleas. He realized he was looking forward to the prospect of crushing some bones. *They didn't do anything,* he reminded himself. And that made him calm down.

That was close. He was really on the edge of doing some crazy shit. Perhaps Teresa was right: He needed better impulse control.

"Mr. Chase, are you all right?" Candi asked.

The girls had witnessed his quick trip to Angerville.

"Fine, and please call me Samson. I'm not *that* old," he tried to make a joke to distract them from what had happened. Or *might* have happened.

"Ok, Samson," Candi replied, grinning as though enjoying the informality.

"So, how did you end up here?" he asked next, steering them back to the topic.

"Well, after Candi so colorfully declined to have sex," Lissa started, "Chad got super mad and started yelling."

"What about the other boy?" He wanted to know.

Both girls made faces. "Dylan is a follower, so he did what Chad did."

Samson nodded. He got the picture. So, Chad was a top dog or at least tried to be one. And that was a shame. When a person who distinguished himself as a leader was a douchebag, as Candi put it, all the minions acted accordingly.

"Chad said I was nothing but a cock tease," Candi revealed.

"And Dylan said I was so stupid I couldn't find a dick even if he put it in my mouth," Lissa added, looking genuinely hurt.

"I hope you told them to fuck off."

"Sure, and then Chad demanded we get out of the car."

"What? He threw you out?" Samson asked incredulously.

"Yes," Candi confirmed. "I said he should at least take us home after being such a disappointment, and he said we deserve to walk for leaving them with blue balls."

"He literally pushed us out of the car. Dylan helped, of course," Lissa added, upset all over again.

"Unbelievable," Samson commented since there were no other words for what had happened. Those boys had left them in the middle of nowhere as an act of revenge.

He wanted to hunt them down and scare them shitless; see how they liked it when the tables were turned. It was time someone taught those boys that no matter how big they got, there was always someone bigger in the shadows.

"The worst part is that they took off with our purses in the car," Candi added.

"They took your stuff with them?"

That was theft.

"Our phones were in there, too."

Everything made sense now, and Samson was very upset by what had happened. Despite their sometimes-colorful language, they appeared to be good girls. At any rate, they didn't deserve this.

"They didn't come back for you, or try to return your stuff?"

Samson hoped they'd had a change of heart.

"I yelled after him to at least throw our things out the window, but he just laughed and drove in a circle around us before taking off," Candi explained.

"They didn't come back," Lissa added. "We waited forever." At that moment, she looked her age, vulnerable, and scared.

It made his blood boil, and he again had to force himself to calm down. They were okay, he reminded himself. It was good they'd found their way to him.

"We waited for about fifteen minutes," Candi corrected, "before we decided to try our luck and start walking."

"These shoes are *not* made for walking," Lissa pointed out, dramatically raising her leg so he could see and sympathize. Samson knew jack shit about shoes, but the stilettos looked dangerous, their thin heels at least five or six inches high.

He nodded dutifully.

"Luckily, we saw the light on at your house," Candi wrapped up the story.

"And you opened the door," Lissa added with a grateful smile.

Candi smiled too, so he did the same in return.

"Well, I'm glad everything turned out okay in the end."

"We're very grateful you let us in," Candi said, placing a hand over his.

He moved away, feeling slightly uncomfortable. "So, who are you going to call? Your parents?"

"God, no," Lissa replied with a snort.

"Can I have some water, please?" Candi asked before looking at her sister.

Samson nodded and poured a glass for each of them.

"Thank you," Candi said, downing the whole thing in one go.

I guess she got thirsty speaking. "Want a refill?"

She shook no.

"I need to call Kristina," Candi said, answering his previous question. "That's our friend."

"She has a car, and she can come to pick us up," Lissa added as Candi started to dial.

" I can drop you off somewhere," Samson offered. They didn't have to bother their friend for that. What if she was asleep? He didn't have anything better to do.

"It's not that simple. Kristina's our roommate, and we need her because—"

"You don't have keys with you," Samson finished in her stead, realizing the problem. If they didn't have their purses or phones, it was safe to assume the keys to their house were missing as well.

"Exactly," Lissa nodded.

Those creeps had messed with them good.

Candi frowned.

"What is it?" he asked.

"Something's wrong," she said, looking at his phone. "I don't think the call is going through."

"Do you have service here?" Lissa asked with genuine concern.

She acted as though they were in the middle of nowhere, which they weren't. Of course, he had service. Always.

"Let me see," he asked for his phone, and Candi returned it.

She patted his hand lightly as she did and Samson brushed it off as an accident. Candi stood from her chair as though interested to see what he was doing.

His phone appeared to be working just fine. He had full bars. Regardless, he shut it down and turned it on again.

"Try now," he encouraged, returning the phone to her. She was still standing too close to him, to the point he could smell her perfume, so he took a step back.

Candi followed him. "You know, this was very nice of you," looking at him with doe eyes.

"Very nice," Lissa added like a backup singer.

"Thank you. You saved us."

"It's nothing. Anyone would do the same," Samson replied, a bit self-conscious.

"Hardly," Candi disagreed.

It was understandable she would be slightly bitter after what happened to them tonight.

Lissa agreed. "I agree with Candi." She then hopped off of the barstool and took the phone from her sister. "Let me try."

"Okay."

Lissa then left the room, leaving them alone.

"Not all men are bastards," he tried to joke again.

"I can see that." Candi was looking him straight in the eye as a small smile danced across her lips.

Samson had experienced real-life death situations in his life, but this girl was making him nervous. Uncomfortable might be a better word for the state he was in at the moment. Especially when she grabbed his forearm and gave it a little pat.

"Samson?"

"Yeah?"

"I hope there's some way I can repay you for your kindness."

Her meaning was pretty clear.

"That's not necessary," he replied, taking a couple of steps out of her reach and only stopping when his ass hit the stove.

Why did he feel so trapped all of a sudden? On a few levels.

That didn't change the fact he was, quite literally trapped, since Candi approached anew. Her tenacity was impressive, as was her confidence.

She leaned against him, placing both hands on his chest. "But I want to," she said seductively, licking her lips ever so slightly.

This is not happening, Samson panicked. Very gently but firmly, he moved her away and strategically moved quickly across the room from her. Retreat was the only thing he could do. He felt much better with the dining table between them.

Despite everything, he didn't want to hurt her feelings. She had gone through enough as it was. Was that the reason she was doing this? Not that he would engage himself in analyzing her behavior. The only thing that mattered was that it needed to stop and for that, he had to set her straight.

"Thank you for the offer, but I'm happily married."

He showed her his wedding ring for good measure. Candi looked at him funny in return. That uneasiness persisted. "Besides, I'm too old for you anyway," he said, trying to make light of the situation.

"You're not old, Samson. You're experienced."

Oh my God.

He was about to reply – he wasn't sure what, exactly – when Lissa saved him from further embarrassment by returning to the kitchen. He practically sighed with relief. That was too close. Not that anything would have happened: He would have turned her down without a doubt. He just felt uncomfortable dealing with it in the first place. He didn't want to be cruel like those boys were, but if she persisted, he would have to be firmer. Luckily, it didn't come to that.

"Did you manage to reach your friend?" he asked her, eager to change the subject. He completely ignored the fact that Candi continued to look at him funny. Was it in astonishment? Wonder? Confusion? Disbelief that he'd said no? He couldn't tell, but he was ignoring it.

What he would do to be that young and confident again.

"Yeah. She's in the middle of something, so she said she'll call me back."

"In the middle of something?" Samson repeated like a parrot.

"She's having sex with her boyfriend."

And she answered? Samson cringed. He'd learned much more than he needed.

He wasn't happy with this turn of events. It was time for these girls to be on their way home.

"If she's home, I can drive you."

"She's not," Candi replied. "She's always at Ted's."

"Okay, then, we'll wait for her to... um, finish," Samson said awkwardly.

"What happened in here while I was away?" Lissa asked.

"What do you mean?" Samson faked ignorance.

"There's a strange vibe going on here."

Samson was about to deny everything when Candi beat him to a punch.

"Samson refused to have sex with me," she said calmly.

He would have given anything not to be in this room.

"He did?" Lissa sounded genuinely delighted by that, but for the love of him, Samson couldn't understand why.

"Maybe he prefers blondes," Lissa said, giggling.

Samson groaned inwardly. This was a nightmare, and he would wake up any minute now. *Any minute.* Unfortunately, nothing was happening.

"He's married and faithful to his wife," Candi mocked.

"I bet we can change that," Lissa countered in a teasing manner, moving toward him.

Once upon a time, this would be a dream come true, when he was a young man and not happily married. This was more night-mare than fantasy.

He raised his hands to stop their advancements. "Cut it out, girls. The fun's over," he said sternly.

"Oh, I think the fun is just getting started."

"Candi please, no more," he begged. "You don't know me. This isn't appropriate."

"We would *like* to know you," Lissa said, pouting.

They didn't believe he was serious. "I'm married, and I don't do these kinds of things."

"What things?"

"Fool around."

They looked at one another before looking at him in confusion. Why did he get the impression they were speaking in two different languages all of a sudden?

Well, you'd better learn their language and fast, because this was going down the path he didn't like being on.

CHAPTER 5

The girls looked at him for a while, as though not understanding his words.

Samson cleared his throat. He couldn't stand the silence. "I'm sorry if I offended you; that wasn't my intention. You are lovely girls, but I love my wife and would never cheat on her," he remained adamant.

"Why not? It's only sex."

"Not to me."

"I don't believe you," Lissa said, folding her arms. "All men cheat."

Candi smiled. "With the right incentive," she added.

"Well, I don't and never will," Samson said sternly, hoping the message was loud and clear, and they'd drop this.

He'd never guessed his evening would turn out like this. Instead of falling asleep in the middle of some carnage, he was declining sexual offers from sisters. *This is some crazy shit.*

"That's sweet of you, Samson," Lissa said, taking him by surprise. "Your wife is one lucky lady."

"*I'm* the lucky one."

"That's sweet, too," she swooned. "Don't you think so, Candi?"

The other girl seemed on the fence. Whether because she didn't believe him or because her ego was bruised, Samson couldn't say for sure.

"Yes, it is," Candi said eventually.

Luckily, they backed off, taking the hint that wasn't a hint but a neon sign, and Samson sighed with relief.

The last thing he anticipated when opening the door for them was that he would end up fending them off. Not in a million years had he seen it coming, that he would get an offer for sex from sisters.

If Malcolm learned any of this, Samson would never hear the end of it. That made him cringe. It would be better to keep this adventure to himself. Too much could be misunderstood, and Samson wasn't going to take any chances. Although nothing had happened, he had no proof that that was the case, and the last thing he needed was for Teresa to get a wind of it.

She would get needlessly upset. It was better to keep his mouth shut and forget this ever happened.

However, he had to admit that the timing was perfect. What are the odds that these girls appear on his doorstep when Teresa was out of town? *Was it a sign from God?* He shook off that thought. It was more like a test. He was proud that he hadn't even been tempted. Not that he needed any reassurance that he loved his wife; it was just the way he was. His moral code meant everything.

An awkward silence fell among them, and Samson didn't know what to do or say. He remained on guard, for which he gave himself a mental slap. These girls were not wild animals that planned to attack him the instant he relaxed.

Are you sure about that?

Your life is almost unbearable. Two young, hot girls are coming on to you, he mocked silently. They wanted to sleep with him, and he was acting as though he was in a life-and-death situation. It was wrong on so many levels.

Sadly, his dick didn't have any moral dilemmas or care that his heart belonged to someone else. Still, it behaved, which was a relief. This evening was stressful enough without further complications.

"Let's go sit in the living room while we wait," he offered, needing to distract himself with something; anything.

"Can I use your bathroom?" Candi inquired. The girls acted as though some kind of a spell had broken, and that they could interact normally once again.

"Yes, down the hall and first door on the left," he explained.

"I'll come with," Lissa said, following after her sister before stopping in her tracks to look at him. "I'll take the phone with me in case Kristina calls," she explained.

"Sure," Samson replied, although they were already gone. He could hear the bathroom door closing behind them, and he sat down, suddenly feeling exhausted. *What a night.* He took a deep breath, exhaled, then repeated the process.

What the fuck was happening here? He couldn't help wondering.

The evening had taken quite a turn after they came seeking help. Samson felt like a tornado had just picked him up and thrown him right down again after giving him a nice twirl or twenty. It was insane. Replaying everything that happened from the moment they'd banged on his door, he still had trouble accepting all of it as reality. Was he being overly dramatic? Perhaps.

Maybe I dozed off? This was no dream. *Maybe I stumbled and hit my head.* Not even a coma could explain this shit.

It was sad he wouldn't be able to share this with his best friend because it was a good story. Not that Malcolm would believe him. Samson wasn't that good of a writer.

He would not have been able to come up with something like this for a novel if he tried. Yet wouldn't that be a great story? Although in his case, he would add that the girls were serial killers or something. Thinking about his next literary project helped him find his bearings.

Feeling slightly silly standing in the living room, he grabbed his beer and sat down. Looking at the paused movie on his TV, he chuckled. He couldn't even remember what it was about. These girls had disturbed everything. Not that he minded, despite the complaints. They needed help, and he was happy to help, despite their strange, misguided behavior.

I wonder why they didn't want to call their parents, he thought as he waited for their return. They were really taking their time. That appeared to be a common trait girls shared: Teresa took forever to do her business, too, although he was sure most of the time she spent in there was wasted on looking in the mirror.

A part of him wished they wouldn't return, or hadn't shown up in the first place. This was too much drama, and he was tired. He had enough on his plate as it was. But that was wrong of him, and it made him feel guilty. They were in need, and it was his duty to help.

Their friend will come to pick them up, and they'll be out of your hair for good. That comforted him.

He debated if he should resume watching the movie. Would that be rude? This was his house. He hit play and took a handful of popcorn.

He checked the time. What was taking them so long? He worried about what they were doing in the bathroom for so long. *Are they taking a shower?* A moment later, they returned.

"Did your friend call you back?" he asked, perhaps appearing too eager to hear the answer.

"Can't wait to get rid of us," Candi teased, picking up on it.

"Kristina will come as soon as she can," Lissa replied.

Samson didn't like the sound of that. "When will that be? Fifteen minutes? Half an hour?"

"Who knows," she replied, nonplussed.

I'd like to know.

"What are you watching?" Candi asked looking at the screen.

He told her. She didn't look impressed. He understood: Dark fantasy was an acquired taste.

"So, what did Kristina say?" he pressed.

The girls shrugged.

Were they playing some kind of game? Samson had a moment of doubt. *Did they even call anyone?* He had never heard a conversation.

You sound ridiculous. He dismissed the new doubts.

It wasn't like being stuck in a house with a middle-aged man was a dream come true for them. They were harmless if not somewhat direct. He wished their parents paid more attention to teaching them how to behave in front of a male stranger that was twice their age.

He pushed that thought aside, too: It made him realize how old he was. He was one to avoid saying things like, "in my time," or, "when I was young." So, as it looked like they were going to be here for a while, he offered them a place to sit down.

"So, is this what you were up to before we showed up?" Candi pointed in the general direction of the flat screen and snacks on the table.

"Pretty much."

She jumped on the couch next to him, startling him a little. "Then you're lucky we dropped by," she said, grinning. "You are in serious need of an intervention."

"Why?" he asked genuinely curious.

"Because this is lame."

"Where is your wife, Samson?" Lissa asked. She was looking about the room, taking in framed pictures of him and Teresa. "She is pretty."

"She's visiting her parents," he explained.

"So, you're home alone?"

He nodded.

They grimaced. "And you're here, eating crappy pizza and watching crappy movies." Candi looked genuinely outraged.

He shrugged. He liked it. All of it. He said as much.

"You should have thrown a party," Lissa tried to reason with him.

Samson wanted to roll his eyes. Also, he noticed how Candi was still looking at him like she was assessing him. *Assessing what though?* He wasn't that interesting or complicated.

"We could help you throw one now, " Lissa offered, her excitement rising. "We know all the right people to call."

"Absolutely not." Samson put his foot down. "Besides, *this* is my party."

"A pity party," Candi grumbled mostly to herself.

"What?" he asked.

Candi waved noncommittally, then scooted closer. "I bet we can make it better." As she said that she placed a hand on his thigh. It was way too close to his junk. One wrong move, and …

Samson jumped from his seat as though his ass was on fire. "Let's not restart that," he warned.

Lissa watched his actions with amusement but said nothing.

"Why not?" Candi asked.

Samson was stunned for a few moments. He couldn't believe how calm she was about propositioning herself to him.

Is this some kind of a joke? Did they have a bet going on who could turn him on before letting him down?

It didn't matter because it changed nothing.

He took a deep breath. "Because I'm not interested. So, let's just wait for your friend to arrive without further discussion."

Lissa sneaked up on him from the right, looking at him with genuine curiosity. "Have you ever cheated on your wife?"

"Never," he replied without a thought. He'd never even been tempted because, for him, it would mark the end of the marriage. Plain and simple.

"Aren't you at least a little bit curious?" Candi asked provocatively as she stretched on the couch.

"We would totally rock your world." Lissa went to join her.

Samson had to look away.

"Are you blushing, Samson?"

"That's so sweet."

"This is highly inappropriate."

"It's only natural to feel curious," Candi continued.

"I'm not," he lied. He was a man with a pulse, so of course the thought crossed his mind, but that didn't mean he would ever act on it. He was no animal, and Teresa deserved better from him. He deserved better from himself.

"Look, Samson, Lissa and I talked about it, and since we both like you, you can have us," Candi declared.

"At the same time," Lissa added, as though that wasn't already obvious.

Samson closed his eyes for a moment. "Girls," he began, turning to face them with resolve, "I don't know what kind of a game you're playing …"

"This is no game," Lissa protested.

"… or if you're just bored, but it's starting to piss me off," he said honestly, not even trying to mask his irritation. " I'm not interested. I'm married. I love my wife, and I won't have sex with you," he ranted.

To his surprise, they burst out laughing.

He had been right: it was just a game. He couldn't decide if that made him feel better or worse.

Then Candi said, "Why are you so serious, Samson? It's only sex."

"Yeah. We don't want to marry you, just have some fun."

Samson groaned. They had missed the point. It wasn't surprising considering their age.

"I don't know how to make myself clearer," he said with exasperation. "No means no, end of story."

"Samson—" Lissa began, probably to reassure him that it was all fun and games.

He was having none of it. "… and if you keep playing like this, and pissing me off, then you're going to have to wait for your friend on the porch." It was not an empty threat.

Lissa instantly righted herself while Candi took her sweet time.

"You're kicking us out?" Lissa pouted, looking surprised and maybe even a little hurt.

"That's what he said," Candi said incredulously.

Samson nodded, unremorseful. "If that's what it takes for you to stop pestering me, then that's what I'll do." He half shrugged.

"But it's cold outside," Lissa whined.

"It's your choice," he pointed out. "Stay here and behave, or you know where the front door is." He pointed for good measure.

Check me out! He'd forgotten how fun it was to behave like an authoritative figure. He'd given the rookies hell while serving, just because he could. This felt no different, although it was for a good cause. These girls had to learn there were limits they shouldn't cross.

This showed him he would ace parenting.

"So, what do you say?" he prompted since they remained silent.

"Candi," Lissa said softly, nudging her sister.

"Fine. Message received," Candi said, crossing her arms.

She was not pleased with this turn of events, but he didn't care. So long as they did what he asked.

"We'll back off," she added.

"Thank you."

"Does that mean we can stay?" Lissa wanted to make sure.

"Sure."

"But only if you have a drink with us," Candi added out of the blue.

Well fuck. He should have known there would be a catch involved. There always was, especially when someone's pride got in the way.

Fuck.

CHAPTER 6

C andi looked at him almost triumphantly as she asked him to have a drink with them, calling his bluff. Samson smelled a trap.

He'd fully intended on kicking them out while he was pissed off, but that had worn off pretty quickly. He knew that he would never do that because his conscience wouldn't let him.

Bored kids will rebel against everything. Candi was no different. Everything she did was to shock, but he saw right through her. She was a good kid deep down; her sister, too.

"What do you say, Samson?" Candi prompted.

"Don't tell me you're scared," Lissa added, her eyes widening in surprise. "It's one tiny drink."

Samson sighed. *Am I going to regret this?*

"Okay," he replied slowly as the girls cheered.

He was going to regret this. Already, he was starting to feel as though he'd made a huge mistake. *Cut the crap; it's one drink, not an affair,* he snapped at himself as he went to the kitchen to grab a couple of beers.

Another beer wouldn't kill him. He'd only drunk one before he was interrupted, which meant he would still be able to function normally in the morning and finish his book.

He paused as he opened the fridge. *Why the hell are you doing this?* He had a moment of doubt. Samson knew these girls were messing with him, but why or how was yet to be determined. That notion irked him. They'd already had a crappy night and lost their phones, and everything else. Shouldn't they be more grateful to him? He was helping out.

Candi offered her gratitude, Samson reminded himself with a cringe. He didn't mean it that way, so maybe "grateful" was the wrong word. *Polite? Mindful?*

"Samson?" They sang his name in unison, impatient that it was taking him so long to get them drinks.

Maybe their current behavior was a defense mechanism. After the shit they'd been through, it was normal to be in a state of shock, even if they were not aware of it, he continued to rationalize. *Offense is the best kind of defense.*

They were attacking him, treating him like a piece of meat, so he wouldn't do the same to them. Not that he would, but they didn't know that. He was a stranger, and to them, just another man who could hurt them.

That's so messed up, he said, stopping himself right there. He'd fallen into his own trap. He said he wasn't going to analyze them or their behavior, and that was exactly what he was doing. It wasn't on him to figure them out. They would be gone soon, and for good. He couldn't ignore the relief he started to feel thinking that.

Without wasting any more time, he grabbed three cans of beer from the fridge, closed the door with his elbow, and returned to the living room, bracing himself. He'd done the same thing, mentally and physically prepared himself, while he was in Afghanistan.

"I've got beer," he stated the obvious.

The girls looked at him with strange expressions. They were standing awkwardly by the sofa. Were they trying to hide something behind their backs? That tingled his inner paranoia, and Samson began imagining all kinds of scenarios. He didn't have to bang his head for long, which was a blessing because all his thoughts went to places he didn't particularly like.

Lissa pulled out the bottle of tequila she'd been hiding. "Look what we've got."

"Is that my Don Julio?" There was a lot of accusation in his voice. Their guilty faces now made perfect sense.

"We found it in the liquor cabinet," Candi explained as though it was perfectly normal for them to go through his things.

Was that the reason they'd stayed in the bathroom for so long? Because they were going through his stuff?

One irritation at a time.

"You shouldn't have done that."

"We didn't think you would mind," Lissa tried to defend.

Yeah, right, that was why they'd hidden it in the first place. Samson was particularly irked since that was a bottle Malcolm got him after they left the military.

"I got us beer," he repeated, putting a stop to this pointless argument. He was impatient. He wanted all this put behind him as soon as possible. He'd agreed to a drink and that was what he would do.

"But we want to do shots," Lissa pouted. She sounded like a whiny, spoiled little girl.

"We already opened the bottle," Candi added.

Samson groaned.

Once again, he asked himself what he'd gotten into. *Why me, God? What did I do wrong to be punished like this?*

"Where are your glasses?" Candi asked as though it were a done deal, then added, "Never mind; I'll find them." She dashed into the kitchen before he had a chance to react.

Lissa grabbed the remote and turned off his movie before finding something else to watch. They'd made themselves at home pretty quickly, he grumbled, setting the beer on a side table.

This was complete anarchy. If this was what it was like having children, then Samson was really glad he'd dodged that bullet. Coming from a man whose previous occupation involved dodging actual bullets, that said a lot.

"So, Samson, what do you do for a living?" Lissa asked.

"I'm a writer."

"Ooh, fun."

Shortly afterward, while Samson mused about the meaning of life, Candi returned with three glasses.

"It's time for some shots," she announced, doing a little dance as she approached.

"You do that. I'm sticking with beer," Samson said. He was still pissed that they'd touched his alcohol without asking first.

They made the same expression simultaneously. It would have been funny if it weren't directed at him. They were definitely sisters; he could see that now.

And then the avalanche of complaints started.

"Oh, come on," Candi started.

"Please, drink tequila with us."

"It's going to be fun."

"Just one."

"It's better than beer."

"Especially the way we do it." Lissa giggled.

On and on it went.

Maybe it would be easier to just do what they wanted, but Samson had never liked tequila. The bottle had sentimental value because it marked a new era in his life.

All that sucking and licking just to get a drink never made sense to him. Not that he said any of that out loud. It was a minefield of double entendre, something he was wholeheartedly trying to avoid. He was many things, but a complete idiot wasn't one of them. *Usually.*

"No, thank you." He stuck to his guns, but the girls were relentless when they were trying to get their way.

"You promised," Candi insisted, but she was wearing a flirty smile.

"And I fully intend on keeping that promise," he replied, making a show of picking up a beer and opening it slowly. He topped that off by taking a small, satisfying sip. "Perfect," he murmured.

The sisters rolled their eyes, and he couldn't help smiling.

Candi narrowed her eyes at him while Lissa said, "That doesn't count. We all have to have the same drink," she pointed out.

That made no sense to him. "Why?"

"Because that's the rule," she insisted.

Whose rule? Was this one of those female logic things he would never manage to grasp in his lifetime? He feared that was the case.

They continued to pester Samson until he cracked. "Okay, okay, I'll have a damn shot with you, just stop."

He was sick and tired of all the cluck, cluck, clucking. *Yeah, keep telling yourself that.*

"I knew you'd come to your senses," Candi said with a grin.

"But just one, okay?" he hedged.

"Do you have any lemons? Sea salt?" Lissa asked enthusiastically.

"No," Samson replied, "so we'd better abandon this silliness."

"It doesn't matter; we'll do them straight," Candi said to her sister, ignoring him. Samson had to accept his fate he was about to have some tequila.

"We sure will," Lissa replied with the biggest smile imaginable.

Samson didn't like that one bit and remained wary. "So, to make it clear: I do one drink with you, and you will behave until your friend arrives," he reminded them.

"One-ish," Lissa commented and Candi looked at him questioningly. "What's the matter, Samson? Worried we'll get you drunk and take advantage of you?"

Although it was meant as a joke, it got him thinking. Samson hadn't worried about something like that until she'd pointed it out. Was that their plan? Try to lower his inhibitions, and then offer themselves again? Candi looked pretty determined to sleep with him, stopping only when he'd threatened to kick them out. Was this a new strategy?

Samson was ashamed of his thoughts. *This isn't some B-rated porn movie, so get your head out of the gutter,* he snapped at himself. Besides, he wasn't a catch. It wasn't like women were lining up to sleep with him because he was so irresistible. These girls were bored, had had a crappy night, and took their chances. They weren't heartbroken he'd said no. The way they looked, they were the ones who had guys lining up to be with them. So, it was just a drink and nothing else.

"Can you even drink legally?" It suddenly crossed his mind.

"Quit stalling," Lissa complained.

Samson didn't press. His mother used to say, *not my circus, not my monkey,* and Samson applied her sage words to this situation.

"Come on, pour the drinks," Samson said, if somewhat reluctantly.

Candi clapped her hands. "You heard the man, Lissa," she instructed.

The younger sister poured three glasses in record time, as though she was afraid he would change his mind.

"What are we going to toast?" Lissa asked handing them their glasses. "To new friends?"

"To new experiences?"

This wasn't something he wanted to experience ever again. Too late, Samson realized he'd said that out loud, but the sisters took it as a joke and laughed.

"Hey, you never know what new experiences are on the way with your inhibitions lowered," Candi jibed with a wink.

"I know exactly what will happen next," Samson started to reply. "I will have this drink, then sit on the couch and watch my movie while you wait for your friend."

"Oh my God, you are such a grownup," Lissa said in exasperation.

Was that meant as an insult?

"With no sense of humor," Candi added.

"And a bore," Lissa jumped in.

Candi sobered. "He's not a bore, he's a wuss," she said, looking him straight in the eye.

Samson made a face. He was a thirty-eight-year-old man, and he didn't blink at such childish provocations. He wasn't going to fall for such obvious incitement. He had nothing to prove, not to these girls or anyone else.

"Is that the best you got?" he decided to tease in return.

"My hand is getting numb while you try to outwit each other," Lissa complained, irritated by what was happening.

Oh, right, this is supposed to be fun. So instead of continuing with this charade, Samson raised his glass. "To your health," he said, downing the contents of his glass.

Oh God, how he hated tequila. His animosity toward it didn't occur by chance. Right before he'd enlisted, he decided it was time to get properly drunk at least once. So, he and a couple of local boys stole a bottle of tequila and drank it, hiding in the unlit part of a park after dark. He didn't like the taste back then either, but he wanted to appear cool to his friends, so he drank it like it was juice. And then the horror started, the throwing up and the pain. He would never forget that night.

"Way to go, Samson," the girls hooted and cheered.

He tried hard not to make a face. It was disgusting. And that cheap bastard, Malcolm, appeared to have bought him the lousiest brand there was. He'd remember to mention that to his best friend the next time he saw him.

Samson then realized that the alcohol tasted strange, but not just because it was cheap. *Can tequila spoil?* What was its expiration date?

There was a definite taste in his mouth and a peculiar powdery texture. He looked at his empty glass but saw nothing strange. That didn't mean something wasn't wrong because there absolutely was.

He looked at the girls, and they looked back at him intently.

Did they put something in my drink? He looked at their still-full glasses. They hadn't touched them, not even a lick. That confirmed his suspicions. They'd done something to his drink.

Samson felt like smacking himself in the face for falling for the oldest trick in the book.

"What di—" he started and couldn't finish.

Well, fuck.

CHAPTER 7

"**W**hat did you do to me?" Samson boomed as the glass slipped through his fingers. He advanced toward them, but they parted like the sea for Moses, giggling all the while.

Was everything a joke to them? *Did they drug me to see what would happen?* All kinds of thoughts passed through his mind as he turned to look at them anew.

There was no doubt in his mind they'd drugged him, but with what? Had they grabbed something from his bathroom, or had they brought it with them? If they brought drugs, that showed intent. The thoughts swirled inside his mind and dispersed at practically the same time. It was hard to keep his thoughts coherent.

"You need to relax, Samson," Candi advised.

"Just surrender to the feeling," Lissa added.

"I asked you a question," he insisted. He was already feeling weird, not only in his brain, which felt as though something was pulling a thick veil over it: His tongue flopped unnaturally inside his mouth, making his words sound funny.

"We said we wanted to party," Candi said matter-of-factly.

Samson was horrified. Didn't they have boundaries? Notions of good and bad? His foggy mind and rapidly declining motor skills made the answer crystal clear.

"This is wrong," he said, as though they weren't already aware.

"We're going to party hard, Samson," Candi approached, as though she needed to make sure he would hear and understand her. "And for that to happen, you need to relax."

"You're too uptight," Lissa agreed. "You need to chill."

This was a nightmare. He couldn't believe he'd let these girls get the best of him. He was an idiot for trusting that he was doing a good deed; he was just a plaything to them. He would not make the same mistake twice.

"I want you out of my house *right now*!" he shouted, pointing at the door before lowering his arm quickly because it felt like it weighed a ton.

The drug was really starting to mess with his system.

"Make us," Candi said, raising her chin.

He couldn't believe his ears. *Yeah,* that's *the shocker, not the fact that they freaking drugged you.*

"This is no game," he was adamant. "I'll call the police," he threatened.

Samson looked about, knowing he had limited time before whatever they'd dosed him with kicked in completely. Since he had no idea what they gave him, he had to assume the worst – that it would completely knock him out. Time, then, was of the essence. It was imperative to get rid of them before that since there was no telling what they were capable of doing. Robbing him blind would be the least of his problems.

Where is it? he stressed.

"Looking for this?" Lissa asked, waving his phone.

"Give it to me," he demanded.

Instead of complying, she threw it to her sister. "Candi, catch."

He went for it, but Candi was faster and tossed it back to Lissa.

"Give it to me," he growled.

"Not a chance," she countered, elated by this game.

Realizing he was just going in circles without achieving anything, Samson stopped and prepared to wave goodbye to his motor skills.

He just hoped that the adrenaline rush that kicked in because he was in danger would last long enough to get him out of this mess. He had to kick these girls out, no matter what.

He didn't care that they were broke, without their phones, or in a part of the city they didn't know. The little bitches deserved to suffer for what they'd done to him. This little stunt was devious enough for him to start doubting their story in the first place.

Stop it. Focus.

"Get out, now. I won't ask nicely again," he shouted, enraged.

They didn't move a muscle, apart from Lissa taunting him with his phone.

"Samson, we've been over this. We're not going anywhere," Candi said calmly, which only further pissed him off.

How dare *she.*

"I'll throw you out if I have to," he threatened, but it did him no good.

They continued to tease him.

"You leave me no other choice," he added, turning to stumble into the kitchen.

Focus, asshole.

Muttering something completely unintelligible, he reached for the landline. Lissa had his cell phone, but that didn't mean he was powerless. He could still call the police and would do so gladly. These girls needed to be taught a lesson, and he was more than happy to oblige. Maybe a few nights in jail would set them straight and teach them not to mess with people.

With white-hot fury, Samson picked up the receiver but Candi took it away. He hadn't heard her walk in behind him.

"What are you doing?"

"I will *not* let you spoil our fun," she snapped.

He recoiled. "The only thing spoiled here is you. Do you think it's okay to go around drugging people?"

"Why are you overreacting?" she accused. "We did it for you."

"*Excuse* me?"

"You needed it."

Yeah, he'd really needed to be drugged tonight.

"You are unbelievable. I'm calling the police," he remained adamant.

"If you try to call the police, you'll regret it," Candi threatened, her face contorting. Gone was the sweet girl who was so grateful for his help. Gone was the seductress who wanted to get into his pants. In her place stood someone he didn't want to deal with.

That didn't mean he was afraid.

"The fun's over. You fucking drugged me, and it's time to face consequences."

"If you call the cops, I'll tell them you tried to rape me."

"*What?*" Samson exploded.

"You heard me," she countered calmly and smirked. "And you know they'll believe me."

She thought she was so smart. There was something strange with that smile. It had no lines. Samson's vision was blurring. *Focus, asshole.*

"I did no such thing," Samson said.

"I'll say you tried to put your dick in my mouth," Lissa added.

Where had she come from? His senses had gone to shit. He was well aware that his time had nearly run out. They'd won.

But he couldn't accept that. He just couldn't. He would fight until the end.

"You're both crazy. Get away from me."

Candi grinned. "You have no idea."

"But you'll learn," Lissa said.

"Now, be a good boy and let the drug do its thing," Candi advised. "I promise, you will enjoy every second spent with us."

"Not as much as we will," Lissa added, and to emphasize that she gave him a little kiss.

He retreated in disgust. "Don't touch me."

Candi laughed at Lissa's joke.

"Come on, Samson. Party with us."

"Not a chance. I'm getting the police." Even if he had to walk to the station.

"You won't get far," Candi taunted.

"You have about five minutes to get lost," Samson warned, trying to reach the front door. It was a bluff, but they didn't have to know that.

"Are you that eager to go to jail for rape?" Lissa asked.

"The local cops will take my word for everything," he insisted, taking a small break. He could feel the drug trying to overpower him, and it took everything in him not to succumb.

"Who do you think they'd believe? Young girls who look like us, or an old man like you?" Candi asked in all seriousness.

How had he wound up in the living room? *Oh no.* It was serious if he was starting to lose time.

"You put something in my booze; that's all the proof I need," he argued. Or at least he hoped that was what he'd said.

"What booze?" Lissa asked, looking about. Every move was extremely exaggerated for show.

Had they already gotten rid of it? Oh no.

Don't panic. There were still things he could do. His blood could certainly be submitted as evidence. Whatever they gave him would be present in his system.

"We're just two sweet, naive girls that made the mistake of asking you for help," Candi said, playing her part to perfection.

Shit. He would believe their act, too, and he knew the truth. He was in some serious trouble.

Samson forced his legs to move, trying one last time to propel himself out of the house. The slight euphoria was overtaking him, claiming his body, and he knew the conscious part of him was in a final countdown. Stubbornly, he refused to give up.

"Get out. Now."

"Samson, this is pointless," Candi chastised.

"I'm ex-army, little girls, so no matter what, I can do some serious damage," he threatened, trying to appear menacing, which wasn't that hard considering how angry he was.

His bark was greater than his bite right now, but they didn't have to know that. Unfortunately, his words didn't accomplish their desired effect. Candi and Lissa were delighted by his outburst and nothing else.

"Come on, Samson. Talk dirty to us some more," Lissa said giggling.

"Tell us what you want to do to us," Candi added.

He felt – and looked – as though he wanted to strangle them both, consequences be damned.

He wanted to reach for something, *anything* to use as a weapon, but he couldn't. His body was failing him. Never in his life had he felt so powerless.

"Get out! Get out!" Something was seriously wrong with his mouth. He wanted to lie down, curl into a ball, and forget this nightmare.

No. Not now, he rebelled. He needed to fight. This pep talk didn't work as well as before.

Stay awake. His determination wasn't enough to overpower what was happening inside his body. Everything was extremely fuzzy, and now, multiple Candis and Lissas were staring and laughing at him.

The argument was a distraction; he understood that now, and it filled him with dread. He was an idiot. They were biding their time until the drug took effect. His accusation was proven true seconds later when Candi approached him and shoved him so he collapsed onto the couch.

No.

No matter what he did or how hard he struggled, he couldn't will his body to move. He couldn't feel his body at all, but his brain still tried to function, on some level.

Am I having an out-of-body experience? He wasn't that lucky.

"Are you ready to party?" Candi sounded strange. She straddled him, and Samson definitely felt that. She patted his arms, torso, and stomach, as though assessing what she was dealing with. She whistled in approval.

"Get off. Stop," he mumbled, each word taking monumental effort.

Why do I even bother?

"What did you say, Samson?" She leaned closer. "You want me to unbutton your shirt? My pleasure."

For a moment she looked at her sister, who giggled.

He followed her eyes, but even that small movement of his head was nearly impossible as it now weighed a ton.

Samson was horrified to see that the other girl was holding a phone, recording everything. It wasn't his phone, either. Even in his state, he could distinguish that, especially because the one she held was a golden rose color, probably an iPhone.

They'd lied about their phones. Discovering that was the cherry on top. Now, he knew they'd lied about everything to get inside his house. *But why?*

The thoughts dissipated from his head.

What is she doing?

Candi was taking her time with his shirt, removing one button at a time, then licking her way down his body. He tried to push her away. He accomplished jack shit.

"Change position; I can't see him," Lissa whined.

Candi readjusted, then looked at the camera. "Is this better?"

"Much," Lissa reassured.

Samson turned away, not wanting to participate in this. It was equal to an ostrich sticking its head into the sand, but it was the best he could do considering the circumstances.

The flowery, sweet smell of her perfume was making him sick to his stomach.

Samson, fight! the thought broke through the fog.

One last time, Samson tried his best to fend off the demon girl in his lap. He raised his arms to stop her but couldn't.

"Samson, be patient," Candi teased.

The girls cheered when his shirt was completely open, and Lissa approached for a closer look.

"You've been hiding a very nice body under these ugly clothes,"

Candi said approvingly, using her nails to explore all the crooks and crannies and causing pain in some areas.

It helped clear his head somewhat.

"Get off of me. Stop," he protested. He didn't want this. This was wrong. He loved his wife. *Please, can someone help me?*

Unfortunately, Samson was powerless to stop what was happening to him. He was nothing more than a puppet in their hands. The removal of his clothes, the filming, and the touching were all happening without his consent. Not that they cared. The notion made him want to rage or cry. Samson couldn't do either.

"Let me go." He wasn't sure he was even saying anything out loud.

"Oh, Samson. We're going to fuck so hard, you'll remember it forever," said a half-frenzied Candi.

"No."

"I'll even let you fuck me in the ass. Or I'll fuck you in the ass; whatever floats your boat," she said a little bit louder for the camera.

"We'll do everything your stuck-up wife never would," she promised.

No, no, no, no, no. Let me go.

The sisters started laughing at that.

Samson was spiraling out of control. This couldn't happen. He didn't want it to happen. They couldn't treat him like this; it wasn't right. It wasn't fair.

"Let's see what else you're working with," Candi announced giddily at some point.

Blissfully, that was the moment he blacked out.

CHAPTER 8

A couple more turns and he would be out of this nightmare; Samson was sure of it. *You can do this.* He forced himself to continue forward, running through one of the abandoned mines, trying to find a way out.

A skirmish between his platoon and some insurgents occurred. They were winning at first but were eventually forced to retreat. The terrorists forced them into this mine and then threw in a bomb that destroyed the main entrance. Samson and his comrades were separated in the blast. Brawn, Martinez, and Macgregor died from the bomb. Samson had to mercy kill Martinez after the man begged him to end his misery.

They were trapped inside, in the dark, but Samson wasn't giving up. He would find the rest of his men, and they would find their way out. He was sure of it.

Samson had hated small, dark places with a passion ever since he was a kid, but he had to put his claustrophobia to the side if he wanted to get out of there alive.

Which way to go? The entrance was destroyed, but there had to be another way to get into or out of this place.

What if there wasn't? Samson halted that train of thought. He couldn't think like that. He wasn't going to allow himself to be buried alive. Those motherfuckers couldn't win.

He had to stop running and resume at a lighter pace. There wasn't enough air here, and he was already feeling short of breath. It was also extremely stuffy and hot. Samson pressed forward, ignoring everything. He heard gunshots, and since the whole place was extremely echo-friendly, it was hard to pinpoint from where they came. He called out for his friends, and no one replied. Why couldn't they hear him?

What if they're dead? If the insurgents were in the mine too, that meant there was another entry point. That notion filled him with hope.

It was hard to move forward when he had to look over his shoulder every other second. His flashlight started to blink, and he had to hit the thing a couple of times before it stopped. *What will I do when my light dies?* He was confident he would be out of there before that.

New paths presented themselves to him at every turn. *What if I'm going deeper underground, and not toward the surface?* That caused a light panic in his chest.

Everything will be all right. You won't die here, Samson. Do you hear me? he screamed in his head.

You won't die; not today. He was too young for something like that. He planned on a long, fulfilling life before he croaked. He planned to find a girl, get married, and have a bunch of children. Dying in this sticky, dirty old mine in the middle of hostile territory across the ocean wasn't in his cards. For any of his dreams to come true, though, he had to find a way out of this hellhole.

A Taliban terrorist appeared suddenly in front of him, and Samson fired without thinking. Luckily, Samson was faster. He wondered if he should take the path the other man came from, and decided that would be the most prudent. It was dangerous because more could be lurking in the dark. That was a chance he had to take if he wanted to see the light of day. As he passed the dead body,

Samson tried and failed miserably to avoid looking at the man's face. *He's just a kid,* he thought with pure sadness.

Keep going. He had to find the damn exit before he suffocated.

Suffocation, gas poisoning, starvation, death by thirst, death by an enemy bullet … who knew there were so many different ways to die while going through a mine? Not to mention a part of the structure could collapse and squash him. He didn't need those images inside his head.

"Connors? Talbert?" he called out for his buddies, but there was no reply. There was a chance the enemy would hear him, but he wasn't worried: He was armed to the teeth.

Maybe he needed to speed up his pace.

However, his legs refused to listen to his brain, and something was weighing him down. He looked, but there were no weights wrapped around his legs. *What is happening?* Was this one of the symptoms of methane gas poisoning? He had no idea.

Of course, it could have just been that he was exhausted. They'd been engaged in this skirmish and cut off from the rest of the U.S. Army for days. The terrorists had ambushed them, cut them off from everyone, and forced them to this suicidal retreat in the mine.

That wasn't such a hot idea, but what other choice had they had? It was that or be gunned down like sitting ducks. This damned place hadn't turned out to be any better. This death was just slower, sneakier.

Don't think like that.

There should have been a sign when entering the mine – *Abandon all hope when entering* – because it felt like he was on a path to hell.

Suddenly, Samson could see a light up ahead. He couldn't resist the urge to rub his eyes before grabbing his gun again. He wasn't hallucinating: There was a light in front of him, and he went toward it with vigor. He couldn't quite tell whether it was a natural light. What if someone was down there with him? Would that person be a friend or foe?

What if one of his buddies had survived? *Maybe I've found a way out.* All kinds of contradictory thoughts and questions passed through his head, but they did not stop him from marching forward.

He would discover the truth soon enough.

Samson tried hard not to get his hopes up that this was his way to freedom and the prospect of putting some fresh air into his lungs, even if it was of the desert variety. Walking much lighter now, he felt like he'd won the fucking lottery.

I found my way out. I did it. He couldn't help but wonder if one of his comrades had managed to do the same. *I guess I'll find out.* Strangely, no matter how long he walked, he felt like he wasn't getting any closer to that light.

What is going on? Was this nothing more than a hallucination? Taking stock, he realized he felt a little off. *Have I been poisoned?* If it was gas, then he was screwed. As he mused about what could be his last moments on earth, the light began to grow. Soon enough, he'd reached a door. It was wide open and light spilled from within.

Who in their right mind would build anything down here? Or maybe it was some kind of storage room or even a room for miners to rest. He'd never worked in a mine; he didn't know how they functioned.

He closed the gap very slowly, gluing himself to the wall. He couldn't hear any sounds from within, but life had taught him that meant jack shit.

Very tentatively, he decided to step inside. He was startled to enter a normal-looking room hollowed out of the mud. There was a mattress on the ground in the corner, a wooden table, and an improvised kitchenette.

A woman stood up from the table when he came into view. She wore a dress with loose-fitting pants, and a chador that hid her hair as was tradition. She looked startled to see him.

"Hello," he said softly, not daring to raise his voice over a whisper. "You are in no danger. I'm not going to hurt you," he reassured her, although he didn't lower his weapon. There was no telling who else could be hiding nearby.

His buddy Ryan had almost lost his nuts making that mistake a couple of months back.

She started yelling in a language he'd never mastered and approaching him. By a whole lot of gesticulation, it appeared, she was trying to kick him out.

"Please, I need help. Do you know a way out of here?" he pleaded.

She screamed, rushing toward him, and although she didn't appear to be armed, Samson panicked and pulled the trigger. Nothing happened. The gun didn't go off.

The woman was on him like a spider monkey, showing surprising strength, throwing him on the old cot in the process. She straddled him.

"What are you doing?" he demanded.

Her veil fell off, and he could see the smiling face of a young American girl. He was startled: She hadn't looked like that a second ago. Freaking him out even more, he knew her.

"Ready to party, Samson?" she inquired.

Without waiting for a reply, Candi started grinding against him. He tried to get her off of him and couldn't. His hands felt numb, although he didn't have time to start panicking about that.

She moved faster and faster, letting out all kinds of noises of pure pleasure, and even slapping him in the face a couple of times.

"Be quiet," she warned.

He wasn't aware he was talking in the first place.

Something was wrong with his eyes. He couldn't keep them open. Soon enough, he couldn't focus on anything else other than the feeling of being inside of someone. The pressure continued to build, Candi became even more erratic with her movements, and he felt like everything was happening beyond his control. He tried to resist, but it was fruitless, and his orgasm soon overtook him. Simultaneously, he felt a searing pain in his left shoulder.

Panting, Samson opened his eyes to see Candi was coming down from her release. She had bitten him on the shoulder.

No! he screamed, realizing what had happened.

Candi laughed at his expression as the other girl continued to film them. "You rocked my world, Samson," Candi said, kissing him on the lips.

He turned away with disgust.

"My turn," Lissa sang.

He wanted to stop them, tell them how wrong all of this was and how violated and exposed he felt, how ashamed he was that he'd just cheated on his wife, but the powerful drug they'd given him pulled him back into nothingness. Soon enough, new dreams and vivid nightmares were there to torment him and violate his mind while the sisters violated his body.

His worst nightmares began mixing with images of the girls having sex with him.

Samson woke up in his bed, completely naked and covered in dried blood and dirt. He had no memory of how that had happened, or how he'd gotten there in the first place.

He heard water running in the bathroom.

"Teresa? You there?" he called out. "Honey?"

She didn't reply.

"You wouldn't believe what a crazy dream I had," he said once the water stopped. He used the moment of privacy to cover himself with a blanket. For some reason, he felt too exposed.

"Oh, I think I can," Candi replied, exiting the bathroom with Lissa following closely behind.

The younger sister still held that damned phone, and Samson was grateful he'd had enough presence of mind to cover himself.

"What are you doing here?" he demanded.

They surrounded him on the bed. Lissa shoved the phone into his face and Candi jerked the blanket off him. "Come on little monkey, dance," she said to his penis.

Samson covered himself with his hands. There was no escape from them. They were everywhere.

"I said *dance*," Candi added more sternly.

Lissa made a sympathetic face. "Maybe we have to use one of those blue pills on him. He *is* old," she taunted.

Samson jumped out of bed and began to run. He had to get out of this house and alert the police.

The girls were right behind him.

"There's no point in running," Lissa yelled after him.

No matter how fast he moved, he couldn't seem to shake them. Couldn't seem to reach the steps, either.

He didn't remember the hallway being this long.

Where are the damn stairs?

And those damn girls wouldn't stop chasing after him, goading him, and saying all kinds of disgusting things to him. He didn't want to hear how his dick felt while Candi sucked him, or if it was too big for Lissa at first.

He had to get out of there. Changing his mind at the last second, Samson rushed through the first door he spotted on the left … and ended up in another hallway.

What is going on? Where am I? He panicked. This was not his house … but at the same time, it was. It was a maze he couldn't escape from. He was lost.

"It's time for you to dance again, little monkey," Candi said, jumping in front of him.

"No," he rebelled.

"It's my turn now," Lissa complained from behind him. He turned his head to look at her, and she was completely naked and sucking on a lollipop. They blocked his exit. He was pinned into a corner.

Candi continued to film him, and the spotlight on the phone was blinding him. "Let me be, you demon girls," he spat.

They laughed.

"You are hot when you beg; do it some more," Candi instructed.

Samson made a mental note to remain quiet. He didn't say anything, even when they advanced on him, touching and sucking him greedily.

Feeling completely overwhelmed and in despair, Samson did something he'd never done before, not even when he was about to die in Afghanistan. He began shouting at the top of his lungs, until all the walls around began to rattle, then shattered as though made of glass. The fragments cut his body in a million places, but he didn't care. He welcomed the pain.

Then everything went dark again …

CHAPTER 9

Samson opened his eyes, and this time, he knew he wasn't dreaming. Unfortunately. *What day is it? What time?* He had no concept of how much time he'd spent under, battling nightmares. His whole body ached in various ways as though he'd gone through a meat grinder, twice.

What happened to me? He had serious memory lapses, but his brain provided a series of very disturbing scenes full of sex and violence so he could piece together the story. The two girls lied about needing help so they could get inside his house, drug him, and rape him multiple times.

Did that really happen? Had been involved in something so debasing? It was him and it wasn't at the same time since they drugged him. He had been high as a kite the entire time and unable to fend them off. The few times he'd regained consciousness painted a horrifying picture, and a part of him was glad he couldn't remember the rest.

A fruit salad of emotions swirled inside of him. *Fruit salad?* Was he hungry? Probably, among other things.

Samson did a quick inventory of his body. He was completely naked and didn't dare think about that other than how it was convenient at the moment, to do his thing. He had scratches all over his body: Both girls had long nails and had used them in abundance.

There were a couple of bruises on his torso and legs, and the side of his neck was pretty tender. *Did they choke me?* He wondered, and then remembered that Candi had bitten him. Samson stopped himself there.

He knew if he thought too closely about last night, he would enter a state he wouldn't be able to recover from, so for now, it was imperative to keep moving, keep functioning, and find a way out of this mess without analyzing anything or thinking too closely about certain events. That was the only way he could survive this.

Unfortunately, no matter the mental freeze, the evidence that he'd had sex with these girls last night was more than apparent, not only on his body but around the room as well. He didn't need to recall anything, nor did he require his body's memory to tell him that. The room he was in painted that picture perfectly.

"Ready to party?" Candi's words popped into his head, making him shiver. He felt like throwing up.

Only then did he realize he wasn't alone. The girls in question – a pair of devious monsters who'd drugged and abused him – slept peacefully, snuggled against him on the couch. Candi was to his right and Lissa to his left, basking in their post-coital bliss.

More images assaulted him. Lissa, on top of him, riding him, moaning, and Candi by her side, watching, with approval, every sick detail the other was doing to him. Samson felt sick to his stomach. He couldn't believe they'd done all that. That he'd done all that. *Not me,* he rebelled. He had been drugged. They'd taken his free will and treated him like an object, a piece of meat they could use and then discard without consequences.

A sudden, overwhelming rage washed over him, and he mulled over how he could easily kill them before they even realized what was happening. Instead of committing double homicide, he pushed them away in disgust. He rushed into the kitchen, reaching the sink just in time to throw up. Samson felt completely violated and wanted to shout at the top of his lungs.

This isn't happening, his mind remained in denial as the heaviness of reality pressed down on him. And yet, it was. Once he stopped and drank a bit of water, Samson forced himself to calm down. This was no time to freak out.

He returned to the living room and began looking for his clothes. The girls were still asleep, and his rage reappeared. It had never gone away, just been pushed down by all other things he felt. The room was in shambles.

They wanted to party, and they had. Condom wrappers were everywhere. *Don't think about it.*

"Hey, lover. Good morning," Candi greeted sleepily in a slightly hoarse voice.

He looked away, refusing to think about why she looked and sounded like that.

"I want you out of my house. *Now,*" he snapped in return, not bothering with pleasantries. Hearing her voice made him homicidal, without regard for what she said.

How could she pretend that what happened last night was okay, fun?

"Look who's not a morning person. Noted."

Samson looked back in disbelief, catching her as she stretched, her naked breasts sticking out toward him. Her full body was on display, and he felt like gauging his eyes out. So much hate and fury mixed with something else – remembrance perhaps? – hit him like a ton of bricks and he turned away again.

He located his boxers and put them on. That small piece of fabric didn't feel like enough. He wanted to put on as many layers of clothes as possible, including winter wear.

"Did you hear me? I want you out."

"Samson, you need to chill," she countered, sounding almost bored.

He was boring her? That raised his blood pressure through the roof. "Are you fucking kidding me?" he yelled.

She looked up at him innocently. "Can we not do this? I need my morning java."

His mind short-circuited for a second before rebooting. "Do *what*?" he snapped. "You don't want to be reminded how you drugged me and then forced me to have sex with you?" *Tough shit.* "What do you want me to do? Offer you fucking breakfast?" he ranted. His tone heavily suggested they were lucky to be alive.

"That would be a good start," she countered instantly. "Also, a simple 'thank you' would be nice."

"Excuse me?"

"Oh, you wanted it, too; you're just too stuck up to admit it," she threw in his face. "We just helped you relax a bit."

He couldn't believe his ears. That was incredible. *I wanted to be raped? Good to know.*

"You are fucking crazy," he realized with utmost clarity. "And I want you out of my house, *right now*," he shouted.

Lissa stirred just then but did not wake. That irked him to no end. Wasn't he loud enough for the princess, or did she just not care?

"*Get out!*" he gave it another go.

"Five more minutes," Lissa murmured through her sleep.

He was about to comment that she'd clearly had a rough night before he bit his tongue, remembering he was the reason behind her sleepiness.

He could never forget this had happened, not for a second. A complete mind-wipe would help in this case and nothing else.

Candi moved closer to her sister, nudging her slightly. "Lissa, wake up."

It took a couple of tries before Lissa opened one eye. "Hmmm? What's going on?" she asked sleepily.

Samson gritted his teeth. She didn't deserve to look so content, so peaceful, after what she'd done.

Samson watched as Lissa slowly come to her senses. This was such a fucked-up scene, and such a fucked-up situation, that Samson didn't know whether he wanted to rage or cry. Probably a little bit of both.

What did I do? What did those girls make me do? he thought over and over.

That wasn't me, a part of him shot back. *It was the drugs.* He still felt immensely guilty. Circumstances aside, he'd cheated on his wife, and that was something he didn't know how to handle, or forgive himself.

Oh my God, oh my God, help me. He started to spiral as panic washed over him. *Teresa will find out what happened and leave me.*

"Why did you wake me up?" Lissa grumbled, snapping him from his thoughts.

"Samson over here wants us out of his house," Candi explained, looking at him defiantly.

"And right fucking now," he growled for good measure.

Lissa wasn't impressed. "Let me sleep," she said and turned over.

Samson envisioned picking her up with the couch and throwing both outside.

"Take your sister, Candi, and get the hell out," he insisted. He couldn't look at them anymore. He was thoroughly disgusted.

Samson couldn't get over the huge mistake he'd made. He'd have never guessed such monsters lurked beneath these innocent-looking faces.

Should he call the police? *And tell them what?*

He had no proof that anything that happened wasn't consensual. Looking around, he saw no traces of the tequila bottle.

"You woke me up," Lissa said, irked. She sat up, trying to fix the hair that was stuck onto her face.

"What is *wrong* with you?" Samson asked them. Apart from the obvious.

Lissa looked at him, and her expression suggested she didn't understand his question. That pissed him off even more.

"I. Said. Leave." he made sure to accentuate each word, so there were no more misunderstandings.

Lissa looked at her sister. "You didn't tell him?"

That confused him. "Tell me what?" he demanded.

"That we're in charge, not you," Lissa said haughtily.

"Excuse me?" He was taken aback.

Candi decided to over. "Let's get one thing straight, Samson. We're not going anywhere."

"We're staying here until we want to leave."

"What?"

"You heard us," Candi said, raising her chin slightly. "We're staying here with you." She grinned, showing all her teeth, and Samson had a flashback of her using them on him. Bile rose into his throat, and he had to force it down.

"So instead of standing there, talking nonsense," Candi added, waving with her hand, "go to the kitchen and make us some breakfast."

"Coffee, too," Lissa added.

That's when Samson lost it. "That's it. You have five seconds to get dressed and get the fuck out of here, or I'll throw you out the way you are."

"Are you sure you want to kick us out?" Candi taunted.

"You deserve much worse for what you did, you monsters."

"Big words coming from someone who has no power," Candi countered calmly, with a sigh.

Her attitude did wonders for his already piss-poor mood. He was barely holding himself from causing serious violence to them, and they were taunting him anyway.

"What do mean by that?" he asked through gritted teeth. "This is my house. This is my life you're fucking with. I have no power?"

"Samson, you have three seconds to calm the fuck down," Candi interjected.

Samson advanced toward her, fully prepared to grab her by the hair and drag her out of his house, not caring how something like that would look to the rest of the neighborhood. He was a ball of rage, and a more rational part of him – one that could point something like that was a bad idea – had left the building.

Candi shoved the phone into his face. The same phone they'd used last night. He remembered it clearly. He remembered Lissa filming, and Candi doing the same.

They didn't, his mind rebelled. But denial was pointless, as Candi reminded him.

She rose for her seat and stood toe to toe with him. "Let me tell you how things are going to go from now on. In this phone, I have videos of you having sex with us."

"For hours and hours," Lissa added, smiling. "And let me tell you, you are a wild beast, Samson," she teased.

"You're lying," Samson rebelled.

Sighing, and with a few strokes against the screen, Candi pulled up one of the said videos and clicked play.

He had an out-of-body experience watching Candi having sex with him. *That's not me. I wouldn't do that.* He felt like weeping.

Samson tried to take the phone from her and destroy it, but Candi was faster, moving out of the way.

"It doesn't matter if you destroy this phone," she said in a rush since he wasn't giving up. "Everything is stored in the cloud."

"We're not stupid enough to keep it only on the phone. Candi and I are the only ones who can access the cloud."

Samson stopped in his tracks, realizing his complete demise. "No, you're not stupid, just vicious and insane."

Candi looked disappointed. "Are you sure you want to be calling us names?"

He wanted to do so much more than that.

"We have all the power. And we can ruin your life if we want to," Lissa said matter-of-factly.

It took him a moment to wrap his head around what they were saying. "So, you're blackmailing me?"

"You can bet your sweet ass we are," Lissa replied with a giggle.

Samson felt the earth shift under his feet. *This can't be happening.* He'd rather be in one of his nightmares right now because this couldn't be his reality. It just couldn't.

"You'd better start behaving and treat us with respect, or these videos will find their way to your sweet wife," Candi said icily.

He was in a fuck load of trouble. He couldn't let these girls send anything to Teresa. She could never know about this. *Never.*

"What do you want from me?" Samson forced himself to ask.

"You already know what we want," Candi said slowly.

"I have some savings in the bank," he started to say.

"We don't want your money," Lissa interrupted him, sounding offended.

She grabbed his discarded shirt and wrapped it around herself. It did very little to cover her naked body as she stood up to approach him.

"Then what do you want?" he demanded. He had nothing else to offer. If this wasn't about money, then he was at a loss. Samson was sure autographed copies of his books wouldn't cut it, either.

Even though he was known to some people who liked a certain genre of novels, Samson was just a regular guy trying to live a regular life. But that was gone. These girls had changed everything.

Don't think like that. Everything will be all right. He just had to figure out what they wanted and comply. In this case, he was more than ready to negotiate with the terrorists because the consequences were too severe and the fate of his marriage wasn't something he was prepared to gamble with.

"I want you to do what I want and what I say. I want you compliant," Candi replied in a voice that suggested it was the most obvious thing in the world.

Would they ask for more of what they'd done last night?

"Oh, Samson, don't look so serious," Lissa patted him in reaction to his expression.

He moved out of her reach.

"We promise this will be fun."

Not to him.

"Just tell me exactly what you fucking want from me," he demanded.

Candi approached him and put a hand against his chest, then she started making small circular motions with her fingers. He took a step back, but she followed closely. There was no escaping this nightmare. He hated that she was touching him, but he couldn't stop her.

"We're going to stay here with you."

Samson opened his mouth to speak, to tell them why that couldn't happen, but she beat him to the punch.

"Just for a week, while your wife's away."

He recoiled. "How do you know about that?" he demanded.

Candi grinned. "Oh, Samson. There's not much I *don't* know about you." She looked directly into his eyes as she said that, suggestively, provocatively.

He looked away, but that brought him little peace as Lissa was right there.

This is a nightmare of a newer kind.

Come on, Samson. Wake up. Wake up!

"So, as I said, Lissa and I will be your guests, and the three of us will party all day, every day like there's no tomorrow. That is what I want."

Samson closed his eyes. This was unbearable to him.

He shook his head before saying, "And if I refuse?"

"If you refuse," Lissa began, "then we will fucking ruin your life."

And here he'd thought Candi was the cruel one.

"You will beg us to end it," Candi surprised him by adding.

Gone were the girls who asked for his help. It was an act from the beginning. "Is this what you wanted from the start?" He guessed.

"Pretty much."

Why him? He couldn't help wondering. How had they known to target him? Fury started to consume him, but there wasn't much he could do about it. Not if he wanted Teresa to remain ignorant about all this. They had him trapped, and by their smug expressions, they knew it.

How am I going to survive this? How could he spend the entire week with these girls?

"What's it going to be, Samson?" Candi prompted, not appreciating his silence. "Are you going to play nice, or will we have to *make you* play nice?"

The words that stuck in his throat nearly choked him, and he watched the girls with pure hatred as he tried to reply.

CHAPTER 10

"Say that again, Samson. I didn't quite catch it," Candi taunted.

Samson gathered all his willpower not to grab her, do some serious harm, and opened his mouth instead. "I said, 'I will play nice.'"

"Yay," Lissa said, jumping up and down and clapping her hands in delight.

Samson, on the other hand, was sick to his stomach. It felt like he'd just sold his soul to the devil. Certainly, wasn't the first time.

What did I just do?

What he'd had to do to save his marriage and his family. There was no doubt in his mind that he would lose Teresa for good if she ever saw any of that footage.

But I was drugged.

That didn't matter. She would be as disgusted by him as he was right now. It was better for everyone if she never discovered his shame.

And if he was being honest with himself, he worried that she wouldn't believe him when he said it wasn't consensual. He had been there, had to endure the torture, and he still had trouble comprehending what happened.

"Smart choice," Candi complimented.

Samson remained silent. What would they expect of him next? Especially since he was on the verge of biting off their heads. He hated being in this position. He felt trapped and powerless.

"This is going to be great," Candi said, hugging him.

He was painfully aware she was still completely naked. "Could you please put some clothes on?" he snapped, realizing too late that his tone was too harsh.

Candi did not react the way he feared she would. Instead, she grinned. "Why?" she asked peeling herself off of him. "Am I making you uncomfortable?"

He remained silent.

"It's not like you haven't already seen all of me, and tasted me," she taunted.

Samson didn't appreciate the reminder. That hadn't happened because he wanted it to; they'd made him. And he hated them for that.

He looked away.

Instantly, Candi grabbed him by the jaw and forced him to look at her. "From now on, you are my slave," she seethed.

"*Our* slave," Lissa corrected.

"So don't try and boss me around. If I want to walk around naked, then that's what I'll do. Understood?"

"Whatever," he grumbled.

Looking irked by his reply, she let him go.

Did she expect him to be amenable just because she'd threatened him? *She's got another thing coming.* Sure, they could ruin his life in minutes, but his will was still his own. And that would not change.

He wasn't about to break down because some girls drugged him and filmed him as they forced him to have sex with them. He was nobody's lap dog. Candi would learn that, and soon.

"Go make us some breakfast; I'm hungry," Candi ordered, trying to maintain authority.

Samson nodded. He would obey this time. It would be nice not to be in their presence. He would gladly cook hundreds of breakfasts for that.

Lissa stopped him in his tracks. She looked pissed off, although, for the life of him, he couldn't say why. Unfortunately, he learned her intentions in the next instance.

"I want to play with him," she informed her sister.

Candi sighed. "Can't I have some breakfast first?"

"I'm horny now." Lissa stomped her foot, and Samson gulped.

When he'd accepted this arrangement, he hadn't stopped to process what it would entail. There wasn't time then, but he was thinking about that now. *Will I have to sleep with them again?* The notion of having sex with either of them made him feel so enraged he could tear down the whole house with his bare hands.

To his horror, Candi said, "Go play," waving her hands as though shooing them. "I'll eat on my own," she added generously.

Samson panicked. He couldn't do this.

As he teetered on the verge of a complete meltdown, Lissa blew her sister a kiss, grabbed him by the arm, and dragged him upstairs to the bedroom. Before he knew what was going on, she'd pushed him onto the bed and jumped next to him.

"I'm not a morning person, but I love *this*," she said with a giggle, as she tried to pull down his boxers.

Samson couldn't believe what was happening. How could she be so relaxed and casual about this situation? He tried to stop her, taking her hands in his. "You don't have to do this," he pleaded, his eyes communicating how wrong this was.

Lissa looked at him with a strange expression, jerking her hands free. "I know I don't have to do this. I *want* to," she corrected.

With that settled, she undressed and jumped on top of him. When she leaned in for a kiss, Samson instinctively turned his head. He might be forced to whore himself for the greater good, but he refused to kiss her.

She slapped him hard, taking him by surprise. He hadn't expected her to be that strong.

"Kiss me. Now," she ordered.

When he didn't move to comply, Lissa leaned closer until their faces were practically touching.

"If you don't do what I say, I'll call your wife and tell her everything you did to me last night," she threatened without missing a beat.

Samson predicted a lot of that happening in his future.

She sat up abruptly and smiled. "I have to say, it's been a while since I had sex with someone so well-endowed. My vagina tingles just thinking about it." But then the smile disappeared. "Would you like me to say that to her as well? Or how your balls ..."

"Enough, stop," he begged.

"Then kiss me," she said leaning down. It didn't stop there.

"Touch me. I'm horny, and I want an orgasm."

It was scary how both sisters tended to go from zero to psychopath in mere seconds. *I'm sorry.* He prayed. Although he wasn't sure who he was apologizing to, himself or Teresa.

Samson complied and did everything she asked him to do. He held himself in control for as long as he could. That was a thing of pride. Eventually, he lost the battle against his biology. He hated that they could entice something like that from him, no matter how much he loathed them.

After he'd given Lissa three orgasms, she let him be, jumping off the bed as soon as she finished for the last time.

"Let's go eat," she said, putting his shirt back on. It was long enough on her that her ass didn't show, but he was sure she didn't care either way. He hated that, too.

Also, he couldn't believe she was still able to walk. Not to boast about his sexual prowess, but there was no way she could be that chipper after everything. *She's young,* he reminded himself.

"Can I stay here?" he replied sleepily. Unlike Lissa, he was pretty wiped out. "I need to rest." He hoped she would leave him to succumb to nothingness and forget any of this happened, possibly soak his body in a bathtub full of bleach. He felt extremely dirty. Last night, the drugs shielded him from the wrongness of the situation. He wasn't so lucky today.

"No," she replied sternly. "Come on, get up."

Was it too late to change his mind and just kill them?

He got up with a sigh, although he didn't immediately follow her to the door. He went to his closet and got dressed. He felt like himself again for a short moment … until Lissa joined him.

"Let's see what we have here," she sang, as though she was shopping, going through Teresa's things as Samson gritted his teeth. She shrugged off his shirt and took one of hers.

"Don't touch her things," he blurted out before he could stop himself.

She turned to face him and put the shirt on anyway. She grabbed a pair of yoga pants next, and Samson felt like screaming. This was wrong. This was *so* wrong. Why couldn't see that?

"Let's go," she ordered.

Samson complied. *Who's the dog now?* He banished that.

"Yuck, what the hell are you wearing?" a still-naked Candi said, her face twisted in disgust.

"I think it's cute," Lissa retorted.

Candi shook her head but decided not to continue. "So, how was he?" she asked instead. She was sitting at the breakfast counter eating sliced watermelon.

Samson hoped she would choke on the seeds.

"Impressive," Lissa countered without a thought. "A little shy at first," she added as an afterthought, snickering.

Among other things, Samson hated how they spoke about him as though he wasn't even there. He felt completely debased. *I am just a plaything to them. Do they ever see me as a human being?* He didn't dare answer that question.

"Did he have any problems getting it up?" Candi asked, eating her watermelon very slowly.

Lissa shrugged.

"That's not so uncommon for men his age," Candi added in reassurance.

Samson gritted his teeth. It wasn't that he couldn't perform. He'd never had problems with Teresa. He just had zero interest in having sex with these girls.

"It was an easy fix," Lissa provided.

In other words, she took matters into her own hands until his dick came to life. Samson almost wanted to chop the damned thing off for making him feel so powerless. He hated the feeling that his body had a mind of its own. His feelings and his thoughts didn't matter; biology took over, and that was that. He even had an orgasm even though he didn't want to.

It made him feel dirty; sick beyond measure.

Stop. Don't think about it.

Samson was only doing what needed to be done to save himself and his marriage. This week was no different from some of his missions in the war. He had a job to complete, and that was that. There was no need for further thoughts. Besides, if he started analyzing things, he knew that what he would encounter had the potential to destroy him. He couldn't allow that. He needed to be strong and stay focused.

That was what he continued to tell himself as Candi demanded some one-on-one time with him, right there in the kitchen. Still completely naked because she had no shame, so she swiveled around on the barstool to face him and spread her legs.

"As you pointed out, I'm an old man. I need more recovery time." He was trying to get himself out of the predicament.

He still had to fuck her.

"Yes," she screeched while he was between her legs.

"Faster!"

"Harder!"

"Don't stop."

Samson prayed to the heavens to make him blind and deaf, simply so he wouldn't have to witness Candi's ecstasy as she reached her peak and hear her scream at the top of her lungs.

Samson wanted to strangle her. That would solve all of his problems. If he killed them right now and buried them in the backyard, then he wouldn't have to worry about them sending those damn videos to his wife. Lissa mentioned they were the only ones who could access the cloud, so with them gone, it would be the end and he could continue with his life in peace.

It would be so easy to get rid of them.

So easy.

When it was done, Samson moved away and pulled up his pants. *I can't do this for the whole week.* There had to be another way. With every passing second, thoughts about finishing them off became more and more appealing.

It wasn't like the girls were innocent. If they died by his hand, who could say they didn't deserve it?

"Samson, are you thinking about killing me?" Candi surprised him by asking as she hopped off the stool.

Samson couldn't reply even if he wanted to. He'd only been fooling himself by thinking he was fit. All this sex slavery business was showing him that he most definitely was not.

Look at him making jokes about his situation. He took that as a good sign. What else could he do? It was either joke or go completely insane.

"Need a minute?" she asked sympathetically.

Samson nodded and went into the living room to crash on the couch.

Candi followed him, and he groaned inwardly. He couldn't have a second of peace. This was hell.

"I would totally off us if I were you," she said casually.

"Are you encouraging me?" Samson managed to say, finding his voice again although he was still somewhat short of breath.

"Am I?" she countered. She looked overconfident and was not bluffing.

Samson was sure she had something else up her sleeve.

She grinned when he remained quiet. She must have recognized something in his expression because she said, "That's right, Samson, I'm always at least ten steps ahead of you. Remember that."

"Yes, ma'am," he drawled, heavy on the sarcasm, although he felt anything but.

"Good little monkey," she said condescendingly.

"I hate you." He wanted her to know that.

Candi leaned and kissed him on the mouth. Her tongue inside his mouth made him want to throw up.

"I don't care," she countered once she moved away. "As long as you continue to behave."

Samson made no promises and by the look on her face, she'd expected that. Did she like the challenge? Not that it mattered.

They hung out the rest of the day, watched some really bad TV, and drank excessively. Samson was forced to do everything they did. It was exhausting.

You can do this, Samson, he encouraged. *They'll get bored with you soon enough. When they finish off the liquor cabinet, they'll leave.*

"You're almost out of food," Lissa said in a judgy voice.

That had been on his to-do list. "I can go get some."

Lissa snorted. "Nice try. We'll order everything we need," she replied, returning to the liquor cabinet.

She hooted as though she'd a jackpot, taking a bottle out.

"Don't touch that!" Samson jumped from his seat, ready to snatch it from her. It was a bottle of wine that he and Teresa received as a wedding gift. They'd planned to drink in on their fiftieth anniversary.

"What?" Lissa asked in return. "Does this bottle of wine mean something to you?"

He bit his tongue, refusing to give them any more parts of him. They could demand his body, but they could never have his heart and his soul. It sounded cheesy, but it was true.

"That's what I thought," Lissa said smugly, going to join her sister on the couch.

Candi accepted the bottle and looked at the label.

"We'll drink this special wine and then have a threesome," she announced.

"Sounds like a great plan," Lissa agreed, gesturing for him to join them. Lissa jumped into his lap as soon as he sat down.

Here we go again.

"Oh, Samson, don't look so glum," Candi observed. "This is every man's sick fantasy. You should be more grateful for the opportunity and enjoy it while you can."

"Not *this* man," he said definitely.

"You'll still fuck us," Lissa demanded.

He didn't answer, but he knew she was right.

"Why are you doing all of this?" he asked after a pause.

Candi chuckled and Lissa laughed out loud. She was the one who replied, "Because it's fun, silly."

CHAPTER 11

Another day brought Samson some new ideas. Who said his brain couldn't function when he was hungover? It definitely could if properly motivated, and he was more than motivated to end this hell.

Since it became more than apparent to him there was no way he could survive being used and abused in this manner day in and day out for the entire week, Samson had to come up with a way to get rid of them. Today.

The more he thought about their devious little agreement, the more he believed he would end up screwed. There was no guarantee they would hold up their end of the bargain at the end of the week, so he decided to do something about it.

Samson needed to level the playing field. Sadly, he had no fucking clue who these girls were, so there was nothing he could use to blackmail them.

After some consideration, he opted for a different plan. It was pretty simple: He would pit the girls against each other. Samson was sure they would leave if they started to fight since all this "fun" would lose all the appeal.

For that to happen, he needed at least some basic information about them. He needed to know what made them tick. He had a rough idea about who they were, but he needed more. Samson needed to know precisely what buttons to push for them to start snapping at one another.

They were sisters, which meant they were bound to start arguing, *right?*

He couldn't just start asking a bunch of questions, so he did the second-best thing. He decided to play the jealousy card, knowing that would get some kind of response.

Samson began pretending to favor Lissa. He picked her, figuring Candi would have a much shorter fuse when she realized she'd been left behind.

He was very subtle at first. Mrs. Connelly, who had been in charge of his drama section in high school, would have been so proud of him.

"Hey Lissa, want me to make you something to eat?" he offered sweetly. "My frittata is to die for."

"Aww, that is so sweet, but you know I prefer something else first thing in the morning."

He suppressed a shudder. "Okay. Come on, then," he said, reaching for her hand while flashing his biggest smile, praying to God he wasn't overdoing it.

Candi observed the exchange and didn't comment. She continued to nurse her morning coffee, clearly fighting a mean hangover. Samson was surprised she was even up after everything she'd drunk the night before. Even so, he noticed that she looked aware of something going on. *Good;* that's what he was counting on. She was the smarter one, after all.

Lissa gave him her hand and they started walking toward the stairs.

"Just her?" Candi asked after them.

Samson suppressed a smile.

"You can join if you want to," Lissa said over her shoulder. Samson remained quiet.

"What do you say, Samson, can I join?"

Was that a taunt? He wasn't sure.

"Slaves don't get to have an opinion," he said, opting for the safest reply even though his tone suggested he hated her guts every bit as much as he'd told her he did many times in the past couple of days.

Lissa and Samson ended up in his bedroom alone. He tried not to think about the fact that he was using his marital bed for such filth.

You can do this, Samson. You have *to.*

"I want you to do that thing with your tongue again," Lissa said at some point, snapping him from his thoughts.

He'd barely managed to remove himself from this situation and what he was doing, and the girls pulled him right back down. There was no escaping this hell.

As he satisfied Lissa, he noticed that Candi was standing by the door, filming them.

Had his plan backfired already? The last thing he wanted was for them to have even more blackmail material. He ignored her.

This was something he needed to do, no matter what Candi did in return. Samson needed to learn about these girls to crush them, and Lissa looked like the easiest mark.

Candi would be suspicious if he started showering her with attention, but Lissa just went with it. She was the easiest target, although she had bitten him in the ass so hard last night that he was still sore, so maybe he should reassess his initial thoughts.

She was as worthy an adversary as her sister. Nevertheless, it looked like his plan partially worked. Candi was intrigued, if not irked by his behavior, which was why she came to spy on them and film them in the first place. Or so he believed.

Samson hoped this little stunt wouldn't do him more harm than good. It was getting pretty dark outside when Candi cornered him in the bedroom while Lissa took a shower.

It had been exhausting playing the clown all day with Lissa, but he did it anyway and was grateful to have some time alone ... until Candi came to ruin his rest.

She'd finally put some clothes on, and Samson felt like cheering. He knew better than to say anything out loud.

"I know what you're doing," she said without preamble, looming over him. The gesture wasn't lost on him. "And it's not going to work."

He begged to differ.

Samson faked ignorance. "What are you talking about?"

"You think I'll get jealous of Lissa, and that I'll call this off."

That worried him. He *did* want to find a way and start a feud between them, but this wasn't it. This was just a test to see if he could learn more about them.

"Are you really stupid enough to think we would let some man get between us?"

He couldn't judge his cleverness just yet, but he hoped at least one of them was dumber than him.

"You can't blame me for trying," he decided to play along.

"Oh, Samson, you're not the first one who's tried this shit, but I suggest you cut it out before you piss me off. This whole week will be more enjoyable if you listen to me."

This girl was on a serious power trip. But it was more than that. She enjoyed putting men in their place. *Can you say daddy issues?*

Then he registered the first thing she'd said. Candi had just shared something with him. He wasn't the first one they'd done this to.

I'm not the first. Unable to hide his surprise, his eyebrows went up. Mrs. Connelly would be very much disappointed in him.

This was a huge revelation. The girls had done this before. When he looked back, it *did* feel like a very well-rehearsed trap. It wouldn't have worked otherwise. Samson would have figured it out. *But you didn't,* he pointed out, as though he needed a reminder.

The knowledge that there had been someone else before him who went through this torture was as surprising as it was chilling. And Candi's smile completed the picture.

She sat down next to him and patted his cheek. "Did you really think you were the only one?" she asked.

He had, but now, he understood his mistake. He was constantly underestimating these girls. He wouldn't do that again.

"You're not even the best we've had so far," she taunted.

"How many times have you done this before?" he asked, unable to help himself.

"Done what?" she asked in confusion.

Torment and rape. "Party," he chose his words carefully.

Her smile was predatory. "That's for me to know, and you to wonder."

"Oh, come on, that's not a real answer. Or are you afraid to tell me?" he countered.

Samson wracked his brain but couldn't recall seeing anything on the news about being held against his will in his home and drugged and raped by a pair of sisters.

He wasn't too surprised. They lived in a world where men were reluctant to admit such things. There was still a lot of stigma revolving around men who admitted to being abused in any way.

Would you? he challenged.

Samson's case was different. He had to keep his mouth shut and play along so they wouldn't ruin his life. He had to bury this so Teresa didn't find out.

"I'm not afraid of anything," Candi snapped, but wouldn't say anything else.

Suddenly, it hit him. If what she'd said was true – that they'd done this before – then there was a reason nobody came forward. The other men had wives, and maybe children, and had to stay as quiet as he would.

Lissa and Candi intentionally targeted married men who had a lot to lose if they opened their mouths. He was sure of it. If they were blackmailing him, then it was safe to assume they had blackmailed others. This was a practiced game.

The realization that they'd forced others into compliance chilled him to the bone. They were even more devious than he'd thought.

As his mental wheels spun like crazy, Lissa finished her shower. To his surprise, she didn't appear in the towel. She had a shirt and yoga pants on again, but he knew she had no underwear or bra.

"What's going on?" she asked after seeing Candi's expression.

Her sister looked ready to scratch out his eyes because he dared call her afraid.

That was an interesting piece of information.

"Nothing," Candi brushed it off. "Samson is learning his place."

I am? He was tempted to ask.

"Hasn't he learned that already?" Lissa asked perplexed.

Candi shrugged. "There was still some defiance left. Or didn't you notice that cheap stunt he tried to pull?"

They were once again talking about him like he wasn't there. This time, he let them. He hoped it would help him discover something else.

"With the jealousy? I noticed," Lissa, replied, looking at him like he was a puppy who'd just peed on the carpet.

So, they were *both* smart enough to realize what he was doing. Luckily, it was never his intention to play with them in that manner.

"Do you get it now?" Candi got into his face, snapping him from his thoughts. "We dictate the rules, and we are the ones in charge."

Samson couldn't accept that. He wasn't born into this world to be some spoiled kids' sex slave. He wouldn't nod and be okay with it: He would fight them until the end.

It was bad enough when he believed he was the only one. Hearing others had gone through this same type of torture made him realize how sadistic they were. In the name of "fun," these sick, twisted, perverted women had victimized man after man, and Samson promised he would be the end of them. He would find a way.

It pissed him off that they'd managed to get away with it before. He would stop them and make sure he was the last one, no matter what.

"I don't think he believes you, Candi," Lissa observed.

It wasn't that Samson didn't believe they were in charge. It was only that he didn't plan on making any of this easier on them.

Samson shrugged noncommittally. "I just don't get one thing," he said.

"What's that?" Candi replied eagerly.

Samson realized she wanted to speak about their adventures, to rub his nose in them, and to put him in his place.

What she didn't know was that it would have a counter-effect.

"Aren't you afraid of getting caught?" he asked innocently.

The girls busted out laughing.

"You really *are* an idiot." Candi looked disappointed.

"It was a good question," Samson defended.

Candi sighed. "We won't get caught because we have men like you under our control," she explained slowly, as though speaking to a child.

"And besides, our daddy would get us out of trouble if someone ever tried something," Lissa provided.

That girl never disappointed. She was smart, but she was reckless. She didn't care what she shared with him, unlike her sister who was always careful and calculated.

For the second time today, he'd learned something new. These girls had protection. There were only two explanations for how their father could get them out of trouble: He had power, or he had money. Probably both. If they were confident enough to could go around tormenting people, then it was safe to assume that their daddy had a lot of it.

Their attitudes could only mean that he'd bailed them out of trouble in the past. All of a sudden, everything fit perfectly. Lissa and Candi were spoiled brats who lived their lives in privilege and had a powerful father who fulfilled their every desire. Those desires grew over time, got twisted, and the girls started doing this, knowing daddy dearest would run to their defense if they ever ended up in trouble. Unfortunately, these girls had also learned how to play it safe and smart.

How had they wound up like this? Or was it unavoidable? They were sadistic, serial rapists with a powerful father.

If he'd never been around, or never disciplined them for their wrongdoings, then it was no wonder they had no concept of right and wrong, no moral values, and were spoiled rotten.

If they'd never experienced consequences for their actions, it was no wonder they lived thinking rules didn't apply to them.

Everything he'd learned today was very helpful. Not in a direct way, but he'd learned a lot that he could use against them. For now, he had to store away this newfound knowledge. He had a part to play, and he didn't want them to become suspicious.

"What do you want me to do now?" Samson said, faking compliance.

"That's better," Candi complimented, getting up.

She gestured with her finger for him to do the same.

"We're going downstairs to get properly drunk and party," she ordered.

He complied.

Samson didn't give a fuck who their father was since he wasn't seeking legal resolution. He would destroy these girls in a way that didn't involve lawyers or judges.

He sought revenge, and he'd already started plotting it.

CHAPTER 12

The girls got wasted pretty quickly, tearing through his liquor cabinet especially once Lissa announced that it was time to make cocktails. It was all fun and games until they turned violent. What they didn't drink, they smashed against the wall.

"Vermouth?" Lissa said with disgust. "Who drinks this shit?" and with that, she flung the bottle across the room with impressive strength that resulted in the bottle smashing into a million pieces against the wall.

Candi cheered as though that was another game to play but Samson was horrified, and not simply because he would have to clean all the shit up. He was troubled that they'd turned to destroying his property and worried whether he would have enough time to fix the damages before Teresa came home.

There was a distinct dent in the wall that could only be fixed by covering it up with a painting in the limited time he would have at his disposal.

His pleas for them not to do that were met with mocks and disdain.

"You are such a grown-up," Lissa said with disgust while making herself another cocktail.

Their drinks weren't real recipes, either: They were mixing whatever they liked at the moment. They forced him to drink, too, and the concoctions were downright disgusting.

With the living room was the center of the impromptu party, Samson was pouting on the couch while Candi jumped up and down next to him, dancing to the extremely loud music they played and screaming the lyrics at the top of her lungs.

Samson was sure one of the neighbors was bound to have enough of all the ruckus these demons from hell were making and call the cops. He couldn't decide if that was a good or a bad thing.

While Candi put on a one-girl show, acting like the star in a music video, Lissa absentmindedly walked around the room, holding a half-full glass of freshly made poison as she picked up all kinds of things, Samson's memorabilia. Most of it was things he and Teresa bought to decorate the central space in this house.

She was particularly fascinated with all the photographs of the happy couple. Teresa loved to take pictures of them, and it showed. There were a ton of framed pictures of them, doing all kinds of things. Lissa looked lost as she picked up a photo of Samson and Teresa grinning with the Grand Canyon in the background.

Despite everything, Samson was grateful they were leaving him alone for the time being, which was a rare opportunity. He was aware that could change any minute. It was pure agony being in their presence without having homicidal thoughts. He wanted to kill them so badly, he actually came up with a couple of scenarios. Snapping their dirty little necks was just one of the options. After everything they'd put him through, plotting their demise was the only thing that kept him sane because his captivity was growing worse by the minute and their demands were getting crazier by the second.

Samson was permitted to wear only a pair of boxers, a comfort he'd had to fight for like a lion. He didn't feel particularly victorious about it. These girls acted like cats in heat, demanding sex non-stop, which made exhausted him.

He was sure he'd lost weight in the past couple of days because he barely ate, always having to attend to their needs. When he rebelled, at least one of them – but usually both – threatened him with the videos until he complied. It was hard being a slave.

I'm only missing a collar. He was nothing more than a lapdog, something he vowed he would never become.

It was hard to remain a principled being when they constantly threatened him with his demise. He was fully prepared to admit that he had a leash on him and would remain bound to them as long as they had those sex videos.

He was trapped, but that didn't mean he was idle. He would find a way out of this predicament even if he had to resort to violence. Looking at them acting so careless, free, and arrogant, doing whatever they pleased, Samson could not help but contemplate the end.

Theirs or mine? That was a good question.

He couldn't envision a happy ending. These girls were too cruel, too vicious, to let him return to his normal life after this, and he was a fool to delude himself for even a second that something like that was a possibility.

Even if they decided to honor their end of the bargain – something he very much doubted – he still planned to ruin their lives, which might bring severe consequences. Especially since they had a father who could potentially destroy him.

That didn't change his mind. Samson needed with every fiber of his being to hurt them as much as they'd hurt him. Maybe that wasn't particularly Christian, but he'd made his peace with that. He was fighting demons, and he believed in the justice he would implement on his enemies.

The real question was about who else would get hurt in this showdown.

Is this revenge worth losing everything? Worth losing Teresa?

It was ironic to answer that with a "yes." He was doing all of this in the first place because he didn't want Teresa to discover the truth.

But that was before he learned he wasn't the only one this had happened to. This wasn't just about him and his life. Samson had to seek revenge for those other men, too.

A loud crash snapped him from his reverie. Lissa was going

around the room, smashing things without discrimination. Was she crying?

Samson instinctively jumped from his seat to stop her. He stepped on some debris, either from the bottle they'd broken earlier or from the ceramic elephant he and Teresa kept for luck, he wasn't sure, but he didn't stop to check.

"What are you doing?" he demanded, stepping in front of her.

He physically kept her from smashing any more things. He was enraged to see that a couple of pictures had been destroyed, among other things. And he was horrified to see she was holding his wedding photo. The frame was one of a kind, something Teresa's maid of honor had designed especially for them. He tried to take it from her, but she wouldn't let go.

That started a tug of war.

"You look so happy in this photo," she said with pure sadness, a few tears in her eyes.

"Let go of it," he countered.

Her expression morphed in an instant. "I hate it!" she screamed at the top of her lungs. She jerked it from his hand with surprising strength before turning to smash the frame against the coffee table, screaming the entire time.

It was an understatement to say she went completely insane. "I hate it! Hate it! Die!"

Samson needed a moment to snap himself from a shocked stupor and spring to action.

As Lissa reached for another piece to destroy – a figurine they'd received as a gift from Teresa's parents – and smash it against the wall, Samson tripped on a piece of frame, and it stabbed him in the sole of his foot. He ignored the pain.

"I hate everything!" Lissa continued to scream as Candi laughed, amused by her sister's mental breakdown.

Not knowing what else to do, Samson approached Lissa from behind and physically subdued her, pinning her hands against her body, so she couldn't destroy any more of his stuff. She'd already wrecked so many irreplaceable things.

"Stop it. Calm down," he demanded.

"Let me go," she started to struggle against him. "I have to break everything."

"Why?"

"I hate it."

That wasn't an answer, but he really expected to hear an explanation for such erratic behavior?

She was much stronger than she looked, but Samson's grip was unbreakable. She wasn't going anywhere.

"Let my sister go!" Candi joined in the party, throwing all kinds of things at him. He couldn't withstand being assaulted on two fronts.

Samson couldn't believe Candi's behavior. Eventually, she started pushing against him, grabbing his hands, and biting him. "Let go."

"She's out of control," Samson tried to reason, only to realize that Candi was equally unhinged.

"So?" Candi threw back at him, stopping with her efforts to free her sister for a moment.

Her response baffled him. "She's destroying my house!" He felt silly for having to point out the obvious.

Lissa was panting loudly, still full of rage, and Samson knew if he let her go, she would finish what she started. That was something he couldn't allow.

"She can do whatever she wants!" Candi shouted at him loud enough to damage his eardrums. "Or do I have to remind you that we own your ass?"

He was sick and tired of hearing that crap. "You're bluffing," he challenged. "Even if you have something recorded, I'm sure everyone would see how I was drugged and uncooperative."

He had a lot of time to think about those videos, and although he'd panicked initially and accepted this damn deal, he was now sure that whatever they'd recorded could only be used against them because it was more than obvious that they'd had sex with him against his will.

It was time for them to lay all cards on the table and be done with this nightmare once and for all.

Without a word, Candi grabbed her phone from her pocket and, with a few clicks, connected it to his TV. A few seconds later, he was watching a video of him having sex with the both of them on the very couch they stood next to.

"Let go of me," Lissa continued to protest as that same girl moaned on the screen.

This was not the image of them having sex that first night when he was so out of it and heavily drugged. In this video, Samson looked perfectly lucid and compliant.

They were still both telling him what to do, but they didn't necessarily sound like commands so much as pleas.

He was completely devastated to be confronted by an image of him that didn't look coerced, forced in the slightest into satisfying those two girls.

No one would believe he'd been blackmailed into fucking them, and the video playing on the TV proved as much. He knew the truth, but Candi's traps were executed to perfection.

"If this isn't enough proof for you, then let me fast-forward to the end," Candi snapped. She pushed play just in time for him to watch himself orgasm all over them.

Candi freeze-framed the image.

He had to look away.

Samson was thoroughly disgusted, hating them with renewed passion. *Look what they made me do.* Who had he become because of them?

"I think Teresa would appreciate this particular video," she continued to taunt. "You had some pretty good moves for an old man."

"And stamina," Lissa chimed in.

He hated them so much, his vision turned red, the color of blood. His hands would be dyed in that same shade after he killed them. His home would be painted in it as well after he put an end to this once and for all. It would be so easy to do something like that, especially since one of them was already in his hands.

"Face it, Samson: We have all the power."

"You won't get away with this," he countered defiantly through gritted teeth.

"We already have," Lissa tormented.

"… and there's nothing you can do about it," Candi finished. "So let my sister go, and don't make me ask again."

He pushed the other girl away from him, tempted to do something else, and Lissa stumbled. Not even that could erase the victorious grin on her face.

Rage completely consumed him. Deep down, Samson knew that Candi had a point. He was trapped; thoroughly fucked, for lack of a better description. Even if he marched out of this house this instant and went to the police to report all the crimes they'd committed against him, there was a big chance the authorities would laugh in his face. There was a chance no one would believe him, especially if Candi released the videos.

It was their word against his, and the videos they had made him look like his participation was completely voluntary. He almost looked eager in some of them.

If he tried to force them out or harm them in any way, there was a chance they would not only release the videos – which would cost him his marriage – but sue him and win. As he figured before, it was their word against his, and Samson feared the law would be on their side. They had a wealthy father who could hire an army of lawyers to spin every event to make it look like Samson was the true villain.

It would be funny if in the end, after everything, Samson wound up in jail for kidnapping and raping them, despite it being the other way around.

Who would believe he was a victim next to these innocent-looking young girls? Who would believe they were rapists and complete sociopaths?

That they didn't look the part made this whole situation worse.

The way he saw it, he had only one option: He had to kill them and end this torture.

There was only one thing that stopped him from acting on it.

Teresa.

No matter how he looked at things, he felt like he was going to lose her. If he killed them, he would have to live with their blood on his hands. Not even their deaths would free him from this nightmare.

Samson was sure he would likely be caught for what he did and jailed for murder. He would be branded a monster who'd killed two young girls because they had a daddy who would seek justice and demand the maximum penalty.

And he would have every right to do so.

Samson was scared shitless that he was doomed no matter what, and that was a bitter pill to swallow.

"You win," he said, falling to his knees. Glass fragments and all kinds of shit that littered the floor scratched his skin, and he didn't care.

"Oh, Samson. It's not that simple," Candi said calmly as he looked up at her.

She took his belt and folded it in two. "It's time for your punishment."

CHAPTER 13

Time was slowly but steadily passing, and Samson was starting to dread the end of the week when Teresa would return home. Unfortunately, his efforts to kick these girls out beforehand bore no fruit.

Teresa called each night and Samson had to speak to her, lying to her as the girls tormented him. Each second on the phone with Teresa was pure torture because he feared the girls would do something that would inevitably lead to Teresa learning the whole truth. He especially hated them for ruining something so precious to him.

The house was completely trashed, and each time the girls passed out from the alcohol, Samson did his best to clean up. He also had to scrub the bloody footprints he left all around from cutting his feet. His back hurt from the lashings Candi gave him for being disobedient, and he had no idea how he to explain that to his wife. But the physical damage was not what worried him the most.

He wouldn't be able to fix the things Lissa had broken in her fit of madness, and he'd already tried to come up with a viable lie. She would definitely notice that all their photos were gone and that some of the other things that were gifted to them ended up in the trash, thanks to Lissa.

The pipe in the upstairs bathroom broke and ruined everything? No. A part of the ceiling came down and ruined the living room? Perhaps. An earthquake that broke only specific things? Who would believe that?

He hated having to lie to her, but what choice did he have? The truth was not an option. She would leave him, there was no doubt in his mind about it, and that was something he couldn't accept. If she left him, then he would go on a killing spree. And he wouldn't stop with these demon girls. He would hunt down their precious daddy as well and deal with him appropriately because he was the reason these girls dared to act in such a manner, and believe that everyone and everything was at their disposal to play with.

However, he was getting ahead of himself. He still had no idea how to get rid of these monsters in the first place. They said they would leave on their own, but how could he trust them? He couldn't. He had to make sure they weren't here when Teresa returned.

And then, I'll tell her vandals broke in and destroyed our house. He even envisioned himself going to the police to report the crime.

But why was I not inside the house? How could he explain his absence? No matter what he came up with or what plan he pieced together, it was always flawed.

And you call yourself a writer, he mocked in exasperation.

He needed to come up with a viable plan, and pronto. Time was running out and murder wasn't an option. He was sure Malcolm would help him cover it up, but he didn't want to put his friend in such a position.

Can I say I spent the night at Malcolm's? That was precisely when said imaginary vandals took advantage of an empty house and ransacked it. He was sure his best friend would lie without missing a beat, but Anita would never go for it. It was another plan flawed and full of holes, like Swiss cheese.

He had to keep thinking, keep scheming and plotting because he didn't have any other choice.

It would be easier to just kill them, came the sudden thought, which he banished immediately. If they had such a powerful, wealthy father

– and there was no reason to doubt that when everything about them screamed trust-fund brats – then he would be relentless in his pursuit to discover what happened to his precious daughters if they fell off the face of the earth. Of course, all leads would lead to Samson.

Especially since videos of him having sex with Lissa and Candi were stored in their cloud. In this day and age, any decent, respectable hacker could access it, and then it would be game over for Samson.

Samson would do the same if he were the father, which led him to a different question. *Did daddy dearest know his daughters were sociopaths?* He couldn't rule that out. He knew nothing about the man apart from that he was prepared to help his children no matter what.

The situation wasn't completely hopeless, though: Samson had managed to learn a great deal about his unwanted housed guests throughout their stay.

"We're out of cereal," Lissa announced in a voice that suggested they were going to starve to death.

"I ordered some food online," her sister immediately reassured her. "It'll be here soon."

Since they'd arrived, everything had been delivered to them because Samson wasn't allowed to leave the house. Of course, he'd had to pay for everything.

"Did you order anything I like?"

"I think so," Candi replied.

Lissa grimaced, clearly irked.

Cereal was the only thing that girl ate. She was more childish and selfish than Candi. At times, Samson couldn't decide how bright she was. She must have been somewhat brilliant in the most devious manner, but at the same time, she was a downright dimwit who always said too much, and said things she shouldn't, especially to him.

Maybe she just doesn't care. Or maybe that was all a part of the game. Samson couldn't rule that out.

Lissa jumped on the couch next to Candi as Samson sat on the floor, painting Candi's toenails.

"What are we going to do today?" Lissa asked enthusiastically.

Samson already knew the answer: Nothing. They would drink, they would smash his house, they would demand sex, and they would pass out. That was all.

"I don't know," Candi replied, inspecting his work.

"That's okay. We already know *who* to do," Lissa said, laughing at her joke. She was the only one.

"True," Candi agreed. She was unusually moody today, and that worried him. Candi was the smarter of the two, not to mention more devious.

The doorbell rang.

"Go. And behave," Candi ordered him.

Samson sighed, grabbed his wallet, and went to accept the delivery.

A teenager greeted him with several bags of junk food and alcohol. "That'll be sixty-five dollars and eighty-seven cents, sir."

Samson's eyes bulged as he counted out the money.

"Here you go," he offered to the kid, who stood frozen, looking past Samson, and turning bright red. He turned just in time to see Lissa passing by, completely naked. Samson rolled his eyes, stuffed the money into the kid's hands, and closed the door.

"Did you have to do that?" he asked her. The last thing he needed was for that kid to spread around that he had naked girls parading around his house.

"No, but it was fun," Lissa countered unremorsefully.

They gathered next to him like hyenas eyeing prey as he dumped out the bags on the kitchen counter.

"Oh my God, you reek," Lissa said to him all of a sudden, her high-pitched voice rattling the glass around them. "Get away from me," she said, pushing him out of the way.

"Well, it's not my fault you won't let me have any time for myself," he shot back, unable to take any more of their bullshit.

The fact that he stank was the least of his problems. He was also sleep-deprived and starving. They rarely let him be. One of them was always demanding his attention. One of them was always horny. He'd barely had time to eat anything, and usually only managed to grab something while preparing their meals. So far, they hadn't let him bathe or even properly dress for that matter. So, he was so sorry that his state wasn't up to their standards. He said as much.

"Well, go now," Candi shooed him with her hand.

His happiness, if he could even call it that, was short-lived because Lissa went with him, and he had to let her play with his dick while he showered.

"You have to stop doing this," he blurted out before he could stop himself.

"What?" She looked genuinely confused.

"This," he pointed at her hands, which held his dick and balls. "This is wrong."

She made a face. "It's just fun, nothing else."

It was more than apparent he wouldn't be able to get through to her. *Why do I even bother?*

He felt like crying. Hitting his head against the tile. Snapping her neck or drowning her in the toilet. The possibilities were endless, especially for someone trained to kill.

"I'm bored," she announced at some point and left the bathroom. Her clothes were dripping wet: She hadn't bothered to take them off. "You have five minutes to finish up and join me in bed," she ordered.

Lissa discarded her wet clothes and took a towel to dry her hair a bit as she walked toward the bed. Samson gritted his teeth. That was the towel he'd grabbed for himself. Lissa was the most selfish person in the world. Not to mention she was shallow to the point of disbelief.

He had no idea why she'd turned out the way she had, but it was safe to say she had no empathy, or even any understanding that what she was doing was wrong.

He was sure Candi was the one to blame for that, at least partly.

Sighing, he turned off the water and went to the bedroom. He didn't bother drying off, wanting to get the next part over with as soon as possible. Lissa didn't mind.

It was fast. He didn't put any effort into it, and she took off immediately afterward, saying something about her cereal before leaving him alone.

Samson sat on the edge of the bed. The place was a complete mess. Candi and Lissa had raided the closet last night and tried on all of Teresa's clothes. After they picked out the ones they liked, left everything else on the floor.

Still, he made no move to clean up the pile. The bed reeked of sex, and he couldn't stand it. He felt like burning the sheets. *Why stop there?*

Samson stood up and went into his closet. He picked something nice to wear and then got dressed, not caring that they would give him shit. He needed to feel like a normal human being, even if just for a little while.

You will survive this. You've been through so much worse.

Somehow, he wasn't so sure of that anymore.

When they started calling for him, Samson went downstairs and found the girls doing lines in the living room. He could hear their snorting from the stairs.

He wondered where the drugs had come from. *Did they call their drug dealer?*

Great. The last thing he needed was for some shady guy to know where he lived.

"Remember what I told you, Lis. Men are dumb animals who are only good for cash and fucking." Candi was sharing wisdom with her younger sister.

Samson paused by the door to hear this special conversation unfold.

"Samson isn't that bad," Lissa countered.

"He's the worst because he pretends to be a good guy, and we both know he enjoys fucking us too much."

"True," Lissa agreed.

That was when Candi noticed him. Her nose was still slightly powdery from all the drugs. "Hey monkey," she greeted, blowing him a kiss. "We need more fuel."

"So?"

"So, buy us some fucking blow."

Sure, because he had a drug dealer on speed dial. He said as much.

"I'll call him," Candi said with an eye roll. "You get the cash ready."

"I'm a little low on money."

"Use your credit card," Lissa provided.

"Right. Any respectable drug dealer has a magnetic stripe card reader with him."

"Shut the fuck up; you're getting on my nerves," Candi snapped, not liking that he was making fun of her sister.

Lissa looked oblivious.

Samson wished he had his phone with him so he could take photos of them snorting all that coke. Unfortunately, Candi had hidden his phone and only gave it to him when Teresa called. He'd been unable to find her stash, which was pretty ironic, considering this was his house. He was supposed to know it better than her, right? Nothing was right these days.

"Your wish is my command," he grumbled.

"And don't you fucking forget it."

She was in a particularly bitchy mood today, and he hated that he could differentiate between her states.

"Lose those ugly clothes," she continued, wiping her nose. "I'm in the mood to fuck."

She adored abusing him, debasing him. It was obvious she hated men and for the life of him, he couldn't understand why. Had someone hurt her? Or had her father neglected her, and this was her way of getting back at him?

Samson bet on the latter. Not that it mattered since the result was basically the same. Candi would still be using him for sex, tormenting him, and making him take drugs regardless of what had caused her damage.

That wasn't what he felt the guiltiest about.

The worst part was lying to his wife. She called him every night to check in and chat quickly before bedtime, and Candi and Lissa were there the entire time. They watched him, mocking him as he spoke to the love of his life, lying to her and pretending all was great.

"How's the book going?" Teresa wanted to know that night.

"Great. Really great," Samson lied like a pro.

"Oh, good!"

Candi started taking his pants down and he knew that was his cue to wrap this up.

He yawned. "I'm beat. Talk to you tomorrow, okay?"

"Sure. I love you."

"Love you, too," he said before disconnecting as Lissa took his dick into her mouth and started sucking.

I love you more than you'll ever know. And that was why he endured.

CHAPTER 14

"I need to work," Samson shouted, enraged.

"You need to do only what I tell you to do," Candi shouted in return.

They were inside his study screaming at one another at the top of their lungs. Samson had gotten up that morning, and after managing to clean some of the mess the girls made, he'd decided to do some work.

It had been days since he'd fired up his computer to write. His deadline was fast approaching, so he decided this was the day to change that. He pushed all the blackmailing and rape to the side and decided to pour his heart, and all the pain, into his newest novel. If he stopped to think about his actions, it sounded insane, so he didn't. It was just easier like this.

It was not that surprising that the girls hadn't reacted well to his declaration that he was taking the morning off from their abuse to write. Especially Candi. She'd followed him upstairs, ordering him to stop. He refused, and this was the result.

"I *have* to write. My deadline is approaching." He tried to reason with her.

"I don't care."

"This is my life we're talking about."

"You have no life, apart from us, as long as we are here," Candi insisted, and he felt like murdering her where she stood. "So, if you know what's good for you..."

She didn't have to finish. Punching the wall next to the door, Samson exited. However, he didn't return downstairs like Candi wanted. She could make her own damned breakfast or starve to death for all he cared. He went to the bedroom and slammed the door behind him. He needed some time alone to vent.

These girls were completely ruining his life.

Isn't that their goal? He jumped on the bed and buried his head in the pillow, only to push it out of the way in disgust seconds later when he recognized Lissa's perfume on it. They were everywhere.

He needed to get rid of them before it was too late because this was unbearable. Things were turning from bad to worse, and he feared that by the end of the week, something even more disastrous would happen.

Don't think like that.

By some miracle, as he stressed about everything, Samson was able to fall asleep.

A loud crash made him jump out of bed and assume a battle position. Through the haziness of sleep, Samson registered that it was night outside, which could only mean he'd dozed off after both girls demanded sex from him. It went on and on for hours, especially with Candi, who was particularly vicious, clearly still upset with him because he'd dared to defy her by doing some work.

Afterward, he'd passed out from sheer exhaustion, Sadly, there was very little rest for him with these sisters inside these walls, because they were forces of destruction incarnated.

They'd decided to continue partying on their own.

Another crash echoed followed by a burst of laughter that sounded on the border of madness. He knew he had to intervene before they managed to destroy the entire house. Opening the door, he registered where all the ruckus was coming from and paled.

Oh, no, he thought, practically leaping to reach his office.

He arrived just in time to see Lissa destroying his computer with a baseball bat.

"No! What are you *doing*?" He shoved her out of the way, shielding the machine with his body.

The monitor was already smashed, and the keyboard was missing half its letters.

"I heard you had an argument with Candi, and I wanted to fix that," she said calmly.

"By destroying my computer?" He crouched next to it to assess the damage. "Why the fuck would you do that?"

She'd opened it up and pulled out all the wires.

"Because now you can focus on what's important: us."

Samson closed his eyes for a moment. "You just destroyed my manuscript," he said through gritted teeth.

The manuscript he'd worked so hard on and was so proud of how well it was going. The manuscript he hadn't been allowed to work on for the past couple of days since he was too busy being held hostage and abused in every way imaginable.

"You're welcome," Lissa snickered.

"Get out!" he shouted. He was sure he would harm her if she said another word; consequences be damned.

To his surprise, Lissa turned and swung the baseball bat down on his leg. The pain it brought had him seeing stars.

"Don't you *ever* speak to me like that again!" she screeched. "I'm sure your book was garbage, anyway."

Candi clapped from the door frame. Just what he needed, a demon child with backup.

"Nice work, Lissa."

"Thank you."

As they chatted, Samson tried to see if there was anything salvageable. Right now, his book was more important than his busted leg. He was no expert, but the hard drive looked trashed. The thing was also wet for some reason. *Fuck, fuck, fuck.*

"Come on, Samson. I want you to wash my hair," Candi ordered, as though nothing terrible had just happened.

He was sorely tempted to tell her to fuck off.

"What did you say?"

As it turned out, he'd said it out loud.

"Do you have any idea what you've done?" He shot daggers at them.

"We don't care," Candi replied in the same tone. "Now get up, monkey, and do what I say."

He didn't move a muscle.

"Teresa will be very disappointed in you," Lissa taunted.

Samson gritted his teeth and rose. His left leg protested a bit. Lissa had one hell of a swing, but he ignored it. He was too angry to feel anything else.

"Do you have anything else to say?" Candi taunted.

It took everything in him to remain quiet.

"Good boy. Now move."

He was at the door when the phone in Candi's pocket started ringing. He knew that ringtone. Someone was calling him.

Sure enough, Candi showed him the screen with glee. It was his wife. Was it that time of night already? He was starting to lose track of time.

"Pick it up," Lissa ordered, clapping her hands. She particularly liked to torture him when Teresa called. She'd pretend she was about to say something, then start laughing; torment him physically, biting him, and even sexually pleasuring him. All to see if he would slip and reveal to Teresa that something was seriously wrong inside the Chase residence.

"No," Samson replied, adamant. There was no fucking way he would give them satisfaction to hurt him even more. They'd done plenty of that already.

"Are you sure you want to be a rebel again, after everything?" Candi pointed out.

"Go to hell."

"Fine. If you don't want to talk to your wife, then I will," Lissa said, reaching for the phone. Samson snatched it first.

"Hello?" he answered.

"Hi, honey," his wife greeted him, and he could barely keep himself from sobbing. It was so good to hear her voice; good and pure torture and the same time. He was living in hell, and her voice was like being reminded of heaven. Lissa and Candi were sadistic to the core.

"Hi." He'd said that already.

"Is everything all right?"

"Yeah, why do you ask?"

"Well, Hunter called me, saying he couldn't get a hold of you."

"That's odd. I didn't hear the phone ring," he lied.

"Call him back; you know how he gets."

"Sure."

Samson wrapped it up pretty quickly. He hated talking to his wife in front of this audience, and before anyone could stop him, he dialed his editor.

"Samson," the other man greeted with relief.

That was Hunter all right, the perpetual worrier. "You called?"

Lissa approached and started whispering, "Put it on speaker."

He ignored her, but she became louder and louder as they played tag down the hallway. Eventually, Samson relented.

"... I was just checking in. How's the writing going?"

Samson cringed. It wasn't going. And by the look of things, it wouldn't go, at least for the time being. There was worse news, but there was no way in hell he would tell the other man he'd lost the entire manuscript.

Maybe I can salvage it. He still had hope.

"He sounds hot," Lissa commented, and Samson tried to mask her voice with a cough.

"It's going great," he rushed to reassure.

Candi started laughing.

"I'm glad to hear that."

To his horror, Lissa began singing, and Candi joined in, saying. "Come on, Samson. Sing with us."

He looked at them in desperation. He didn't know what to do with his phone. There was no way Hunter hadn't heard that.

Samson wanted to strangle these girls for continuing to ruin his life. He wanted it so badly that his fingers tingled.

"Samson, are you having a party?" There was no accusation in his voice, but Samson took it that way.

"No, I have some friends over for dinner," he tried to smooth it over.

The last thing he wanted was for this editor to think he was slacking off and partying when he should be writing. The reality was so much worse. He entered the bedroom, trying to move away from all the noises the girls were making.

They followed behind him.

"O-kay," Hunter replied slowly. He hadn't bought Samson's explanation, but there was nothing he could do about that right now. The damage was done, all thanks to those two girls that were hell-bent on ruining his life.

"Bye, Hunter. Talk to you soon." Samson disconnected.

"He sounds hot," Lissa said again.

"Can we meet this Hunter?" Candi taunted.

"Can we play with him?"

"Do you want to completely ruin me?" he shouted. It wasn't enough that they'd smashed up his house, done what they pleased with his body, and threatened him daily with Teresa. Now they had to fuck with the last good thing he had in his life. That was crossing the line.

"Yeah, pretty much," both girls agreed.

"It took you long enough to figure that out," Candi added.

Samson frowned. "You really shouldn't push me any further. You're not going to like the consequences."

Lissa hugged herself, pretending to shake from fear as Candi approached him. "What would you do? Hurt us?"

Samson remained quiet. There were no words for the things he wanted to do.

"I dare you to try," Candi said, interpreting his silence as a challenge.

"When I snap, I won't try anything. I will *succeed*, and I definitely won't stop at just hurting you," Samson explained, so furious that he sounded extremely calm. That was bad news, and it meant he was hanging on by a thread.

"So, you want to kill us," Candi continued, looking at him like he was the most fascinating animal in the zoo.

Badly. He didn't say that out loud, but he was sure the truth was plain to see in his blazing eyes.

"He totally wants to kill us." Lissa smiled in delight. "But why? We are as sweet as a pair of kittens."

Candi smirked.

There was something seriously wrong with these girls if they were reacting positively to his threats. Normal people would run away as fast as possible, but they were cheered by it. That was not normal. Then again, knowing what he did about them, he wasn't surprised.

"Tell me, Samson, how does it feel?"

"What? The desire to kill you?" he countered.

She shook her head. "To be so powerless. To have to fulfill our every desire while hating us so badly you want us dead," Candi replied.

"Take a look in the mirror. I am sure I hate you less than you hate yourselves," he threw in her face, and she slapped him, hard.

"Hit a nerve, I see," he commented, licking the blood from his busted lip. For some reason, the exchange was starting to help him calm down.

"You don't have the balls to kill us," Candi insulted, or at least tried to.

"I've killed a lot of people in my time," he said to her. "Adding another name to that list – or two," he appended glancing at Lissa, "– would make no difference."

"Our father would destroy you if you tried," Lissa snapped. Speaking about their demise had ceased to entertain her.

You would not be any less dead. "And your daddy is a real bad motherfucker," Samson jibed. "Rich and powerful."

"Exactly. He's your worst nightmare, the scariest adversary, a relentless sociopath, and a master of nightmares, wrapped into one."

"I'm so scared," Samson replied, unimpressed.

"You should be," Candi said calmly.

If all that were true about their father, it was no wonder they'd turned out the way they had. Hell, if even half of the things they said were truthful, it was still too much.

"Scary stories don't scare me. I write that shit on a boring Thursday night," Samson said, intentionally provoking the two.

"What scares you then?" Candi asked, intrigued.

Too late, he realized his mistake. He'd wanted to hear more about their father but had inadvertently thrown them a bone they wanted to pick at.

Lissa's next words confirmed as much. "Yes, Samson, tell us."

He sat on the bed, remaining quiet.

"Start talking, Samson," Candi snapped, losing patience.

"Yeah, or I'll send a very juicy video to your wife. Showing her every wife's worst nightmare," Lissa shouted, stomping her foot.

Her reaction was so severe even Candi objected. "Chill, sis."

Samson knew what would happen if he refused to play the game.

"Fine, I'll tell you," he capitulated with a sigh.

They jumped on the bed and snuggled next to him as though he was about to tell them a bedtime story.

I hate myself.

"While I was in Afghanistan fighting, at wound up buried underground. It took me three days with practically no food and a limited amount of water to find my way out."

He couldn't help shaking from the memories. Although he recounted it calmly and without emotion, inside, he felt anything but. Those were the darkest moments of his life. Samson was sure he would die down there. He'd screamed a lot, cried a lot, and prayed, but no one came to rescue him. He'd had to find his way out or die trying.

He'd fought stubbornly until the end. He was so far gone that in those last moments, he'd believed he was hallucinating his way out.

Not even when his fellow soldiers appeared to help him did he believe that they were real. He'd wept, believing he reached heaven.

Samson left the army for good after he was discharged from the hospital, a decision he'd made while in the tunnels. He couldn't stomach all that anymore. Even after all this time, some things still plagued him. Even the basement in his home made him feel uneasy, which was why he'd installed the brightest lights available and an additional exit, just in case.

Candi smiled as he spoke, enjoying how unsettling this was to him.

"That's some crazy shit," Lissa commented once he finished.

Yes, it was, he thought, *but so is this.*

CHAPTER 15

"Tell us another one," Lissa urged, nudging him as though needing to make sure he understood how much she enjoyed his torment.

Samson was glad someone found his gruesome war experiences amusing.

"I'm done talking about it," he replied, suddenly exhausted. Thinking about war and everything he endured always put him in a foul mood, and he didn't want that now. He was already struggling with everything that was going on; he didn't need any more shit on his plate.

"You're done when we say you're done," Candi warned.

He was sick and tired of her attitude as well. Whenever she heard something she didn't like, her immediate response was to threaten.

Isn't that to be expected? He was held here against his will after all, and Candi had to assert her authority to achieve anything.

Samson looked at her long and hard before replying, "Aren't you tired?"

"Of what?" she replied defensively.

"Of yourself," he snipped.

Lissa snickered.

Candi narrowed her eyes. She didn't like being laughed at.

Samson didn't give her a chance to reply before continuing, "Is this how you want to spend your days? Don't you want to be better?"

"Ugh. You sound like our father," Lissa commented.

Good.

"You must realize this can't be good for either of you," Samson almost pleaded.

"Shut up!" Candi screamed.

He'd clearly struck a nerve.

"All of this is wrong, and you know it," he continued to press.

"I don't care about your psychoanalyzing bullshit."

"Yeah. We only want you to do what we tell you and nothing else," Lissa added.

"Because it's fun?" Samson challenged.

"Yeah."

"This is not fun; this is torture," he pointed out, needing to confront them with themselves and what they were doing. They had to know all of this would eventually have consequences.

"Yeah, it's so torturous that you have to have sex with two hot girls," Lissa mocked.

She still had no idea how wrong this was. Worse, she believed she was doing him a favor. It made him sick to his stomach.

"I won't let you get inside my head," Candi seethed, looking at him like a wild animal. "So shut the fuck up, or I'll cut out your tongue."

He fully believed she was capable of something like that. Not that he would let her, but still. She was vicious enough to do much worse than he initially believed: He had scabs from the lashes to his back to prove it.

Samson ignored their outbursts, already knowing where this was headed. They would threaten to talk to his wife, share videos with her, and so on.

He needed leverage, and asap since he figured with a stalemate, mutual destruction was the only result.

These girls were crazy but they weren't stupid, and they

wouldn't do anything to jeopardize their comfort and their "fun." All he had to do was find something to threaten *them* with and it was game over.

Sadly, that was easier said than done.

"Do you want me to shut the fuck up?" he quoted. "Or do you want to hear another war story?" he challenged, heavy on the attitude.

Candi figured out what was doing as Lissa cheered. "We want another story, of course."

The other sister let it slide, and he smirked. Small victories meant more than they should these days.

"Well, you're in luck because I have plenty of them," he told Lissa in a jolly manner although he felt anything but.

"Yes," Lissa said, snuggling even closer.

"My first week in Afghanistan, my friend Jarrod and I were in a patrol, and he stepped on a land mine," he started. Samson didn't even have to think about what story to share because so much shit had happened over there. It was kind of depressing when he thought about it, and that was precisely why he tried not to. But fuck it; he had a role to play.

"What did he do?" Lissa asked, clearly invested.

"The worst thing he could have," Samson replied. The girls looked blankly at him, so he decided to elaborate. "Jarrod panicked and tried to run away."

"What a moron," Lissa commented as Candi asked, "Did he die?"

"No," he countered much to their disappointment, "but the mine won that battle."

"How come?"

"He lost both his legs, and I had to carry him back to the base." All the while Samson prayed like hell his friend would not bleed out.

"So, he became a cripple?" Lissa sounded almost disappointed, or disgusted. "Better he died."

That was such a hurtful thing to say that Samson didn't know how to reply.

"A whole lot of people *did* die over there, so have some respect," Samson snapped.

"Whatever," Lissa replied, rolling her eyes.

"Is that the whole story?" Candi prompted.

Samson nodded.

"What else happened in that war of yours?"

"It wasn't my war," Samson felt the need to correct.

"Whatever. What happened next?"

"With Jarrod?"

"No, with you."

"One time we were flying over in the helicopter when the Taliban started firing on us."

"Really? What happened?" Lissa asked, moving so she could look into his face.

"One of their missiles hit the tail of the helicopter and we started spiraling out of control. The pilot did his best, but we crashed hard in the middle of the desert."

"Did you get a nice tan?" Lissa asked completely straight-faced.

Samson groaned inwardly. These girls didn't take anything seriously, and it was infuriating.

"A lot of bad things happened to you, Samson," Candi said, sounding almost impressed.

"Well, I was in a war," he pointed out the obvious.

As he started to tell more stories about his time in Afghanistan, the lines between reality and all the bad memories began to blur. At times, he almost felt like he was back there again, with the smell of gunpowder mixed with scorched earth inside his nostrils. He could nearly hear the shouts of his brothers, feel the heat against his skin as his body pumped with adrenaline, and crave action.

"The village was supposed to be abandoned, but our intel was wrong. Some women with children and elderly had refused to evacuate, and the terrorist used that to their advantage."

"How?" Lissa urged.

"They took them as hostages."

"Aren't they like the same people?" Candi wondered.

"That didn't matter to them. The terrorists demanded we surrender and give them our weapons or they would start killing them."

Of course, their commanding officer wasn't in the mood for negotiations, resulting in a massacre. Nearly all of them died, both terrorists and innocent people. Samson could still see a boy, no more than four years old, killed right in front of him. He was running, barefoot, toward Samson when a gunshot rang out. Bang! And he fell to the ground. His wailing mother clutched the child in her arms, cradling him like he was just asleep.

When the next loud bang echoed around them, Samson jumped on the floor next to the bed and covered himself. If one bomb fell, another would be close behind. There was never just one. His heart was beating so fast that he had trouble hearing anything else. Even so, something broke through. *Was that laughter?*

Samson concentrated hard. It was definitely laughter. He looked up, bewildered. The girls were laughing at him.

Girls? There were no girls with him on that mission. That freaked him out for a moment until more details bled through. He was not crouching next to the armored vehicle as he believed. He was hiding next to the bed in his room. He was home and not across the world. *That war ended a long time ago,* he reminded himself. He was safe.

Well, sort of, he corrected, returning to reality.

"Look at him." Lissa was clutching her stomach and pointing.

Candi stood up to look outside. "It was just a car backfiring, you coward," she chuckled.

Samson sat up slowly. He needed time for his body to return to normal, and realize it was not in danger. That was the hardest part. Although his head was fully in the here and now, his body continued to behave as though he was in danger.

"You're such a coward, Samson. Scared of some car," Lissa mocked in disgust.

"A complete wuss," Candi added, returning to bed. "I can't believe you went to war."

"He made everything up. I'm sure he hid in the base the whole time, wetting his bed," Lissa said with a laugh.

That's it. Samson exploded, jumped to his feet, and started advancing toward Candi, who stood up as well.

"Don't you *ever* speak to me like that," he boomed into her face. "I'm a decorated soldier. I defended my country."

"Sure. Just like I saw you defending yourself from a car," Candi taunted.

He felt sorry for her.

"You wouldn't last an hour on the battlefield. Out there, there are no blackmail sex tapes. Out there, nobody gives a shit who your daddy is. And if you cross paths with someone who is a better killer than you, you die. Period."

"We're shaking with fear," Lissa piped up, but Samson was too focused on Candi to care what her sister had to say.

He could reach for her, kill her, and feel nothing afterward.

"So, you're telling us that you were always the better killer?" Candi asked with a smirk.

Samson shrugged. At times, yes. At times, he was just lucky. A lot of things could and did go wrong while he was fighting. Fortunately, he was never alone. His brothers had saved his skin more times than he could count, and he'd done the same for them. Not that these spoiled, ignorant bitches could ever comprehend such a complex, divine concept of unity.

Candi made a face. "Did I hurt your feelings when I called you a coward?" She was still playing, and it pissed him off further.

"You'd better stop messing with me."

"Or what?" she challenged. "What will you do?"

"To you? Or your sister?" he clarified.

"You would kill me? Kill Lissa?" she continued to taunt.

It irked him to no end she believed his threats were empty. "Don't tempt me."

"I have to; it's so fun. How would you do it?"

He smiled humorously. "I could kill you in so many different ways. I sad that you only have one life to give."

"Would you choke me?"

"That's too easy."

"Really? Come on and show me." There was a strange glint in her eyes as she said that. Did she want to die?

"Come on," she urged, "grab Lissa," she offered as though they were discussing what to order for lunch. "I want to see you choke her to death." Candi was so excited now that her voice vibrated.

"Excuse me?" Lissa voiced, moving away from them. "I'm right here, and I don't want to be strangled."

Unlike her sister, Lissa grasped the gravity of the situation. Or maybe Candi just didn't care what happened to Lissa.

"Come on, Lissa; it'll be fun," Candi said to her, although she was still looking at Samson.

"Stop joking around," Lissa complained. "I don't like it."

The kicker was that Samson wasn't joking. He was on the verge of committing a double homicide. It took everything in him to not act on his impulse. The most insane part was that Candi wasn't joking, either. There was a strange, macabre curiosity in her, and she wanted to watch him kill someone. Even if it was her sister.

Realizing that helped him to calm down. *This is not who I am. I am not a killer. I don't do biddings for a sociopathic little girl.*

That did not mean he couldn't have some fun.

"I don't want to feel my hands around Lissa 's neck," he said taking a step toward Candi. "I want them around yours."

"And I hold your leash," she said defiantly, although he could detect a trace of fear in her eyes as she said it.

"Are you sure?"

"Do as I said," she commanded.

"Candi!" Lissa screamed.

Samson stood down.

"Relax, Lissa," Candi said, flipping her hair. "I was just joking."

Lissa stood up and crossed the small distance to stand next to her sister, managing to avoid Samson. *Smart move.* "It didn't look like that to me."

"It's just fun to rattle his cage, that's all," she defended with an eye roll.

"Well, it wasn't fun for me, telling him to choke me to death," she whined, and her voice started to shake. She was genuinely upset about this, and Samson was glad.

He remained quiet. He felt no need to reassure her that he would never do something like that. It was better that she believed he was more than ready to kill her.

"What would you do if he came after me?" Lissa wondered aloud.

Candi took her time answering.

"*Candi*," Lissa urged.

"I'd stop him, of course."

Lissa wasn't buying it. "Right."

"Stop overreacting," Candi said, irritated.

"Whatever," Lissa said, throwing her hands in the air and then storming out of the room.

Samson smiled at Candi. It couldn't be helped. He'd won. This was a small battle, but he'd won, and Candi knew that.

She stormed out after her sister, leaving him alone.

He sat on the bed. *That was close.* Too close for comfort. He was scared shitless of how close to the edge he'd been. If Candi hadn't been so eager to see her sister choked to death, he might not have been able to recover in time. That act of madness from Candi had allowed him to start thinking rationally again.

He didn't like what had happened one bit. It showed him how the raging beast that was always lurking inside of him, was just beneath the surface and ready for its moment. However, he couldn't succumb, no matter what.

There was a silver lining, though. The sisters weren't as tight as they proclaimed to be. This little stunt showed proved as much.

If there was tension between them, then that was something he could use to his advantage.

Samson just had to find a proper pressure point to divide them for good. And he knew just where to start.

With Lissa, of course.

CHAPTER 16

After the sisters left – presumably to continue arguing in a different part of the house – Samson enjoyed some peace. Although his mind was preoccupied, being alone helped him to calm down.

He hated how easily Candi had managed to provoke him and infuriate him, but it wasn't all her fault. He'd struggled with PTSD for a long time and refused to seek help. He'd deluded himself to think he could handle it on his own, and this was the result. He'd almost made the biggest mistake of his life.

Samson put his head into his hands and took a deep breath. There was a mantra, a prayer really, that he'd recited to himself in combat, and he repeated it now as well.

It took him three tries, but eventually, he began breathing normally and managed to lower his heart rate. Now his body, mind, and soul were once again steady and in harmony. He couldn't say he was "at peace" because he was far from that. There would be no peace while he was being held against his will, blackmailed, and abused.

But he was working hard to change that.

Although he was ashamed of his relapse today and how he'd

allowed himself to be triggered by a car backfiring, it had shown him something new. He couldn't believe how eager Candi looked while goading him to go after Lissa.

Would she really have let me choke her sister? he wondered. Seeing her expression, he had his doubts. Although she'd defended herself and said she would have stopped Samson when Lissa accused her of crossing the line, he wasn't so sure. Candi seemed pretty blood-thirsty.

As it turned out, Lissa noticed as well. Candi was a different kind of monster than he thought, and this turn of events was something he would use to his advantage. But he needed to act now, while Lissa was still upset with her sister.

Samson went downstairs just in time to see sisters going their separate ways. It was clear that the atmosphere between them was still tense, although Samson was sure Candi did her best to smooth things over. Lissa's expression made it clear that Candi wasn't completely successful in her endeavors.

Candi went to take a bath while Lissa retreated to the living room to watch TV, clearly still pouting.

Samson grabbed some cereal and decided to join her in the living room. He offered some to the younger sister as he sat beside her. She refused.

"Are you all right?" he inquired, faking concern.

"Why wouldn't I be?" she asked with a smile. She looked slightly off.

"I'm sorry for what happened," he said next, figuring it would be a bad move if he started trashing Candi right away.

Lissa looked at him with a blank expression. "What?" she asked.

Samson couldn't decide if she was intentionally pretending not to understand him, or if she was that dense.

"I'm sorry I lost my temper back there," he said. It wasn't techni-cally a lie.

It seemed like she was about to make a joke out of the whole situ-ation, and brush it off, but he wasn't going to let her. This was his chance, and he had to take it.

"Candi shouldn't have taken advantage of that and tried to get me to choke you. She's your sister, and that was crossing the line," he said sympathetically.

"Candi was just playing around." She brushed it off as he knew she would although Samson could see on her face that the words didn't match her emotional state. She was rattled by what happened.

Good.

"Are you sure?" he pressed a little.

"Of course I am. It was a joke. We always look after one another," she recited, raising her chin.

"It didn't look like it to me."

"Really?"

"Yes, it looked like your sister got carried away."

Lissa remained silent.

"And if you won't get mad about it, I certainly will," he said, earning a pair of raised eyebrows. His words had surprised her.

"Candi is a sociopath who only cares about having fun. She showed today how little loyalty she has for you," Samson said harshly.

Lissa wasn't any better, but unlike Candi, she appeared to genuinely love her sister and would do anything for her. Samson could not say if Candi loved anything or anyone.

However, right now, he needed to shock Lissa so she would start thinking things over and hopefully begin to have doubts. That was his only way out.

"She's not that bad," Lissa countered, her tone not completely convincing.

"No; she's worse," Samson was adamant.

"What have you been saying about me?" Candi inquired, entering the room. Her hair was wet and stretched down to her ass while dripping all over his wooden floor.

"Only the truth: That you don't care about who you hurt as long as you're having fun," he countered without missing a beat.

Lissa slapped him. "You're wrong. Candi loves me, and she wouldn't do anything to hurt me."

Was that for the show because her sister had appeared, or did she mean it? *She wants to believe it's the truth.*

"Of course I wouldn't," Candi agreed, leaning over to kiss her sister on the cheek. Her eyes stayed on Samson the whole time.

That was a message. He was right, but he couldn't do anything about it.

"I'm the only family she has," she continued, "and we look after one another."

"Loyal to the end," Lissa finished.

That was obviously some kind of a mantra they told one another when things got tough.

"Just you and her against the world, huh?"

"Always," Lissa and Candi said almost in unison.

"How does your daddy fit into that picture?" he asked slyly.

He couldn't say whose reaction disturbed him more.

Lissa hit him again and Candi began screaming at the top of her lungs and breaking things. She threw the remote, and it cracked the TV screen. He felt like he'd just lost a limb. But so many other things were happening just then that he didn't have time to properly process any one thing.

"Don't you ever mention him again," Candi screamed at him. "You don't know what you're talking about. You know nothing."

His eardrums were throbbing, but he was pleased to have found a sore spot.

"He obviously doesn't love you enough," Samson commented, which earned him a couple more hits.

"Shut up! Shut the fuck up!"

He jumped from the couch, moving away from the two screaming banshees.

"So, I guess he doesn't know about or approve of your little hobby."

"If you don't stop talking about him, I'll hurt you so bad, you'll think of me every time you try to sit down," Candi threatened, and she looked so enraged and deranged that Samson could envision another lashing in his near future.

That didn't stop him from saying, "You must be a real disappointment to him. Especially you, Candi."

Objects started flying around as he ducked out of the way, retreating to the kitchen. In retrospect, that was a bad move. There were various very sharp objects at their disposal in this room.

As they circled him, Samson raised his hands into the air in a universal gesture of surrender.

Candi hit him with her fist. Samson shook his head to clear it and grinned. "I was only kidding. It's all just harmless fun. Right, Lissa?" He looked at the other girl.

"Don't get cute," she snapped.

Maybe he'd gone too far.

"You're not on our level, so stop, before you make us hurt you," Candi added.

"That would be a shame," Lissa made a face. "We like playing with you so much."

Samson nodded. With that little nudge from him, they'd revealed a lot.

It sounded like their father wasn't as supportive as they'd initially boasted. There was drama going on there; serious drama based on the girls' reactions. Samson took that as good news. Terrific, even.

Samson was sure their father was to blame for their behavior. He was sure he had spoiled them rotten and given them all the things money could buy. It was questionable how much love they received from him, but that didn't matter to Samson.

He was also sure that they'd made quite a few messes and their father had had to intervene. If that was their cry for help or way to seek attention he couldn't say, but he also wasn't their shrink.

Now, Samson wondered if daddy dearest had had enough. If they had been this wild for years, maybe their father had put his foot down. That would explain their recent outbursts. They acted as though he'd betrayed them.

If their father learned about the current situation, would he try to help them? Drugging and raping was a much different scenario than some of the more juvenile misdemeanors they could have committed in the past.

There seemed to be no love lost between them, and they used him just like they used other men in their lives. Lissa's comments about how Candi was her only family accentuated that.

So, daddy dearest isn't pleased with how his two princesses turned out. Samson was sure the man in question had only himself to blame for that.

"I need a drink," Candi announced, snapping him from his thoughts.

"Me too."

Samson cringed. This was the wrong time to point out how they'd already drunk everything in the house. That was why he said, "Let me order you some tequila." He asked for his phone and Candi ignored him, deciding to do the shopping on her own.

As they made a list that would burn another hole in his bank account, Samson continued to muse.

All this drama about their father had made him wonder about their mother. Who was she? How did she fit into this picture?

They'd never mentioned her, not even once, which he found odd. It didn't matter if their mother was dead, divorced from their father, or still around but completely useless, it was obvious they cared less about her than they did about their father.

Samson was sure there was one incident that could be somewhat related to their relationship with their mother. It was bizarre how Lissa acted while looking at his wedding photos. She screamed and smashed them all, like she couldn't stand the happiness and had to destroy it. That could point to the state of their parents' marriage.

These girls had a lot of issues, and the list grew every day. The question was how to take all these bits and pieces of information and use them against them.

There had to be some way he could take all the daddy issues, sprinkle them with mommy issues, and use them to his advantage. *But how?*

This wasn't something he was taught in school or the military.

He couldn't suddenly start acting like he cared, showing them all the love they never received from their parents. They'd never buy that, especially since he had been on the verge of strangling them mere hours ago.

At the same time, things happened in these kinds of situations. Stockholm syndrome was real, but for that, they would probably have to spend months or years together, and he didn't have that kind of time.

Can I speed things up? Not to develop that shit, but just start acting like he had. He had never been that good of an actor, but he had to try something, and he was certain that their father was the key to everything.

Then, inspiration struck. *Maybe I can threaten to tell their father everything.*

He liked that idea, but there were a few problems. One, he had no idea who their father was. No name or occupation either, so they would just laugh at him.

Even if he managed to learn something like that, Samson still had no proof to bring to the gentleman. Besides, what if the other man was the monster his daughters painted him to be? What if he was a gangster?

When they'd first mentioned him, Samson had some kind of a white-collar businessman in mind. What if that was the wrong assumption? What if their father operated on the other side of the law? It could explain the sisters' behavior.

Sociopathic tendencies can be hereditary. Samson could very easily find himself six feet underground if he said or did the wrong thing. No father in the world would like to hear that his precious daughters were monsters.

As always, Samson was getting ahead of himself.

I don't have to go and see the man, just make the girls believe I will.

Still, it would be tough to sell the fact knowing nothing about that man, not even his freaking name.

If he could just find a way to provoke them into spilling the beans, he would be golden.

Of course, like everything else in his life, that was much easier said than done.

CHAPTER 17

I t didn't take long for the girls to forget everything and demand his presence once again, an encounter that included playing naked Twister without the Twister.

"We're bored," Lissa announced at some point, already quite tipsy. She was drinking wine right from the bottle and not sharing it with anyone. He didn't mind. Samson avoided alcohol at any cost and drank only when he was forced to.

"Entertain us," she whined, yelling directly into his ear.

"How?" Samson asked in return, preying like hell this wouldn't turn into another sex game.

He'd started to hate sex, and he was physically disgusted each time he had to satisfy either of the sisters. He was repulsed each time they touched him.

Don't think about it.

"I don't know," Lissa countered, helpful as always. It was better that way. The longer it took her to think of something, the better.

He didn't care for Candi's expression, though. He so didn't want to hear any of her suggestions.

Samson was about to offer to prepare something to eat. Playing naked chef was much better than playing sex slave. Although he was sure they would demand sex from him regardless of what he offered them now.

Candi beat him to the punch. "How about you tell us more about war?"

The strange expression on her face made him immediately understand why. She liked how he lost his temper. She enjoyed seeing him triggered the last time he spoke about his war experiences, and she was hoping for more of the same.

She was so devious that Samson needed to invent another word for it. Part of him couldn't believe the fact that he'd almost killed them had turned her on. Another part could.

When a person lived for "fun," it was imperative to maintain the same levels of excitement, which wasn't easy. Repeating the same actions causes boredom, and eventually, the activities must be more creative, bolder, and crazier. The same could be said for any addiction. Over time, a single dose isn't enough; a person needed more. Not that Samson was trying to make excuses for her. That was the last thing he would do.

"Why do you want to hear about war?"

"Because it's so educational," Candi replied with a smile.

Right, like he was buying that. He knew exactly what she wanted.

There was no way he would allow Candi to trigger him in any way again. He was aware of that possibility now, which meant he would avoid it like the plague.

At the same time, this was an opportunity he couldn't pass up. He wanted to try something he'd been thinking about for a while, and there was no moment more perfect than now.

"You know, there's a reason I ended up in the military," he said carefully, making a face, as though that thought only now popped inside his head.

"What reason?" Lissa asked as he knew she would.

"My fucking father," he added some extra heat as it said it but worried he'd overdone it.

"How come?" Candi asked, looking genuinely curious.

He mentally patted himself on the back. *So far, so good.* He needed them engaged.

"I don't like talking about him," he replied with a hand wave. "The man's a bastard."

"Oh, come on. Tell us about him," Lissa complained.

He almost expected her to start pulling at his sleeve to urge him to continue. He was almost completely naked though, so he had no sleeves to pull.

"You can tell us anything, Samson. We know how to keep a secret," Candi said seductively, her meaning clear.

Samson pretended to be on the fence. He had only one shot at this, and he didn't want to blow it.

"I can't. I hate the guy," he said eventually, pacing around the room.

"Samson, speak," Candi said a bit sharply.

"Fine," he grumbled as though not pleased with this turn of events, sitting on a chair opposite them. He always tried to keep as much distance from them as possible when they allowed it.

He took a deep breath before starting. *Don't overdo it.*

"My mother met my father when she was still very young."

"Were they high school sweethearts?" Lissa inquired.

Samson shook his head. "No. She was a waitress in a restaurant he frequented."

"Was he older than her?" Candi asked next.

"Yeah. He was already a very successful businessman, and he swept her away."

"What did he do?" Lissa asked, getting excited.

Samson shrugged. "The usual rich-guy crap. Took her to expensive restaurants for dinner, bought her presents, flew her to a different city to listen to her favorite band play ..." He trailed off. "You get the picture."

"Classy," Lissa commented.

"He sounds like a catch," Candi approved.

Samson made a face. "Yeah, that was what my mother thought,

too. As it turned out, he was nothing but a spoiled rich guy who wanted to get into her pants."

"There are other, more simple ways to get into woman's pants," Candi pointed out, playing the devil's advocate.

"Like drug her?" he asked before he could stop himself.

Her eyes flashed with undiluted fury.

Lissa saved him from Candi's reaction. She moved closer, sitting on the floor. "What happened between your parents?" she urged.

"They were madly in love, or so she believed," he replied before looking away. Then he added, "Eventually, she got pregnant with me."

"And how did he react?" Candi asked although it was obvious, she knew where this was going.

"He went ballistic. He accused her of being a gold digger, said she got pregnant on purpose, and gave her money for an abortion," Samson explained.

"Did she have it?" Lissa asked, on pins and needles to hear his reply.

Samson looked at her. There was no way she was that dense.

"No. She decided to keep the baby – *me* – and raise me all by herself."

"I'm sure he loved hearing that," Candi commented with a half-smile.

Samson shrugged. "He forced her to sign some kind of a document that she would never seek him out or initiate any kind of legal dispute against him."

"No child support?" Lissa was aghast.

"No child support," Samson confirmed. "He thought having me around would jeopardize his future political career, especially since he considered my mother very socially undesirable."

"Socially undesirable?" Lissa repeated, making a face as though not understanding the meaning.

"Poor," he clarified.

"She signed that shitty document?" Candi was horrified.

"She just wanted him gone. But because of that, he never gave us a dime."

"How sad," Lissa said simply.

"Did you ever meet him?" Candi asked next.

Samson shook his head. "No. Never wanted to, either."

"I can understand that."

"It irks me to no end when I see him on TV, doing speeches and campaigning with his wife and kids next to him, smiling proudly while I know he's a complete bastard."

Lissa and Candi looked slightly uncomfortable hearing his tale. Did his story ring true to them? He hoped so.

"He's that famous?" Lissa exclaimed.

Samson nodded. "He's living his dream, and my mother had to have two jobs so we could survive. She suffered until the day she died, and that bastard couldn't have cared less," he seethed.

Candi suddenly started laughing, taking him completely by surprise.

"I can't take it anymore," she managed to say through the cackles, and Lissa joined in.

Samson was confused. He had no idea what was happening. *Did I overdo it? What did I do wrong?* He wondered since this was not the reaction he was hoping to achieve.

He wanted them to feel sympathetic; connected to him. He hoped that a shared, painful experience would create a bond he could later exploit.

That was not happening.

"I'm glad my life story is so amusing," he decided to give it another go, looking at them with anguish. That was no act: He was, just not for the reasons he was offering.

"Cut the crap, Samson. The fun is over," Candi replied, managing to calm herself long enough to say that.

"Excuse me?"

She gave him the look. "I know the story you just told is complete bullshit," she announced.

What? How? Did he make a slip of the tongue? Had he said something during his blackouts? All kinds of questions swirled inside his head, but he didn't have to wonder long.

"We researched you a little beforehand."

"What?" he exclaimed, completely aghast.

"We like to know who we're dealing with," Lissa said innocently. "I don't want to party with some stranger. What if you turned out to be a psycho?" She giggled at the bad joke.

Samson was looking at Candi. "You *researched* me?" he accused. That meant nothing was by chance. He was chosen, and that was how they knew when to appear on his doorstep. The realization was downright devastating.

"Yeah," Candi replied as though it was no big deal. "I know your father wasn't a politician," she accused, as though what he'd done was bad and what she and her sister continued to do was completely legitimate.

Blind rage consumed him, and he had to bite the inside of his mouth to stop himself from shouting.

"I mean, the part of not knowing your dad is true," she corrected. "However, he was not a businessman or a politician. Your father Zack was a soldier, like you, who died in action."

He was horrified. There was nothing he could say to that.

"I guess you were right, in a way. You *did* end up in the military because of your father," Lissa concluded.

"You knew all along?"

They nodded.

"We just wanted to see where this would all go," Lissa explained. "You painted a very sad picture for us, Samson. Thank you."

"But what did you hope to accomplish?" Candi wondered.

He remained silent.

"Oh right, you hoped we would feel sorry for you," she guessed.

Lissa started laughing. "You're such an idiot."

His mind was still spiraling from the last revelation.

"How did you know the truth about my father?" he demanded, standing up.

That wasn't something they could read online. He was a soldier who died during a covert mission. Not even his mother knew the whole truth because the military documents were classified. And yet somehow, these girls knew. He was shaking from anger.

Candi rose as well, with a self-satisfying smirk. "Don't you get it by now? We know everything about you. I know everything that goes on inside that head of yours," she added, approaching slowly, predatorily. "Just know that whatever you try to do won't work. I'm smarter than you, and this crap won't fly."

There was nothing he could say to that. He knew when he was beaten. Once again, Candi had proven that he was not their equal.

Am I just to accept my fate? He couldn't do that, either.

Samson was furious, and it took everything in him not to pounce on her. Mostly though, he was angry with himself. His plan to entice sympathy in them, upset them, and make them trust him and build a bond based on a shared traumatic experience had backfired. He was the only upset individual here; they looked very amused.

His plan to gain more info about their father, and maybe even turn them against one another had tanked. The revelation that they'd done their homework on him and knew intimate details about his past was chilling if not downright disturbing. The fact that they'd done a background check before picking him for this fun experience and entering his life just to ruin it, showed him a completely new dimension of their criminal enterprise.

They were not just party girls looking for fun and seizing an opportunity when it arose. They were serious predators who chose their victims carefully.

He already knew they looked for someone committed, probably with children, who could be manipulated and blackmailed with compromising videos, but this went beyond that. *Did they know about my PTSD, too?* He didn't want to know the answer but feared he already did.

As Candi had said, she was at least ten steps ahead of him. That was daunting and utterly terrifying.

Samson knew he was screwed before this, and now, he felt ten times worse, and the notion left him paralyzed.

CHAPTER 18

.

Samson's head hurt. He had been forced to do shots with Lissa, and he couldn't remember why or even what they'd ended up drinking. It was all a blur of her laughter and Candi's smugness seasoned with a lot of sex during which the sisters continued to tell him what an idiot he was for telling that story.

Naturally, it all was taking a serious toll on him. He was devastated by the fact that no matter what he did, he couldn't win. Alcohol wasn't helping in that department, either: It just made him feel worse and more depressed. Samson had never been a drinker. He'd grab a beer or two with his buddies every once in a while, but that was that, so he had no tolerance. He also wasn't young anymore, and it showed.

Candi appeared as he mused about his uselessness. She was a white blur, and it took him a couple of tries to focus on what was going on with her.

"Look at me, everybody," she said cheerfully. "I'm Teresa, and this is the happiest day of my life," she continued to mock, dabbing at her eyes with a tissue.

He raised his head, which caused a series of problems, but he ignored that and focused on the fiend in front of him.

Oh no. Samson was horrified. Candi was wearing Teresa's wedding dress. It instantly sobered him up.

His wife adored that dress, and after their wedding, she'd placed it in a special wrapping to hold it as a keepsake. And now, that evil girl was parading around in it.

Lissa laughed, looking at her sister. "That thing is hideous."

"I know. I can't believe someone wanted to be married in it."

"Samson, your wife has no taste," Lissa told him.

"Well, she married *him*," Candi deadpanned, and they laughed.

Samson gritted his teeth at seeing Candi. He'd had tears in his eyes when he first saw Teresa in that dress. She was the most beautiful woman in the world to him – still was – as she walked down that aisle toward him. He remembered thinking that he couldn't wait for her to become his wife and hoped the minister would keep it short. Teresa took his breath away when she'd said yes.

"Where did you get that?" he demanded.

"The closet," Candi replied.

"Take it off," he growled. They'd already destroyed too much; he couldn't allow them to ruin this as well. The mere notion that Teresa would see her dress marred in any way broke his heart.

"So eager to see me naked," Candi teased in return, giving him a little show by folding the skirt with her hands and showing her privates. Lissa laughed even harder. He should not have been surprised that Candi had no underwear on.

"I said take it off. The fun's over," he insisted. On some level, he knew what he was doing was counterproductive, but he couldn't help it. Every part of his being rebelled against this. He couldn't let these girls defile everything and destroy every good memory he had. He just couldn't.

"What's the matter, Samson? Upset about the dress?" Candi continued to taunt while slowly approaching him.

He knew it was a trick question.

If he said he wasn't bothered by her wearing his wife's dress, then she would continue to wear it and things could happen to it.

These two were the sloppiest human beings he'd ever had the misfortune to encounter. Pigs in the mud had nothing on them.

But if he told the truth and revealed how much he was bothered by this, he was also screwed because she would continue wearing it to spite him and go to even greater lengths to torment him with it.

Rock, hard place, meet Samson.

"Tell me, Samson. What would you do for me to take this dress off?" Candi challenged.

Another trick question. There was no way he could say anything because knowing these girls, that could very well be the death of him.

"What do you want?" he asked instead.

She crouched next to him. "Everything."

They stared at one another, battling wills, then she looked toward the stereo. "Lissa, turn it up; I love that song."

As the girls started dancing, Samson had to endure watching Candi in his wife's wedding dress.

I'm sorry, Teresa. I'm sorry for being so useless.

He felt powerless, and that hurt a lot. Nothing was sacred to them and nothing scared them, so how could he fight against that?

He had no idea.

Candi returned to his side. "Come on, Samson. Fuck me," she said with a glint in her eyes. "It's my wedding day."

Like anyone would ever marry you. He managed to bite his tongue just before saying that out loud.

She laughed as she straddled him, kissing him passionately.

These had been the longest days of his life. He tried and failed to remember what it felt like when Teresa kissed him. It freaked him out to no end.

Don't think about it.

Lissa laughed, cheering, and saying all kinds of nasty things "to the happy couple." Samson felt like weeping. He had his eyes closed the entire time, not wanting to ruin the memories he had involving Teresa, their wedding night, and this beautiful white dress.

Teresa was glorious that night. She was practically glowing with happiness, and he was so in love with her that it felt like he was walking on clouds. Consumed by passion, they hadn't even managed to get the dress off for the first round of lovemaking. They took their time the second time around. And the third. To this day, their wedding night was one of his favorite memories of them together. He wouldn't let these monsters take that away from him.

"Samson. Look at me," Candi ordered.

He did, but only after she'd slapped him a couple of times.

"Have you ever fucked her like this?" she taunted, sliding up and down against him.

"She doesn't have a sister to watch us," he replied definitely.

She slapped him again.

If she expected him to ever say she was a great lay, he wouldn't. She was nothing, especially compared to Teresa, and he was sure Candi could read that all over his face. She hated him for that, and he took great pleasure in that notion.

"Hurry up, Candi. I want my turn, too," Lissa complained.

"Only after he comes."

Samson thought about his friends in the army getting killed. He thought about all kinds of diseases, natural catastrophes, and so on, anything to avoid the inevitable.

Candi began riding him faster, squeezing him harder, and eventually, his body did what she demanded. She collected his cum with her fingers and licked them clean before kissing him one last time.

"He's all yours," she said to her sister, getting up.

"But he's no good to me now. I'll have to wait, and I hate waiting," Lissa whined like a spoiled brat.

Samson put his head down against the sofa cushions. He felt like screaming.

"I hate you," he said through gritted teeth, righting himself.

Candi looked at him over her shoulder. "I still don't care."

Sometime later, Samson was lying on the bedroom floor with no memory of how he wound up there when he spotted Lissa moving about. She was dancing, humming to the music in her head as she stood next to Teresa's vanity. She was playing with Teresa's jewelry box, taking things out and examining them. Every once in a while, she put something in a purse she'd taken from the closet.

Just now, she had a couple of earrings in her left hand. She held them against her ear, looked at herself in the mirror, and then tossed them into the bag.

Is she taking those?

"What are you doing?" he demanded, although it was pretty self-explanatory.

She jumped a little before turning to look at him. "Do you think this goes with me?" she asked about a huge silver bracelet Teresa liked to wear on special occasions. "It doesn't matter," she continued without waiting for him to reply. "I like it."

The bracelet disappeared inside the bag, too.

"What are you doing?" he repeated the question.

"Looking at what you've got here."

"And taking what you like?" he guessed.

Is that my watch? Teresa had bought it for him for their fifth anniversary.

"So?" she asked. "Oh, I know someone who would die seeing this necklace. Candi," she added, giggling.

He couldn't believe this was happening. *Really? After everything else?* Still, he couldn't believe this rich, spoiled bitch was no better than a common thief. She couldn't just take his stuff.

Are you sure about that?

Samson jumped on his feet to stop her. Big mistake. His head felt like a disco ball, giving the world a little swirl, and he started to teeter. Being tipsy and exhausted could do that to a man.

He balled his hands into fists, trying to find the strength and will to push forward.

Lissa smiled seeing him approach. "Wanna help?"

Hell no. "I won't let you take or destroy any more of my belongings," he said sternly. There was no way he would let this girl steal Teresa's jewelry. This madness had to stop somewhere.

Are you sure?

Lissa's smile faded, replaced by a look of confusion. "You don't want me to have a keepsake from you?" she asked, sounding almost hurt.

That pissed him off further. He took the bag from her and started returning things to the jewelry box.

"But that's mine," she whined.

"Nothing here is yours," he snapped, getting into her face. "Everything you took was by force, and I won't let you have any of this."

Lissa began screaming as loudly as she could. To his credit, he didn't bat an eye. He was quite used to her tantrums.

Was that a good or a bad thing?

Candi came rushing upstairs. Samson gritted his teeth. She was still wearing the goddamn wedding dress.

"What's the matter?" she demanded, approaching her sister.

Lissa stopped immediately and pointed at the bag. In some weird way, Candi understood her perfectly.

"Give that back to her," she commanded.

"No," Samson replied instantly. "This is too much. You've already destroyed my house, done what you wanted to me, and abused me. I won't let you steal from me as well." He had to draw a line somewhere.

"Is that so?" Candi challenged.

Samson nodded.

Candi left the room without further exchange, leaving Lissa still fairly agitated. Not that he gave a damn. Nobody was taking his stuff. Period.

As he was about to go to bed and hopefully sleep for at least ten hours, Candi returned, looking furious and holding the baseball bat. He was on the receiving end of her first swing, which connected squarely into his solar plexus and brought him to his knees.

He gasped for air.

"You said we destroyed everything? I disagree. There's still plenty we can do," she screeched as Lissa giggled.

Candi smashed the vanity mirror before proceeding to bash everything else. Her sister joined in.

It was complete chaos that resulted in Lissa flinging a chair through a closed window. Samson was sure the crash could be heard two blocks away.

"No!" he shouted, but the damage was done.

The girls cheered.

"Let's move downstairs," Lissa offered, and Candi agreed.

Samson followed them like a dog, trying to stop them but was fruitless in his effort.

Suddenly, red and blue lights appeared in front of his house, followed by the unmistakable sound of a siren.

I knew it. Samson knew one of his neighbors would call the cops.

"You're done now," he said and smiled genuinely for the first time since this torment started.

The girls looked uneasy for the first time. He was ecstatic.

"What is it, Candi? Was this not part of your ten steps?" he taunted.

"Shut up," she growled.

He just laughed harder.

"You'd better keep your mouth shut," she threatened.

"Or what?"

There was a knock at the door and Samson didn't have an opportunity to hear her reply because both girls retreated. He wasn't sure where. *Is this it? Am I free now?*

The knock became more aggressive. He rushed to open the door, realizing a little too late that he was once again wearing nothing but a pair of boxer shorts. It was too late now to rethink his fashion choices. Not that this was his choice anyway.

Two police officers greeted him. "Hello, sir," a one with a name tag Preston added. "We received a complaint about the noise."

On top of Candi's vandalism, the music was blasting like they were in the nightclub or something, pretty much shaking the entire house.

Instead of trying to lie his way out of this, say he was sorry, that he would turn the music down, Samson decided then and there he had enough of this shit. It was time he was free from those monsters once and for all. Besides, they needed to be punished for what they did to him, and all other men.

"Thank God you're here," he said with obvious relief.

The police officers tensed immediately. "What happened, sir?" Preston demanded.

"Two girls broke into my house while my wife is away. They drugged me, assaulted me, and now they won't leave, and they're blackmailing me with sex tapes. Please, you have to help me," Samson rushed to explain, words coming out of his mouth, in a complete jumble.

The police officers looked at one another. To his chagrin, they didn't believe him. *They think I'm a drunk fool.*

Officer Dawson's next word confirmed as much. "I wish I had your problems."

"Yeah," the other agreed with a small smile.

"Please," Samson started and didn't know how to finish. There was nothing he could say to convince them. Even if Candi and Lissa were standing right next to him, it wouldn't make a difference.

"Just keep your partying down, okay, buddy?" Preston warned.

They left after that, and Samson looked mournfully after the car as it drove away. He didn't know how to process the fact they hadn't believed him. They didn't bother to investigate if he was telling the truth; they just drove away without helping him.

To serve and protect, my ass.

This was his biggest fear, right here, coming true. That no one would believe him. That everyone would think he was making up a story to cover his mess.

He was right.

"Samson?" Candi called out.

His whole body went numb realizing they'd just hidden, not run away. He turned reluctantly.

"Could you please remind me where we were before being so rudely interrupted?" she sang, wearing a smug expression.

He didn't have to be a genius to know they'd heard every word. They knew the police officers had brushed him off.

Lissa closed the door before taking him by the hands, leading him toward his doom. "The real fun starts now," she practically cheered.

Well, fuck.

CHAPTER 19

After the cops dropped by and laughed at his story, things changed dramatically from bad to worse. The girls were intoxicated by the notion that they were untouchable and took it out on him.

The cops wouldn't believe his story because he had no proof, which gave the girls absolute power over him. And they definitely used it. Or more accurately put, abused it.

If he thought they were nightmares before, it was nothing compared to what he came afterward. Samson thought he knew the meaning of abuse, pain, and humiliation before. He soon learned differently.

A certain kind of pattern developed. They would torture him to the point he thought he couldn't take it anymore, so he would try something – an act of defiance or petty revenge. It would backfire, and Lissa and Candi would start to break shit in a fit of rage that would result in the cops returning. Again.

They did jack shit to help.

He continued to get off with warnings, although the last time they visited, he begged to be arrested. They looked at him like he'd lost his mind.

Maybe I have.

Today would be different, Samson promised himself. Today, he would be smart and not react out of anger or spite. Today, he would think before he acted and hopefully get himself out of this mess because he couldn't continue like this. His house was trashed, and the place reeked of alcohol, drugs, and sex. He was a mess, too. He couldn't remember the last time he showered, and he hadn't picked up a razor since before these demons set foot inside his house.

Teresa liked him clean-shaven. No, he couldn't do that to himself. Thinking of Teresa caused him too much pain. Not to mention how ashamed and humiliated he felt for allowing something like this to happen in the first place. He was an utter failure.

Don't think like that. Today, his luck would turn.

Candi was so full of alcohol and drugs that she'd forgotten to take the phone from him after his last chat with Teresa. He nearly began to weep as he hid the phone in the bedroom to use it later on. He had to make sure the girls were passed out before calling for help because otherwise, they would do everything to stop him, threaten him, and torture him. He only had one shot and needed to choose the perfect moment for this covert operation.

If the police wouldn't help him, then he was determined to help himself. Thankfully, he knew Malcolm would assist him in that endeavor. They had been best friends since high school, they'd enlisted together and survived a war watching each other's backs. Samson knew his friend would help him this time around as well. But for that to happen, Samson had to choose the right time to call his friend. He had no idea what day it was; his concept of time had completely disappeared. But he prayed the weekend wasn't approaching because Malcolm liked to get out of town from time to time and take kids camping or go hunting. He needed him to be home. He prayed for that.

Samson patiently waited to make his move.

Lissa went to the kitchen to make herself some cereal while Candi danced in the living room, and she was wavering. She'd pass out in a matter of minutes. Sure enough, she tripped and stumbled onto the couch. She didn't move again. It was lights-out for her.

One down, one to go. On tiptoe, he went to see what Lissa was up to. She had dumped the cereal on the kitchen counter and was placing only specific colors in her bowl.

That would keep her occupied for a while, Samson realized, rushing upstairs.

He grabbed his cell phone from under the pillow to make his call. He ignored all the messages, missed calls, and other notifications that assaulted him the instant he fired it up.

I can't believe this is my life, sneaking away from two underaged girls who are holding me hostage.

That was about to change.

"We need more cereal," Lissa said, bursting into the room with an empty box of cereal before realizing what he was doing. "No!" she screamed, lunging toward him. They struggled for the phone. To his chagrin, Samson hadn't managed to dial the entire number. It was all in vain.

"No!" It filled him with so much anger that he wanted to demolish everything and everyone in sight. This was his shot, and he was going to take it no matter what. This ended *now*.

"Give that to me," she ordered, and he ignored her. His life depended on that phone. He needed it.

Lissa once again showed remarkable strength, which resulted in him dropping the phone. Samson lunged for it as Lissa kicked it out of the way.

"No," he growled.

"Bad monkey," she said, slapping him.

On reflex, he hit her back. She fell to the floor and grabbed the phone. Laughing victoriously, she got up and ran out of the room without missing a beat.

Samson was right behind her in hot pursuit.

They ended up in the living room. Samson wanted – *needed* – that phone back. It was his only way to call for help. The girls had pulled out the cord on the landline days ago. This was it. His only shot.

"Give me my phone!" he boomed, consumed with fury and a dash of desperation.

"Yeah, right."

He advanced, determined to get the phone from her, but Lissa ran. They started running laps around the couch, and by the look of it, Lissa enjoyed being chased, which made him even madder.

All the noise caused Candi to open her eyes. "What's happening?" she demanded.

"I caught Samson trying to make a call," Lissa explained before squeaking as Samson almost got her before she slipped through his fingers.

"What?" Candi exclaimed, suddenly completely alert. The notion Samson would end her fun had sobered her instantly.

"He did what?" she asked, trying to block his advances. It was hard to do anything when they ganged up on him like this. That didn't mean he was giving up. He couldn't.

Candi looked at him as though she was the principal, and he'd broken the window to her office. "You just never learn."

Samson was beyond caring. "Give me my phone back, now."

"You can't have it," Lissa countered stubbornly.

Samson advanced even though Candi was standing in front of him, fully prepared to steamroll her if he had to. He couldn't listen to another threat about Teresa getting an eyeful of him fucking them. Samson had had enough.

Candi realized she could not fight the raging bull and moved out of the way. "Give me my fucking phone, or I'll kill you," he shouted.

Lissa threw the phone to Candi.

"Your threats don't scare me," she said, raising her chin, "but you should be terrified of mine."

Samson smiled. Well, it was more that he bared his teeth aggressively. If he were an animal, he would already be ripping her to shreds. "Oh, we are *so* past threats. This is where you die." He meant every word.

Suddenly, an all-consuming pain washed through his body, leaving him paralyzed. He fell to his knees and tumbled over. Lissa had used a Taser on him. And by the feel of it, it was on maximum voltage.

"Take *that*, you piece of shit," Lissa screamed, giving him another zinger. He convulsed like a fish on dry land.

Where did that thing come from? He had no time to dwell on that because he passed out shortly afterward.

Then a couple of voices broke through the darkness.

"Did you kill him?"

"I don't think so."

"Is he breathing?"

"I don't want to check."

The girls' voices came through the haze. He couldn't have a moment of peace from them, even while passed out. It was hard to open his eyes. Had they put weights on his eyelids?

Somehow, Samson managed to open them and sit up. The girls looked at him intently. *I can't move. Why can't I move?* Before he could panic that he was paralyzed, he realized that he was tied to a chair. *Oh, joy.*

"What's this?" he demanded. It wasn't enough that Lissa had almost tasered him to death; they had to tie him up as well?

Candi made a face. "Our time together has run out, Samson." She looked genuinely sorry, but he wasn't buying it.

They were excellent actresses. But then, he registered what she's said. *They're leaving?* This wasn't ideal, but he would take it. As long as they finally left him alone, he was a happy camper. … One that would one day track them down and chop them to pieces.

"Don't let the door hit you on your way out." He grinned.

"Not so fast," Lissa replied. "We still have time for one last party."

"A final hurrah, if you will," Candi added.

"Yes!" Lissa jumped with excitement.

"Believe me, Samson," Candi leaned into his face, "it's going to be the one you will *never* forget."

"I can't wait." Lissa grinned, pushing a bottle of water to his mouth and he gulped it greedily.

"I would normally say how sad I am to see you go, but we all know that's a lie," he said after finishing his drink.

He was very much aware of how much better that line would have sounded had he not been naked and handcuffed to a chair.

Why am I naked?

Candi mentioned "one last party." Suddenly, everything inside of him went dead. He'd endured so much already; he could survive this, too. He had to. During his little pep talk, he started to feel it: The tingle, and the slow seduction.

He looked at Lissa. "You didn't," he accused, and that bitch giggled.

"You drugged me again," he exclaimed.

He shouldn't be surprised. They were forever in search of ways to screw him over, and he fell for it every time.

"Nighty-night," Lissa said, blowing him a kiss.

His vision was already hazy. This had kicked in much faster than last time. Unfortunately, the dose wasn't strong enough to completely spare him from what followed.

The girls took turns having sex with him, and he could feel he was out of his bonds at some point, but in his state, there was nothing he could do about it.

While being high on coke and other things, they took the game to the next level. They took photos while sodomizing him, and they whipped him with a lamp cord.

Lissa laughed the whole time while Candi went nuts with the cord. His chest, his stomach, and legs burned like crazy.

"Now he has a matching set," Candi said at some point, slightly out of breath from the workout, referring to the bruises he had on his back from the belt.

"Stop. Please," he begged.

"Oh, come on, Samson. You can do better than that," Candi taunted, striking him to the rhythm of her voice. "I want to really hear you beg."

"I think a few tears would be nice as well," Lissa mocked.

He was so desperate just then, there was nothing he wouldn't do or say to get them to stop hurting him. His ass hurt like hell, and it was very difficult sitting down. It took all of his willpower not to think about why was that the case.

He was miserable, to madness and back.

"Please, Candi. I'll do anything, just stop," he pleaded.

"I don't believe you mean that," she countered.

"I do, I do."

"Okay then. Tell me I'm the best fuck you ever had."

Samson hesitated. He didn't want to utter something like that. It felt blasphemous.

"Say it." She swung with the cable and hit him even harder.

"You are the best fuck I've had in my entire life," he said in desperation.

"Better than your wife?"

"Yes."

"Say it."

"Better than my wife."

Lissa approached with her phone, recording every second. He didn't expect any less. They loved to torture him.

"Say hi to Teresa," she taunted, and he looked away.

"Did you get all that?" Candi asked her sister.

"Every word," Lissa replied, showing her the phone.

"Good." Candi was pleased, and that scared him shitless.

Lissa fumbled with her phone, then grinned. "Aaaaaaand send," she announced.

"Congrats, Samson, the life you knew is over," Candi mocked.

"*What?*" Samson exclaimed in a panic. Her words could only mean one thing, but his brain refused to acknowledge it. They wouldn't do that. Although there was only evidence of the contrary so far.

"I hope your wife loves our gifts and will appreciate our little movies," Lissa said, patting him on the head.

"What did you do?" He cried out in desperation, straining against his bonds.

"We've been sending her all kinds of things all day," Candi said with a small shrug.

"She hasn't responded. Not even a thank you. Rude," Lissa complained.

Samson struggled harder. "You sent her videos of us?" he asked like an idiot.

"Of course we did."

His brain shut down. *This can't be happening. This can't be happening.* Not after everything he'd endured. Samson was ruined.

The look on Candi's face made him realize that was the point all along.

There was no chance this would have ended any differently. This was their end goal. Their little agreement was a lie from the start, and on some level, he'd known that. That was the reason he'd fought them so hard.

He felt sick to his stomach, then started vomiting as he pictured Teresa receiving all that filth.

Oh my God. Oh my God.

"Ewwww," the girls screeched, taking a step back.

They'd ruined his life, just as they planned. Everything else, the pushing him around, was just additional fun to see how long he would endure. Samson felt like crying and opted for the second-best thing the instant he stopped throwing up. Samson started to rage. Actual growls escaped his mouth. "I will fucking kill you, you bitches."

"We love you, too," Candi taunted, blowing him a kiss. "I'll miss you and your massive dick."

"We have to go, though. So many others we want to fuck over." Lissa giggled.

"You are done. Dead," he continued.

"Besides, we don't want to be here when Teresa gets home." Candi pretended to shudder as she collected her things. They robbed him blind despite his best efforts.

"I wouldn't want to be you, Samson," Lissa mocked, following her sister toward the front door.

"You are *dead*! Do you hear me?" Samson shouted after them.

"Bye Samson."

"It's been fun."

Lissa turned around and returned to his side in a rush. "I have to do this one last time," she said, grabbing his dick, and he tried to bite her face as she leaned in.

She laughed.

"I will find you and kill you," he continued to rant long after they'd left.

They'd taken everything, and he wasn't talking about the money, jewelry, and his phone.

They'd taken his dignity and his life.

Samson had nothing left.

CHAPTER 20

"**S**on of a bitch!" he screamed at the top of his lungs, then screamed some more, as his throat started to protest.

They'd left him like that, handcuffed to a chair. At the same time, if they'd released him, then he would have definitely killed them both. This was a smart move for them; terrible for him.

He was naked, partially bleeding, tied to a chair, and completely screwed in more ways than he could count. At the moment, the only thing he could think about was Teresa. She must be freaking out right about now after everything those girls sent her, and his heart was breaking in two.

He could guess what she must think of him now because he felt the same way. The worst part was that he couldn't call her and try to explain everything or prepare her for what she was about to see because the devil children had not only taken his phone but hand-cuffed him to a fucking chair. He couldn't break the chair; it was made of metal. Teresa had insisted they buy them for the kitchen, but now, he realized it was the biggest fucking mistake of his life. Apart from letting those two monsters inside his home, of course.

He stopped his antics for the briefest of moments. He had another problem, and he didn't mean the need to go to the bathroom at some point. He couldn't remember how many days had passed since Teresa had left to visit her parents. *Is she coming tomorrow night or the day after that?* And then it hit him. If she'd received those videos – and he knew she had – knowing her, she would be on the next flight home to confront him. There was small comfort in that, but he was also terrified to see her.

Once again, Samson started screaming at the top of his lungs. He hoped the neighbors would call the cops on him again. It was better that some police officer free him than Teresa. Much better.

"Please, can somebody help me?" he screamed and screamed, but eventually, he completely lost his voice. No one came to his rescue.

"Please," he continued to say, even though no one could hear him. *What can I do?* he asked in desperation for the hundredth time.

He couldn't stay rotting in the chair and wait for Teresa to find him. He would die.

What if she doesn't come home at all? The terrifying thought entered his mind. *What if she got so angry after seeing all the filth that she decided to stay with her parents for a while?* He could die in this chair, for real. Samson started to panic. *Don't think like that.*

But what else could he do? Only think, stress, panic, rage, and cry.

"Please God, help!"

Samson couldn't take it anymore. He started to thrash about. He needed to get out of this. *Why wouldn't anyone help him? Please, help me.*

He sobbed.

At some point, he passed out from exhaustion and surrendered to the nothingness, enjoying the speck of peace amid all the agony.

A shooting pain snapped him back to reality. He couldn't feel his legs because they'd been in the same position for a long time. There was no way he could pick up the chair and walk around with it on his back. The same could be said for his arms. They, too, were completely useless, numb to the point that he wasn't even sure they were attached to his body.

He had to go to the bathroom, badly. He held it as long as he could.

Samson began crying again as he relieved himself. *Why is this happening to me? Am I such a bad person?*

He had tried to live his life as honestly as possible. Had he made mistakes? Sure. Had he always done the best thing? No. Nonetheless, he loved his wife with all his heart and did his best to make her happy. *Doesn't that count for something?*

Was this karma for killing in the war?

No one can change the past. And one day, all of this would be a history that he would move past, he tried to reassure himself. However, it was hard to see a way out, and a happy future, as sat in his own waste. Samson sobbed inconsolably.

The hunger and thirst hit next, and since he had no other choice, he endured that as well. He retreated deeper and deeper into his mind, trying to picture other, happier times in his life, and that helped a little.

"Oh, my God!" Teresa's scream woke him up.

He must have dozed without realizing it. Then a door slammed, and he panicked that she'd run away after seeing the state of the house.

"Over here!" he yelled, or at least tried to.

Teresa recoiled when she entered the room where he was confined. He knew he must be quite the sight. He wished there was some way to hide his shame, his state, his naked, marred body, and the evidence of his confinement, but he couldn't. It was driving him mad.

The smells were poignant as well. His nose receptors had burned out a long time ago, and he barely noticed it. Small favors of God and all that.

"Thank God you're here," he cried. "Please help me."

"Samson …" she stammered.

"Please help me. They left me like this."

Teresa's face darkened. "You deserve much worse, you cheater," she screamed in rage.

Samson panicked. No, she couldn't believe that. He was the victim! But she gave him no time to defend himself.

"I can't believe you did this to me. To *us*," she accused.

"Teresa, please," he begged, but she wasn't listening.

"How *could* you, in our home! How *could* you?" she demanded.

"They came, and—"

"Oh, I don't want to hear about your whores. I saw the videos. I thought they were a bit too young for you, but I guess you can buy anything these days," she threw in his face with disgust.

Samson cried out, "It's not what you think! They drugged me."

"Yeah, right," she replied dismissively. "With what?"

"I don't know."

"How convenient."

"It was in the tequila."

She scoffed. "You don't drink tequila," she announced, her voice raising as though she'd just caught him in a lie.

He was wrecked. His worst nightmare was coming true.

"Please, Teresa," he begged through sobs. "You have to believe me. None of this is what I wanted," he pressed her to understand as tears streamed down his face.

"I bet it's not. You expected the best fuck of your life and got this!" She waved in his direction and then pinched her nose as though she couldn't stand being in his presence. "You really know how to pick them!" She shook her head. "Not only did they fuck you, they fucked you over, and good."

She was getting it all wrong. He said as much.

"Oh, I see the truth. I see you, and I can't even look at you. You disgust me."

And then she said something that hurt like nothing else ever had.

"I can't believe I married you."

Samson closed his eyes. He might as well die here and now if that was how she felt. And then, he reminded himself she was just upset. He was, too.

"Could you please help me?" he pleaded in a small voice. "I can't feel my legs."

"How?" she asked, waving her hands. "It's not like I have a spare key. I didn't even know you owned handcuffs."

"They aren't mine."

"Oh, my God," she covered her face.

"The key is in the kitchen, in the first drawer to the left," he explained. Candi had put it there to taunt him, knowing there was nothing he could do to reach it.

He'd hoped Teresa would help him. In her current state though, Samson feared she would storm out and leave him helpless and covered in shit.

To his relief, Teresa went to get the key.

Thank you, God, he wept. He was an emotional wreck. The fact that Teresa had seen him like this was unbearable. He was so ashamed, it was maddening.

She returned with a ruined wedding dress in her left hand and the key to his freedom in her right.

"Teresa, I—"

"*No*, Samson," she snapped. "Don't. I had a lot of time to think things over on my flight back, after watching all the videos that kept coming. I don't want to hear another word from you."

She didn't allow him to say anything.

"I don't know what sick game that was, or why you felt the need to send me all that, but I'm glad you did. Because now I know exactly who you are," she seethed.

Teresa was getting it all wrong, and it broke his heart. Each word she uttered caused immense pain. *She can't mean all that. She's just angry because she doesn't understand. I was drugged and raped repeatedly.*

"I'm sorry, Teresa," Samson said quietly. He meant it from his heart. Everything he'd done in the past several days was to spare her from all of this. Unfortunately, it was unavoidable. The demons had plotted against him and ruined his life. They'd hurt Teresa.

"I bet you're sorry … for getting caught."

With that, she moved forward to take the handcuffs off of him. She made a face, disturbed by the foul smell coming off of him in waves.

That was just one more reason to be ashamed.

The instant she'd freed him, she moved away as quickly as possible. She didn't attempt to help him, and that stung, too. He was in so much pain – physical and mental – that he felt like there was no point in going on.

Things can't end like this, a part of him rebelled. They couldn't. He had to make Teresa see. She had to hear the truth.

Although he was free, he still couldn't move. His arms and legs refused to cooperate.

Come on, you useless piece of meat. Being angry and focused on his body helped him ignore all the other thoughts and feelings. Like the fact that his marriage was over.

Teresa left the room again. *No, this can't end like this.*

"Oh, my God," he heard her exclaim a couple of times as she went through the house and took in all the damage.

Samson closed his eyes and fell to the floor.

This was worse than a nightmare because there was no waking up from this. He was powerless to change anything. It was like watching the car wreck in slow motion but being too slow and insignificant to stop it.

This was all Lissa and Candi's fault, and he would make good on his promise. Samson would track them down no matter what and have his revenge if that was the last thing he did. Now that they had completely ruined his life and turned Teresa against him, there was nothing to lose. That additional fury helped him regain some control over his body. Everything hurt like hell, but he endured. The physical pain was nothing compared to the one inside his heart.

Something hit him in the face. He didn't notice that Teresa had returned, throwing some clothes at him.

She was still clutching her ruined wedding dress close to her heart. He hated seeing her like this.

"Teresa …" he tried again.

"Get dressed," she commanded, her voice cutting the space between them like a knife.

He was dirty, bloody, and covered in all kinds of bodily fluids. He had to shower first. "I can't. I need to—"

"*Get dressed, now*!" she repeated on the verge of hysteria.

CHAPTER 21

"I fucking hate you," Samson argued, finishing another bottle of Jack Daniels. The list was so long that it was hard to say to whom he referring just then. He was alone in his room, but his mind continued to plague him with all kinds of images.

"This is my house," he said after some pause.

In the next instant, he was crying. "I love you so much."

A week had passed since his life as he knew it was ruined. One agonizingly long week.

After Teresa had so gracelessly kicked him out without allowing him to explain what had happened, he went to see Malcolm and collapsed on his doorstep.

"Oh, my God, Samson. What happened to you?" Malcolm was beside himself.

"Teresa kicked me out," he sobbed.

"I heard."

Of course he did.

"You don't look so good. Should I take you to the hospital?"

Samson's whole body clenched. He couldn't let people see what had happened to him. "No. No hospitals," he managed to croak out.

"Okay, okay. Whatever you want," his best friend agreed.

And that was how he ended up in this stinky hotel room talking to himself. Malcolm drove him here because Anita wouldn't allow him to inside their house. She, too, believed the worst. Of course, the fake version of events had spread like wildfire throughout their community, making him a pariah.

After eating something, Samson demanded to be left alone. Malcolm looked unsure but respected his wishes all the same.

"Call me if you need anything, okay?"

Samson nodded.

He took a long bath, trying to wash all the filth from his body, but no matter how hard he scrubbed his skin, he continued to feel dirty.

He got out, bought a couple of bottles of alcohol, and hadn't stopped drinking since.

Today, Teresa sent him some of his stuff, chopped into pieces. Apparently, she was still very upset with him. His ruined clothes perfectly mirrored the state of his life.

Samson grabbed the phone that Malcolm had given him and called Teresa. She, of course, didn't answer.

"Pick up the phone," he slurred.

How could he talk to her if she wouldn't pick up?

An empty bottle on the floor filled him with anger. Who'd drunk his whiskey? There was nothing left, and that meant he would have to go outside and buy more. He hated going outside.

Samson felt too exposed while walking on the streets, as though everyone who looked at him would know his dirty little secret.

"I did *not* cheat on my wife," he grumbled. He'd tried to save her. Because that was what he did. He was a soldier, and it was his job to save people.

Reluctantly, and in a piss-poor mood, he stood up. The bed squeaked in protest, and the ground shook beneath his feet. He was much drunker than he realized, and he fell down almost immediately and passed out.

Samson woke up in a panic as he realized that he was once again chained to a chair.

"No, not again!" he yelled, struggling against the restraints.

Candi was examining which cord to use on him as Lissa held a big dildo, playing with it.

"Please, no more," he begged, but the girls just laughed. They were amazed by his tears.

As they circled him, the door opened, and Teresa walked in. "Samson, how *could* you?" she accused.

"It's not my fault! They made me do it," he tried to defend. "Please help me."

But she acted like she didn't hear him. "You disgust me, you filthy animal."

"All men are filthy animals," Candi agreed.

The girls continued to chant that as Teresa berated him.

"Teresa, please. You have to believe me."

"You disgust me. Get out!"

"Teresa, no. Don't do this."

"Get out, you filthy whore. I don't want to see you ever again." She looked at him with so much hate in her eyes that Samson was completely heartbroken.

"I can't. I'm chained to this chair."

"I said get out! I hate you!" she screamed at the top of her lungs as Lissa and Candi laughed.

"Oh Samson, you are so pathetic," Candi taunted.

"Soooooo pathetic," Teresa agreed, joining in the laughter.

"No, no, no. Leave me alone!" Samson shouted.

With a jolt, Samson woke up covered in sweat and something else – his own vomit – gasping for air.

His nightmares differed little from reality. He was screwed, ridiculed, and tormented in his dreams every bit as he was in real life.

At least in dreams, he could still see his wife's face even though she was screaming at him, telling him how much she hated him, and looking at him with eyes filled with a mixture of fury and disgust.

He didn't possess that luxury in real life. *Samson, you really are pathetic.*

Waking up like this, completely alone in a stinky hotel room, alienated from everyone, stigmatized, and troubled by everything that happened to him, Samson felt like blowing his brains out. Not that he had a gun. Maybe he had a razor. *I can't even die properly.*

How had he wound up here, anyway? Not rolling on the floor in his vomit – thankfully, the shag carpet had soaked most of it up – but in general. How had he become a victim? *What did I do wrong?*

Oh right, he felt like smacking himself on the forehead. *I opened the door for two innocent-looking girls and tried to be a good Samaritan.*

He would never make that same mistake again.

Samson picked himself up from the floor with some effort. He could feel that he was still a bit drunk, so he crashed on the bed once again.

Why bother? There was no point in living like this. He'd rather just wait for death.

His phone rang, and he moved to glance at the caller ID. Once he made saw it wasn't Teresa, he curled up again. At this point, only a fucking miracle would have her calling him. She hated his guts. Still, he sympathized with her and made excuses for her behavior.

You are beyond pathetic. A new word should be coined in your honor.

The phone kept ringing. Malcolm was determined to get his attention, but Samson wasn't ready to face his friend. He might never be. He was so ashamed that it ate him up inside.

"Shut up!" he yelled at the phone.

The man was persistent; he had to give him that. Malcolm had been trying for days to get him out of this room, put some food in him, and force him to tell him what happened but Samson couldn't. How could he share something like that, anyway? Even to this best friend. He couldn't even put words to something like that. He could barely deal with it in his head, and not at all without freaking out, while liquored up.

Samson started weeping. He was so alone, and he didn't know what to do.

How could he, as a man, admit to another man what had happened? What he'd allowed two girls to do to him. It was unfath-omable. Samson couldn't. It was better that everyone believed he was a bastard who'd partied all week than learn the truth about his abuse, rape, and torture.

If he wasn't capable of defending himself when it counted, then he deserved everything that happened to him. That was what people would say, anyway.

Every time he closed his eyes, he saw Candi rubbing her hands all over him, or Lissa slapping him. It made him nuts. It made him nauseous. Luckily, he'd stopped eating a while ago, so there wasn't much to vacate from his stomach.

Apart from leftover whiskey, he reminded himself. He might try to drink that up again since his bottles were empty. That thought disgusted him. There was no more booze for him. He would have to dwell in his sorrows completely dry. Besides, all he'd done since Teresa had kicked him out was drink and think about his mistakes.

What else was there, anyway? He didn't want to be around people, and he didn't want to write.

He couldn't even if he'd wanted to. It wasn't like he had his computer anymore; Lissa had made sure of that. His manuscript was lost in that demolition. All of that hard work, and all of the sleepless nights thinking of the best twists and subplots, were gone.

If he hadn't already been thoroughly depressed, he was now, thinking about his ruined career. Everything else was ruined, too, that was just the cherry on top.

If only he could close his eyes and escape this wretched existence; go into oblivion. But that was not happening any time soon, and every time he closed his eyes, he could still see those two monsters raping him, laughing at him, and taking pleasure in his pain. So, sleep was not an option.

Teresa was the newest addition to his nightmares. And he was pathetic enough to feel grateful to see her, even if it was during a nightmare while she joined the girls in their abuse.

Everybody had turned on him. Pete had called twice before he learned what was happening. Theresa was on the warpath, warning everyone about him.

Malcolm was the only one who stuck around. He was such a good friend, but Samson wasn't capable of reciprocating just yet.

The only person he wanted to see or talk to was the last person who wanted to see him — Teresa. She refused to speak with him but had sent him a message a couple of days ago saying he should expect to hear from her lawyer.

He couldn't believe what those girls had managed in such a short time. He'd lost everything. He had no home, no wife, no job, and all his friends had deserted him since it was generally accepted that he'd had a wild affair that went badly and was now getting what he deserved.

He would never cheat on his wife. Didn't she know him better than that? Apparently not.

A loud banging snapped him from his thoughts. Fear washed over him, and adrenaline kicked in. It was the terrorists; they'd found him. Samson crawled under the bed. He wouldn't surrender without a fight.

Where is my rifle? he thought, bewildered. Patting his leg, he realized he was missing his knife as well. He cursed. The banging persisted, and he was sure they would break inside any second. He prepared himself for a fight. He lacked a weapon, but that didn't mean he was powerless. He would fight with his bare hands if he had to.

"Samson?" What are you doing?" Malcolm demanded, horrified.

Samson recoiled. "Malcolm?"

"Yes, it's me," he approached warily.

What had happened? A second ago, he was sure he was back in Afghanistan. He was losing his mind.

"Oh, man. Look at you."

Samson took a step back. "I'm fine. Leave me alone."

"I had to come. You weren't answering your phone."

"My battery died," he lied.

"I promised to give this to you." Malcolm offered a big manila envelope.

Samson had a decent idea of what was inside. "So now you do her bidding," he accused.

"You know it's not like that. Take it."

"No," Samson rebelled.

"I'm so sorry, man."

He couldn't stand being pitied. He grabbed the envelope and practically ripped it in half in his endeavor to open it. Sure enough, divorce papers were inside. He saw that Teresa had already signed them.

Wow, she works fast. He would have been impressed if it hadn't marked the complete ruination of his life. It had taken her just a week to write him off completely and banish him from her life.

Samson crumpled the papers. "You did what you came for, now leave," he said through gritted teeth. On some level, he was aware of shooting the messenger, but it couldn't be helped.

"Samson, you can't keep going like this," Malcolm tried to reason with him, not understanding he was too far gone for reason. "Come on; let's get you cleaned up."

Samson freaked out when Malcolm touched him on the arm, and hit him. "Don't touch me," he shouted before rushing out of the room.

"Samson? Where are you going?" Malcolm yelled after him in vain.

He reached the street and kept running. He couldn't take it anymore. The pain was too great, and he was completely alone in this world.

Part of him was glad his mom wasn't alive to see him like this. A completely ruined man, abandoned by all.

The only person who vowed to always be there for him, to love him no matter what, to take care of him in sickness and health, had left him. She was loud and clear that she didn't want to have anything to do with him.

That pissed him off. *How dare she.* Samson had given her every-thing. He'd bought the house she wanted and was a devoted husband. He'd given up having children for her and this was how she repaid him? Sending him divorce papers without giving him a chance to explain himself, like he was nothing? It was devastating that she'd assumed the worst. *How can she think so low of me?* Didn't he deserve a chance to be listened to? They'd spend eight years together; didn't that count for something? Apparently not.

She had the videos, and that was enough for her. Somehow, as he argued with his wife inside of his head, Samson ended up on a bridge. He looked at the murky water below.

Maybe this was the answer to his problems. Maybe all he had to do was jump and be free from everything. There would be no more pain, no more shame, and no more anguish that his wife had left him.

She didn't want him anymore, but she still demanded payment for the house repairs, and he had no clue how he could afford them. His publisher had taken back the advance for the book that no longer existed, and that left him living on alarmingly lean savings.

It was better to just die and be done with everything. It was a nice evening after all, and the scenery around him was almost soothing.

What would Mom think of me now? That stopped him in his tracks. She would be disappointed, and not because of what happened, but because he was contemplating suicide.

Momma raised no quitter. No matter the difficulties in life, he could not do something like that. It would be a sin. So, despite all the pressure, pain, and sorrow he felt, Samson managed to find a pay phone and make a call. It was time to ask for help.

doctor decided he needed a sedative. He wasn't going to take it anymore.

"I want to discuss it *now*," Samson countered, but before he'd managed to finish the sentence, the nurse had already plunged the thing into his arm and administered the drug. Samson could only stare.

"Wow, you're quick," he mumbled, strangely impressed.

Then again, considering his role at the hospital, the guy probably had to be quick on his feet and capable of giving shots to crazy people in extreme circumstances.

Wait. Is that politically correct? Samson mused. Should he be calling those troubled people crazy? Samson decided it was okay because now, he was one of them.

"Good night," Steve said, leaving the room.

Samson could hear the door lock behind him, and then, he went like a light.

He was woken by the sound of his door opening. He was horrified to see Lissa and Candi enter, giggling.

How did they find me? How did they get in here? Samson panicked.

"No!" he shouted. "What are you doing here?" He thought they were done with him. That was what they'd said anyway, after leaving him handcuffed to a chair, naked. "Get out!" he screamed, glancing at the door in hopes the nurses would be alarmed by the noise and come to his rescue.

"Did you really think you could run away from us?" Lissa snickered.

"Samson, really," Candi's voice was patronizing. "You should have known better by now."

Samson retreated to the corner of the room, as far away from them as possible. "Help me!" he hollered. "Please, can someone help me?"

The girls continued to laugh at him.

"You are pathetic," they mocked when no one came to defend him.

"No! Get away from me!"

"We're going to have so much fun now."

"Noooo!"

"You'll never forget us."

"We are the best fucks you've ever had."

"No, leave me be."

Samson opened his eyes to see the same nurse holding him down on the bed.

"No! Don't touch me. Let go of me," he protested as panic started to consume him.

"You need to calm down," Steve said as another nurse tried to restrain him enough to tie him to the bed.

That triggered him even more and he began thrashing about, defending himself like a lion. He had to get away from them.

"No. Please don't."

Samson felt another small prick and knew he'd been hit with another dose of sedatives. He felt like weeping. Once again, he succumbed to darkness, which was just a prelude to another nightmare.

"You are so pathetic that I can't even look at you. You disgust me," Teresa lectured, then spit on him.

Samson was on his knees in front of her, begging for forgiveness.

"Please, Teresa, you have to listen to me," he pleaded as tears streamed down his face.

"Shut up," she snapped, turning away from him. "I don't want to hear your lies. I know everything."

"No, you don't," he argued.

"I saw everything you did with those girls." She turned to look at him and her eyes were glacial. "You pervert," she spat in disgust.

He could only imagine what those bitches had sent her. Samson closed his eyes. "It wasn't my fault," he wailed.

"It was *all* your fault," Teresa boomed, creating a hole in the ground with the power of her voice through which Samson fell into.

Oh no, not again. He was back in that tunnel, and he knew this time he would die there.

"Samson, where are you?" He could hear through the darkness.

"We'll find you."

He was sure they would. They always did.

It was dawn the next day when Samson finally opened his eyes and knew he wasn't sleeping or in one of his nightmares. He'd survived the brutal night, but that didn't mean his agony was over. Reality did not bring with it any peace. He was restrained, and that freaked him out to no end. Beads of sweat covered his face. He did his best to remain quiet, biting his lower lip while every part of his being wanted to break free.

Still, he did his best to remain calm so he wasn't drugged again. He couldn't survive another round of nightmares. Although it was unfathomable, this was the lesser evil.

Everything is all right. No one is harming you. Despite his soothing thoughts, laying there and looking at his restraints was pure agony. He'd come here to heal, but everything they'd done so far had made him feel worse. He'd checked himself in voluntarily, but something told him that getting out wouldn't be so easy.

I want these off of me, he screamed inside his head, balling his hands into fists and testing the restraints for the hundredth time. They were pretty tight. They reminded him of Lissa and Candi.

Don't think about it, he warned, which was easier said than done.

At least this time he was clothed. If the ridiculous hospital gown could be considered proper attire.

By the time a nurse came to check on him, he was covered in sweat and hyperventilating. She looked at him, perhaps contemplating if he needed another dose of sedatives.

"I'm fine," he lied. "I just need to go to the bathroom."

To his chagrin, she provided him with a bedpan.

Maybe this hospital thing had been a bad idea. Everything triggered him, causing him pain and forcing him to revisit all the bad things that had happened.

Don't think about it; just do it.

There was not a person happier than him when the nurse set him free. Of course, she first made him promise that he would behave.

He would promise her anything for the opportunity to scratch his nose.

"You have an appointment with your doctor today," Nora, the nurse, informed him.

He did not fail to notice how she said doctor and not psychiatrist. Was that by design? Or was he just paranoid about wrong things? Probably the latter.

Either way, Samson was ecstatic to meet his doctor, who was bound to fix him.

True enough, he was escorted into Dr. Nancy Meyer's office after breakfast. He sat in an empty chair across from her as she looked at some papers. She was a middle-aged woman with fiery red hair. This was not the same doctor who admitted him last night.

Part of him was glad. He felt like he wouldn't be able to share all his misfortunes with another man. Maybe that made him a wuss, but he didn't care.

She looked at him and smiled. She had kind eyes.

"You came here saying you tried to commit suicide," she dove right in, and he recoiled. He had never been in therapy, but what he saw on TV suggested that the therapist tried to ease a person to open up. TV was wrong.

He nodded.

"Why did you want to kill yourself?" she asked next.

Why wouldn't he? It was a hefty list. Samson wasn't sure how to properly answer that question.

He was weak, briefly. He was overwhelmed, and sad, but not even that description felt true.

"I heard you had an eventful night," Dr. Meyer commented, deciding to change the subject.

"You could say that," he tried to joke, too late in realizing that this was maybe not the right place or time for humor.

"Can you explain what happened?" she prompted.

Can I? he asked himself. *You came here to talk and work on your issues, so talk, you asshole,* he snapped at himself.

"I had nightmares," he managed to choke out, deciding to start with something light. Although that was true, admitting he needed help was still hard. And he was not sure he could do this.

"Are they recurring ones?"

"You mean did I have them before?"

She nodded.

"Yes, I had nightmares, especially after I left the military."

"Were you in a war?"

"Yes, in Afghanistan."

"So, after you returned home, you started suffering from nightmares? Anything else?"

He recognized this was a perfect opportunity to mention his PTSD but didn't for some reason. "Yes, but they lessened over time. These are new ones."

"When did they start?"

When he "met" Candi and Lissa. "About a week ago."

"Was there an event in your life that could cause such bad dreams?"

You could say that. He nodded instead of replying.

"We don't have to talk about that if you're not ready," she reassured.

Her smile was so warm and genuine that Samson relaxed ever so slightly. He was relieved she'd said that. He'd rather not talk about certain events. He didn't want to talk about Teresa, Lissa, or Candi either, but that was a different story.

At the same time, how would he get better if he clammed up? This doctor wasn't a mind reader. Which was a good thing. He didn't want her to know everything that was going on in his head. He didn't want her to see what had happened to him. This way, he was in charge of what information she received. That made him feel a little better; more in control.

"Samson?"

"Yes?"

"We don't have to talk about your nightmares either, at the moment."

"Okay."

So, were they just going to sit here in silence? That didn't sound very productive.

"We can talk about anything you like. Is there something you want to share?"

He knew there was a catch.

He said the first thing that popped into his head. "I didn't like being restrained last night."

Dr. Meyer nodded. "The on-call personnel said you reacted violently."

"That was because they drugged me," he defended. "They triggered my nightmares, plus they were touching me."

Unconsciously, Samson hugged himself.

"You don't like to be touched?"

He shook his head no.

"I see."

She scribbled something down on her notepad before continuing. "The restraints were not there to harm you, but to prevent you from harming yourself or others," she explained.

"I get that," and he did. He'd tried to get that through to his screwed-up brain the entire morning, as he sweated and panicked. "It's just hard."

"Do you want to tell me what made you so agitated?" she prompted.

"I dreamt about my wife. Well, my soon-to-be ex-wife," he corrected himself reluctantly.

"Is the divorce the reason you ended up on the bridge?"

Samson thought about it. "Partially."

"What is her name?"

"Teresa."

"What's she like?"

He didn't know anymore. Once upon a time, he'd thought she was a great person who loved him dearly. Now, he had his doubts. Maybe he'd only seen what he wanted to. So he shrugged.

"Tell me about her."

"We've been married for eight years; happily, I think. I fell in love with her the instant I met her. She's a real estate broker and a very good one. She has her own company and everything." He had always been particularly proud of how capable she was. There was nothing she couldn't do if she put her mind to it.

For some reason, it was easy to talk about her. That easiness helped him get out all the rest. Although he thought he wouldn't be able to speak about the rape, as it turned out, the words poured out of him like an unstoppable flood. He went with it, letting it all out.

"It started when Teresa went to see her parents, and I had to stay home and write. Later that night, these two girls – Lissa and Candi – appeared at my door asking for help."

As the story progressed Samson became more and more agitated.

"They wouldn't let me dress, not even my underwear," he screamed.

Norman the nurse entered to see if the doctor needed help.

"Everything is all right," Dr. Meyer reassured, kicking him out. "Carry on," she encouraged.

Surprisingly, Samson did. The dam inside him had broken, and he was able to tell her everything without holding back for fear that she would judge him. But it didn't come without pain, sorrow, anguish, and a lot of hate.

"They did stuff to me while I was powerless to defend myself, and not just because they threatened me. They tied me up and drugged me."

It was extremely difficult speaking about that last night.

"They used all kinds of toys on me, and filmed the entire time."

He was grateful that she didn't have any follow-up questions or try to interrupt him. He needed to get this out.

"Teresa found me like that, handcuffed to a chair, sitting in my own shit," he wept. "I will never forget the look on her face."

He had to pause there, and Dr. Meyer offered him a tissue. Once he managed to calm down enough, he continued.

"And then she threw me out like I was nothing to her. Like I was garbage," Samson concluded, getting angry all over again. "She wouldn't even listen to my side; she just assumed the worse. And she still won't take my calls."

"How did the confrontation with Teresa make you feel?"

"Angry … ashamed … hurt," he started to count.

They talked for what felt like hours, although logically he knew it couldn't have been more than an hour.

"Okay. I think you did an amazing thing today, Samson," she complimented, "and we'll continue all of this tomorrow."

He nodded. "But what about …" he started, then stopped.

"About what?"

"The restraints."

"I will note that no one should touch you, but if you have another violent outburst, the staff will have to act accordingly."

He understood, but he wasn't too happy about it. Especially since the nightmares were a given.

As he left the office, Samson felt changed. Not cured and not better, but definitely lighter, as though sharing his burden helped him breathe more easily. It was a strange feeling but not completely unpleasant.

This became a pattern. He freaked out at night, then talked about it during the day. But he was getting better over time.

At least, that was what Dr. Meyer kept telling him.

She was pretty amazing. Dr. Meyer was the first person who listened to him and believed what happened. She encouraged him to get it all out and confront his demons, although she protested when he called Lissa and Candi demons.

They are nothing more than a couple of girls who are bad people. There is nothing subhuman about them. Those were her words.

"I'm very impressed with your progress. And I believe it's time we lighten your medications."

Samson was glad to hear that, although he couldn't explain why. "Woohoo!" he pretended to cheer.

"I know you feel like you haven't accomplished enough, but I disagree. This is a marathon, not a sprint."

Wasn't he painfully aware of that? In this race of mental health, he was a freaking snail, and he said as much.

"You are extremely brave to seek help and for doing the work to get better," she countered.

"*Brave*?" He tested the word. It sounded weird.

"In a society that struggles with taboos and condemns men who ask for help, you are very brave," she was adamant.

"I don't feel brave."

"How do you feel?"

He took his time answering. "Broken," he replied honestly.

"You're not broken, Samson. I would not be recommending you be discharged if you were broken. You're just cracked, like the rest of us."

It felt nice to have someone in his corner.

"If you say so," he replied eventually.

She leaned forward and folded her hands on the desk. "You know when you cut yourself and end up bleeding?" she asked.

"Yeah," he replied, not sure where she was going.

"Well, afterward, with time and treatment, the wound starts to heal. It looks ugly at first, and scabs over. And it might take some time, but eventually, it looks like nothing happened," she concluded.

"It leaves a scar though," he pointed out.

"Sure, there could be some scarring, but that would only serve as a reminder that you are a survivor."

He liked that. He was not a victim; he was a survivor.

He was discharged one month after the day he stepped into the hospital.

Dr. Meyer advised him to immediately find another psychiatrist and continue his treatment. He was a long way from healed. He still had to properly deal with his PTSD and all the rest of his crap.

Samson felt like crying when he saw Malcolm waiting for him outside, leaning against his car like a chauffeur. They hugged.

"How do you feel?" his friend asked.

"Like crap," he joked. He didn't feel quite ready to face the big, bad world, but here he was.

"Good, because you look like crap," Malcolm countered without missing a beat.

Samson laughed, and it felt good. "Good to know."

"Come on, let me take you to breakfast."

Samson felt blessed to have such a good friend in his life.

CHAPTER 23

Samson woke up and felt like patting himself on the back. Last night marked the first night since he'd left the hospital that he hadn't woken up screaming or felt disoriented. He knew exactly where he was: In his new crib, so to speak. The fact that he hadn't screamed his lungs out didn't mean his night was nightmare-free. Samson still had those, unfortunately. Only now, he didn't get triggered as badly as before.

Am I getting used to them, or am I getting better? He couldn't say for sure. All the same, Samson was certain his new therapist, Dr. Johanna Valarezo, would tell him what was happening and that was good enough for him.

He stood up and stretched, impressed that his shirt wasn't soaked with sweat. *I guess this is what they call progress,* he joked, in a surprisingly good mood.

He hated that the progress was so slow, but it was still happening, and that was good. Life could be good as long as he screened his thoughts and made sure to stay in the moment and not think about the past, which wasn't always easy.

Five weeks had passed since he'd moved here. Malcolm and Anita were generous enough to let him live rent-free in their guest house while he got back on his feet. Teresa had taken pretty much everything he had to remodel the house. By her calculations, he still owed her big time. But he wasn't about to dwell on that today.

Samson refused Malcolm's offer at first, not wanting to be a burden. But his friend had insisted, and Samson was pathetic enough not to want to be alone. He wasn't suicidal anymore, just lonely and depressed. And he felt like he would bring a lot of trouble into their lives.

It helped to know this was something Anita was okay with too. Samson didn't know how Malcolm had managed to convince his wife to do this, but he was grateful.

Their generosity wasn't without consequences. Teresa wouldn't speak to them anymore, and some other friends had chosen her side as well. Samson wasn't too heartbroken about that, and luckily, neither were Malcolm and Anita.

"Screw them all," were Anita's exact words.

To respond to their kindness, Samson sat them down and, with a lot of effort, told them what exactly had happened. He didn't go into as many details as he had with his psychiatrist, but he shared plenty. At first, he wasn't sure if Anita believed him, especially since Teresa told everyone who would listen how he invented the ridiculous story so he wouldn't have to take responsibility for his behavior. Now, he knew better.

Malcolm and Anita fully supported him.

On the other hand, Teresa was unyielding. He'd written her a couple of letters, sharing everything with her, telling her how sorry he was, but it had accomplished nothing. She believed he was nothing more than a liar, and her words hurt his feelings.

The fact she still refused to speak with him after all this time was as infuriating as it was hurtful. He no longer recognized the person he'd married, which was ironic because that was exactly what she was saying about him.

At times, he got so mad he wanted to piss on the divorce papers she kept sending to him but managed to refrain. Behavior like that wouldn't help his case in the slightest. The goal was to make things better, not worse.

For now, his strategy was to ignore her lawyer and refuse to sign the papers in hopes that would enrage her enough to want to meet with him. So far, his strategy sucked.

His alarm went off, reminding him it was time to take his medicine. He hated he had to take pills, and he hated that he had been forced to ask for help in the first place, but that was a moot point. He was all in or all out; there was no middle ground.

He swallowed the damned things since despite the inner hate, he wanted and needed to get better. Although at times he felt like a failure, he knew this was what he needed to do to achieve the results he wanted. Plain and simple.

Of course, the road back to mental stability wasn't easy and was definitely not a straight line. It was full of turns and rocky obstacles. At times, he felt like he was moving backward, especially after a tough night. But it wasn't all so bleak. He had a great psychiatrist who helped him see things in a different light, showed him how to accept things he couldn't change, and most of all, accept himself for what he was, with all the good and bad.

And today, I woke up like a normal person. That had to count for something.

With a little help from his shrink, Samson gathered enough courage to visit his publisher. He didn't go into details about what had happened or why he'd ended up in a mental hospital, but with a bit of sucking up and a lot of remorse shown, he was forgiven, and the publisher gave him another chance.

So, his book was once again scheduled for publishing. The due date was a bit tight, but he was eager to prove himself, so it was manageable. The best part was that he would work with the same editor, Hunter, and that was great because the other guy got him and understood his writing style.

However, none of that would matter without the most vital part: the manuscript … the ruined one, of course. With a little – read: huge – help from Malcolm, Samson got his busted computer back from Teresa.

She was reluctant to return it and tried to blackmail him into signing the divorce papers first, but eventually, Malcolm managed to bribe her with some free carpentry work.

Thanks to Lissa, his computer was busted, although he still hoped some data could be salvaged from the hard drive. He took it to a repair shop, and a few people laughed in his face when he showed them his computer. Then he stumbled upon a small computer repair shop where the owner and the only employee named Ben promised they would check it out, which brought him some hope.

Ben did everything in his power, surpassed Samson's expectations, and eventually managed to recover a large portion of his old manuscript. He got more than seventy percent back, and thanks to the notes he'd taken, he was able to recreate what he once had. If he was to be so humble, he believed the new pages were even better than the lost ones.

The new developments gave Samson the will and motivation to start writing full-time again, but even that wasn't without its challenges and difficulties. At times, especially if he was having an emotionally hard day, it showed in his writing. It was hard when the fantasy world he was trying to create for his protagonist, Marc, and his real, broken world kept colliding. He continued to paint an already dark book even darker shades, but Hunter was blown away by them. Samson hoped that was a good thing.

Thanks to Dr. Valarezo, things in his life started to improve greatly. He continued to have nightmares and preferred not to be touched, but the way he handled the stress that followed had changed. Samson now knew just the right way to calm himself without freaking out or getting triggered. The notion that he was once again in charge of his life and in control of his body pushed him further down the road to full recovery.

He hadn't touched alcohol since the night he'd tried to kill himself, not a single beer during a game he watched with Malcolm. In retrospect, it was foolish to turn to the bottle to relieve his pain in the first place. Not only because it made matters worse, but because it was what got him into trouble in the first place.

"Oh, come on. Take one beer," Malcolm said to him once.

"No, thank you."

"I promise I didn't spice it up."

Samson gave him a look.

"Too soon?" His best friend made a face.

"A bit."

And then they both laughed, and Malcolm never pressed again.

Samson was aware he had a lot of issues to deal with, but he also wasn't at rock bottom anymore, which was huge progress.

All the same, no matter how many hours he spent with Dr. Valarezo, the thoughts about revenge haven't left his mind. His body still burned with the desire to find the girls and ruin them.

However, he put all that to the side for time being. He knew he had to get better before going on the hunt. Perhaps that didn't make much sense to an outsider – getting better so he could go on a killing spree – but it made perfect sense to him. Samson wanted to enjoy that event as much as possible, and for that to happen, he had to break the cycle he was in and completely free himself from their control. Only when he was one hundred percent free could he do what needed to be done.

That was what motivated him to get out of bed in the morning, go to therapy, work out, and write. The notion that he would kill those bitches one day soon put a smile on his face.

That was what his shrink called a "future goal," and she would be very proud of him if she knew he had one. He might be crazy, but he wasn't crazy enough to share something like that with her. Samson would only end up in a padded room, and that was something he wanted to avoid at all costs.

Finished with his work for the day, he left the guest house and went in search of his friend. It was freeing that Malcolm and Anita knew what had happened to him and believed him because he could be himself around them without pretending he was all right. They knew he wasn't, although he was working hard to be. The notion they accepted him the way he was, broken and all, meant a great deal to him.

Entering the main house through the kitchen, he found Malcolm at the stove.

The kids were at school and Anita was at work, so Malcolm was home alone making lunch for them.

Malcolm was a contractor and had a lot less work in the dead of winter, which meant he could hang out with Samson after doing the chores around the house.

"Perfect timing," Malcolm greeted.

"What's that? It smells great."

"My mom's secret recipe. Try this." He offered him a wooden spoon filled with some kind of sauce. "Is it too salty?"

"No, it's perfect," Samson replied honestly. "And now I know why Anita married you. You are a perfect wife."

"Bite me, asshole."

After they finished with their usual ritual of heckling one another, they settled in to eat. In front of a TV, of course, because Malcolm was also watching some game.

"How are things going?" his friend asked between bites.

He wasn't asking that simply to fill the silence; he was worried, and rightfully so. Malcolm had seen him at his worst. The first night he moved in, Samson screamed so loudly during his nightmare that Malcolm had broken in with a baseball bat.

Samson wasn't repulsed by their talks. Quite the contrary, they felt nice. He liked that he could talk about certain things with a person he didn't have to pay.

"The same, I guess." And then he remembered how he hadn't screamed last night and shared that.

"See? Things are getting better," Malcolm tried to comfort him.

Samson remained quiet. He wanted to believe that, but he still felt like a fraud most days, going through the motions while feeling crappy. The same way he'd felt for months.

"Samson?"

"Yeah?"

"You *do* believe things will get better, right?" Malcolm pressed.

"Honestly, I don't know," he said with a sigh.

"Why?"

"I can't get over what happened to me. And I don't see how I ever will."

"Hell, man. I won't pretend I can understand what you're going through, but you have to try because what's the alternative?"

"Padded white room," he tried to joke.

"Exactly. So, you have to push forward without looking back, like we did in that place."

There was no need for him to clarify what place he was referring to. They had been together in Afghanistan.

Samson knew his friend was right, but there was still something holding him back: Burning rage and the need for revenge.

"You know what eats at me the most?" Samson heard himself asking.

Malcolm looked at him questioningly.

"I'm worried that some other guy will end up with his life ruined like me and those poor bastards before me." Samson knew those girls were unstoppable. They would continue to party and seek their form of "fun" until someone stopped them.

Samson couldn't bear the thought that they were still out there, free, roaming around and tormenting men, all in the name of fun. They had completely perverted the meaning of that word.

He said as much.

"I hear you," Malcolm replied.

Samson was glad his friend understood him.

"It doesn't feel right to just move on and forget everything," Samson summed it up.

Malcolm nodded. His friend was deep in thought for a while before he spoke again. "How about you hire a lawyer or private investigator to help you find them?" he offered. "Since the police are useless," he added, making a face.

When Samson told his friend how the police had treated him, how they'd laughed in his face when he'd begged for help, Malcolm was so furious, he wanted to go down to the precinct, find those officers, and have a chat with them.

His precise words were, "I think I'll go there and give them something to smile about: A mouth full of broken teeth."

Samson had managed to calm him down, and not from the goodness of his heart. He planned to kill those bitches, and he didn't want the attention on him from the men in blue.

Malcolm's idea was a good one, but he wasn't so happy about having to share his horrific experiences with strangers.

On the other hand, what was the alternative? How could he find them on his own? He couldn't. Once again, he needed help.

But there was a small catch.

"I don't know if I can afford something like that. It sounds expensive."

He was spread thin as it was.

"It costs you nothing to give it a try," Malcolm pointed out. "Meet with a few of them and hear what they have to say."

"You're right," Samson agreed.

"So, you'll do it?"

"Yeah."

Malcolm looked happy with their little talk and continued eating. Samson followed his example.

CHAPTER 24

Through online research, Samson found a list of people who he believed could help him find Candi and Lissa. He was concerned that the two hadn't given him their real names. If that were true, he would be doomed, but then he realized he was probably stressed out for nothing. They were arrogant enough to use their real names. They also couldn't imagine a scenario that one of their playthings would try to track them down. He would use that to his advantage ... he hoped.

However, there were some difficulties right from the start.

Finding someone willing to help him wasn't as easy as he'd hoped, and Samson discovered pretty quickly that he wasn't a desirable client.

He figured it would be better to work with a lawyer than a private detective. He couldn't afford both, so he concluded that a lawyer would serve him better. Plus, many had private investigators on their staff anyway, so it would be like getting two birds with one stone.

Or so he believed.

He was wrong.

It was nearly impossible to make an appointment, and those he managed to speak with weren't kind. Among those who offered a consultation, a couple laughed in his face after hearing his story; others were just plain rude. It was difficult to keep his temper in check in that kind of situation.

He saw a dozen lawyers that week, all of whom he thought were professionals, but it was one fiasco after the other.

Samson saw red and had to count to ten to calm down when, after hearing his story, one guy straight up told him to stop trying to build a case to cover up his affair.

Samson was so enraged, he nearly forgot how to count. He couldn't believe the guy. He wasn't only an asshole but a stupid one. Samson was twice his size and in excellent shape.

"Excuse me?" Samson snapped, jumping from his seat. He wanted to strangle the man with his bare hands, but he knew Dr. Valarezo would frown upon it.

The prick in question shrugged. "You asked for my legal advice, and that's it. Give up. No one will believe your story."

"It's not a story; it's the truth!" Samson was adamant.

"Whatever, Mr. Chase. I think we're done here. I don't have the time to take your case," he recited.

That pissed him off further. "Are you calling me a liar?"

Some of the smugness disappeared from this jerkoff's face as he sensed he was about to get his ass kicked. "Calm down. It wasn't my attention to offend."

"Yeah, right." Samson picked up his stuff, and then stormed out of the office before giving in to the temptation to bash the man's head against the table.

The rest of the encounters were only marginally better. Two guys canceled their appointments with him and had their secretaries lie about them being too busy in court to take on any new cases. These bastards clearly talked to one another, which meant Samson was screwed again.

What could he do if no one would take his case? *Don't think like that.* He would find someone who was a decent human being and wouldn't assume the worst. Someone who became a lawyer out of a desire to help.

Okay, maybe he was reaching.

Everyone refused to take his case. Samson felt like a leper. It wasn't bad enough that the police didn't believe him and that Teresa and his friends thought he was a liar, too. Now, he couldn't even capable find legal representation because people assumed the worst.

What kind of man would invent a story full of torture and abuse to cover up an affair?

In the first story, he was a victim and a weakling. In the second, he was a stud and a superhero to a lot of guys who dreamed of scoring with sisters.

It made no sense to him that he would insist on something that wasn't true. Apparently, the rest of the world thought differently.

Not everyone, he corrected. There were still people who believed him and wanted to help him. He would find a lawyer, too; he just had to dig a little deeper. So, he persisted.

Without much luck.

Samson couldn't say who pissed him off more: the ones who enjoyed a good laugh at his expense or the ones who thought he was sick enough to invent that story.

Either way, it was depressing. How could he seek revenge if no one would believe him?

If lawyers – people who were paid to help – didn't believe his story, he was either screwed or crazy and had imagined the entire week with those girls. *They didn't exist*, he mocked. *I did all that to myself.*

What was happening to him was pure insanity.

Why can't I catch a break? Some would say the universe was conspiring against him because he planned to kill those bitches, and murder was wrong. How else could he explain his streak of bad luck? Luckily, he didn't believe in that nonsense.

I can't give up.

Malcolm greeted him as he returned home.

"How did it go?"

Samson gave him a look and plopped on the couch, defeated and exhausted.

"That good, huh?" Malcolm guessed sitting next to him.

"Let me put it this way: I didn't kill anyone today, even though I wanted to."

"Son of a bitch."

Samson's sentiments exactly.

"The ones who laughed were the better ones I visited."

"What?"

"Yeah. Today, one bastard told me I should just admit to the affair instead of trying so hard to cover it up."

Just thinking about that asshole and his smirk made Samson's blood boil. He had half a mind to return to his office and teach him the importance of people skills.

"He *said* that?" Malcolm was aghast.

"Yeah. I barely stopped myself from strangling him."

"I'd feel the same way," Malcolm said, shaking his head in disbelief. "What a jackass." And then, he brightened up. "I'm sure you'll have better luck tomorrow." That was Malcolm, all right. An optimist to the end.

Samson wouldn't get his hopes up, not after all the interviews he'd had. He also wouldn't give up.

It was hard not to lose hope in humanity after everything that had happened. And he wasn't even talking about the two evil creatures who'd ruined his life; he meant the normal people who looked the other way, laughed, or told him to stop lying.

Are there no good lawyers left in this world? Not one of them is brave enough to take a chance with me?

The more people turned him down and the more frustrated he became, the more determined Samson was to have his way. He would prove to all these people that he was not a liar, and that what happened to him was not a laughing matter. He would find someone to help him, and with their help, he would track down those girls and expose them to the world for what they were: A couple of sociopaths who fed on human misery.

Samson would find his white whale even if he had to visit every attorney in the city.

Hell, he would even branch out to another city if he had to. There was no way in hell he would give up. That wasn't an option.

Samson would not let these girls get away again. They were going to pay for the crimes committed against him and all the other men who'd fallen into their trap.

He would find and stop them because too many things were at stake. Repairing his reputation was at the bottom of the list at the moment because, for all he knew, Lissa and Candi were tormenting some other guy right now. That notion drove him insane, and it also made him that much more determined to find them.

Some might call him obsessed, but Samson was just a man on a mission. And once he found them, with a little help from the lawyer he still had yet to retain, God help them.

Samson would deal with Candi and Lissa in his way.

Malcolm thought Samson planned to sue them, and Samson didn't correct him. He didn't want to burden his best friend with the fact that legal action was the furthest thing from his mind.

Samson did not want this to turn into a media circus. He had zero desire to be portrayed as a man who'd allowed two girls to drug and rape him repeatedly.

Once he discovered where these girls were, he would happily be their judge, jury, and executioner.

He'd already picked a nice little spot in the forest to take them to bury them after he'd killed them.

CHAPTER 25

Why is this so hard? It was so absurd that Samson felt like laughing. The city was filled with lawyers, but here he was, still looking.

As another one turned him down, this one didn't bother with an excuse for refusing to take his case. He didn't even allow Samson to present his case. Samson had barely sat down when the lawyer told him he couldn't help.

Samson was perplexed. He could only stare at the other man for a couple of heartbeats.

"Then why did you agree to see me in the first place?" Samson demanded. This could have been done over the phone; had better things to do than drive downtown to meet this clown, just for him to say no.

"I made a mistake," he countered.

Could I use the same excuse to throw an ashtray at him? Samson wondered.

"No. I'm the one who made a mistake, assuming you're a professional," Samson said before storming out.

What a dickhead.

What was that about? Did this guy just want to meet the guy who cried rape so he could have a funny story to tell his other lawyer friends? If that was the case, then Samson wept for humanity.

Come on, universe. Throw me a bone. He was at the end of his rope. He'd promised himself he wouldn't give up, but all this drama was seriously wearing him down.

Maybe I should ask Dr. Valarezo for advice. Maybe he was doing it wrong?

What, talking? He had done that his whole life without a psychiatrist by his side to guide him. This was just so frustrating and was giving him serious doubts about himself.

He knew he was right. He knew what had happened to him was wrong, but the whole world was telling him differently. It was maddening.

Samson looked at his list. There was only one more name on it. Even looking at it now, he had second thoughts. Perhaps he should leave this one for tomorrow? He'd had enough rejection for one day.

The last lawyer's office was across town from where he was now, and he didn't feel like driving all that way to be shut down again.

Still, Samson got into the car and drove to his last appointment. He sang to his favorite tunes while driving, and that helped ease his stress a little.

Samson was treated to a little surprise as he pulled up to the building: The office space was settled in an old shoe repair shop, and in its front window there were still some tools left and figurines of gnomes repairing shoes.

This looks promising. Not even that discouraged him from proceeding. *Here I go.*

A woman sat in a smallish room that had just enough space for a desk and a huge collection of books behind it, intently reading some papers in front of her.

She looked fairly young, slim, and petite, with long wavy black hair. *This must be the secretary I spoke with,* Samson deduced.

Where was the lawyer's office? He saw no additional space or even another door.

Nevertheless, he approached her. "Hello," he greeted.

"Hello," she countered, rising from her seat.

"I have an appointment with Mr. Chang," he explained.

The woman smiled. "I'm Melissa Chang. You have an appointment with me," she explained.

His lawyer was a woman? Not that she was *his* lawyer, or that it mattered she was a woman. This wasn't the eighteen hundreds, and he shouldn't act like a caveman. Besides, she would probably turn him down like all the rest had anyway.

"Great," he said, before remembering to say. "My name is Samson Chase."

Although if she had an appointment with him, she already knew that. He was acting all kinds of stupid today.

They shook hands before she offered him a seat.

Taking a pen as though preparing to take notes, she said, "How may I help you, Mr. Chase?"

"I have a unique problem," he began. He was sure all clients believed that about their misfortunes. *Focus,* he reminded himself. "I'm sure you've already heard about me from your colleagues. I've visited quite a few."

He regretted saying that the instant the words left his mouth. *What is wrong with me?* Now she knew that she had not been his first choice. *More like the hundredth.*

There was no point in stressing over that now; the damage was done. Samson prepared himself for a quick exit.

However, she countered, "I don't pay attention to gossip, especially if it's coming from my colleagues."

"Good to know." Samson liked that, but he didn't dare hope that meant she would take his case. Everyone else had said no; why would she be any different?

He felt she was.

"Tell me about your problem, Mr. Chase," she prompted.

Where to begin? Although he'd done this part plenty of times before, he still struggled. Talking about this wasn't easy, and no matter what people said, it didn't get easier with time, especially when he'd had such bad experiences with people lately.

"Someone wronged me, and I want to do something about it." Why was he acting so vague all of a sudden?

"You want to file a lawsuit?"

"I guess."

"What is the name of the defendant?" she asked.

"That's where it gets a bit tricky."

She looked up, raising an eyebrow, and he understood why. The name of the person you wanted to sue should be the easiest part.

Sorry, lady. Not in this case.

"I only know their first names," he explained.

"All right. What are their names?"

"Lissa and Candi," Samson said as she wrote it down. Each time he said their names out loud still left a bad taste in his mouth. He feared that would never change.

This would be a time when Dr. Valarezo would caution him about his pessimism.

"What did they do?" the lawyer asked next.

Me. Of course, he didn't say that out loud. "They assaulted me."

"Do you have any medical reports about the assault?"

"It wasn't a typical assault," he began. "They drugged me and raped me." Samson clenched his hands into fists as he said that. He figured it was the easiest to just get it out, like ripping off a Band-Aid.

Her expression remained the same. He appreciated that.

"And the DA's office didn't want to press charges against them?" she asked without missing a beat.

"I never completely reported the crime. I had a misfortune with the police officers, and that warded me off."

"What do you mean by 'a misfortune?'"

"They laughed in my face when I tried to explain to them what was happening to me."

"I see," she said, putting down her pen. "I think I'm going to need some more information to better understand what we're dealing with here. Can you tell me exactly what happened to you?" she asked gently.

And so, with nothing to lose, Samson dove in and told the young attorney everything.

"My wife was out of town when these two girls, around twenty years old, knocked on my door in the middle of the night and asked for help."

"What happened to them?"

"They said some guys had mistreated them during a date and taken their stuff, so I invited them inside to use my phone, so they could get a ride home. It was all a lie."

"What happened afterward?"

"I made the mistake of agreeing to have a drink with them. They put something in my drink."

"They drugged you?"

"Yes. And then they raped me, repeatedly, while filming it."

Samson chose his words carefully but managed to cover all the bases, from how they blackmailed him and tormented him for days, to how they'd trashed his house.

"You said the police came?"

"Several times, to warn me about the noise. The neighbors complained about a "party" at my house."

He tried his best not to sound bitter but couldn't help it.

"And they did nothing to assist you?"

"They laughed at me. They thought it was a joke."

"Do you remember their names?"

Samson shook his head.

"It's not important," she reassured. "I can find that out with one phone call. Tell me what happened next."

"Things escalated when I rebelled. They tied me up and declared it was time for a farewell party. That was when they drugged me again."

He skipped most of what had happened that night, not only because he couldn't remember much of it but because he didn't want to disgust her. He glossed over the torment and rape.

To her credit, she didn't flinch once or look at him as though he was some poor schmuck. He hated when people felt sorry for him.

"They sent all the videos to Teresa, my wife."

That was the hardest part to retell because it was what hurt the most. He could deal with the trauma, but Teresa's betrayal was something he didn't know how to handle. She was supposed to love him more than anyone, but she'd abandoned him the quickest.

"After she kicked me out, I spent a month in a mental institution, and that's that," he concluded.

Samson was very proud of how calm he was.

Ms. Chang nodded. "First of all, how you are feeling now?" She surprised him by asking. "Have you sought help to deal with the trauma?"

"Yes. I'm going to therapy."

It was one of the terms of his early discharge.

"Good. I think that's very important, especially considering you want to get into this legally. I'm telling you now that it won't be easy or stress-free."

"I'm aware of that, and I'm ready for it," he reassured.

She nodded. "Okay, then. Let's dive right back in. Tell me everything you can remember about those girls, how they looked and how they behaved."

Samson tried but there wasn't much he could share. Apart from being rich, he didn't know anything about them.

Ms. Chang noted that too.

"Would you be willing to work with a sketch artist? It would help a lot if we could have their pictures."

"Of course," he replied without a thought.

She looked pleased by his answer.

"I will set that up, then," she said, and since it looked like she was mostly talking to herself while writing something down in haste, probably a reminder, Samson remained quiet.

"You mentioned that they recorded the whole experience. Do you by any chance have copies of the videos?"

"No. My wife is the only one who has them, apart from Lissa and Candi."

Or so he hoped.

"To the best of your knowledge?"

"Yes."

"I know this is a delicate situation, but do you think we could get copies from your wife?"

Samson gave her a look. "Teresa hates my guts. She won't help me."

"I understand," she said, although she looked disappointed.

Speaking of those videos, Samson was surprised Teresa hasn't shown them to anyone, although she talked about them non-stop to whoever was willing to listen. Samson was grateful for that small gift. His life was fucked up enough without having to deal with being an internet sensation. He could just picture the hype. *Novelist caught in a sex scandal. Favorite positions of a dark writer.*

He shuddered at the thought.

Ms. Chang continued to ask him questions, and Samson answered the best he could. He wasn't always helpful, but she never looked bothered. They went back and forth for a while.

Ms. Chang asked a lot of good questions, questions he should have asked himself that had never occurred to him. He supposed that was why she was a lawyer and he wasn't.

They talked a lot about how he felt while under the influence of that drug. She even fired up her computer to do an internet search, in hopes something would come up.

"Well, based on your symptoms, I think they drugged you with ketamine," she said after some time.

It was all the same to him, but for some reason, Ms. Chang took this as a positive thing.

"I'm not a medical expert, but that's what the internet search provided me with," she hedged. "We could consult with an expert and see what he has to say."

"*We*? Does that mean you will take my case?"

"Yes, I will."

Samson was overjoyed and relieved. "Thank you very much," he said honestly.

"Don't thank me yet," she said with a smile.

He smiled in return. "So, what's next?" he asked with renewed vigor.

"Do you think your therapist would be willing to testify about your trauma?"

He didn't know. He was sure there was some kind of a patient/doctor entanglement to think about and was sure Ms. Chang was better informed about it than he.

"I can ask," he replied.

"Great. That would help us a great deal."

"So how do you plan to track them down?"

"There are a few ways, but as I mentioned before, I want you to sit down with a sketch artist to see if we can identify them that way."

"Okay," that sounded like a promising start. "Whatever you need."

"Also, something else came to mind. You said they bragged about doing this to other men?"

"Yes, but I don't know if they were telling the truth."

"Either way, that's an avenue we should explore."

"What do you mean?"

"I think we should try to locate the other victims and see if they want to join in the fight. That way, this could turn into a class-action lawsuit," she explained.

"You think that's the best course of action?"

Samson had his doubts. Did he really want to meet and get involved with the rest of them?

"The way I see it, to build a solid case against these girls, it would be better if we had more plaintiffs," she explained.

He never thought of that. Maybe it was a good idea.

That was why he said, "Okay. Proceed how you think is best."

"My team and I will handle everything," she reassured him.

"Ms. Chang, I'd like to be involved in the process."

"That's not standard practice."

"I know, but I want to help."

"Mr. Chase—"

"Please, hear me out. I won't get in your way, I just feel like it's something I need to do to find closure." *To find redemption.*

She thought about his words for a moment. "All right," she said eventually. "Under one condition."

"Name it."

"We will work within the law and make sure these girls get what they deserve that way."

Her words took him by surprise. Did he have a neon sign on his forehead that said, "I want revenge"?

He smiled. "Of course," he said, lying like a pro.

CHAPTER 26

Samson couldn't wait to share the good news with Malcolm. He finally had a lawyer, and she seemed truly motivated to help him.

Samson was in Ms. Chang's office for about three hours, talking things over and developing strategies. Something was finally happening, things were moving forward, and that filled him with hope.

"Hey, Samson. What's up?" Malcolm greeted as he entered the house.

Anita waved at him with a knife as she chopped vegetables for dinner.

"You're looking at a man who finally has legal representation," he announced.

"That's great, Samson," Anita said.

"Yeah," her husband agreed. "Good for you."

"It wasn't easy, but I think I landed a good one," he said, leaning against the counter.

"Is it that guy we saw on TV?" Malcolm asked, handing Anita a plate full of chopped potatoes. They were a well-rehearsed team, and it was always pleasant to watch them while they cooked. Samson found it soothing. He'd liked watching his mother cook as well when he was a kid.

"No, he was a dick," Samson replied, snapping himself from those memories.

"Then who?"

"Melissa Chang."

"Cool. What did she say? Is there hope? What's her first move?" Malcolm started bombarding him with questions and Samson didn't mind. He was excited, too.

"She said a lot. You should have seen her; she was amazing. She's so normal and down to earth."

Which was refreshing after all those douchebags who looked down on him like he should feel lucky and honored that they'd blessed him with their presence.

"And she's really smart."

Some kind of ruckus began upstairs, and Malcolm groaned. "They've started fighting again."

Anita and Malcolm's children were going through a phase where they didn't like one another and fought constantly.

"I'll deal with them," Anita said wiping her hands against the dishrag. "You got this?"

"I got this."

Once she left, Malcolm resumed the conversation.

"Tell me more."

"Well, I told her everything and she took me seriously," Samson said, unable to hide his amazement.

"I knew she would," Malcolm said confidently, although a few minutes ago he hadn't known she existed.

Samson felt no need to point that out since Malcolm was simply being his usual optimistic self. There was nothing wrong with that. Especially on a day like today, when everything was good and anything seemed possible.

"She also suggested we should find out about the other men. Maybe some of them know something we can use against the girls."

"That is pretty smart," he agreed.

"And she said she'd allow me to help."

Malcolm stopped to look at him. "Do you think that's a good idea?"

"Yeah," Samson replied instantly and only slightly defensively. "I mean, I have to do something. Waiting around will only drive me insane."

"That's true," Malcolm agreed.

"Besides, she warned me that I would have to behave. No taking matters into my own hands."

"It's like she knows you already," he joked.

"Oh, and tomorrow, I'm going to sit with a sketch artist," Samson remembered.

"To get Candi and Lissa's pictures?"

"Yes."

"That's a great idea."

"It was all Melissa's idea."

"Oh, it's *Melissa* now," Malcolm jibed with a small smile.

Samson rolled his eyes. "Grow up," he grumbled.

"Is it just my imagination or have you developed a small crush already? I mean, it's Melissa this, Melissa that," he teased.

He was like a dog with a bone.

Samson made a face. "Dating is the last thing on my mind, believe me." Besides, it wasn't like he was a chick magnet. Sociopathic girls who liked to drug and rape aside.

He was still a basket case who could get triggered and spiral out of control with the slightest provocation. He also couldn't stand to be touched. *Who wouldn't want to date a stud like that?*

Malcolm got serious, sensing this was no joking matter. "And what's on your mind these days?" his friend asked.

Samson decided to come clean.

"I'm constantly thinking about what I would like to do to them after we find them."

"For example?" he probed.

"I want to kill them, Malcolm," he replied looking his friend straight in the eyes. "I want to punish them, make them scream in terror for everything they did to me. I want them dead. And I want it to do it with my hands."

He needed to see their life draining from their bodies and know it was because of him.

Malcolm sighed, rattled by this revelation. "How long have you felt like this?"

"Since the first time they drugged me," Samson replied without a thought.

Malcolm cursed, rubbing his head, as though that would help with the thinking process. And then he cursed again once he noticed he was burning dinner.

"When things get bad, that's the only way I can calm myself," Samson continued to explain. "Thinking about their demise pushes me forward. Without it, I don't think I would even get out of bed. I need this."

Samson needed his revenge, plain and simple, and he pleaded with his friend to understand. He knew he was asking a lot, but he couldn't change how he felt. Those girls had messed him up and good.

"Fuck, man," Malcolm said eventually. "That's so fucked up."

"I know," Samson said, looking away.

"I'm sure I would feel the same way if I were you," Malcolm surprised him by saying.

"Really?"

"Hell yes. Even now, I want those girls dead for what they did to you."

"But?" Samson prompted, knowing what would follow.

"I'm afraid your pretty lawyer is right. You have to seek legal satisfaction because nothing good will come of you taking matters into your own hands," he warned. "As much as those girls deserve the worst possible suffering and death for all they did to you, the legal way is the only way."

"You think I don't know that?" Samson snapped. "I just can't change the way I feel. I'm still barely containing an urge to rage every time I think of them."

"I know it's hard."

"You have no clue what it was like to go through all that. And for that, I need them dead." Samson raised his voice before remembering they were not alone. He didn't want Malcolm's children to hear any of this.

"Death is what they deserve. And if we lived in a lawless society, that would be exactly what they would get. However, we fought against such things, remember?"

As much as he hated rational Malcolm, it was hard to argue against it.

"Yeah, I remember," Samson grumbled.

"And I want you to remember something else: No man who is violent against two girls will ever be perceived as a victim," Malcolm pointed out, landing a final blow.

Samson felt like punching something.

"It's not fair that everyone assumes I'm lying, that I wanted all this to happen. It's like my pain counts for nothing."

"Unfortunately, we don't live in a perfect world that believes men can be victims, too."

He hated the word victim. He was a survivor, but he understood Malcolm's sentiment.

"It is what it is," Samson replied with a shrug, feeling frustrated to no end.

"That doesn't mean you should give up. You have to keep fighting."

"I know," Samson replied. He didn't plan on giving up. Especially not now that he'd found a lawyer who believed him and wanted to help.

"By the way, how did you know she was pretty?" Samson asked as an afterthought.

"Who?"

"Melissa Chang."

Malcolm grinned. "She *is* hot, isn't she? I knew it."

Samson rolled his eyes. Malcolm was no better than his children.

He went back to his room after dinner with the Northrups but found he couldn't sleep. His brain was wide awake working through possibilities.

At times, it was hard getting out of his head. Despite all the good news, his brain continued to torment him with all the bad. Teresa still wanted to divorce him and refused to see him, although he'd gone to see her one day and she threatened him with a restraining order.

Since there was no news from Ms. Chang and Samson felt ready to explode, he did the only thing he could considering the circumstances: He went to see his therapist to share his feelings, thoughts, and frustrations with her. It hurt his pride to be so powerless, which frustrated him to no end, but he'd promised himself that he would do what needed to be done to get better, so there he sat, crying like a baby on a stranger's couch.

Samson also shared his homicidal fantasies with Dr. Valarezo.

"It's completely normal to feel like this, as long as you understand you cannot act on it," she explained.

But he very badly wanted to act on it, and he shared as much. "I even started sketching all these various murder scenarios in one of my old notebooks."

"Murder scenarios?" she repeated.

"Yeah. How I want to end them, and in what way. Do you want to hear it?"

"If you think it would be beneficial for you," she hedged.

Samson thought it might. He said as much.

"Okay then."

"First of all, I picture bludgeoning Lissa to death with a baseball bat." She'd used it on him a couple of times, so he believed it was only fair to return the favor. "However, I would also like to simply smother her with a pillow, as she screams and begs for mercy."

"Is that all?"

"No. I've also contemplated pushing her off the roof but ruled against it."

"How come?"

"It seemed like too quick of a death, and I want to savor it."

"It wouldn't be if the height isn't sufficient. Then she would end up with several broken bones and a lot of suffering," Dr. Valarezo pointed out.

Samson's jaw dropped. His therapist was really cool. He couldn't believe he was engaging in this kind of discussion with her.

"You have a point," he allowed.

"What about Candi?" Dr. Valarezo asked professionally, as though they were discussing ways to deal with insomnia and not indulging in his murderous fantasies.

Then again, she was a psychiatrist. She'd probably heard it all in her dealings with crazy people like him.

Samson hated Candi a little more, so he'd put a lot more thought into the ways she could die.

"I would like to drown her," Samson started. It wouldn't be a quick endeavor; he would drag it out. He wanted to submerge her in water and bring her to the brink of death before pulling her to the surface. After giving her a chance to recover and breathe for a bit, he would repeat the whole process.

The images almost put a smile on his face.

"Then I would like to choke her to death, so I can see the terror on her face as I do it." Samson wanted her to know he was her doom, and that there was nothing she could do about it, no way to stop him. He was not her toy or her lapdog but the master of his own life.

"Most of all, I would like to tie her up and cut her slowly, and wait for her to bleed out in agony." Of course, he would tell Candi that he would set her free if she told him a story that amused him, and each time she disappointed him, he would cut her anew.

"Is that all?"

"Actually, I just came up with another one. I want to bury them alive in the same box."

Naturally, he would have a camera installed to watch what was happening. He thought that would be a fun way to go. Fun for him, terrifying for them.

Dr. Valarezo continued. "All right, hypothetically, let's say you go through with your plan. You capture them and kill them."

He liked this story already. "Okay."

"What would that accomplish?" she surprised him by asking. "Would it make you feel better?"

"Hell yes," he replied, not even having to think about it.

Of course it would make him feel better to know those two weren't breathing anymore. Because that would mean they were all free of them. The ones they hurt and the ones they didn't get a chance to. Samson was sure their "game" would only progress over time, and get more complex, more devious. They could evolve into killers, and then Samson would have the blood of those men on his hands because he'd done nothing to stop them. Or so he told himself.

"Temporarily, yes," Dr. Valarezo hedged. "However, all your problems would remain. Killing them wouldn't stop your nightmares or inability to allow physical contact. It wouldn't erase the bad memories. So overall, their death would accomplish nothing."

Samson didn't know how to respond to that.

"The only thing you would accomplish by killing them is to destroy your life," she continued. "You are at a crossroads now. You can choose to get better, or you can choose to continue walking down the destructive path, but know this: If you choose the latter, it would mean that they won again."

Hearing those words rattled him. He didn't want them to win again, not after everything they'd put him through. Not after they'd taken everything from him: his wife, his job, his life. They'd destroyed his life once, would he let them do that again?

The next time around would be even worse because he would be helping them. He would be the one doing the destroying.

"So what do I do?" he asked in a small voice.

"Give yourself some time to mourn your old life, and then embrace the opportunity to build a new one. Stop worrying about those girls. They will get what they deserve regardless. Focus solely on yourself and your healing."

It sounded so easy when she said it like that.

"I don't know how to do that," he replied honestly.

"Focus all your energy on achieving peace of mind, and the only way you can ever do that is to start forgiving yourself."

Forgive myself? That shook him to the core and gave him something to think about. He wasn't aware of how angry he was at himself for letting everything happen to him. Rationally, he knew it wasn't his fault, but he still blamed himself. As always, Dr. Valarezo was spot on.

Forgive myself? Could he do that?

"I don't know how to do that, or even if I *can*," he choked out after some time.

Dr. Valarezo offered a small, comforting smile, pleased they reached some kind of a breakthrough. "You will most definitely get there, with a little help."

"From you?" He wanted to make sure.

"And from life."

"Okay." He was ready to try anything. He didn't want to end up all alone and haunted for the rest of his life, locked in some cell.

"For now, I want you to make a list of things you like about yourself; things you are good at. We'll discuss it during our next appointment," she concluded.

Great. Achieving a breakthrough meant he now had homework. His life was complete.

Nevertheless, he said, "Sure."

Samson meant what he said. He would do anything in his power to not let those girls ruin him completely, and if that meant getting rid of his anger and hate for them while forgiving himself, then that was exactly what he planned to do.

Piece of cake.

CHAPTER 27

I t wasn't easy adjusting to a reality where killing Lissa and Candi wasn't an option, but he knew Dr. Valarezo was right. He couldn't let them win. So, he would do his best to move on, work on himself, and not think too much about them.

Which wasn't easy since he was working with Ms. Chang to find them. The way he saw it was that the faster he dealt with it, the better for him. Luckily, his lawyer called and shared some good news with him.

"I found them," she said without preamble.

Samson had to sit down; he honestly hadn't thought it would happen so fast. She was good. She'd managed to find them with only their names and a couple of sketches. Already, she was worth every penny he'd spent.

"I can't believe you managed to do that," he said.

"What can I say?" she joked. "I'm very good at my job."

"Yes, you are."

"When can you drop by my office?"

"Right now?"

"Perfect. See you in a bit, then."

"See you," he replied before hanging up.

As he got ready, he walked about in a daze. *She found them.*

Samson was so focused on this first step on the road that he hadn't stopped to consider what would happen next. *Should I confront them?* Would he meet with the other men? Would they all file a lawsuit against the girls?

What if they end up in jail? What if they get acquitted?

Samson had to sit down again.

You're getting ahead of yourself. For now, all he had to do was go to the lawyer's office and learn their identities.

Calming, Samson sat in his car and started driving. He wanted to break every law known to man or teleport himself to her office, but instead, he wound up in a traffic jam.

Just what he needed. He honked at the idiot in front of him. "Come on! Move it."

Samson needed to know who those girls were, and now, but here he was, wondering who allowed all these incapable people to get driver's licenses.

Morons!

Luckily, the universe had mercy, and the line moved again, allowing him to reach Ms. Chang's office in record time.

"Who are they?" Samson demanded the instant he stepped inside, not bothering with the pleasantries. He wasn't even sure he'd locked the car; not that he cared just then.

"First, sit down."

So, the news is that good, he thought. Samson complied, but it was hard to remain calm.

"You were right; they're heiresses."

He cursed. "Which family?"

"Their full names are Candi Marie and Lissa Marie Bellwether."

It was good he was sitting down because this news drove the air from his lungs. *Bellwether? They were freaking Bellwethers?*

"As in Donald Bellwether?" Samson asked, needing to make sure.

"Yes," she said, making a face. Samson understood the sentiment perfectly.

"As in Marissa Bellwether?"

"Yes. She is their stepmother and Donald is their father."

Samson's mind was blown. He'd expected them to have a rich father, but this was some next-level shit. Donald Bellwether was not only rich and powerful, but he was also famous and legendary.

Donald Bellwether was one of the richest men in the U.S., maybe even the world. He was a businessman known for his ruthlessness who made money by buying and selling companies. Hostile takeovers were something he was most famous for. It was like he enjoyed ruining companies others created and making money in the process. Shortly put, he was a son of a bitch who only cared about money.

Marissa was a typical trophy wife. This was Donald's third marriage, and Marissa was a famous supermodel before she married the business mogul. Nowadays, she just followed her husband around and ignored all the controversy around him.

Samson had trouble comprehending that Donald was responsible for bringing those two monsters into the world, but it also made perfect sense. It was expected that a man like him would have daughters like that. They were cut from the same cloth.

"Candi is twenty and Lissa is nineteen," Ms. Chang continued, unaware of his thoughts. "And they are enrolled in the most prestigious private college in the country."

"Daddy's?" Samson asked snidely.

"Yes."

Typical. Daddy bought a college for his little girls because he didn't want them to struggle too hard and actually earn their degrees.

I should go see him, came a sudden thought. *Just to say hello.*

No.

He should track them down. Now that he knew who they were, it would be easy to get their address.

Assuming they were not currently in some poor bastard's house, tormenting him to death.

He gritted his teeth. Their days of torture were over. He'd abandoned his plans of murdering them but he still planned to stop them for good. Samson would confront them and make them pay for everything they did to him and to all rest of the men they'd tortured.

He'd made peace with the fact that he could not take their lives, but no one had said anything about light torture. And then he would send *that* video to their father.

He could just picture their faces once they saw him. Samson would make himself comfortable and wait for them to return home. They would be startled to see him sitting in the dark, and he would smile and enjoy their discomfort.

"I told you I would find you," he would say with a smile to break the heavy silence among them.

Lissa would start laughing.

No. She wasn't supposed to do that. But she was, he could see it perfectly in his head.

She would laugh. "Look who followed us home, Candi. Our little monkey."

And Candi would roll her eyes and shake her head. "Oh my God, Samson, you are so pathetic," she would say with disgust.

Samson's heart went into overdrive. He couldn't stop the images from unfolding in front of his eyes.

"Let's play another game," Candi suggested.

"Yes! We will have so much fun," Lissa squeaked in excitement.

Samson couldn't breathe. Why was there no air? Air was supposed to be all around him, but he couldn't catch a breath no matter how hard he tried.

"Samson? Are you all right?" Melissa Chang asked, rushing to his side.

What was she doing here?

Wait, where am I? He started looking about. Lissa and Candi were gone. It took him a moment, but he remembered that he was sitting in his lawyer's office.

"Do you hear me?"

"Yes, yes I'm fine," he reassured. "I'm sorry for that."

"Would you like some water?" She still looked freaked out, and Samson couldn't blame her.

He couldn't believe he'd allowed himself to get triggered like that. He should be more careful of what he thought about. The temptation was almost too great now that he knew who they were.

Since Melissa continued to look at him intently, he remembered she'd asked him a question. "Yes, that would be great."

She offered him a small bottle that she'd fetched from a fridge he spotted for the first time.

"Thanks."

"Do you need to take some medication?" she inquired.

"No, I'm okay. I just got overwhelmed for a moment."

"You don't have to explain. I understand," she said, offering a smile.

Samson drank his water, not knowing how to respond. She had just witnessed how much of a basket case he was and didn't look at him as though he belonged in a mental institution.

"Feeling better?" she asked after some time.

He nodded. "It was just a lot to take in."

"I would feel the same way."

"And now that you've witnessed me falling apart, I think it's only appropriate to call me Samson," he tried to make a joke.

"All right," she agreed.

"So, what's next?" he wanted to move past this unfortunate incident. Samson needed a distraction.

"Are you sure you want us to do this now? If you need to rest, we can reschedule this for some other time," she offered.

"No, no," he was quick to reassure. "I want this." He *needed* this.

"All right." After taking a deep breath, as though needing a second to collect her thoughts, she continued. "I still believe that finding the other men that Lissa and Candi assaulted is what we need to do before anything else."

"How so?"

"They're Bellwethers. We have to have a tight case before making our move. And we don't want to tip them off too soon," she pointed out.

"Smart." And he meant that. Donald Bellwether would bring an army of lawyers to defend his daughters, so Samson's case needed to be bulletproof.

That felt like mission impossible since they had no clue who these other men were. They also had no evidence of the sisters doing anything wrong.

One problem at a time.

He was so wrapped up inside his head, he didn't realize that his lawyer was speaking.

"Samson?"

He nodded to whatever she'd said, before adding, "Let me know when you have more info for me."

He was about to leave when she stopped him. "Could you please promise me something?"

He turned and looked at her expectantly.

"Don't do anything rash while I track down the other men. We need to be very smart about all this considering who we're going up against."

That almost made him smile. She knew him all too well, although they'd only known each other for a short time. Samson nodded. "Of course. I won't do anything rash," he promised.

They said their goodbyes.

Samson was going to be very smart and deliberate while planning a double murder. The urge to track them down and be done permanently was so strong, it was the only thing he could think about. It would be so easy to succumb to his desires. Especially now that he didn't have to work so hard to find them. Melissa provided all the relevant information. *The Bellwethers*, he seethed. All his dreams could come true with a couple of clicks in the search engine.

Should I strangle Lissa? Should I cut Candi into pieces? A small part of him still fought against these thoughts.

A very small part, and it was getting smaller.

Samson hoped he could talk about all this with Malcolm once he got home. Unfortunately, his friend was out. *Just my luck to want to commit murder on a day Malcolm is out on a job.*

Joking aside, Samson was close to convincing himself that killing those two would be beneficial to the entirety of mankind, consequences be damned.

Do you want them to win? the question broke through all the rest of the crap swirling inside his head.

They would still be dead.

Despite what Malcolm had said and what Dr. Valarezo had told him, deep inside his core, Samson still felt that this was something that needed to be done.

The world would be a much better place if they were dead. It was easy for everyone to tell him that murdering them would be wrong. They hadn't lived through all that hell and torture. They didn't endure being raped repeatedly and being forced to fulfill each fantasy the girls had for fear they would retaliate by ruining his life. Which they did anyway. And now, he couldn't even see his wife.

They couldn't understand what he was dealing with.

Samson needed this, plain and simple, and he was sure the rest of the men they tortured would be on his side.

How do I track them down? Sure, he could easily find their address, but there was no guarantee they would be there. They were demon girls in constant search of fun and trying to stick it to their rich dad by tormenting men, so there was no telling where they were. He needed to find them, now.

And then, he had a thought. They'd taken his phone with the rest of his things – *keepsakes*, Lissa called them. There was a tracking app on his phone.

But she wouldn't be stupid enough to still have his phone on her. *Would she?*

Excited now, Samson fired up his new computer and logged into his account. From there, he could only stare. A small red dot marked the location of his phone on a city map. And it wasn't in his old house.

Samson was perplexed by the fact the girls not only had his phone on but were apparently using it. Someone was keeping it charged, and Samson bet on Lissa.

It never occurred to her that someone could use it to track them. Their confidence had no limits.

Samson zoomed in so he could read the name of the street. It was an off-campus house. Of course, Daddy's little girls wouldn't be living in some stinky dorm room.

The temptation to march there right then and confront them was so great that he already had his car keys in his hand. *What if they were in some poor schmuck's home, raping him?* While he sat around having a moral debate about killing them, someone could be getting a stick up his ass. Samson's head started to pound. What to do? He had to go right now and rescue the man they were playing with.

What if there was no man? What if they lived with roommates? Some normal girls who had no idea that Lissa and Candi were monsters. He had a moment of doubt.

Samson could not traumatize an innocent just to get his revenge. That would make him a monster.

Through the window, he saw that Malcolm was home.

Thank God. He picked up the phone and dialed his friend.

"Hey, buddy. What's up?"

"Come to the guest house. Now," he said, hanging up.

Malcolm arrived twenty seconds later.

"Please help me," he said, looking at his best friend.

"What's the matter?" he demanded.

Samson glanced at his screen. That red dot was still so inviting.

"I don't understand. What's that? What are you looking at?"

"Melissa found them. Lissa and Candi Bellwether."

"As in Donald Bellwether?"

"Yup."

"Wow, so is that like their address?" Malcolm guessed.

"Possibly. That's my phone."

"The one they took?"

Samson nodded.

"Wow."

"And I have an all-consuming urge to go there, right now," he confessed.

"You can't do that." Malcolm's voice was very firm.

"Why?" Samson needed a good reason to stop himself.

"Because it would be wrong."

"I don't give a fuck about that."

"Okay, okay, because you can't. I won't let you."

Samson gave his friend a look. They both knew who would win in a fight.

He closed his eyes for a moment. "I want to kill them."

"You can't."

"Yeah? What's stopping me?"

"Teresa," Malcolm said, taking him by surprise.

"What?"

"You want to get back with her, right?"

"Right," Samson replied, although he felt weird saying that.

Malcolm looked relieved. "Well, you can't win her over from a maximum-security prison while you wait for the needle on death row," he pointed out not so subtly.

That was exactly what Samson needed to hear. *I don't want to die. I don't want my life to be meaningless.*

As it turned out, Samson loved himself more than he hated them. Who would have known?

He said as much.

"So, you won't go on a murder hunt?" Malcolm wanted to make sure.

"No, I won't," Samson grumbled in return.

"Great, now be a good little boy and forward this info to that pretty lawyer of yours."

"Hey, don't push it. I can still kick your ass."

"Just send it."

He did as he was told. As he fully calmed down, a more rational part of his brain took over. He'd lost his shit twice today, and that was alarming. On the other hand, he'd reined himself back in with a little help from the people in his life. And that was good.

He couldn't believe how close to the edge he'd gotten. But that was over now.

Samson still wanted to kill them – badly – but he wouldn't. He could ignore the small voice in the back of his head that told him that was the only way to recover his manhood.

He could ignore it because he didn't want to end up broken completely. Malcolm had painted a very sad, realistic picture for him, and it was a wakeup call. He needed to be better. He *would* be better.

To prove that, he would let Melissa do what she did best and find a legal solution for his troubles. He was sure she would find a way to make these girls pay.

"I sent it," he informed his friend.

"Great. Are you okay now?"

"Yes."

"Sure? Because I want to shower, and I'm not in the mood to have to chase you down the street soapy and naked."

Samson cringed. He didn't need those mental images. Malcolm sometimes had a really strange sense of humor.

"I promise that won't be necessary. Ever."

"Good to know. See you later." He started walking toward the door.

"Oh, and Malcolm?" Samson called back.

"Yeah?"

"Thank you."

"Sure. That's what are friends for."

CHAPTER 28

Samson decided that during this extremely stressful time in his life, he would go to therapy every single day. He didn't want what happened in Melissa's office, and later at home, to happen ever again. He needed help with that, and a lot of it.

He had been overconfident before, and now, he knew better. Relapse wasn't an option, although he knew there was a realistic chance it would happen again. Something could happen to trigger him in a big way, and Dr. Valarezo would do her thing so the story would have a happy ending. Or so he hoped.

The next test of his mental health occurred a couple of days later when his lawyer called to share that she'd located the first victim. It was a strange feeling to know there was another person out there in the world with the same experiences he'd had.

Part of him hoped that when the girls mentioned other men, they were just saying that to rattle him. He prayed that was only a part of their torture. Unfortunately, they had been telling the truth.

It did make sense that they would tell the truth about something like that. They were sadistic enough to want to brag about it.

In the next ten days, Melissa located five men who could have been abused by the girls.

Samson was fascinated to learn how Melissa had managed to

track them down because none of them had reported a crime. Samson theorized that was because they had been blackmailed like he had. He just hoped the sisters hadn't done to them what they'd done to him, although he knew the chance of that was slim to none.

Once again, she rang him on the phone to share the good news. She'd found five men.

"You are amazing," Samson complimented.

"Oh, it was pretty easy."

Samson was sure she was being humble. "How did you do it?" he asked, genuinely curious.

"Well, since I knew who the girls were, I pulled out their photos and did a simple video search on the Internet," she started to explain.

"Okay, and?" Samson would never think of doing something like that.

"And I ended up with a bunch of results."

He wasn't too surprised. These new generations posted everything online. *It must be exhausting to be so self-absorbed.*

"I focused only on sex videos," Melissa continued, and her words snapped him from his reverie.

"Excuse me?" he asked since he was sure he heard that wrong.

"Yeah, there are a lot of sex videos with them, on all kinds of porn sites."

"Did the girls post them?"

"I'm not sure, but I suspect so."

"With these guys?"

"Well, I hoped so. That's why I did an image search of their partners and cross-referenced it with those who got divorced or lost their jobs, and came up with this list."

"That's brilliant, Melissa," he praised, and while doing so he realized something. His videos could be on there as well.

"If they posted sex videos on porn sites," *for all to see*, "does that mean—"

"Please, Samson. Don't," she interrupted him.

He was right.

"Did you find me, too?" he demanded. He didn't want to hear the answer but couldn't escape seeking it.

She remained silent.

"Melissa?" He needed her to say it.

"Yes, I did."

He closed his eyes. Samson was glad they were just on the phone. He didn't want her to see him like this. "I knew it," he muttered.

Of course those evil girls had one last ace up their sleeves. It wasn't enough for them to ruin him on a personal level; they wanted the whole world to see his shame and judge him.

He felt sick to his stomach.

"I didn't look at them," she reassured.

"Can they be deleted?"

"I don't know. Probably only by the person who posted them."

He cursed. "Tell me the names of those sites." He needed to see for himself, although God only knew why.

"I don't think that's a good idea."

"I need to see them."

"What good would that do?" she argued. "Seeing yourself like that will only upset you more."

More? More. Oh, he begged to differ. Everything that had been happening to him since he met those girls was beyond reason, so why would this be any different?

He had every right to see the extent of their destruction because no matter what he did and how hard he tried to move on, those girls still found new, devious ways to screw with him, hurt him, and destabilize his already ruined life.

"Samson, are you there?"

"I am."

"Promise me you won't look for those videos," she pleaded.

"I can't do that," he replied honestly.

"They will only cause you pain. Don't do it."

"Would you take that advice if the tables were turned?" he asked.

That made her pause. "I don't know."

That didn't make him feel better. "But I *do* know I would like someone by my side who would try and persuade me not to do it."

He could see her point. "All right," he said reluctantly.

He could hear her sagging with relief. *Are they that bad?* he wondered. Then again, she said she hadn't watched them. This was all for his benefit, not to get hurt. Or hurt even more.

"Tell me about the other guys," he said to try and distract himself from the fact that videos of him in the most private, disastrous moments of his life, were on the internet for everyone to see. He was going to throw up.

"The first one I managed to find is an IT guy. He moved here ten years ago from Texas ..."

As she talked, Samson did his best to focus on each word she said because otherwise, he would completely lose his shit. There was no doubt in his mind he would have to call Dr. Valarezo after this for an emergency session. This bombshell could not wait until tomorrow. Samson felt like screaming and feared if he started, he wouldn't be able to stop.

I'm a porn star. He wondered in what genre he was in. *Rape and torture?*

Did it matter?

"And that's about it," she concluded.

He hadn't heard a word she said; he was too wrapped up inside his head. He'd tried, but his thoughts were pulling him in other directions.

"You did an amazing job," he complimented. "And all by yourself."

"Well, I was motivated."

And then something occurred to him. "You did all that all by yourself? What happened to your team?"

He remembered how, when they first met, she'd told him her team would work on his case. Yet so far, he'd met only her.

"Well, I have a confession to make," she started, and his interest was piqued. "There's no team; only me."

"Only you?"

"Yeah, I'm sorry I lied, but I didn't want you to think I was an amateur. I wanted to work on this case."

She did that to get his case? Other lawyers couldn't wait to get rid of him, and this woman lied so he would choose her. That was weirdly flattering. He was speechless.

"You're forgiven," he said without thought.

She had surpassed all of his expectations so far, and now he was even more impressed, knowing she was responsible for all the ground they'd covered in such a short time.

"Thank you for understanding."

"No problem. I have to go now, but we'll talk later."

"Okay, bye."

They disconnected.

Despite the short uplift from Melissa's revelation, Samson's thoughts inevitably returned to the matter of the porn sites. How could he make peace with something like that? Then again, the only thing it changed was that he now knew they existed. For all he knew, they had been circling the internet for months. That didn't make him feel any better. He called his therapist, who also advised that he didn't look for them.

"I'm not that weak," he raised his voice. "I will not fall apart seeing those videos."

"Why do you feel the need to see them in the first place?"

He shrugged. "I don't know. Maybe to see what Teresa saw."

"Would that change anything?"

"Maybe. Maybe I would understand why she won't speak with me."

"I see. I still advise against it," she added.

"Why?"

"Because you're doing it for the wrong reason, and it will only cause you pain."

"I don't understand."

"You're trying to find excuses for your ex-wife's behavior instead of accepting the simple truth."

"Which is?"

"That your marriage is over, and you have to deal with that pain."

Was that the reason he was doing all this? Did he want to see the videos because he couldn't deal with the fact it was over between him and Teresa?

He remained quiet for a long time. "Maybe you're right," he said eventually, feeling defeated.

"I know it doesn't feel like it right now, but this is a good thing, Samson," she tried to reassure him.

He didn't feel reassured. He felt like crap.

"There's something else I wanted to discuss," he said, changing the subject.

"Oh?"

"Melissa, my lawyer, managed to find five guys who could have been Lissa and Candi's victims."

"Really? And what do you plan to do with that information?"

"Well, we can't be sure if we have the right guys until we contact them."

"Would you be in charge of that, or are you going to let your lawyer handle it?" she asked.

"I thought about it, and I think I should be the one to make contact."

Dr. Valarezo thought about it, then nodded. "I believe that would be best, too."

"But I don't know what to say."

"It's a very delicate situation, and it's imperative to do this the right way. You can't know what mental state these men are in."

He hadn't thought of that. If he was struggling even after seeking help, then there was no telling how others were fairing. Especially if they refused to get help, as he had in the beginning.

"That's a good point."

"You have to leave room for them to turn you down or contact you when they're ready," she advised.

Samson nodded. "I was thinking of writing them emails."

"That would be a good start, and if they want to hear more or get involved, they can contact you."

"Right."

Feeling all over the place, Samson returned home. Everything he'd discussed with his therapist was bouncing around his brain.

As he promised Melissa, he didn't fire up his computer and start Googling his sex videos, although he was tempted. Was he a masochist? Was it some kind of a macabre curiosity? Or was Dr. Valarezo right? Was he focusing on the wrong things so he wouldn't have to deal with reality?

It was probably the combination of everything, and that was depressing.

Feeling like he should do something, he grabbed the list Melissa had sent him. On it were the names and email addresses of the men. He was glad he'd told Dr. Valarezo about it, and that she agreed that emailing them was the best course of action. That way, it was up to them whether they wanted to speak with him.

He thought about it a lot, and spoke with Malcolm, too, and they agreed that his showing up on their doorstep was the last thing he should do. Samson wouldn't like someone ambushing him in that way, and the person who did something like that get a fist in his face.

The best approach was to fire off a short email and if they wanted to meet with him, they could call or write back.

He was aware that not all of them might be ready to talk about it. What had happened to Samson was horrible, and he still struggled with everything. He was sure that would continue for years to come. It was safe to assume the others felt the same way. So, if they wanted to talk to him and help him bring the girls down, great. If they didn't want to have anything to do with him or those girls again, that was okay, too. They had the right to make their own decisions, do what felt right, and live with those decisions.

With his mind set, Samson turned on his computer and started to compose a letter. He wondered how much he should say. After some thought, he decided to not go into too many details but share enough that they would know he was a fellow survivor.

Okay, here I go.

"Mr. Valmont," he started since adding Dear, Greetings, or anything else felt creepy and wrong.

"My name is Samson Chase, you don't know me, but I have something to share with you regarding Lissa and Candi ..."

Samson tried to keep it concise, stating who he was, why was he approaching him, and mentioning their shared experiences. He invited the other man to contact him, either by replying or calling, if he was open to working together to bring the girls to justice.

Once he was satisfied, he hit send.

Then, he wrote four more.

All that was left to do now was wait and see if he would get a reply. And everybody knew how much he enjoyed doing that.

Maybe I need a hobby? he mused.

CHAPTER 29

The next couple of days dragged on. Samson had sent his emails full of hope, but no one had responded, so that hope was slowly and steadily fading. Luckily, he had a ton of work to keep him busy.

What do you think, Marc? Should I make you bleed now? Some would find it strange, but Samson always spoke to his main characters. They never lied to him.

He was pretty amazed that he'd managed to write amid all this craziness. At the same time, he had no choice: His deadline was approaching.

Let's make it a truly bloody experience.

Unfortunately, not even putting his main character through hell and back managed to stop him from stressing about the other men. He wondered if any of them would contact him. *They need time.* He understood that receiving a letter like that must have been quite a shock.

What would I do if the tables were turned? Would I ignore it, or reach out? He wasn't sure.

He received his first response on the fourth day.

He woke up that morning after a full night of sleep and grabbed his phone to check his messages, as he always did.

Not many people wanted to get in touch with him these days, but Malcolm tended to send him funny videos, stupid memes, and things like that, which Samson appreciated. It was a good way to start a morning. That morning, he spotted an email reply from a man named Tom Sorkin.

It took him a moment to register who that was.

Oh, my God. He sprang to his feet as though opening the email couldn't be done from the bed.

He sat at the table and opened it.

Samson read it twice, even though it contained just one line.

"I think we should meet," Tom wrote him. He'd left a phone number.

"Oh, my God."

This was happening. This guy had contacted him and wanted to meet, which could only mean that he'd gone through a similar hell with the evil sisters.

Samson was excited and wanted to share the good news with Malcolm, Melissa, and his shrink, but most of all, he wanted to talk to this man.

Checking the time, he decided it wasn't too early to call.

He was on pins and needles as he waited for the other man to answer. "Hello?"

"Hello, this is Samson Chase. Is this Tom Sorkin?"

"Yes, this is he."

And then they went silent, as though they needed a moment to appreciate the magnitude of the event. Samson recovered first. "I think we have a lot to talk about."

"It appears so."

Tom had a gentle voice and spoke in a calm, slightly monotonous manner, and Samson was glad when the other man agreed to meet with him. Considering the nature of their conversation, they agreed that they didn't want to meet in a public space. How could they openly discuss rape and torture in a coffee shop? Tom decided to come to Samson's house, or Malcolm's to be more precise, since Samson still lived there.

While he waited for Tom to arrive, he wanted to call Melissa and share the good news. She was as invested in this case as he was and deserved to know, but he reconsidered at the last minute. She would want to be present, and Samson believed this first meeting should be just between him and Tom. They would both feel more comfortable that way, he was sure of that.

A couple of hours later, a skinny redhead with bright blue eyes and skin so pale it looked translucent knocked on his door.

He looked a bit nervous. Samson could sympathize; he felt the same way.

"Tom?"

"Samson?"

"Yes, come in."

They shook hands before retreating to the guest house. In haste, Samson explained how he'd come to live there.

"Your wife kicked you out?"

"Yes."

"I'm sorry."

They looked uncomfortable assessing each other, wondering why the sisters picked them from all others. Considering the circumstances, who could blame them?

"Sit down, please," Samson remembered his manners. "Want something to drink?"

No amount of alcohol could smooth this talk; not that Samson was willing to try. However, if Tom needed something to calm his nerves, Samson would provide it without judgment.

Ton shook his head. "I was surprised to get your letter," he started.

"I can imagine."

"I didn't know there were others," he said, looking at the floor.

"I knew there were. They ... bragged about it."

Tom looked up, and his eyes were haunted. "How did you find me?"

Samson didn't want to answer that. They'd been through enough without having to add sex videos on porn sites to the mix.

"My lawyer did," he replied without going into detail. He was sure Tom would eventually find out the truth, but it didn't have to be today.

"Well, thank you for reaching out."

"Really?" he blurted out before he could stop himself.

"Yes, I would love to help as long as we stick to the law."

Tom and Melissa would get along great.

"Really?" Samson repeated. "Just like that?" He didn't even try to hide his surprise.

He expected this guy to be a little skittish. It wouldn't be easy to go public and admit to the world they were raped. Samson had struggled with that himself before he'd managed to reach peace. As it turned out, he would need to waste no time convincing Tom that this was the right thing to do.

Tom shrugged. "What can I say? I have nothing more to lose. My wife left me, and my kids ignore me. I lost my job, so why not go forward and try to do everything in my power to prove my innocence?"

Wow. He liked how this guy thought.

"So, if you have a plan, I'm on board."

"May I ask ..." Samson started but stopped himself midway. He was about to ask a very personal question, and he didn't know if it was completely appropriate. He couldn't assume this guy was comfortable sharing his story with a man he met fifteen minutes ago.

Samson briefly shared his story in the email, but that was only because he wanted Tom and the rest of them to know he wasn't a lunatic but someone with shared trauma. He shouldn't expect Tom to feel the same way. However, Samson would be lying if he said he wasn't curious about Tom's time with Lissa and Candi. He didn't need to know all the details, just how they'd tricked him, and things like that.

In short, he wondered if they used the same techniques and if they'd drugged him. That was probably something Melissa would be interested to hear as well. It would help this case a lot if their stories matched in some way.

Even with that in mind, Samson felt extremely uncomfortable asking.

He had not thought this through when he invited Tom over. It didn't occur to him how they would feel discussing the extremely private, most difficult events of their lives.

"Never mind," he added.

"It's okay. You want to hear how it happened?" Once again, Tom surprised him by asking.

Samson nodded. "If it's not too painful to talk about it," he hedged.

Tom looked out through a window for a moment, lost in thought. Although he was only thirty-two years old, he looked like Samson's senior. Pain and grief could do that to a person.

"It happened about six months ago," he started. "My wife went to visit her father in Wisconsin since he had just had a hip replacement and needed help. And since it was summer break, the kids wanted to go with her."

"You stayed behind?" Samson asked, already finding similarities in their stories.

"Yeah, I had to. I had a job booked and had to stay to finish it."

Tom mentioned that he was a roofer, and like Malcolm, he had the most work when the weather was fine and was allowing such huge repairs.

"One day, after I came home exhausted from work, I fell asleep and woke to someone ringing my doorbell. That was when I realized it was the middle of the night."

"Lissa and Candi?"

"Yes, they appeared on my doorstep asking for help."

So far, it was the same M.O. Marissa would like that.

"They told me how someone had stolen their car, just pushed them out of it, and threatened him with a gun, while they waited for a red light. They looked freaked out. So, I invited them in."

"Big mistake," Samson murmured, but Tom heard him.

"Yes, I know. Before I knew what was happening, they drugged me, and—" That was where he paused. "Well, I'm sure you know the rest."

"Yes, I do," Samson replied, looking at anything but the other man.

So that was what they did. They shared some sad story with the owner of the house, knowing that would insure an invitation. And then, they found a way to drug him. He was sure they could break inside, but this way was more fun for them. It was more exciting if there was a challenge.

"How long did they stay?"

"Ten days."

Samson gulped. That was longer than his experience, and it was hard not to feel sorry for the other man.

"They ruined the entire house and took any valuables they liked."

"They did the same to me."

Neither one of them looked cheered because of that.

"What happened afterward?"

"They told me that if I cooperated, they wouldn't tell my wife what happened."

"Let me guess: They lied," Samson replied.

Tom nodded. "They called my wife Ruth on the phone and told her everything, while I had to listen, tied to a bed."

"What?"

"Yes, and when she said she didn't believe them, Lissa sent her all the videos they'd made." He shrugged. "And that was that."

"They left afterward?"

He nodded. "Leaving me tied up. I was trapped like that for two days because my wife couldn't find an earlier flight."

Samson was horrified. This guy was lucky to be alive. Those girls were monsters. Not that there was any doubt before.

"I'm sorry," Samson offered, not knowing what else to say.

"I lost everything because of them; my wife, my two kids."

"Do you see them?"

"Ruth decided to stay with her father. Besides, I don't want them to see me like this, broken and ruined."

Samson sympathized.

"We sold the house. I lost my job because I couldn't show up, and I couldn't afford to do all the repairs. It has been hard ever since."

"Did you seek help?" Samson asked, feeling like that was the most important question. *Money can be earned and relationships can be mended, but none of that is possible if he didn't first take care of his mental health.* "I know it's hard, but it's also necessary."

Tom sighed. "I've been going to therapy, but that's not enough for me. I want my life back."

Me, too.

Samson no longer believed that was possible. Lissa and Candi had made sure of that.

"You said it yourself: Your wife decided to stay with her father, and you sold your home. There is no 'back,'" Samson said. He didn't want to come across as cruel; he was just stating facts.

"We have to accept that our wives and closest friends don't believe us." It was hard, but they didn't have a choice. They had to move on.

A small part of him was comforted that Teresa wasn't the only one who'd reacted so poorly.

"She wants to believe me," Tom surprised him by saying.

"What?"

"Ruth wants to believe me, but she needs some kind of proof that they drugged me, which I don't have. So, I was hoping that this was a way to prove my innocence."

Wow. Samson was floored. "That's great," he said eventually.

"Do you by any chance have some proof against them?" he asked, full of hope.

"Not yet."

"That's okay. I have a good feeling about this."

Tom reminded him of Malcolm. Tom was a real stand-up guy, peaceful and full of optimism despite what those girls had done to him.

How could he achieve that, too?

He didn't look angry or resentful. He was just a man who wanted his family back. Samson wanted that for him as well. That was why he said, "Me, too. I'm sure that we'll find a way to help each other and make sure those girls get what they deserve."

Tom grinned. "I like the sound of that."

Samson knew he would get along great with this guy.

"I'm still waiting to hear from others, but I'm very optimistic."

"How many?"

"Four more."

"Six of us? That many?" A shadow passed over Tom's face.

"That we know of," Samson hedged.

"Well, let me know if anyone else contacts you. I would like to meet them."

"Of course." It was implied that they work together, and he was glad Tom was on the same page.

Once Tom left, Samson met with Malcolm at his favorite bar.

Once in a while, Anita would kick Malcolm out, so he would retreat to this place, a sports bar. Conveniently enough, it was just a couple of blocks from his house. Even when he got drunk, he could walk home.

"You'll never believe what just happened," Samson greeted.

"Tatiana Weston won Miss Universe?" Malcolm deadpanned.

"What?"

"What?"

"I met with Tom."

"From the list?" Malcolm quickly caught on.

"Yes?"

"What was he like?" he asked with interest.

"Completely normal and completely fucked up at the same time."

Malcolm understood his meaning perfectly.

"Will he help with the lawsuit?"

"Yes, he was totally onboard."

"You think the rest will reach out, too?"

"I don't know. I hope so," he replied honestly.

Malcolm wanted to pat him on the back but stopped midway, and Samson was grateful. "You know what? I think this calls for celebration. Two beers," he yelled to the bartender.

"Soda for me," Samson corrected.

"Still don't trust me?"

"I trust you with my life, just not with my drink," Samson joked, and they laughed.

CHAPTER 30

Three out of the other four men reached out in the next couple of days. Samson couldn't believe his luck.

The first man called the day after Samson met with Tom. His name was Sam Weatherby, and he had been a thirty-four-year-old trash collector with a loving family and his own recycling business before Lissa and Candi had destroyed his life. His wife and their two sons left him when the scandal broke, and he was forced to close his business after losing the patronage of all the local businesses and community.

He had struggled ever since and, like Tom, was surprised to learn that this shit hadn't happened to just him. Sam was very tall and slim, with a goatee that was almost blond, in strange contrast to his brown hair.

On the same day, Eric Stokes also emailed him back. He was a thirty-eight-year-old computer expert who worked for a major company before being forced to spend the weekend with the girls. He was a huge teddy bear of a man who still couldn't get over the fact that his fiancée had called off their wedding after seeing the sex videos. She believed that his bachelor party had gotten out of control and left him.

Even his parents had stopped speaking to him. On top of everything, he'd lost his job due to a morality clause in his contract. He too was comforted in some strange way by knowing that there was a group of guys who'd gone through the same thing.

A couple of days later, Carl Valmont wanted to meet him. Carl was a twenty-nine-year-old photojournalist whose life and marriage were also ruined thanks to the Bellwether sisters.

They all had basically the same stories. All had lost families, friends, and jobs thanks to the scandal, leaving them completely brokenhearted, broken, and broke.

As he spoke to each man, Samson discovered that everyone but Tom shared one more thing: None of them had much hope of getting back what they lost. And much like Samson, they were all focused on moving on, forgetting everything, and had no desire for revenge. That didn't mean they didn't like Samson's idea about finding a legal solution to make those girls pay.

Surprisingly, when Samson asked why they hadn't reported the crime, each man answered the same: The thought had not crossed their mind because the damage was already done.

"Who would believe me anyway?" Sam summed it up the best.

They were unfortunately right: Samson experienced that firsthand.

Regardless, they agreed to meet with Samson's lawyer and discuss their legal options.

"We could file a civil suit," Melissa started to explain. "Five testimonies that share so many commonalities exhibit a distinct pattern of behavior."

"Do you think we have a shot?" Sam wondered.

"It will be hard without any concrete evidence, but I think your testimonies carry a lot of weight. I also believe we should convince the DA's office to open a case against the Bellwethers."

"Would they go for it?" Samson asked for the group.

"That's hard to say. However, a criminal case plus a class-action suit would ensure you get justice."

"We don't have any proof," Eric pointed out.

"Yeah. Right now, it's our word against theirs," Sam added.

"And you know a jury would believe them and not us," Carl provided.

Samson agreed with everything they'd said.

"I'm not saying it's going to be easy. It's going to be extremely hard considering who the Bellwethers are."

"Thanks for sugarcoating it," Eric muttered.

"I'm hoping a "but" is coming," Sam grumbled.

"But," Melissa did not disappoint, "I believe we have a case, and I believe you should pursue it no matter what."

Is it a strong case or just a publicity stunt? Samson wondered, and it was on tip of his tongue to ask, but he forced himself to remain silent. This was hard enough. He didn't have to sprinkle additional doubt; there was enough of that flying around without his help.

"I think we should do it. The criminal case *and* the civil suit," Tom spoke up for the first time. The rest of the gang agreed.

Is this happening? Samson didn't dare hope. Things tended to go to shit each time he did.

Then again, none of them was an idiot. They needed to tackle this beast on two fronts. The civil case would compensate them for the physical destruction, and the criminal case would ensure the girls were punished and brought to justice. The civil suit would hit Donald Bellwether where it hurt the most. No amount they were awarded would bring back what they'd lost, and it wouldn't erase the pain of the hours and days spent with the monsters who tortured them. But it would provide comfort and allow them to focus on piecing their broken lives back together.

On the other hand, in the ideal scenario, the sisters would go to jail for a long time as well. That was not an ideal scenario for Samson, who would rather kill them. That was off the table though, so he would settle for the next best thing: Life in prison.

After he'd lost everything, Samson believed they deserved at least that much in return.

"So, we are all in agreement?" Melissa wanted to make sure.

They nodded.

"Should I draft the lawsuit now, or would you like to wait a little longer and see if the last man will reach out as well?"

For some reason, they all looked to Samson.

Brian Grant was the last man on the list, and he'd declined to participate. He'd called Samson a while ago and said as much.

"Let's wait a little bit longer. I'd like to talk to him again," Samson said.

"Need some company?" Tom asked.

"I think it would be better if I went to see him alone."

Samson drove to Brian's place after the meeting. The cheap motel wasn't much better than the hotel Samson had checked into after Teresa kicked him out.

After a brief conversation with the receptionist, Samson got Brian's room number.

He knocked.

"Fuck off," he heard from inside.

Samson liked him already. He pressed.

An extremely tall and muscular man opened the door. Colorful tattoos decorated both arms and the side of his neck. His beard and hair were long and unkempt.

"What do you want?" he demanded.

"Hi, Brian. My name is Samson Chase," he greeted.

The other man grimaced. "Man, I already told you, I don't want to have anything to do with your little club," he said defensively.

"I understand, but I think you're making a mistake."

"What?"

Maybe I should choose my words more carefully.

"Give me five minutes. Hear me out."

Brian took his time answering. Samson was sure he was being vetted and judged, but he had gotten used to that in the military, so he let it slide.

Eventually, Brian stepped to the side and let him in.

As expected, the place was a mess. It reeked of stale beer, body odor, and something even more poignant, but Samson ignored it all. He had been at this exact place a couple of months back, so he wasn't judging. Hitting rock bottom was not easy, and that was why Samson was here. He knew he could help this guy if he let him.

"You have five minutes," Brian prompted.

"I understand your reluctance," Samson started, and Brian scoffed as he pressed on. "But I think we have a chance to accomplish something, but only if we step forward together."

"Pass."

"All I'm asking you to do is to come and meet the guys, nothing else."

"And you're going to press charges or whatever, even if I say no?"

"Yes."

"Do you want the entire world to know two girls raped you? Because I don't."

It was a good point.

"They need to be stopped," Samson insisted.

"And you think you can do that?"

"It won't be easy, but it's still the right thing to do."

Brian laughed humorously. "The right thing to do would be to put bullets into their sociopathic little heads."

It was eerie how much this guy sounded like Samson only a couple of weeks ago. *Had I been this angry, too?* Maybe even worse, considering he had to deal with war trauma on top of everything else.

Focus, he snapped at himself. He didn't matter right now, Brian did. It was imperative to get him onboard.

"I know you're hurting, but killing them isn't the answer."

Part of him couldn't believe he'd uttered those words. *Check me out, being all reasonable and shit.* If only Dr. Valarezo could see him now.

"You know? *You know*?" Brian's yelling snapped him from his thoughts. "You know jack shit."

Samson didn't want this to turn into a pissing contest, but Brian had pissed him off. "They tortured and raped me too. We're all in the same boat."

"I seriously doubt that. The girls dropped by just when my wife went into the hospital. She was pregnant with our first child, and the pregnancy was difficult. She and the baby almost died during an emergency c-section, and I wasn't there for them. I was too busy being raped in the ass and blackmailed to witness my baby girl coming to the world."

It was hard to remain calm and expressionless after hearing that.

"Not that it did me any good in the end. Those bitches still told my wife everything. It was the perfect baby shower gift, a video of me being fucked in every way known to man."

"Oh, man. I am so sorry," Samson said from the bottom of his heart.

"I don't need you to be sorry for me," Brian spat back.

"I didn't mean it like that. I want to help."

"If you want to help me, then tell me where those two are so I can deal with them the right way."

"The right way? As in killing them?"

"Hell yes."

Samson made a mental note not to divulge the girls' where-abouts. And he needed to warn the others to be careful about what they talked about in front of Brian as well.

But maybe he was getting too ahead of himself. Brian hadn't agreed to meet anyone. He could barely tolerate Samson being there.

"Look, I get it. I was right where you are now. I even picked a burial spot."

"So, what are we waiting for?" he said, cheering. "Let's go kill them. Now."

"We can't do that to the rest of the guys."

"What?"

"I promised."

"What about *my* promise? I promised to take care of my wife and daughter. I promised to always be there for them, and I failed."

"It wasn't your fault. None of what happened is your fault," Samson tried to get through to the other man, who was spiraling out of control.

"You don't get it. It was. And because of my fuckup, Sandra won't let me see the baby. I've never seen my daughter. If I don't do this, then I have nothing to live for," he said in a rush.

"You have *everything* to live for, and that's precisely why you can't do this. You have to think of your daughter, you have to live for her and not ruin your life for revenge."

Brian was shaking his head even before Samson finished. "I don't want her to know me; not like this. It's better this way."

"Don't say that."

"Look." Brian showed him his wrists. The scars there showed evidence of once-deep slashes on the skin. "I'm so useless, I couldn't even kill myself properly."

"I've been there, but I see this as a chance to make things right."

"Really? You tried to kill yourself?" Brian sounded surprised.

Samson smiled humorously. "Yeah, I tried to jump off a bridge. Ended up in a mental institution instead."

"Really?

"Yeah."

"I guess I misjudged you."

"By the way, my wife hates my guts, too."

"That doesn't make me feel better, but at the same time, it kinda does," Brian said honestly.

"I know what you mean."

Brian scratched his head and sighed loudly. "When do you guys meet?"

"Tomorrow at eight o'clock at Raging Bull," Samson recited before the other man had second thoughts.

"I'll be there."

CHAPTER 31

Samson never would have believed that six men, who went through hell and back thanks to the Bellwether sisters, would be having dinner together.

It helped that they didn't spend too much time swapping horror stories. Instead, they took their time getting to know one another, who they were before tragedy struck, and who they were striving to be going forward.

The biggest surprise of the night was Brian showing up. Samson thought there was about a seventy percent chance the other man would change his mind and decide not to show, but he was happy when Brian proved him wrong. He wasn't the most talkative of the group. He mostly just sat, drank, and brooded, but he was there, and that meant something.

Looking around the table, it was obvious that Brian was the most difficult of the group. He was still very bitter and angry, Samson hoped he would seek help before he exploded, which was bound to happen.

That was a headache for another day. For tonight, he focused on being grateful that Brian had shown up to meet the rest of the gang.

Now that they were all in one place, Samson couldn't help but notice how different they looked. They were physically distinct, but they also differed in age and career. One of the only things they had in common was the fact that they all had families.

We all had something to lose.

And every last one of them had lost everything. Lissa and Candi had made sure of that because that was what made them tick.

Also, they were all middle class, which coincided with something Samson determined about the girls as they turned his life into hell. They looked down on everyone and believed they were superior, which gave them the right to treat people – particularly men – this way.

Probably the most fascinating thing to Samson was the fact that they all looked so normal. Nobody looking in from the outside would ever guess they shared such a dark secret, that they'd all managed to fall prey to such skilled, devious predators. They didn't look like rape victims, but then again, who did?

Survivors, he corrected himself. *We are all survivors.*

"So, who's victim number one?" Eric asked as soon as their waiter had brought their drinks and walked away.

Everyone was startled by his abrasiveness.

"That would be me," Brian answered reluctantly.

"How did they get you?"

Although Eric was the one who'd asked, they were all curious and waited for a reply.

Brian took a sip of his drink before replying. "I worked as a gardener at the Bellwether estate."

"You worked for their father?"

"Yeah," he confirmed through gritted teeth.

That was news to Samson. He wondered why Melissa hadn't told him that. Maybe she didn't know.

"I'm telling you, it's a coin toss which member of that family is the most devious."

Samson didn't have to be a mind reader to know Brian harbored a lot of suppressed anger toward the family. After everything he'd been through – what they'd *all* been through – who could blame him?

"So, you were their test subject, and afterward, they decided to branch out," Eric commented.

"What are you implying?" Brian snapped, leaning aggressively toward the other man.

"He was just making a joke," Samson interjected, trying to calm him before the situation got out of hand. The last thing they needed was to start trading punches in a public place. Collectively, they had already had enough bad press for ten lifetimes.

"A bad one at that," Tom added.

"Well, I don't like it," Brian said, remaining tense.

Eric shrugged. "My shrink says I use humor as a defense mechanism. Every time I feel bad or get uncomfortable, I start cracking jokes."

"Well, do that again, and I'll start cracking skulls," Brian threatened.

"Whatever," Eric replied, nonplussed. If anyone could take Brian down, Samson's money was on Eric.

"My therapist says I should socialize more, but I don't think this is what she meant," Tom said as an afterthought, but that was all they needed to hear, and burst out laughing.

Tom, the peacemaker, apparently knew just what to say at the right time. The conversation resumed and they all shared their stories, experiences, and struggles. It wasn't as bad as Samson had envisioned.

Through talking, they created a timeline. The girls' path of destruction, as Eric called it. He was victim number two, and the girls did basically the same thing to him as they'd done to Brian.

"The training wheels were definitely off," he said at some point while looking at Brian. "There were moments I felt like dying was the only way to escape."

The men nodded at that.

Victim number three was Carl. They found him in a motel where he was staying because he was a traveling businessman. He was in the middle of an important report when they knocked on the door to his room.

Sam was the fourth, and Tom was the fifth.

Which made Samson the sixth. Of course, they couldn't be one hundred percent sure there were no other men out there who'd suffered from the sisters' hands.

They couldn't rule out the possibility there were more of them out there. Maybe the sisters had decided not to post everything online, to keep the most terrible cases to themselves. Samson stopped himself there; that was some heavy shit.

He wasn't the only one whose thoughts went in that direction.

"Are we sure there are no more men like us out there?" Eric wanted to know, subtle as ever.

"We can't know that for sure," Samson replied honestly.

"What we *do* know is that they take time off between," Tom provided.

That was true. A certain pattern arose as they created the time-line, and there was always a gap of a couple of months between them.

"Scouting for their next victim takes time," Brian said grudgingly, finishing another drink.

"They came well-prepared despite the chaos they brought with them," Samson thought out loud, and the rest nodded. "I mean, they knew stuff from my past that only a few people know."

"Money can buy that kind of intel," Eric mused.

"So, what are we going to do about them?" Tom asked, bringing them back to the main issue.

"What *can* we do?" Carl wondered out loud.

Brian smiled snidely. "There's nothing we can do," he insisted.

"That's not true," Samson interjected. "We can come together and decide to sue them."

Brian chuckled. "Good luck with that."

"You don't want to sue them?" Eric asked.

"Nope," Brian replied simply.

"You don't think it could work?" Tom guessed.

"I *know* it can't," he corrected.

"How come?" Eric asked.

"Because it doesn't matter how many round-table meetings you hold; what you eventually say or do will make no difference."

"Why?" Samson pressed.

"Because their daddy will step in and get them out of any trouble you throw their way. That is what he does. What he *always* does."

"You think he would do that even with this?" Samson expressed his doubts.

After everything Samson had learned from the girls about their shaky relationship with their father, he wasn't so sure he would act like Brian described he would.

"Of course, he would," Brian insisted. "He has in the past."

Looking around the table, Samson could see the other men begin to waver. He couldn't allow that. They needed to represent a united front if they hoped to accomplish anything. That was why he said, "I'm sure it wasn't as serious as this."

"It doesn't matter," Brian argued. "That guy hates bad publicity. Trust me."

Samson gave him a look. "He hates bad press? The guy that's always in the news, one way or the other?"

"That's all well-construed. He has a very capable PR team that would do anything to make this go away."

Brian knew the guy on some level since he worked for him, so Samson had no reason to doubt him. At the same time, his gut was telling him the other man was wrong.

"I'm not sure that's the case," Samson spoke up again, and all eyes were on him. "When they were with me, whenever I could, I tried to get any kind of information out of them."

"Really? You did that, despite everything?" Tom asked with slight amazement.

"I needed to learn about them to know how best to take them down."

"And how'd that end for you? You still got fucked over good, just like the rest of us," Brian pointed out.

It was like he was intentionally trying to start a fight, and it didn't even matter with who. Samson didn't take the bait.

"Anyway," Samson continued, "I get the feeling they weren't close."

"How come?" Tom asked for details, so Samson explained how Candi had screamed at him when he'd mentioned daddy dearest. "She trashed half my house when I commented that Daddy must be proud of what they'd become."

He also mentioned Lissa's odd reaction to his wedding photos, how she'd smashed everything as though she couldn't stand them. Samson was sure it had something to do with her relationships.

"That's all speculation," Brian wasn't giving up.

"I found all of you based on speculation, too."

"He's still their father."

"Do you think that means anything to a guy like Donald Bellwether?" Samson challenged. "It's obvious to me that their dynamics and relations changed from when you knew them."

"You believe he won't support them?" Tom asked.

Samson knew how much all of this meant to him, so it was no wonder he needed to believe that. If they didn't go forward with the lawsuit, then he couldn't get his wife back.

Samson shook his head. "I don't think he will. I think he'll wash his hands of them and move on."

"That's cold," Carl commented.

"They're terrified of him."

"Could you tell me one more time how you came to that conclusion?" Brian asked.

Samson took that as a good sign, so he did his best to remember everything to the smallest of details when recounting those scenes.

In the end, Brian looked intrigued. *Have I won him over?* Samson dared not hope.

"If you're right, then that changes everything," Brian allowed.

"You believe me now?" Samson asked, and the other nodded.

"Does that mean you're on board, too?" Tom prompted.

"Yes. I'll do whatever the rest of the Scooby Doo gang decides to do," he said reluctantly.

Samson was glad. They'd come to an understanding, and that meant a great deal. He was sure Melissa would feel the same way.

Now that they were all together, and had agreed to work toward a common cause, they could accomplish something. And by something, Samson meant throwing those two in jail.

"Okay, I'll text Melissa and let her know what we decided."

"What's next?" Tom asked him.

"Our road to stardom," Brian answered.

They all struggled with the fact that they would have to speak publicly about their trauma, but Brian was taking it to a whole new level. Samson decided not to indulge him. That was why he said to Tom, "I'm sure Melissa would like to speak with all of us individually in the next couple of days."

"To get our stories on the record?" Tom guessed.

"Yes, so make sure you're available," Samson insisted, looking at Carl. He needed to stay in the city a little bit longer, although if they planned to sue, perhaps it would be more prudent for him to move here for now. Samson made a mental note to talk about that with him later on.

"So, are we done now? Is settled?" Eric wanted to know.

They all looked at one another. "I guess we are for now," Samson replied for the rest.

"Good, because I'm starving," Eric announced. "Let's eat."

They started laughing and Samson could feel some of the tension disappear.

We can do this.

"Sounds good to me," Samson agreed.

They grabbed menus.

We can do this.

CHAPTER 32

Getting together and working toward the common goals of clearing their names and putting the Bellwether sisters in jail was just the first of many obstacles in front of the men. Even united, the road that led to justice was extremely rocky. At times, Samson wondered if it was worth the energy and time. But what other choice did he have? This was it, the best he could do. Besides, this wasn't just about him anymore; five other men needed this, too, and that's why he endured despite everything.

Melissa set up individual meetings with each of them since it was imperative to get their stories on record.

That was part of the road Samson didn't particularly care about, but he knew it was necessary. He knew that from now on, he would have to speak about his experiences to various people, including reporters, and probably even in court while enduring public condemnation, so he had to get over thinking about hard it would be, and fast.

He knew it wouldn't get easier with time, but he would cross that bridge when he had to. For now, he focused on his interview and even wrote down some notes ahead of time so he didn't forget anything. Melissa said every little detail, no matter how insignificant he thought it might be, could mean a great deal in the grander scheme of things.

Samson did his best to be concise and emotionless as he described how the girls slithered into his life and caused havoc. It was traumatic, hard, and uncomfortable, and the only thing that kept him going was thinking of the others and Melissa's gentle face. She was of enormous support and very considerate, offering to stop the interview each time he looked close to the edge. But he didn't fall over.

He was relieved and exhausted when it was over. The notion that he would have to repeat this over and over made him want to run away. Of course, he was constantly working to banish such overdramatic thoughts from his head because they did no good. His desire for revenge remained, and although he had to change his preferred method, he would stick to it. He would see those two locked up for life if it was the last thing he did.

Afterward, he had a session with Dr. Valarezo. They spoke at length about his decision to seek a lawyer, team up with the other men, and file a lawsuit.

She was impressed by his determination and courage. He was determined but didn't feel courageous. He just did what needed to be done, no matter the consequences. To him, that sounded more like stupidity than courage.

Dr. Valarezo smiled upon hearing that. "Sometimes, there's a thin line between the two."

"Good to know," he replied, cracking a smile.

"How do you feel, overall, about the lawsuit?"

"All over the place, to be honest."

If he felt like that, then it was safe to assume the rest of the men felt the same way, which meant Samson was particularly worried about Brian since he looked like the most unstable member of their brotherhood. He shared as much with Dr. Valarezo.

"I know it will get challenging as the case progresses, but you can't force treatment on someone. You have to want help to receive it."

"I know, but I'm worried he'll do something stupid and jeopardize everything."

"You said he had a change of heart," she pointed out.

"Yes, but I'm still worried about him."

"I know it sounds cliché, but try not to worry about things that haven't happened. Instead, focus on everything that *did* happen that went in your favor."

That was good advice, but could he follow it and focus on the good for a change?

He was impressed with how Melissa organized everything. He'd known she was skilled – she'd located the men, after all – but it was different to watch her in full-blown lawyer mode. She was really on top of things, made even more impressive because he knew she was a one-woman show.

The fact that she genuinely wanted to help them as opposed to doing this as some kind of publicity stunt was the most important thing to Samson. It was something he was grateful for, and he thanked God that he'd decided to meet with her that day because it had changed his life for the better.

And she continued to fight for them. Currently, she was trying to figure out the best way to file a class action suit by getting the DA's attention and convincing him to open a criminal case against the Bellwether sisters.

Samson knew it wouldn't be easy with no proof, but because he had a new view of life and tried to look at things in a positive light, he hoped for the best.

The district attorney's name was Jacob Manningham, and from what Samson gathered, he was an obnoxious prick who only accepted cases that he knew beforehand he could win.

That meant that until they had the proverbial smoking gun, they were screwed.

Samson suspected that was because the DA's office was just a stepping stone for Mr. Manningham. He was an ambitious prick, too, and he wanted to shift to politics. This was the easiest way. He wouldn't be the first one to make such a leap.

Samson wouldn't normally care, but a lot was on the line. Lives depended on Mr. Manningham's whims, so he spent hours talking about it with Melissa.

She was worried about their civil suit, and how it would be even more difficult to prove everything in court if the DA's office declined to prosecute.

Although the cases addressed different areas, they were still intertwined. A lot depended on appearance, public opinions, and the way the case was perceived, and getting the girls charged with rape would carry precious weight in their civil case.

"I'm sure he'd go for it if he could meet with you."

"So, let's set a meeting," Samson replied, not seeing the problem.

"Believe me, I'm trying."

It took some time, a lot of begging, and a few favors for the right people, but DA Manningham agreed to meet with them.

Everything depended on that one meeting, but that wasn't why he was nervous. Either way, when the day came, he wrote down as much as he could, not wanting to think about what was to come. Then, he drove to Melissa's office. Both sides agreed that the meeting needed to be discreet, so it made sense to hold it there.

This could potentially be one of the highest-profile cases in the past decade, and Melissa and the DA insisted the meeting remain a secret for now.

Mr. Manningham looked like a typical government employee. There was nothing remarkable about him, and he had an easily forgettable face, but he held power, and it showed in the way he interacted with others.

He wanted to speak with each man separately, go over what happened to them, and take notes. It was nearly the same drill they'd gone through with Melissa, only a CliffsNotes version. In his words, Mr. Manningham wanted to get familiar with their stories but not get bogged down with the details.

The last one to speak with the DA was Brian, and Samson hoped like hell the loose cannon wouldn't punch the other guy, or worse.

Luckily, there was no incident.

After everything was said and done, Mr. Manningham promised he would do some additional research and then let them know his decision about whether to press charges.

Samson saw how Mr. Manningham started to sweat as soon as Melissa mentioned the name Bellwether. It wouldn't be easy for him to go up against such a powerful family. On the other hand, his job was to punish those who broke the law, no matter who their daddy was.

The question was whether the DA would do something like that. Some people would cower and bury the case, not wanting to poke the bear.

Samson hoped he would use this high-profile case to his advantage. This was a case that could make or break a man, and it would be impressive to have something like that under his belt, especially for someone who wanted to delve into politics. Public image was everything, and that image said he would fight for the little man.

As it turned out, the DA was more focused on the other side of the coin. Meaning, what it would be like if he lost. Being on Bellwether's shit list was something no man wanted.

Samson wasn't too surprised, just disappointed, to learn Mr. Manningham didn't want to risk his neck for them.

After weeks and weeks of waiting, the DA asked for another meeting. The others assumed that meant good news, but Samson knew better. *So much for looking at things in a positive way.*

He was right.

"Unfortunately, I can't press charges against the Bellwether daughters."

"I knew it," Brian spat.

So maybe Samson wasn't the only pessimist in the group.

"You're too scared of Donald Bellwether to persecute his daughters. How do you sleep at night, being so spineless?"

DA's eyes flashed with fury. He didn't care to be called a coward.

Samson approved of Brian's words. He would have spoken up himself had Brian not beat him to the punch.

"Think what you like, Mr. Grant," Mr. Manningham replied, raising his chin. "Nonetheless, in truth, you have no case."

Samson believed this guy would be an excellent politician because he sure already sounded like one.

"All you have are six statements, and that's it."

"That's it? Doesn't it mean something that the six of us have the same story even though we've never met before this?" Tom argued.

This was the first time Samson had seen him lose his temper, and he felt the same way. The DA didn't even try to sugarcoat this for them.

Mr. Manningham looked at him as though he were an imbecile. "You have no concrete evidence, so it comes down to your word against theirs. The public will only see it as your way of extorting money from their father."

"*What*?" a couple of them exclaimed.

"That's ridiculous."

"That's the most disgusting thing I've heard in my life," Tom replied.

"I call it as I see it," Mr. Manningham said, remaining adamant. "And if I came forward with a case like that – with no concrete evidence – I would be torn to pieces, my reputation destroyed."

Of course he only thought of himself. Samson had no doubt about that.

The men looked at Melissa as though seeking validation for what Mr. Manningham had said, and none of them were happy about her expression.

Everything that bastard said was the truth.

The DA turned to look at her, too. "Honestly, I can't believe you called me for this. This was pretty unprofessional of you, and you should have known better."

Samson frowned. Had he just *scolded* her? Melissa spoke up before Samson could get a word in. "I was hoping we would get there with your help, except, as it turned out, the only unprofessional person here is you."

"I'm sorry if you don't like my decision." He didn't look sorry at all. "However, to win a case like this you need compelling evidence; a smoking gun, if you will. And you don't even have a toy water gun."

"I guess that means we'll just proceed with our class-action lawsuit then," Tom spoke up, trying to brighten the mood.

"I would advise against it," Mr. Manningham surprised them by saying.

"What? Why?" they jumped to ask.

"As I said before, you have no case," he said after they'd calmed down. "To go forward against the Bellwether family with nothing would be absolute lunacy." He paused before adding, "You *will* fail."

"You can't know that for sure," Tom argued.

"I can. Besides, think of it this way: If you press forward now, the suit will name you as their accusers, and warn them of what's going on."

"And that would be bad because …"

"Because it would give their father a chance to prepare a defense, or in the worst-case scenario, help them escape justice, fly them to some exotic island, and you would end up with nothing."

"So, all of this was in vain?"

Melissa stepped forward, looking remorseful. "I hoped I would find something with time, but they've covered their bases pretty well."

"If you can find evidence to support your claim, give me a call," Mr. Manningham said halfheartedly before taking his leave.

No one said a word.

"I knew it would turn out like this," Brian said, breaking the silence.

"We knew it wouldn't be easy from the start," Melissa pointed out.

Brian scoffed. "It was nice knowing you," he added before storming off.

The rest of the guys followed pretty quickly after, disappointment written all over their faces.

"I'm so sorry," Melissa said to each one of them.

"It's not your fault. It is what it is," Tom reassured her before leaving.

Finally, only Samson remained.

"I'm very sorry things turned out like this," she said to him, too.

"Yeah, me too."

"I know it looks bad right now, but this isn't over," she added after some thought.

Samson wished he could believe her, but he couldn't. Not after the cold shower Mr. Manningham had delivered.

"See you around, Melissa," he muttered as he exited.

What could he do now?

"Samson?" she called after him.

"Yeah?"

"Please don't give up. I will continue to fight this."

"You'll be the only one," he said, getting into his car.

He couldn't believe how everything had turned to shit so quickly. One conversation had changed everything.

One *man* had changed everything.

This sucks.

The look on Melissa's face in the rearview mirror was devastating, but he couldn't deal with her feelings right now when he was so overwhelmed with his.

CHAPTER 33

All of this was for nothing, Samson thought on his way home. Melissa had warned them from the start that it wouldn't be easy, but she hadn't prepared them for this. He was convinced that the DA didn't believe their story. If he did, he would fight for them. That was devastating. There was a small chance he *did* believe them but was too afraid to act on it, and that notion was infuriating. Either way, it was over.

He should have known that killing them was the only way to go. He should have done it as soon as he tracked them down. But no, it was wrong, Malcolm had said to him. It wouldn't solve anything, Dr. Valarezo had warned.

How is this any better? he argued with himself.

It wasn't. He shouldn't have listened to the voices of reason. Life would be so much better if they were out of the picture for good. He was with Brian on that.

Because now, Lissa and Candi would continue to do what they pleased, enjoy life, have fun, torment, and rape innocent men because there was nothing he could do to stop them.

It would be the understatement of the fucking century if Samson said he had trouble accepting that. How could he live in a world where evil people roamed free, unpunished?

He was no idiot or a child who believed that life was full of rainbows and sunshine. He knew firsthand how hard, even horrific, life could be. War had taught him that life could get even a step further than that.

He had believed there was some kind of divine justice in this world, that good would eventually triumph over evil. He didn't anymore. Not after this.

With all the negative thoughts swirling inside his head, Samson could feel himself sinking deeper and deeper into depression.

Life sucked. He was frustrated and angry to no end.

Our word against theirs. Why did their word count more?

To be fair, this case wasn't the only one with this problem. Each time someone is accused of rape, the victims tend to get dragged through the mud instead of the accusers. Especially if there is no proof. This type of crime is the hardest to prove.

Villains deserved to be punished for what they did, and in this story, the villains were Lissa and Candi. Not that anyone would believe the men who'd been victimized.

Our word counts for nothing.

He passed a liquor store on the way home and acted on impulse, making an illegal U-turn and parking in front of the store. Tonight, he would drown his sorrows in alcohol. That technique hadn't been very successful in the past, but he didn't let something silly like that stop him from going inside. Samson hadn't had a drop of alcohol since the night he wound up on the bridge. A smart man would assume he would've stayed away from the stuff the moment those girls drugged him, but no. He had to learn that lesson twice.

And here he was, returning for more. It was time to end the abstinence, anyway. After a day like today, Samson felt like he had every right to get properly drunk and try to forget his troubles for a little while.

He bought two bottles of Jack and went home to get thoroughly drunk. Drunk he got, and pretty fast, too, finishing the first bottle in record time. Unfortunately, it didn't stop his brain from tormenting him: It threw gas on the fire instead.

The thing kept plaguing him with things he didn't want to think about, showing images of people he didn't want to see, and reminding him of events he would like nothing more than to forget. Samson was in hell, and there was no one but himself to blame.

Nobody would believe us. Why would they? We're six strong, adult men, and they are two young girls.

If the situation had been reversed, everyone would believe the girls, but arranged this way, it was unthinkable. Sweet, innocent girls couldn't be monsters.

Samson gritted his teeth. Monsters came in all shapes and sizes, Samson knew that all too well, while the rest of the world preferred to turn a blind eye. It was easier to live in ignorance than admit something so troubling existed.

Is that the reason Teresa left me? No, no, no. He couldn't think of her. Not now. It still hurt too much.

He also couldn't stop.

Samson gritted his teeth. He hated his life, and he hated Lissa and Candi for what they'd done to him. Most of all, he hated Teresa. She'd abandoned him when he needed her the most.

Why couldn't she be on his side? Why couldn't she listen to him just once? He'd sent her letters, and she never replied but to ask him to sign the divorce papers.

Why was she so cruel? Had she ever even loved him? It was high time Samson found out. He grabbed his phone and dialed.

Whoever invented the speed dial was a pure genius. There was no way Samson would be able to hit all the right numbers in his state. Maybe it was invented to help drunken people in the first place.

"Why are you calling me, Samson?"

Teresa's voice snapped him from his musings and took him by surprise. Although he should have been better prepared since he's the one who called her.

"Did you sign the divorce papers?" she asked.

He was so thrown that she'd answered the phone that he forgot why he called in the first place.

"Answer me," she demanded.

Her attitude brought it all rushing back. It was time he got his answers.

"Why are you acting like this? Why are you doing this?" he demanded in return.

"What?"

"How can you treat me like this after everything we've been through? Don't I deserve the benefit of the doubt?"

"Benefit of the doubt?"

"Yes. I'm your husband. You should have more faith in me," he stated, raising his voice.

"Are you drunk?" she asked, her voice dripping with disappointment and something else. Disgust?

He couldn't understand how his inebriation was relevant.

"I loved you with all my heart, and you abandoned me when I need you the most," he cried out.

"You *cheated* on me!" she screamed. "You destroyed my home. And you want sympathy? Really, Samson?"

"For the last time, they drugged me and did things to me no person should ever go through," he countered, losing his temper.

She had no idea what he'd had to endure in the name of his love for her. As it turned out, she didn't even care.

"Continue to tell that stupid story if it helps you sleep at night, but I know better. I know it's all lies," she screamed with all her might.

"Were you always this heartless?" he wondered out loud.

"You're the heartless one, continuing to torment me like this. Samson, if you don't stop bothering me, I will file a restraining order, you bastard." With that threat delivered, she hung up.

She was unbelievable. Samson growled in frustration, throwing his phone across the room. He couldn't believe that after all this time, nothing had changed. Teresa remained as bitter and angry as the day she'd found him handcuffed in their trashed home. She'd freed him from the chair, but she completely refused to listen to reason afterward. Not once had she allowed the possibility that he was telling the truth.

If only there was a way to rub her nose in the truth. And then it occurred to him: He could call the other five guys and show up at her house.

See if she can call all *of us liars.* That would show her. Samson stood up, preparing to go to Teresa's, when there was a knock on his door.

That was quick, he thought cheerfully, and then realized he hasn't called anyone yet.

He opened the door and saw Brian on the other side. *Did I call him?* Samson's brain was fuzzy. *I don't think so.*

Still, he said, "Hi, Brian."

The other man eyed him with suspicion. "Are you drunk?"

Why does everyone keep asking me that? "Thoroughly," Samson replied honestly.

Brian shrugged it off and said, "Can you believe that guy?"

Samson needed a moment to put the pieces together. *What is he talking about?*

Oh right, the meeting with DA. You know, the reason you're drunk as a skunk right now.

"Melissa warned us it wouldn't be easy."

"Oh, screw her," Brian snapped.

Samson didn't appreciate the criticism of his lawyer.

"And screw everyone else," Brian continued, unaware of Samson's musings. "It's time you and I do something about this. Bring some real justice to the girls."

"What do you mean?" Samson asked as his alcohol-soaked brain continued to refuse to work properly.

"Let's finish this once and for all. We don't need lawyers, judges, or sniveling DAs to solve this for us," Brian countered. He was pretty worked up, and that worried Samson.

"Look, man, I've been where you are, and that road is not good for either one of us. Come inside, let's talk things over."

"There's nothing to talk about," he insisted, but still stepped through the door. "I want them dead." He grabbed the unopened whiskey bottle and after unscrewing the top and started drinking straight from it.

Samson didn't feel like sharing but let it slide. They were in all this shit together.

"Need a glass?" he tried to make a joke.

Brian's eyes flashed with fury as he pulled the bottle away from his lips. "How can you be so calm?"

"I'm not calm; I'm drunk."

He'd hoped numbing his senses would help him deal with the situation. Instead, all it did was remind him of how he felt when the girls were with him. He stopped himself there.

"I'm *not* calm," he repeated. "I just don't think," – *anymore* – "that killing them is the best course of action. There has to be another way."

He couldn't think of any at the moment.

"Don't be naive," Brian grimaced. "Killing them is the only way," he insisted, waving the bottle around like a weapon. He had more to say, but something caught his attention.

"What's that?" he demanded, approaching Samson's computer.

Oh, fuck. Samson hadn't turned off his computer.

From time to time, he liked to watch the red dot that represented his phone that was with Lissa and Candi. And now, Brian would learn the truth.

"Nothing," Samson lied, trying to turn off the screen. The other man wouldn't let him.

"Why do you look at a place on the map?"

Samson remained quiet. Even in his state, he could see the instant Brian figured out the truth.

"Is that where Lissa and Candi are?" he demanded.

Samson could lie, but there was a hundred percent chance Brian wouldn't believe him. So, he told the truth.

"Yes."

Brian narrowed his eyes and got into his face. "You knew where they were all this time?"

"Why, didn't you?"

"Believe me, I tried to track them down, but they rented a place in someone's else name. Now answer my question: You knew all this time?" he repeated.

"Not all this time, but yes."

"How?"

"Lissa took my phone, and that was how I found them."

"And you did nothing?" He looked outraged. "Unbelievable."

"As I said before, killing them would change nothing."

"It changes *everything*!" he roared. "Maybe you're all too afraid to do what needs to be done, but I'm not," Brian said and stormed off.

"Brian, wait. Where are you going?" Samson had a sinking feeling he knew the answer.

He tried to follow the other man, but Brian was too quick, fueled by unbridled rage, determination, and a thirst for blood. That, and Samson was too drunk.

He rushed back inside – or at least that's what it felt like – to get his phone.

"Where *is* the damn thing?"

It should come with an alarm or something. *Oh, right, I threw it.*

Locating it under the bed, he picked it up, and as his head swirled, he suppressed the urge to throw up before deciding he should. After evacuating a substantial portion of the alcohol he'd drank, he began to dial. He had to alert the other guys to Brian's plan.

Eric had a bone to pick with him for keeping the girls' location from them, but Samson hung up on him. There wasn't time to get into that discussion right now. This was an emergency.

That settled, Samson got into his car and then … did nothing. He was in no state to drive, and he felt like smacking himself in the forehead.

As providence wished, Malcolm wasn't home to play designated driver.

Next, Samson called Melissa, who thankfully answered.

"Can you come and pick me up?" Samson asked without preamble.

"Why? What happened?" She was on high alert.

"I did something stupid, and now I'm afraid someone will get hurt."

Or multiple someones.

"I'm on my way."

CHAPTER 34

S amson willed himself sober while waiting for Melissa to pick him up. *Come on, come on,* he urged, slapping himself a couple of times. It accomplished nothing.

Melissa came in record time, and he jumped into her car. "Let's go," he urged.

"Where are we going? And why?" She wanted to know.

She had every right to ask, but part of him didn't want to answer. *Man up, asshole.* Samson recited the address, and Melissa's eyes widened in surprise as she recognized it.

"You *knew*?"

"Yes, now please can we go? We have to stop Brian from doing something stupid."

"Like what?" Melissa pressed as they sped down the road.

"Killing them."

"Oh, my God."

Surprisingly, Samson and Melissa arrived first.

"There he is," Melissa exclaimed while parking.

Brian was waiting outside the house, pacing around like a caged animal. To make matters worse, he had a huge knife in his hand.

Where did he get that? Not that it mattered right now.

"Oh, my God. Oh, my God," Melissa panicked.

"Everything will be all right," he tried to reassure her.

Samson got out of the car before it was even in park.

"They're not home," Brian yelled as he spotted them, and Samson sighed with relief.

Maybe there was a God because this was nothing short of a miracle. A tragedy was averted in the simplest of ways.

As it turned out, Samson's celebration was premature and Brian's next words confirmed as much. "But I'm ready for them." He grinned, and as though to emphasize his words, he started slashing the air with his knife.

What am I going to do? Think, Samson. Unfortunately, his brain was still sluggish. There was no telling what that madman was capable of doing in his state, even to them.

As Samson pondered the best course of action, Melissa began to approach Brian with her hands raised to show she posed no threat.

Samson groaned. That silly woman would get herself hurt. He followed after her.

"Mr. Grant," she started in a calm, soothing manner. "Please try to calm down."

"I'm calm," Brian countered. "I found my peace the instant I embraced my faith."

Oh, no. This crazy man was planning a murder/suicide mission. And to kill Lissa and Candi there was no telling who else he would drag with him.

"This is not the way. Please come with us so we can talk," Melissa pleaded.

"I'm not going anywhere. I'm staying here until I see those two bitches."

Okay. Seeing them isn't so bad, Samson tried to rationalize.

"I want to slash their throats, stab their beating hearts, and watch them bleed out."

There it is.

Fuck, fuck, fuck.

"Harming them won't solve anything," she pointed out.

Samson moved by her side, ready to intervene if needed.

"They're not worth ruining your life. And you'll end up in jail," she tried to reason.

"So what?" Brian shouted in return. "It's not like I have anything to live for. They took everything. They destroyed my life and laughed while doing it."

It was hard not to sympathize with the man. Samson had gone through the same thing. Was still going through it. So maybe they *should* just kill them? He had a moment of weakness before pushing that thought away. There had to be a better way.

"So what?" Melissa said. "Now you want to help them finish the job?"

"Shut the fuck up," he shouted at her.

"I will *not*. Someone needs to tell you the truth."

"The truth is that everything will be better once they're dead, once I get my revenge for all of us," Brian insisted.

Samson could only stare at him. It was eerie how much he sounded like Samson a while back. It was like looking in the mirror, and the experience was as sobering as it was chilling.

I guess this is a stage we all have to go through. Samson had managed to pull himself out of this state of mind, but Brian, on the other hand, was still a slave to it.

"Mr. Grant," Melissa tried again. It was impressive how much determination and will to help she possessed. Samson was in awe of her. "I know you are angry with them, and that you're hurting."

Samson flinched. That was the wrong thing to say, and the way Brian reacted suggested he felt the same way.

He narrowed his eyes and took a menacing step toward them. Samson moved to stand slightly in front of Melissa, shielding her with his body.

"You know? You know?" Brian was enraged. "You have *no* idea what it was like to be chained like an animal, beaten, tormented, and raped. To watch, powerless as they destroy your life and laugh in your face like you're nothing."

There were tears in his eyes, and Samson felt his pain.

"Do you have any idea what it feels like to be reduced to nothing? *Less* than nothing?"

Melissa remained quiet. Whether that was because she didn't know what to say or because she was startled by his outburst, Samson wasn't sure, but it didn't matter.

He stepped forward.

"I do," he said simply. "I know what it feels like." Taking another step toward Brian, he added, "I know exactly what it feels like when you wake up with no memory of the night before, but you know it was bad because you're covered in blood and aching all over."

"I know it, too," Tom said.

Samson was so focused on Brian and his knife that he hadn't noticed the rest of the gang appear behind him.

"I know what it's like looking at the ones you love as they leave for good, and you have no way to stop them."

"I know it, too," Eric said next. "I know what it's like to pray for death."

Brian was openly crying now, and he wasn't the only one. A few treacherous tears fell down Samson's cheeks, too.

"I know it, too," Carl was next. "I know how it feels to struggle every day not to get mad or be consumed by anger."

"Me, too," Sam said \last. "I know what it feels like to hit rock bottom and lose everything."

"We all know what it feels like, wishing them to die," Samson added, taking the last step and reaching the other man. "Despite everything, I'm telling you that this is not the way. This is not the way."

"I can't let it end like this," Brian countered, but he'd lost some of his passion.

"If you continue like this, there's only one way this can end: with you in jail, maybe with a life sentence," Samson pointed out, as a scene of someone else telling him that very same thing flashed through his memory.

"I have to. Without it, I have nothing."

"That's not true," Tom spoke up. "You have us."

Brian was prepared to say something in return, but Samson beat him to it. "Besides, it isn't like you really thought this through," he pointed out.

Samson should know everything about thinking things through: He'd written a book about how to kill Lissa and Candi.

"What?" Brian asked in confusion.

Samson pointed at his hand. "You came here with a knife."

"So?" he asked defensively.

"That's not the smartest choice. It's big and bulky, with a short range. One of them could get away."

"So what? I'll get the other."

"True, but even if you manage to catch one of them, killing someone with a knife is not as easy as it seems," he pointed out.

Samson couldn't say if he was doing the right thing. There was a fine line between persuading Brian to give up and giving him tips to improve on his next murder spree. Either way, he had to try something – he'd drag him out of there if he had to – before the sisters returned home.

They could never find out they'd been here, in front of their house, convincing a man – one of their victims – not to kill them.

Oh, the irony.

"How would you know?" he challenged. "You're a writer."

"Before that, I was an infantry combat soldier. Trust me, I know everything a person needs to know about killing."

About the price one pays having something like that on his conscience, too. He said as much.

"I don't care about price. I'll gladly pay it because revenge is all I have left. Without it, I'm nothing." Brian began to get worked up all over again.

This is pointless, Samson realized. No matter what they said to him, Brian was not giving up. His mind was too far gone to see reason.

"I wish you hadn't said that because now I have no choice," Samson replied, wearing a humorless smile.

Brian looked confused.

To everyone's surprise, Samson lunged and punched the other man straight in the face. Vaguely, he heard Melissa's sharp intake of breath.

Samson's balance was seriously compromised due to the whiskey but his muscle memory took over and his body did what needed to be done. Fortunately, Brian was also drunk and lacked military training.

That didn't mean taking him down was easy. Brian was fueled by blind rage and the need for revenge, and that made him extremely dangerous.

They trading punches. Brian had a mean right hook, and when he nicked Samson once, he actually saw stars. He made a mental note, in what was left of his brain, to avoid it at any cost.

Samson's main goal was to get the knife. He didn't want to hurt Brian. Despite what he'd said, Samson believed he deserved help and not additional pain. Unfortunately, this confrontation was a necessary evil.

Seeing an opportunity, Samson spun and kicked, knocking the knife from Brian's hand. The other man roared and ran toward him.

"Get the knife!" Samson yelled just before Brian reached him.

It felt like being tackled by a linebacker, and Samson felt the air leaving his lungs in a woosh. They ended up on the ground, rolling around and punching.

Using his remaining strength, Samson used a maneuver Malcolm taught him a long time ago, to get atop Brian. Without missing a beat, he started pummeling the other man. It was imperative to incapacitate him.

"Samson!" Melissa yelled at some point. There was fear in her voice.

Was she afraid he would go too far?

"Say you'll stop," Samson demanded, hitting him again.

"Say you'll stop this madness."

"Say you won't kill them."

"Okay, okay, I promise!" as soon as Brian stopped struggling, he began sobbing.

Samson remained on top of the other man for a couple of seconds to make sure it wasn't a bluff before climbing off. He sat on the grass, panting. His knuckles were bloody and had already started to swell, but he didn't care. His head, on the other hand, wasn't so easily ignored. It hurt like hell.

I'm going to have one helluva hangover tomorrow. Brian knew how to punch. Samson's head felt like the inside of a bell.

Brian, meanwhile, was curled on his side, crying. "I miss my wife," he wailed. "I miss Lilly."

Samson assumed Lilly was the name of the daughter he'd never met. Samson moved next to him. He wanted to comfort him but didn't know how. They were all so fucked up.

They let Brian cry for a while before Eric and Carl picked him up from the ground. Sam helped Samson. He still felt drunk, despite everything. Luckily, no one had called the cops on them, so they returned to their vehicles and drove away.

Brian didn't want to be taken to the hospital, so Melissa drove him back to that rickety old motel. There, they helped him get to bed.

"Do you think he will be all right?" Eric wondered.

Brian looked pretty out of it. He passed out after having that good cry.

"I'll stay with him," Samson reassured.

"Want someone to sit with you?" Tom asked.

Samson shook his head. "Thanks for your help, guys."

They returned home.

"We'll talk about what happened tonight, tomorrow," were Melissa's parting words.

"Yes, ma'am," Samson replied tiredly.

This was one hard night.

One way or the other, aren't they all? Nothing bad had happened tonight, and he took that as a win.

Samson looked around. The place was a mess. With nothing better than do and not wanting to sit and do nothing, he grabbed a couple of garbage bags and started cleaning.

Brian stirred at some point. "Thank you for stopping me," he mumbled.

Samson nodded. "No problem." Brian went quiet again, so Samson continued cleaning the other man's room.

Once he'd finished, he went to grab some ice to put on the left eye that had started to close up.

Brian was fully awake and staring at the ceiling when he returned.

"Do I have your word that you won't try this shit again?" Samson demanded, not seeing the point in beating around the bush.

"I need to see them punished."

"Me too."

Brian turned to look at him. There was so much pain and anger in his eyes. Samson recognized the haunted look because he saw it every time he looked in the mirror.

"That's why we'll keep fighting until we find a way to bring them down," Samson said reassuringly. Whether to comfort himself or Brian was yet to be determined.

"Okay," Brian said slowly.

Samson sighed with relief.

Brian closed his eyes as though planning to sleep. Still, he said, "Just so you know, when all of this is over, I never want to see you or anyone else involved in this ever again."

Samson wasn't offended.

"Fair enough."

CHAPTER 35

I
t was morning when Samson decided it was time to head home and get some rest. However, he wasn't leaving Brian not before he made sure the other man was truly okay … as okay as he could be in this situation, anyway.

Reaching his house, he practically fell on the bed. Unfortunately, his early arrival did not go unnoticed.

"What on earth happened to you?" Malcolm demanded, horrified.

"You should see the other guy," Samson mumbled against the pillow, trying to make a joke although his jaw still kind of hurt.

"You got into a fight?"

"It was necessary, trust me," Samson moved his head ever so slightly so he could look at his friend.

"Are you all right?"

"Yes. I'm not having a breakdown or anything," he said. "I was just helping a friend."

Malcolm didn't understand a thing but also didn't press, and Samson was grateful. He was far too tired to explain right now.

Once Samson woke, he showered and shaved. The shiner on his eye looked like it would stay there for a while, but he didn't care. He worked from home, so it wasn't like he was going anywhere.

During lunch, he filled Malcolm in on the latest developments.

"Wow. I don't know what to say. How is he now?"

Samson shrugged. "I don't know. Only time will tell."

He hoped Brian would seek help, but as Dr. Valarezo told him, something like that couldn't be forced upon him. He had to want it.

On a more personal note, Samson decided not to drink again, at least not to such excess.

What had happened the previous day with the DA and then Brian was a serious wake-up call for everyone, so after some group texting, they decided to meet with Melissa again and discuss where to go from here. They all agreed that they shouldn't give up on their search for justice. But how to proceed?

They spoke at length, sharing their frustrations and anger with the DA who had so easily dismissed them like what had happened to them didn't matter.

"If the DA needs evidence, evidence is what he will get," Sam said, as though that was the most natural thing in the world.

"If only it was that simple," Samson replied, feeling the need to play the devil's advocate. They couldn't stay idle, but they needed to remain realistic about their limitations.

"All the evidence from our houses is gone. As far as what we were drugged with, we don't have proof it was taken involuntarily and it disappeared from our systems long ago. There is no evidence."

Lissa and Candi had been meticulous. Samson hated how much he sounded like the DA just then.

The only thing that they'd left behind were fingerprints. They could easily explain that away by saying they were invited to a party. They could use the same excuse for the drugs. Once again, it would boil down to the sisters' word against theirs. It was a no-win situation.

"They must have missed something in the houses," Tom thought aloud.

"Even if that's the case, there's nothing we can do about it. None of us live there anymore. You sold yours," Samson replied to Tom.

"That's true," he said in a small voice.

All the same, even if their wives hadn't kicked them out or forced them to sell, could any one of them return there after everything that had happened to them? Samson had an afterthought.

He seriously doubted he could have continued living there as if nothing bad had happened. The trauma was just too great to overcome.

"We have to find another way," Carl spoke up.

"What are our options?" Eric tuned in. "Without evidence that they were inside our houses and drugging us, what's left?"

"A confession would be the best proof you can find," Melissa answered.

"Right, like they would ever willingly go to the police station and confess to what they did," Brian grumbled.

"They don't have to go to the police to confess. If one of us confronts them and they confess, that would be enough," Samson thought out loud.

"But then we'd need proof the conversation occurred because if not, it would once again be our word against theirs," Sam argued.

"We live in a one-party-consent state," Melissa stated. "So, if you get them saying anything compromising on record, that's the only proof we'll need," she explained.

Samson was cheered by that.

"What does that mean, 'one-party consent?'" Tom inquired.

"It means they don't have to be aware we are recording them. We don't have to have their consent," Samson replied with a big smile.

Thanks to that law, all the videos of them unwillingly participating in all kinds of sex games were online legally. Samson saw some kind of poetic justice in the notion that they could use the sisters' methods against them.

He liked the idea of doing to the girls what they'd done to them, minus the rape and torture part. He said as much.

"I think we should try and goad them into confessing everything."

They were so confident and prideful, it would never cross their

"Yeah, you convinced me."

Samson couldn't help but grin.

"How do we set a trap for them?" Brian said.

"And where? It's not like we can walk up to them in a public place and start talking about all the fun we had," Tom pointed out.

That was true, they would be more inclined to mind their manners in public or surrounded by friends. That they were party girls was no secret, but this wasn't something they would share with friends. That was why Samson's idea to expose them was such a great plan.

"Maybe I can help with that. Well, at least with the technical part of the plan," Eric said.

"What do you mean?" Brian asked him.

"I can hook us up with some wearable cameras."

"Really? Nice," Carl said approvingly.

"Wouldn't they see through that? Especially if we start asking questions or demanding a confession?" Sam pointed out.

"The cameras can be hidden in lapels, buttons, even glasses," Eric explained.

"And they won't think anything of it, even if we do start asking questions," Samson interjected. "They love to brag about their accomplishments."

It must kill them that they can't tell anyone.

"Cool, so we're going undercover," Carl joked.

The rest of the group looked excited, too.

"Can you get a bunch of those hidden cameras?" Samson asked Eric.

"Yeah, as many as we need, why?" he asked in return.

"Well, I was thinking we should all wear them, to make sure we get everything captured."

It would be disastrous if they went to all this trouble and were forced to face their tormentors only to discover the gear malfunctioned or that their confessions couldn't be heard because the person recording it was standing too far away. This way, all their bases were covered. There was no room for error.

"Okay, yeah, that's a great idea," Eric complimented.

"Wait, you want all of us to go together?" Brian wondered out loud, looking slightly uncomfortable.

Did he fear facing them? Samson wondered. He wasn't that happy about it either, but this needed to be done.

"I thought it might shock them to see us all together. That way they're bound to make a mistake. Besides, safety in numbers, right?" he tried to joke, but no one laughed.

"I see your point. Let's do that," Brian agreed, and Samson was relieved. For this to work, they needed to stick together.

"The rest of you agree?" Samson asked and everyone nodded.

"So it's settled. We'll wait for Eric to get the cameras, and then we'll go and confront them," Samson said. It sounded so easy, but he knew it would be anything but.

"We still need some kind of plan," Tom pointed out.

That was true. Ambushing them during dinner at a restaurant, in a club, or while they were at some lecture at school was out of the question.

For this to work the way they wanted it to, they needed to catch the girls alone.

"We will think of something," Samson reassured, although he believed he'd already found a solution.

"Do you need me for anything?" Melissa wanted to know.

All men looked at one another. Bringing a lawyer to an operation like this wasn't the best idea. Besides, the girls knew all of them, and they might not talk in front of a strange woman. The point was to get their tongues loose, not make them suspicious.

"I don't think so," Samson replied for the group.

Melissa looked only mildly disappointed. "Okay, just remember one thing."

"And what is that?" Brian asked like a four-year-old.

"You have to play by the book and abide by the law."

"And if we don't?" Brian asked stubbornly.

Samson rolled his eyes. He didn't understand why he needed to do things like that.

"Do you want to get hit again?" Samson warned.

"Samson, it's okay," Melissa told him before turning to look at Brian. "If you don't, then the evidence is useless. It will be dismissed by the court, and everything you are working so hard for would be for nothing. Is that a good enough reason for you?"

Brian remained silent.

"So, we all agree? Do things the right way?" Samson insisted.

"Agreed," they all said, except for one.

They all looked at Brian, who rolled his eyes. "Whatever … agreed."

CHAPTER 36

They didn't have to wait long for Eric to set everything up. He was highly motivated to confront the girls and get their proof as soon as possible.

Samson wanted to talk with Dr. Valarezo about everything that was happening, and she helped him remain calm. This was all very stressful for him, and with some techniques that she showed him, he dealt with stress a lot better. Also, he vowed when all of this was over, he would start doing meditation to help calm his mind. If he wanted to get better, then he needed to commit. But one step at a time. First, they had to bring the sisters down.

Samson didn't like how Melissa felt left out. She had been with him from the beginning and was the first person besides Malcolm and Anita who believed him and had faith in him. He knew how much she wanted to help, so he found something for her to do while they confronted the Bellwether sisters.

Since Eric had to be with the rest of the men, meeting Lissa and Candi, Melissa would monitor the equipment and make sure everything worked properly.

She received a crash course from Eric, who showed her what to do if anything went sideways, but he assured her this equipment wouldn't fail. There was only one problem: The cameras had a limited range, so they decided to rent a van and put all the equipment inside.

They would meet the sisters in their house and Melissa would stay outside in the van, monitoring the feed. It was a true spy van, and the guys joked about it while Melissa drove them to Lissa and Candi's house.

It was also to release tension. This was hard on all of them, but they also understood how important this was for their future.

After some discussion, the guys decided to confront Lissa and Candi inside their home. They would have much-needed privacy that way. Besides, it appeared as some kind of divine justice. The two of them had come into their homes and caused havoc; now, it was time to return the favor.

They didn't come up with a more elaborate plan or rehearse what to say. Samson was sure the shock of seeing them together would be enough to start a conversation and get the confession they so desperately needed out of Lissa and Candi. They were too overconfident, and that would be their downfall, Samson was sure of it.

"What are we gonna do if they aren't home?" Tom said, and silence followed.

In all the madness, no had one thought to ask that very important question until now.

"We'll wait for them," Brian replied, but even he looked unsure. Could they stay in the van indefinitely? *No.* Besides, what if the reason they weren't home was that they were in some other man's house, having "fun?"

Fuck, fuck, fuck.

Glancing at others, it was obvious they were thinking the same thing. *They'll be home,* Samson tried to reassure himself.

As Melissa parked in front, they could see lights on in the house. They were home. The men were relieved, which, considering what they were about to do, felt kind of weird.

"Good luck," Melissa said as they got out, offering a big smile to each of them.

She was a special woman, and Samson was once again grateful to have her in his life.

"It's like a clown car," Eric joked as they got out, but they were all too tense to appreciate it.

This is it. This is the moment that will make or break us, Samson thought. He felt a little sick to his stomach as they walked toward the front door.

Brian knocked. Samson stood right behind him, feeling like he had to have an eye on the man, just in case.

Voices could be heard from within, so Brian knocked harder.

"Come in!" Candi yelled from within.

Brian looked at them in confusion.

"You heard the lady of the house. Let's go," Eric prompted.

Brian opened the door, and the men followed him inside.

The girls were in the living room, turned away from them, sitting on the floor, giggling at the TV.

Samson was horrified by what they were watching. It was one of the homemade videos, with Brian being sexually assaulted. It was an original, unedited version, and it was plain to see that he was not a willing participant.

Brian balled his hands into fists and cleared his throat. Samson was impressed with how well he'd handled himself so far.

"It was about time you came, you fucker," Candi commented, not bothering to turn around and greet them. She'd obviously confused them with someone else.

They were high as kites, with residue from whatever shit they'd snorted scattered on the table.

Brian grabbed the first thing he got a hold of, a laptop, and flung it across the room above the TV, where it shattered against the wall. "You crazy bitches!" he screamed at the top of his lungs.

Perhaps Samson had spoken too quickly. *There goes doing this calmly.* Maybe his expectations were too high, anyway.

As expected, Lissa and Candi jumped to their feet and turned to face them, and the looks on their faces were priceless. These six men were the last people on earth they were expecting to see. Was it just

Samson's imagination, or could he see some discomfort, maybe even fear mixed into the shock? He was projecting.

As always, Candi recovered quicker. "What are you doing here?" she demanded.

"What are we doing? I'll show you exactly what I'm doing," Brian advanced and luckily, Eric blocked his way, and Sam joined in, the two of them managing to hold the infuriated man back.

Candi blew him a kiss, trying to rattle him further.

They didn't need this scene on camera. The last thing Brian needed was to be arrested for threatening them.

"Brian, shut up," he snapped harshly. Seeing no other way, stepped forward, taking lead. This was not a good start.

"Samson," she greeted almost cheerfully. "What the fuck are you doing in my house?" she added almost conversationally, wiping her nose. Brian's little tantrum had put her in a good mood. They fed off that shit; he was aware of that.

"Remember why we're here," Samson could hear Tom whispering to Brian, trying to calm him down.

That was good advice.

Samson put his hands on the back of the couch, leaned forward, and looked Candi straight in the eye. Now that this moment was finally here, he felt nothing. No fear, no anger, only determination to see their downfall.

That was what gave him the confidence to say, "Just checking in to see if you two are having fun with someone else."

"And if we are? What are you going to do?"

Samson straightened up and shrugged.

"Jealous?" Lissa taunted.

Hearing her voice made his skin crawl. God, how much he hated them. "Not in the slightest."

"So how did you all guys meet?" Candi wanted to know.

"You brought us together," Samson replied with a forced smile.

"Aww, that's sweet," Lissa commented.

"So, did you come to party with us?"

Lissa clapped her hands. "That would be amazing. Best present ever."

Samson suppressed a cringe. "Nope. I'm still recovering from the last party you threw in my house."

"Not enough stamina," Candi replied while nodding. "Lissa, we have to remember to pick a younger guy next time."

"It wasn't a stamina problem," Samson countered. "I didn't care for the part where I was drugged and raped."

There. He'd said it, on camera, in front of them.

Candi rolled her eyes as Lissa giggled.

"Oh, you loved it."

"I did *not*," Samson replied.

"Nor did I like it when you sent everything to Sandra," Brian said through gritted teeth. He still looked on edge, but he wasn't trying to kill them. He was calmly standing next to Eric, so Samson took that as a good sign.

Lissa started laughing. "Oh, that was funny. She was in the hospital, and we put Brian in diapers."

Candi laughed, too.

Samson hoped Eric and Sam had a firm grip on Brian because with shit like this coming to light, there was no telling what could happen.

Maybe I'm worrying about the wrong man. Maybe Tom will try to strangle them. You never knew what was inside someone's head.

Focus.

"Was it also fun when you made me sleep in the basement?" Tom spoke up.

"Of course," Lissa replied. "You were a bad dog and needed to be taught a lesson."

"You behaved better afterward," Candi agreed.

"How about when you put me in drag and forced me to fuck you while calling me Didi," Carl chimed in.

"That was a good day," Candi said, looking almost wistful.

"How about when you tied me up to a chair and left me to shit myself?" Samson added. He was proud that his voice wavered only once.

Candi grabbed her heart and turned to look at her sister. "Do you hear this, Lissa? They're recounting our greatest hits."

"I know. It's so cool."

It was not cool to them.

"If you'd like to continue reminiscing, we can show you everything on video," Candi offered.

Samson couldn't tell if she was being serious or trying to taunt them. Both options were plausible since she was crazy.

"Every little detail," Lissa added. "Even the bits you were unconscious for."

As they bragged about their accomplishments, the evidence of their viciousness was playing on the TV in the background. Samson noted how on the video they commented how quickly the drugs worked on Brian, then proceeded to talk about what they were going to do to him, what would be the most fun, and things like that, so Samson, shifted ever so slightly to position himself at the right angle and make sure he was recording all of it.

"You filmed everything?" Tom asked.

"Yes, of course," Lissa replied as though thinking that was a stupid question.

"Are you proud of yourselves? You did all that without our consent? You raped us," Sam said, no longer able to hold his silence.

"Yes. So what?" Candi challenged. "It was super fun. Besides, it's not like you didn't get anything in return."

They'd done it. They'd gotten them on camera admitting everything.

Stay cool, Samson. This isn't over.

"You had a fun time with this sweet ass," Lissa added, slapping herself in the process.

"Something that would never happen in your real lives," Candi concluded.

Samson couldn't believe their depths of self-delusion and deprivation. Now, he too had pretty clear homicidal thoughts.

"Right. We *wanted* to have our lives ruined by you. It was so worth it," Samson mocked. "And FYI, you're not that good in bed," he couldn't resist throwing in their faces.

"Especially since you have to force guys to sleep with you," Tom chimed in.

Candi's eyes flashed with fury. She didn't like being made fun of, he remembered that about her. But this time, there was nothing she could do about it; she was the powerless one.

"Is that why you came here?" she asked as she approached him. "To cry 'rape' to me? Is it an apology you seek?"

"Are you a little bitch?" Lissa interjected with a snicker.

Samson smirked. "Nope. We came here to tell you the party is over."

Candi rolled her eyes. "As always, the party is over when we say it is."

"Damn straight," Lissa said with attitude.

"And you coming here like a bunch of old women, nagging us, changes nothing."

"We'll see about that," Samson replied.

"What's that supposed to mean?" Candi demanded.

"Just what I said."

Candi looked at him for a heartbeat or two, sizing him up, before replying, "What's this about, Samson? Some kind of intervention?"

"I don't give a fuck about your well-being."

"Then what? Are you going to tell?" she guessed. She sounded almost excited by the prospect of it.

That's because she thinks we have nothing on them.

"We're going to tell everyone who you really are," Tom replied instead.

Lissa and Candi burst into laughter.

"Are you serious?" Lissa said through her cackles.

"No one will believe you," Candi pointed out. "I mean, look at you, and look at us."

"Even if we can prove it?" Samson said calmly.

That stopped the laughter.

"You have nothing," Candi snapped in return, finally getting emotional.

Samson would be lying if he said he wasn't enjoying this confrontation a little. It was good for his soul.

"We'll see about that," Samson replied, irritating her further.

"Even if you *do* have something, Daddy will make it go away," Lissa bragged, dismissing his claims.

"Are you sure about that?" Samson challenged. "I don't think Donald will like having rapists as daughters."

Lissa looked stunned; she hadn't expected them to know who they were.

"It doesn't matter. You have nothing," Candi insisted.

"And no one will believe we raped you," Lissa said.

"I'm not sure that's true either," Samson countered. "I mean, there's plenty of evidence of your wrongdoings."

"Name one," Candi demanded.

"You stole my watch and Teresa's necklace," Samson began, and the rest of the group joined in, naming all the things the girls had stolen.

Candi waved them off. "Those were all gifts, given to us willingly because you were so in love and desperate to make us stay."

"Why would I give you my phone? That doesn't make any sense," Samson wondered.

"What?" Candi asked making a face. "We didn't take your phone," she argued.

Samson looked at Lissa, who threw a guilty face toward her older sister. "Sorry," she mouthed.

So, Candi didn't know. *Interesting.*

"That doesn't matter. Petty theft is something Daddy can take care of just like that," she said with a snap of her fingers, trying to appease her sister, who was pretty rattled by this revelation.

If Lissa did more things on her own, then that could ultimately bring them down. Samson really hoped so.

"It certainly wouldn't be the first time," Brian pointed out.

So, Donald really had pulled them out of the jam before. Samson wasn't surprised. Then again, this was another matter altogether. Misdemeanors and felonies were different things, and Samson was sure Donald Bellwether would act accordingly.

"Exactly," Lissa said smugly.

"We will discuss this later," she told Lissa. "And you," she looked at the men, "I think I want you all gone. You're ruining my fun."

"What's the matter, Candi? Not ten steps ahead anymore?" Samson couldn't help jibing a little.

"Twenty," she countered, but Samson knew she was full of it.

"Are you really so confident that daddy dearest will come to your rescue this time?" he challenged.

"Not likely," Brian provided.

"Serial rape is a serious crime, and I don't think he'd like being associated with something like that."

"He got us out of trouble before, and he'll do it again," Lissa argued, but Samson could see her smug façade begin to crack.

"We're not in trouble; they're bluffing," Candi insisted.

"Denial doesn't become you."

"I'm not afraid of you," Candi said, raising her chin. "Even if you do try something, my father's lawyers will destroy you."

"I don't think so. But good luck explaining all this to your father."

Samson looked around. Maybe it was time to go.

"Why would I tell him anything?"

"Because you'll have no choice," Brian said, grinning.

"What's that supposed to mean?"

"Say cheese, you sociopathic maniacs." Brian laughed. "You're on hidden camera."

"What?" Lissa looked around.

"We're all wearing cameras, so we have your confessions recorded," Samson explained.

"Not to mention you had that on while we were here. Talk about a smoking gun," Sam added, pointing at the screen.

Lissa stood in front of a TV as though to shield it from their eyes. "No. You can't do that. We didn't know."

It was beautiful.

"We can, and we did."

Candi started screaming and charged toward Samson as though to strike him, but he caught her effortlessly. He wasn't drugged or being blackmailed this time around, so he could fight back. He said as much. "You're no match for me, little girl."

"Let me go," she struggled.

"I am only subduing you so you won't hurt me," he said for the camera's sake. This was self-defense.

"Give me that camera," Candi insisted. You can't do this to us."

"Watch me."

"Lissa, do something," Candi whined.

"Do you really have us on tape?" Lissa asked in a panic.

"Yes," they replied.

"Are we, like, going to jail?"

"For a long time, sweetheart." Brian laughed like a madman.

"Lissa, help me," Candi urged.

Lissa didn't move, as though the notion that it was game over for them petrified her.

"I think it's time to leave," Samson said.

"Yeah, we got what we came for. Thanks," Brian jumped in.

"No! I won't let you leave," Candi said, struggling even harder. She was trying to rip his clothes and discover where the camera was, so Samson pushed her away and she fell to the ground.

"You will *not* get away with this!" she threatened.

Looking at her like that, on the ground, Samson almost felt sorry for her. Then again, she deserved much worse.

"You're missing the point. *You're* the ones who won't get away with what you did," Samson threw in her face, and with that, they left.

As they walked outside, they could hear Candi screaming. It put the biggest smile on Samson's face.

We won.

"That was freaking awesome," Eric said.

"Yeah," the rest agreed.

"I can't wait to watch the video and see the expression on their faces when they realized they were screwed," Brian said, laughing.

"I told you to trust me," Samson said to the other man.

Brian nodded. "You were right. Thank you."

"Don't thank me yet. We have a long way to go."

They reached the van, and Melissa jumped from it. She was smiling from ear to ear. "Well done, boys," she congratulated.

"Do we have them?" Tom asked her since she was the one who'd monitored the live feed.

"We have them," she replied as they all entered the van.

This was an epic win, and a great day for them all. But the war wasn't over. Still, they had an upper hand now, and they were ready to use it.

It's time to bring them down.

CHAPTER 37

I t was hard to explain the atmosphere inside the van as Melissa drove away from the house. They heard screams as the van sped away, as Candi ran into the street and shouted after them, but what she was saying couldn't be deciphered. They'd won, and the mood inside the vehicle reflected that. It was a strange kind of mixture of shock, wonder, disbelief, and euphoria.

Samson couldn't remember the conversation during the ride, but at some point, they all began to laugh. Brian started it, as though realizing what they'd just accomplished, and everyone followed suit. It was freeing to laugh together like that and enjoy the moment.

Melissa drove them to Eric's so he could look at the footage immediately. Naturally, they stayed to watch with him and see what they'd managed to capture.

Despite Melissa's words, Samson was still a little worried that they hadn't gotten enough, or that something went wrong to make them lose everything.

Stop that. He forced himself to think positively.

"Make yourself comfortable," Eric said as they entered his apartment. "There's beer in the fridge."

They all declined, even Brian, which Samson took as a step in the right direction.

Once Eric fired up his computer, he helped them to take their cameras off. It wasn't hard to do, but no one wanted to take any chances.

The videos they'd captured were already uploaded to Eric's cloud, and it took him no time at all to retrieve them.

"Are you ready?" Eric asked as they huddled around his computer screen.

"Just press the damn play button," Brian urged.

Together, they watched all six videos, getting the scene from all angles. Samson was glad they'd worn multiple cameras because they'd been able to capture each word the sisters spoke, loud and clear.

"I can't believe we did it," Carl said after the first video ended. That was the camera Samson wore.

"We did," Samson insisted.

"What are we going to do now?" Tom asked after they finished the last video.

"Where should we post them?" Sam joined in.

"I think we should edit them first," Eric suggested.

"What do you mean?" Tom asked.

"Well, how about we merge all six videos, choose the best angles, and publish it that way?" Eric explained.

"Maybe we could add something to them as well," Samson piped in.

Six pairs of eyes looked at him in confusion, and he cleared his throat. "If we describe what happened to us at the beginning of the video, maybe more people will watch it and understand it better."

"That makes sense," Carl said, and the rest nodded.

"Can you write something for us?" Tom wanted to know.

"Sure," Samson replied.

What should he say? How should he begin? Then, the writer in him kicked in and all kinds of ideas started to appear in his head.

As Eric started to edit, the rest of the guys offered suggestions on what pieces looked the best, where was sound the clearest, and things like that. In the meantime, Samson constructed a couple of sentences. He wanted the message to be concise but not cold. At the same time, he had to make sure it didn't sound too pathetic. Samson wanted to incite rage in people and nothing else.

Of course, the footage alone would do that even without their part at the beginning. However, an intro would provide important context.

Instead of speaking individually, Samson envisioned them standing together. They had been together from the start of this endeavor, and that should be portrayed in the first cut, too. So that was exactly how Melissa filmed them with her phone, sitting together in Eric's living room. They stated their names, and then Samson described what had brought them together and how they'd fallen prey to Lissa and Candi Bellwether. After he finished his part, Tom added why they believed it was necessary to share this video with the world.

And that was that. After that part, an edited video of the girls confessing how they'd tormented the men followed. After everything was complete, they watched the full video one more time. Samson had to admit it was kind of disturbing, although he'd lived through it.

"It turned out good," Brian said afterward.

"If by 'good' you mean 'distressing,'" Tom mirrored Samson's thoughts.

"Hey, we want people to know the truth, and the truth is ugly," Brian explained with a shrug.

That was true.

"Can't argue with that," Eric replied.

"So, what now?" Tom asked what was on everyone's mind.

"Now, we pull the trigger," Brian replied.

The guys decided to go home but agreed to complete the next step at the same time. They posted the video to their social media with the simple caption that said, *The Truth About Me.*

Samson had avoided social media all this time but figured if there was a time for a comeback, this was a spectacular one.

Carl also used a few contacts that he had left in the business and sent them the video, hoping it would reach the right people.

As it turned out, it wasn't necessary to stress that no one would watch it. *Everyone* watched it. The hype literally crashed the internet.

The view count was changing by the second as more people watched and then reposted it, and in a matter of hours, they were viral. The video spread like wildfire, and it looked like that was all people could think about, talk about, and post about. Not only in their hometown or the U.S. but worldwide.

It was a miracle.

Samson could only stare as he started to read some of the comments from his friends, and then continued to read messages from strangers. There was nothing but love and support. It brought him to tears.

And then something even more miraculous happened: His fans got involved. The community he was so blessed to be a part of rallied behind him, showing support and outrage, overwhelming Samson with gratitude and appreciation. They demanded the Bellwether sisters be arrested and tried.

And then, the phone calls started.

Samson started receiving phone calls from all kinds of reporters and story seekers wanting exclusive interviews and begging for comment. And at first, Samson was so stunned by it all, he didn't know how to react or what to say. However, he reminded himself that this was why they'd done this in the first place. They wanted and needed their stories to be heard.

Journalists weren't the only ones who sought his attention. Friends from his previous life, ones who had sided with Teresa, started calling as well. They expressed sorrow and offered support, and Samson let them. He could forgive if they were willing to admit they were wrong.

"It's very courageous of you to speak up like that," Katja, one of Teresa's clients, applauded him.

"Thank you for your kind words."

"Stay strong," she said before disconnecting.

A few even apologized for assuming the worst of him, and Samson appreciated every word.

During all the madness, the guys remained in constant contact with Melissa, asking for advice and wondering about their next steps.

"I can't get away from all the reporters calling my house," Sam complained.

"Me either," Samson agreed.

"They even got a hold of Ruth," Tom added, making a face.

"I know it's hard, but media exposure is good," Melissa pointed out.

They were well aware of what kind of society they lived in. A public outrage could put additional pressure on the DA to do his job.

"I got a call from some TV show," Brian said.

"Me too," Eric added.

"You should go on and tell your story."

Carl and Eric looked more reluctant about the whole affair.

"I've got an idea," Samson spoke up.

Since they'd decided to come forward as a group, they began appearing on all kinds of TV shows in the same manner.

Safety in numbers.

Samson felt like throwing up the entire time the news reporters peppered them with endless personal questions, but he got through it. He would be lying if he said it got easier over time. As the public's curiosity about them rose, so did the media's demands. Nonetheless, they had one thing in common.

"Why do this?" a particularly unpleasant reporter asked them.

She tried to appear impartial, except she belonged to one of those channels that saw this as just a publicity stunt, a way to extort money from Donald Bellwether.

"Why did you post this video online instead of going to the authorities for help like any other citizen would?"

She looked almost smug, as though thinking she'd managed to corner them.

"We couldn't," Tom replied.

"What do you mean you couldn't? Did you fear for your lives?"

They did now. They were making a huge splash, and there was no telling how Donald would counter.

"Nobody believed us," Eric chimed in.

"Two police officers laughed in my face when I tried to explain to them what was happening to me," Samson said.

It was almost amusing to watch her reaction. She didn't know how to respond, so she changed the subject and moved on to a different question.

Naturally, Samson didn't care how uncomfortable they made her feel. The goal was to reach as many people as possible and make them believe. And they started to believe, especially after watching the video and hearing their stories.

Malcolm was of great support in those moments. He showed it in his usual style, of course.

"Can I have your autograph, Mr. TV star?"

"I was on TV plenty of times before this," Samson pointed out.

"Yeah, but that was for boring books. This is the scandal of the century."

Samson rolled his eyes.

"Joking aside, I'm proud of you, man."

"Thank you."

Despite all of the good, one thing remained a thorn in Samson's side. During all the madness and media hype, one person did not reach out in any way.

Teresa. It infuriated him that she'd ignored everything. And he wasn't the type of person to call her first and rub her nose in the truth.

Why isn't she calling?

Her parents had called him, for crying out loud, saying how sorry they were he had to go through everything. But there was complete radio silence from her.

Luckily, Samson didn't have the time or energy to sit around wondering what her problem was or how it made him feel, apart from mildly annoyed. That woman had already broken his heart too many times in the past, and he wouldn't let her do it again.

A couple of days had passed since the video went viral, and it didn't look like things were going to slow down any time soon. The public demanded justice, as did they. It was kind of beautiful seeing so many people and strangers come together to fight for them.

Samson continued to work on his book, or at least he tried to. He felt lighter these days, which provided him with a lot of vigor and inspiration, but he lacked time to get the words out. It didn't help that his phone rang every time he sat down to write. It was either one of the guys, Melissa, or someone from the press.

As if on cue, his phone started ringing, and Samson groaned.

He felt like he should relocate to a deserted island until he finished his book. He had a deadline to meet.

He had received a call from his publishing house, and his editor reassured him that he didn't have to meet the deadline while dealing with such turbulent times. Those were his precise words. Samson was fascinated with how creative people got when trying not to say certain words like "rape" and "torture."

The writer in him appreciated the effort. However, although they were full of understanding, Samson decided to stick to the original agreement and do his job.

He was relieved to see that this time around, Melissa was calling him.

"Hello?" he answered.

"I have news," she said excitedly, skipping a more formal greeting.

"What is it?" he prompted.

"The DA is willing to talk with us again."

Those were the words he'd been waiting to hear from the start, so it was good he was already sitting down.

"Samson, did you hear me?" she asked after a moment.

"I heard you. He wants to talk. When?"

"As soon as possible."

Well, it was about fucking time.

CHAPTER 38

A few days later, Samson met with Melissa and together, they went to DA Manningham's office to give a formal statement.

Leaving the house that morning wasn't easy. Somehow, the press had learned where he was staying and were staking out the house. He was shocked by their behavior. He wasn't a celebrity, so that kind of hysteria made no sense. They'd already heard his story. How many more times could he repeat it before they moved on to the next sensation? Samson was afraid he would find out.

Either way, with a little help from his best friend, Samson managed to slip into Melissa's car.

"Busy morning?" she commented as they drove away.

Samson shook his head. "This is getting ridiculous. I'm not a rockstar."

"You are to those who were sexually abused," Melissa pointed out.

And that made him pause.

Although this had started so he could get some closure and heal himself, it had turned into so much more. Samson never wanted to be a crusader, but many saw him as one. That was a strange role to be in. It came with a lot of responsibility, and he wasn't sure he was up for it. Still, it wasn't like he had much choice. The whole world was looking to him, and the rest of the guys, waiting to see how this would play out. He had no choice but to push forward.

"I don't understand why they have to camp in front of my home," he said stubbornly.

To make matters worse it, wasn't even *his* home. Although Anita and Malcolm were very supportive, he knew this was disrupting their lives as well.

"The macabre sells," Melissa replied.

Samson sighed. "Don't I know it."

If that wasn't the case, then none of his books would be a success. Speaking of his books, thanks to all the madness, the sales of his novels had skyrocketed, which he found confusing. Not that he was opposed to having more money. His bank accounts were depleted, so he wasn't complaining. It was just strange that people had started buying his books because he was on the news.

"Here we are, ready?" Melissa announced.

"Ready," Samson said because he had no other choice.

He braced himself and entered the justice department.

The DA looked in an even worse mood than the last time Samson saw him. He obviously resented having to deal with this.

Well, tough shit.

"I really wish you hadn't done that," the DA commented as they stepped into his office.

There was no need to elaborate: Samson knew he meant the video they'd posted.

"We felt like we didn't have any other choice," Samson replied honestly.

"You could have come to me."

"And you would have done what?" Samson challenged.

He was sure the other man would do everything in his power to prevent them from stepping forward if they'd brought him the video. Samson had noted before how the DA didn't want to step on Donald Bellwether's toes.

Now he had no choice, and Samson didn't give a shit if he didn't like it. It was his job, and thanks to the online video, people were demanding that he do something besides build his political career for a change.

"Let's begin, shall we?" Mr. Manningham said instead of continuing this discussion.

The man was smart, and he knew when he could win and when he could not.

Samson and Melissa came so he could give a formal statement. The six men came separately because the crimes committed against them were of such delicate nature. Eric had already provided the DA office with all the evidence they'd collected, handing over the unedited original footage.

It was hard to give a detailed account of those events, partly because he still wasn't comfortable speaking about it, and partly because his memory was flaky. There were serious gaps in his memory due to the drugs they'd forced him to take. While he was grateful that he didn't know the full extent of the torment he'd endured, it also made his time in the DA's office more agonizing. DA Manningham asked him to repeat his story many times and asked a lot of personal questions. At times, Samson felt he was intentionally looking for cracks in his story to prove they'd made everything up.

That wasn't the case so Samson did his best to remain calm and answer all of the questions to the best of his ability. In the end, the DA declared he had everything he needed.

Samson spent all day in that stinking office, but Melissa made this experience a little better than it would have been if he'd had some other lawyer.

Melissa was present when each man gave his statements too, and she told Samson in confidence that Brian's interview was the most difficult.

Samson wasn't surprised.

"Did he punch the bastard?" he asked.

If not, Eric owed him twenty bucks.

"He didn't, but it was close."

"Want me to talk to him?" he offered.

"I think that would help."

In the following week, they all gave their statements, and they weren't the only ones the DA wanted to see. Samson heard that even his shrink – the one from the hospital – came to answer some questions.

Samson knew his whole life would be on display, but that didn't make being under so much scrutiny any easier. It didn't seem fair to him that they were the ones jumping through all the hoops when Lissa and Candi were the ones who'd committed the crimes. The men were the survivors, didn't that earn some respect? Not yet, at least. Not until Lissa's and Candi's guilt was proven.

After Samson did his part, they waited to see the DA's next move. Would he issue an arrest warrant for the sisters? The suspense was killing them, and it was hard not to stress over all the decisions he'd made in life.

While he was trying to force himself to write, his phone rang. It was Tom.

"Turn on the news. Now," he said excitedly.

"Hold on," Samson replied, jumping to his feet. He ran into Malcolm's house since he didn't own a TV.

His best friend was watching a game and yelling at the referees when Samson grabbed the remote from him and changed the channel.

Malcolm was about to protest when Samson's expression stopped him, and he understood that something was happening.

Sure enough, DA Manningham was about to start a press conference. Samson could feel his heart start to beat a little bit faster. The cameras showed the DA standing in a corner talking with a few of his associates. Suddenly, he turned and walked toward a small podium. He adjusted his microphone and began.

"I will make a brief statement today, and there will be no Q&A at this time," he began formally.

"First of all, I want to inform the public that I've heard your complaints loud and clear, and I can assure you that this office is doing everything in its power to protect its citizens like it always has, and always will."

Come on, come on. Get to the good part.

"Regarding the cases of Eric Stokes, Sam Weatherby, Samson Chase, Carl Valmont, Brian Grant, and Tom Sorkin, I've issued a warrant for the arrests of Candi Marie Bellwether and her sister, Lissa Marie Bellwether. The DA's office has decided to press charges against the Bellwethers on several counts. I promise you that they will be tried for all crimes committed."

He shuffled some papers before proceeding. "I know this is a trying time for our nation, but I am here to guarantee you that this office is here to keep you safe and protected. Always."

And then, after another dramatic pause, "Thank you, that will be all." With that, DA Manningham stepped away from the podium.

The room exploded with activity and noise, with news reporters shouting questions. He never looked back. The live feed was cut, and a couple of reporters with some analysts in a studio talked about what just happened.

Samson tried to process everything as he sat next to Malcolm.

"So, he grew some balls," Malcolm commented.

"Did you see it?" Tom asked, startling Samson.

While watching the press conference, Samson had forgotten his friend was still on the phone.

"Yeah."

"He's going to arrest them."

"Yeah." Samson knew he was repeating himself, but he was stunned and needed a moment to process this. He wanted to savor this moment and the feelings that came with it.

They were close to victory now.

"Let me call you later."

"Sure," Tom said before hanging up.

"So, when do you think the actual arrest will happen?" Malcolm asked.

"I have no idea."

They didn't have to wait long to learn the answer. The media stations televised the girls' arrest during a full media circus in front of the Bellwether mansion. The media had already come up with a cute nickname for them, the Bellwether Party Girls, which Samson found disgusting.

After the guys' little visit to their house, Lissa and Candi fled to Daddy's. Samson expected as much. Not that it did them any good.

The police officers gained access to the home and came back out shortly after with Lissa and Candi in handcuffs. They struggled the whole way, especially Candi, and the officers had to drag them to the patrol car. Along the way, reporters tried to get their comments on this turn of events.

Samson noted how no one else from the house came out with them. No family members, and no lawyers, either.

Interesting.

Lissa cried, struggled, and begged to go back home, but Candi was livid.

"What are you looking at?" she screamed at one reporter who got too close.

"How do you respond to the claims you raped multiple men?"

"Candi! Over here! Did you do it?"

The reporters were relentless.

"What did your father say?"

Candi looked back toward the house. "Damn you, Donald!" she shouted, enraged. "Damn you! I hate you! Do you hear me?"

"I want to go home. Please, let me go home," Lissa sobbed.

"Do you have anything to say to the men who accused you?"

"I hope their limp dicks fall off," Candi spat at the camera.

And with that, they were pushed inside the police car and driven away.

Sometime later, their arrival at the police station was also televised.

It was as though they were the most notorious criminals in the city, and they behaved in kind. Lissa wailed and Candi threatened. Samson tuned out after that. He'd heard enough.

He wasn't the only one who'd noticed their father's absence during this scandal, and it remained that way.

Samson was prepared for a nasty battle with the father of those demons, but as it turns out, Donald decided to get himself out of the game. The father of the Bellwether Party Girls refused to make a statement. A member of his PR team sent a press release in which he stated there would be no comments on this case from the Bellwether family.

Samson felt like pinching himself to make sure this was all happening and wasn't just a figment of his imagination. It felt surreal to him. The girls had been arrested, and Samson couldn't wait for his day in court. He wanted to be a nail in their coffins.

"This is all happening thanks to you," Malcolm complimented.

Samson nodded. He didn't feel that way. It was a group effort, and none of this would be possible if one attorney hadn't taken him seriously. In his mind, Melissa was the driving force behind everything and for that, he would always be grateful.

Melissa called at some point to tell him that Donald Bellwether's attorney had visited DA Manningham.

"What did he say?" Samson demanded.

"They spoke behind closed doors."

"But?"

"I heard he was reassured that Donald would fully cooperate with the authorities. He denied any involvement in his daughters' crimes."

"Wow."

"Also, he promised that Donald wouldn't assist them in any way. They are all alone in this."

Just as I predicted. "He washed his hands of them."

"Seems that way," Melissa remained a bit skeptical. "I still feel like we should celebrate."

Samson agreed. He rang the other guys, and they met for dinner. They found an obscure place, a small family restaurant, and made reservations under a false name so the media wouldn't bother them.

"We did it," Tom said, excited.

"This is just the beginning," Melissa cautioned.

"But it feels so fucking good. I wanted to record the moment that they were hauled out in handcuffs," Brian said in his usual manner. In this case, Samson had to agree, so he raised his glass.

"To the battles still ahead of us, and to the ones we've already won," Samson made a toast, and they raised their glasses to that.

CHAPTER 39

The video they unleashed on the world had such a massive impact that Samson could only stare in wonder. Not only had the DA decided to get involved, which led to the girls getting arrested, but a lot of other men and women came forward to share that they had been abused by the sisters as well. As it turned out, their path to sociopathic rape and torture was a long one. However, one thing remained the same throughout the years: No matter where they were no matter what they did, they destroyed everything in their wake.

Due to their colorful past, and the fact that many people now felt courageous enough to step forward and speak their truth after watching the video, the DA had plenty of evidence against them in addition to all of the valuables they'd stolen and the original videos the police had collected from their home.

The detectives even tracked down a guy who'd done the background checks for them, and he sang like a canary, fearing he would face jail time. It went without saying that the guys had enough evidence for their civil suit as well.

Samson heard some others had planned to sue the sisters, too. He didn't pay it much mind. In all this madness, he needed to stay focused.

Samson was grateful that he'd listened to reason when he hit rock bottom. He was grateful he hadn't resorted to violence when thoughts of revenge consumed him because this turned out better than he could have imagined. He appreciated everything other people were doing for him. If it weren't for the strangers who demanded justice for him and the other five men, none of this would have been possible.

He was thankful for so many things.

At the same time, he was no saint. And it felt good seeing the media shred the Bellwether family and crucify Lissa and Candi.

The girls didn't fare any better in court. A public defender was appointed to their case after their father refused to hire an attorney. Samson felt sorry for the poor schmuck who had to defend them.

Donald Bellwether completely cut them off, but many remained disappointed by his behavior. Samson knew he would do the same, but it still came as a shock. Donald didn't act like a parent at all. He almost treated it like he was getting rid of a pair of undesirable employees.

He remained in hiding and refused to comment on anything. Marissa did the same, and the public did not respond kindly to that. They felt he should offer an apology for everything his daughters had done. It got so bad for them that Samson saw in the news that Donald and Marissa had fled the country.

They retreated to a private island and lived there for the duration of the trial. Samson couldn't find it in himself to pity the guy. In a way, he'd created those monsters. A part of Samson wished Donald was the one on trial as well. Some people should go to jail for being bad parents.

Seeking justice was an exhausting endeavor, as Samson learned. The criminal and the civil cases were happening simultaneously, which meant Samson was always in court. He made a point to attend the criminal case every time, and he was not the only one. All the other men came as well, and they were of tremendous support to one another during their testimonies.

Although the deck was stacked against them, the Bellwether Party Girls didn't go down without a fight.

Lissa had fits of hysteria and would start crying uncontrollably each time she heard something she didn't like. Candi was even worse. She used the public's curiosity and agreed to an exclusive interview. Samson was sure at least half of the city watched when it was aired.

At first, he didn't want to watch it, knowing it wouldn't bring him anything good, but he caved to the pressure at the last instant.

Candi didn't disappoint. She turned everything around, portraying her sister and herself as the ultimate victims. She also tried to cry, which made Samson sick to his stomach. She was an amazing actress.

There was one problem with that though. Because everything around them was unraveling, Candi changed her story so many times throughout the trial that Samson wasn't sure even she knew what was real anymore. But that kind of unraveling showed him that she was more than aware of the situation, she and her sister were in.

"That was entertaining as fuck. Next time I'll make popcorn," Brian texted him after Candi's interview aired.

Brian had turned a one-eighty. Everything that was happening had a strange, therapeutic effect on him, and Samson was confident the other man would pull through, just like the rest of them.

As for Candi, at first, she simply denied everything, then she claimed it was all a conspiracy. "The six of them are trying to shake Daddy for some money," were her exact words.

However, when the reporter reminded her how their father had disowned them, Candi's demeanor changed.

"He did that for us," she snapped.

Naturally, the reporter prompted for more information.

"He hoped that would stop these vicious men from telling all these lies about me and Lissa."

It was painfully obvious, at least to Samson, how much she struggled to put the pieces together into a plausible story.

When more information came to light, Candi once again changed her tune. She admitted she knew them all quite intimately. All the same, she kept insisting that whatever happened between them happened because all parties wanted it to.

"Are you saying everything was consensual?"

"Of course," she insisted, looking outraged that someone would suggest otherwise. She stuck to that story during the trials as well.

Unlike her sister, Lissa did not do any interviews. In court, she mostly cried. And she was not put on the stand.

Samson almost felt sorry for her. *Almost.* It was hard to feel sorry for a person who'd done all those heinous things and laughed. The only reason she was acting this now was that she'd gotten caught. There was not a speck of remorse in her, only self-pity.

While Lissa cried and felt sorry for herself, and mourned the fact the party was over, Candi raised hell. She was especially obnoxious during his testimony.

At some point, she jumped on her feet and started shouting, "Stop lying! Tell them the truth. It was all consensual. Stop punishing me for not loving you back!"

Since she wouldn't stop no matter how many times the judge warned her, the guards had to take her away. The trial resumed only after her lawyer managed to calm her. She did the same to the rest of the guys as well.

It was also no surprise she demanded to be put on the stand to "set the record straight."

Samson was, of course, in the courtroom during her testimony. And at times, it was very hard to remain calm. She went into painful detail trying to convey how everything they did was pure fun, and how they all wanted to be treated in that way.

"We all have our kinks, you know. Did we go overboard at times?" she asked rhetorically. "Maybe, but none of them ever told us to stop."

A "Ha!" reverberated through the courtroom. It was Brian of course, and the judge stared him down, so he immediately apologized for interrupting.

After such an intro, she spoke of each man individually.

"Honestly, I had no idea he was married," she said when her lawyer asked her about Samson. "But to be perfectly fair, Lissa and I didn't ask, either. We're two single girls who like to party. That shouldn't be a crime."

She droned on and on, and each word brought him new, fresh, anguish, but he endured. They all did.

The group was excited when it was the DA's turn to cross-examine her after a lunch break. Samson felt pure joy watching him do his thing, although he still thought the man was a douchebag. Even so, the man came prepared and asked her good questions without going to the most obvious first.

"You never noticed there were wedding pictures on the walls? A band around his finger?" he asked in a calm, professional manner.

"Lissa and I weren't there to look at his interior design, if you know what I mean. And he wore no wedding ring when we met him."

"What a liar," Tom grumbled.

"Did you expect her to tell the truth?" Eric countered.

The judge hushed the gallery.

Candi did her best to wiggle her way out of DA's questions, but he was meticulous and knew how to set traps.

And then, he went for the jugular, asking if she'd ever drugged any of them. Had she raped them? Candi lied without missing a beat.

"No, I would *never* do something like that. I would *never* harm another human being."

She can say that because she doesn't consider us humans, simply playthings.

"I'm innocent."

"Please answer only the questions I ask," Mr. Manningham countered.

When he told her there was evidence that they'd paid a specialist, Mr. Martin, to find men for them of a certain type and do thorough background checks, she started crying.

"Those are lies."

"You deny you made the last payment to Mr. Martin with a ring you took from Mr. Valmont?" he challenged.

"Of course I deny it."

Luckily, not one juror fell for her act. After weeks and weeks of stressful trials and one quick deliberation, they had their verdict.

The men were on pins and needles as they waited for one of the jurors to read the verdict.

"It's going to be guilty; I know it," Brian mumbled.

The judge called for order. The foreperson had a lot of ground to cover since the sisters were accused of several things, but everything boiled down to one word.

Guilty.

On the multiple accounts of trespassing, kidnapping, sexual assault, blackmail, vandalism, and theft, the jury found them guilty.

The men jumped to their feet and started cheering. The judge had to call for order again as the Bellwether sisters received their sentences.

Lissa was crying, of course, and Candi tried to run away.

"This isn't fair. We didn't do anything wrong!" she stuck to her story. And then she spotted Samson, who was grinning like this was the best day of his life.

Instantly, she morphed into Candi he knew and hated. "This is all your fault!" she screeched, running toward him.

The officers caught her easily before she reached him. Her days of torturing innocent people were over.

Good riddance.

"No! Let go of me!" She struggled.

As she was dragged from the courthouse, she threatened everyone. She cursed Samson, promised she would destroy him for this, and even threatened she would kill the judge.

"Someone has completely lost her mind," Brian said gleefully.

In the end, Candi was sentenced to thirty years in prison while Lissa received twenty-five. Samson was satisfied with that.

"They'll still be pretty young when they get out of jail," Tom pointed out.

"So what? The whole world will be watching them," Eric replied.

Meaning, good luck doing anything more illegal than jaywalking.

Besides, Samson planned to be at every one of their parole hearings. He would stay diligent and make sure they stayed in prison for their full sentence.

"I can't believe we won," Carl said, voicing what was on everyone's mind.

"We did it," Brian sounded amazed, too.

"It feels good," Sam observed.

Samson agreed. It made him feel much lighter.

After the trial ended, the six of them and Melissa left the courthouse as an army of reporters swarmed around them. They demanded to know how they felt after the trial. Were they pleased with the sentencing?

Samson looked at the group. This was such a monumental day, he knew he would remember it forever. He was overwhelmed but in a good way. Also, as he noted before, he felt like a huge weight was lifted from his shoulders. Lissa and Candi were sent to prison, and they would stay there for a long time. Also, Samson's name was cleared. He was no longer a dirty philanderer. He was a survivor of a sexual assault.

I am a survivor. And I won.

He just didn't feel like talking about all that right now. He nudged Melissa forward, so she could give a statement in their stead. She deserved her day in the spotlight. She was as responsible for this victory as the rest of them.

The civil case against the Bellwether sisters ended in much the same manner, with the judge ordering them to pay substantial damages to each of the plaintiffs. Even before that, Samson had decided to give his share to charity. Keeping the money would make him feel dirty. So, with Melissa's help, he found a few causes he liked and wrote them checks. It felt good, and it was the right thing to do.

They went to lunch after everything wrapped up, with everyone talking about what they would do next.

Brian and Tom were going to try to repair their marriages, while others planned to move on and starting fresh in a new town. Carl was going on a trip around the world.

Samson had no idea what he wanted. He knew he could never return to what he had, and somehow, that was all right with him. As long as he had his work, he knew he would be just fine.

That was the last time the six of them were together, and that was all right, too.

skin. His name was cleared, and everyone knew the truth, and that was freeing.

Even the insurance policy kicked in after it was proven the Bellwether sisters had vandalized his home, so he got some of the money back that he'd spent on house repairs.

Now that he thought of it, he should decide what to do with the house. He wasn't using it, nor did he ever plan to again. *Should I sell it and split the money with Teresa?*

A part of him didn't want the hassle, so maybe his ex should get it. Samson wasn't hurting for money at the moment, so maybe he could afford this act of generosity.

Putting all those unexpected thoughts to the side, Samson decided it was time to return to work. He loved his new book and the new characters and was impatient to discover how would it all end. *With tears, blood, and death. The question is, whose?*

The doorbell interrupted his thoughts. *What's with all these people today?* He needed to work, and the universe wouldn't allow it.

Samson had recently signed a three-book deal and was pretty pumped about it. So much so that he contemplated doing a trilogy.

Opening the door, Samson recoiled. "Teresa?" he greeted, although it more sounded like a question. He hadn't expect to see her.

"Hello, Samson. Can we talk?"

He let her come in.

This was the first time he'd seen her in forever. Actually, this was the first time he'd seen her since that day at the house. She hadn't contacted him during the trial, not even when he won. No phone calls or no texts.

Teresa looked mostly the same, although her hair was much shorter now.

She looked around, checking out his new condo before settling her gaze on him. "You must be pretty surprised to see me," she observed.

"Yes," he replied simply. He couldn't understand what prompted something like this. It appeared quite random.

"Well, I wanted to tell you something, and didn't feel like doing it over the phone."

Is she getting married? He banished that immediately. "Okay ..."

She sighed before starting. "As you can imagine, everything that happened was very difficult for me, and I needed time to deal with it all, but I'm finally ready to forgive you."

Samson's mouth fell open. "Forgive me?"

"Yes."

What in the actual fuck?

"I mean, no one can blame me for acting the way I did," she said as she began to defend herself. "Finding you like that ..." she paused, making a disgusted expression. "And considering all your other issues, and dealing with your PTSD, it was understandable that I couldn't believe your story. But now, after some soul-searching, I'm ready to move past all that misfortune and give us another chance."

Samson felt like sitting down but remained standing. He couldn't decide which part of her little speech troubled him the most. All of it was scandalous.

First of all, he hadn't done anything wrong, so her forgiving him was a joke. She needed time? What about him? He was the one who was tortured and put to shame. And it was *his* fault that she couldn't trust him? That amazed him the most.

"The trial ended six months ago," he said conversationally.

"I know," she replied, missing his point.

"Where have you been? Why didn't you call?" She never even asked how he was doing. She'd failed to inquire even now, and that was a thing any normal human would do, especially if they cared about someone.

"I needed time to let it settle in. I needed time to erase those images of you with them from my mind."

Samson couldn't take it anymore. "You needed time? I was the one going through all that hell, not you." Where was she when he needed her the most?

Had she always been this selfish? If so, why hadn't he noticed it

CHAPTER 1

"Benny! Dinner," Carrie called out, trying hard not to cry. It was just one of those days that everything came crashing down.

"Coming, Mom!" her son yelled from his room.

He always had his head stuck in a book or was too focused on a game he invented to remember even the simplest of things like eating or cleaning his room. Considering how kids his age played video games all the time, Carrie considered his little quirks a blessing.

She quickly wiped away her tears, not even aware she'd shed them, as she set the table for the two of them. They'd been alone for a long time, and she didn't know how much longer she could go on like this. She was at the end of her rope, both physically and mentally.

It was a miracle that the electric company hadn't cut their power since she had to spend all the money she earned, and then some, on the rent for their tiny apartment. It was a shoebox, really, with one small bedroom, one bathroom, and a living room that was also a kitchen, but it was the best she could afford at the moment.

Forget the electricity, she thought. She had no idea what they were going to eat until her next paycheck. Although she had two jobs and

Benny received a small amount of Social Security, they were struggling. There was never enough money no matter how much she tried to save on everything.

Maybe we should move someplace else, she thought. Los Angeles was by no means a cheap place to reside.

Benny ran the short distance from his room to the table and sat down, clearly in high spirits.

"What have you been doing?" she asked.

"Homework."

Carrie smiled despite herself. She had a wonderful, special kid. Her son was her biggest joy. Her only joy at the moment.

"Do you want one or two slices of bread?"

"One, please."

When her husband died and they were forced to leave their home on the base at Fort Carson, Colorado, Carrie thought it was best to move someplace else. Start fresh and away from all the bad memories and heartache. In the end, instead of taking the map and picking a place at random, she simply returned to her hometown, to L.A., because despite everything, it was familiar to her and safe.

But not easy.

She was wrong, thinking her life would be better in any way simply because she decided to return home. Her parents didn't want anything to do with her—or their grandson, for that matter—so she struggled to make ends meet on her own. Even after all this time, they held a grudge against her and hung up the phone when she tried to speak with them.

They had never forgiven her for running off after high school to marry Marco. Her mother forbade her from seeing him, but Carrie hadn't listened. Her father had big plans for her and wanted her to become a lawyer, so her getting knocked up and marrying some soldier really screwed that up for him.

She screwed herself up as well, but that was a different matter altogether.

Fuck them. If they couldn't put their feelings aside to think about hers, they didn't deserve to be called parents in the first place. There was nothing she wouldn't do for her Benny, so she couldn't under-stand parents who could so easily turn their backs on their flesh and blood. Their pride was bigger than their love, plain and simple.

Fuck them.

If Carrie made mistakes in her life, that was her prerogative. It was *her* life, after all. Parents' expectations be damned.

Besides, no matter if they were right regarding Marco, no matter how disappointing her short marriage had turned out to be on so many different levels, she never regretted a second of it because it gave her Benny. She would never trade her son for anything. Not for all the money in the world, not for fame, and certainly not for her parents' approval.

He was the reason she'd managed to go on, continuing to fight when everything around her, her whole life, fell apart. Twice.

"Mom?"

"Hmm?"

"Do we have some more orange juice?"

Carrie nodded, stood up, and opened the fridge to get it. In truth, she could have simply reached for the fridge door while sitting down, but she liked the exercise.

Trying to banish her troubled thoughts and failing miserably, she poured him a glass then threw the container in the trash. Another item added to the grocery list.

She sat down and continued to eat, but stopped shortly after when Benny looked at her oddly.

"What is it, buddy?" she asked in concern.

"There's not enough juice for you as well," he stated.

"That's OK."

"You can have half of mine." He offered her the glass.

Carrie suppressed a sob. He was such a sweet kid. She was truly lucky. Although her mother called him a curse, he was nothing short of a miracle to Carrie.

"Thank you, but I don't feel like drinking orange juice."

He looked at her as though he couldn't fathom someone refusing orange juice but shrugged it off and continued eating. As he ate, he chatted about all the interesting things he learned about time while reading his lessons in advance.

Carrie was thinking of time as well.

What are we going to do? They were running out of time because they had almost completely run out of money. It became more than apparent that they could not continue living like this. *What if we end up on the street? No.* Carrie would figure something out. She had to.

Unfortunately, she lost all hope that she would get death benefits from her husband. *The death benefit* was a rather morbid coining, as though there could ever be any benefit from death. Benny had lost his father, for crying out loud, and no amount of money could ever compensate for that. Sadly, the Army was trying to stiff them for that as well.

Marco had been an Explosives Ordnance Disposal Technician, which was still considered one of the most dangerous jobs there were, and he died in Afghanistan in an explosion.

All she could gather in all this time since the Army could be pretty tight-lipped about the details was that after a thorough investigation, they blamed him for trying to disarm a massive homemade improvised device despite his instructions to secure the perimeter then stand down. Two other people were also killed on that day.

Marco had always had problems with his ego, but Carrie believed with all her heart that he did what he did with the belief that he was doing the right thing. If he thought the people in the area were in danger, he would do everything in his power to defuse that device and save lives or die trying.

Of course, the Army didn't care about her opinion. So, after five long, exhausting years of deliberation over whether she should receive a death gratuity, they were still no closer to a decision no matter how many letters she sent to the command. There was a lot of military red tape involved, and she was seriously losing hope.

Everything was so fucked up.

The military had completely abandoned her and Benny, kicked them out of their home, and didn't want to pay for them to survive in any way. Her parents had practically disowned her and ignored the existence of her son because that didn't fit into their plans for her. And because Marco had been so young, the amount of Social Security Benny received was barely enough to cover the water bill. And yet none of that mattered.

Carrie would continue fighting and finding ways to provide for her son because she didn't have a choice. She had a kid she had to take care of, to make sure he was healthy and happy, so it didn't matter how miserable or tired she was.

Carrie would make sure he had a better life than she had. She had lacked nothing material in her childhood and still felt like she was missing the most important thing, love. No wonder she ran away with the first person who said he loved her.

Perhaps it was a bit ironic that she was this jaded considering she was only twenty-six, but after everything she'd been through, it was hard not to be.

"Mom?"

Her son's voice snapped her from her reverie. "Yes?"

"What are you thinking about? You look so sad."

Ah, yes. She had to remember her son was too perceptive for his age.

"About work and how I don't want to go."

That wasn't technically a lie. She hated leaving him alone to work a night shift. Benny loved to snuggle with her, and that was her favorite part of the day as well, reading together before falling asleep. Not to mention she was constantly worried something might happen to him while she was away.

What if there's a fire? Of course, it was a stretch, but electrical fires happened all the time, especially in an old building like this one. *There can't be an electrical fire if you don't have electricity.*

"Can we read tonight?" he asked her.

Carrie checked the time before replying. "Yes, for about half an hour, and then I have to go to work."

If the piece-of-shit car will start. If not, she was fucked.

"OK," he replied glumly.

Carrie understood why. They couldn't finish their book tonight, and he was already looking forward to starting another. Benny was such a bookworm, it was endearing. He could read on his own just fine, but he still preferred her reading to him like when he was a baby. It was a ritual they both enjoyed.

It broke her heart leaving him alone so often, but they needed the money, and the diner she worked at paid better for the night shift. She couldn't afford a babysitter.

Besides, she didn't trust some stranger staying over with her son. There were a lot of psychos in this world. Better to be alone, even if she missed him terribly. Benny was a reasonable, responsible kid. She could trust him not to do anything dangerous while she was away.

She couldn't decide if it was a good or a bad thing that he was forced to grow up a bit too soon. Realizing this line of thought was dangerous since she could once again question whether she was a good or a bad mother, she stopped.

After dinner, Benny took her phone to watch cartoons while Carrie cleaned up.

She just about finished, and Benny was looking at her expectantly to announce that it was reading time when her phone rang. It was an unknown number. Frowning, Carrie answered.

CHAPTER 2

"Hello?" Carrie answered a bit timidly, since the last time she answered an unknown number, she was informed that her husband was killed in combat. That was not a fun conversation.

"Hello, am I speaking with Carrie Pace?" a pleasant female voice inquired in return, which somewhat put Carrie at ease.

"Yes, this is Carrie," she confirmed. "And you are?"

"My name is Maggie Courtland, and I represent a client who would like to remain anonymous for the moment but who wants to hire you as a surrogate mother," she declared.

Carrie had to sit down. "What?" she mumbled. None of what this woman said made sense. A *surrogate?*

"Are you or are you not the Mrs. Pace who registered at The Future Clinic as an egg and surrogate donor?"

Then it dawned on her.

Benny looked at her with interest, so she reconsidered her position and decided to step outside. For some reason, she felt like her boy didn't need to hear the rest of this conversation.

"Yes, I registered as a donor," Carrie confirmed.

A few years ago, her friend Veronica convinced her to do that to earn some extra cash, yet nothing came of it. *Until now,* she corrected herself.

"Great, because my client is very interested in hiring you. So, what I need to know now is, are you still available?"

"For what?" Carrie asked as though she'd lost all her sense. She was acting like an idiot, but it couldn't be helped. This conversation was very confusing, shocking, to say the least.

"For surrogacy, of course," the other woman replied patiently.

Am I available? Carrie asked herself. She'd been desperate when she went to that clinic. *And you aren't desperate now?*

Looking around, she didn't have to think long to reply. "Well, I am available and interested in meeting your client," she hedged.

She couldn't say yes straight away. Even back then, she'd made a clear decision that she would only help if she liked a couple. Carrie wouldn't carry someone's else child just for the money. She would have to meet the future parents and see if they were good people before deciding to help them.

For the right fee, of course. Money wasn't the only major motivator, but it was the biggest one. Carrie would have to dedicate herself, her body, to someone else for almost a year, and for that, she had to be compensated fairly. She and Benny needed the money.

"I am glad to hear that. Now, tell me, if the meeting goes well and you accept the offer, would you be willing to relocate until the child is born?"

"Relocate?" Carrie repeated like a parrot.

"My client would like the surrogate mother to live on the estate with the family—in a separate guesthouse, of course," she added.

"I have a child," Carrie countered. There was no way she would abandon her child, no matter the money.

"I know. I read your file, and that is not a problem. He is welcome to come as well."

"Then, I suppose I wouldn't have a problem with relocating," Carrie replied honestly. So long as she and Benny were together, they could live at the North Pole, for all she cared. Besides, the guesthouse sounded much better, much cleaner, than the apartment they currently lived in.

"Do you suffer from any serious medical conditions? Do you have high blood pressure, diabetes, suffer from migraines, epilepsy, or things like that?"

"Um, no."

"Did you have any type of cancer, go through chemotherapy?"

"No."

"Do you have a history of addiction?"

"No."

The questions asked by this intermediary were a bit invasive, but Carrie understood why the other woman had to ask. If she were picking some woman to carry her child, she would make sure to find the best candidate as well.

"You said you have a child."

"Yes, Benjamin."

"Is he your only child?"

Carrie understood the meaning. "Yes, he is, and I have never had an abortion or a miscarriage," she added, presupposing the next question.

"Thank you for taking the time to answer all my questions. I truly appreciate it."

"No problem." Carrie wondered what would happen next, so she asked.

"Would you be willing to meet my client tomorrow, Mrs. Pace?"

Perhaps it was a bit silly, but Carrie was shocked to hear that. She'd never done something like this before, but all the same, it felt kind of sudden, as though things were moving too fast.

Some poor woman is dying to have a baby. Of course, she's impatient to find her surrogate, Carrie rationalized. But then she thought about the request.

"I have work tomorrow," she replied. Given her current circumstances, she really couldn't afford to miss a single shift.

"I see. My client is willing to offer you fifteen hundred dollars as an advance payment for this meeting alone. I hope that will compensate you for missing work," Maggie offered.

Carrie's eyes bulged. *Fifteen hundred?* That meant one month's rent.

"That is very generous of your client," Carrie said in return, still trying to grasp the fact that someone would pay simply to meet her.

"Well, there is something they would require in return."

Carrie shook her head, even though the other woman couldn't see her. She should have known there would be a catch. No such thing as a free meal, her mother used to say, but Carrie banished that though since she didn't like thinking of her mother in any context.

"What?" Carrie asked halfheartedly.

"My client is a rather famous person, and you would have to sign an NDA before the meeting."

"An NDA?" Carrie had heard of those but didn't know what it meant.

"A non-disclosure agreement. Just a precaution to prevent you from speaking about my client."

"Speaking to whom?"

"The press, for example."

"I see."

"My client values their privacy above all else, so it's essential to keep all this private business, well, private."

"That makes sense, and I agree, private should remain private."

Some things simply should not land on the front page of some paper to satisfy the curiosity of the masses.

Carrie wasn't stupid. She lived in L.A., for crying out loud. Everyone in this city was either an actor or a producer, a director, or a screenwriter. Or they'd like to be one of the above-mentioned.

Whoever this famous person was, if anyone learned about this whole surrogacy ordeal, it would be the sensation of the month. That kind of news would land on the front page of every tabloid in the city, if not the country, and Carrie could understand how something like that could be harmful. Some things should remain private, and that was that.

"So, what do you say? Can I arrange the meeting?" Maggie asked hopefully.

Carrie bit her lower lip thinking about it. Should she accept the meeting? It would be paid, after all. And the meeting didn't automatically mean she would have to go through with it. If she didn't like this person, she could walk away and simply forget about it.

And I would be fifteen hundred dollars richer. She had a lot of pending bills, and with the money offered, she could settle those *and* buy Benny a lot of orange juice.

Closing her eyes, she heard herself say, "I will meet with your client."

"Great, I'm really happy to hear that. I will send you a text with the details about the meeting."

"OK."

"Looking forward to meeting you in person, Mrs. Pace."

"You, too."

They disconnected.

What did I just do? Carrie asked herself, staring at her phone as though it could provide her with some answers. Returning inside, she was still in a daze. *I'm going to a meeting to see someone who would like to hire me to be a surrogate.* She couldn't wrap her head around that concept. Carrie didn't have a problem being pregnant, but the logistics revolving around it were eluding her.

Stop thinking about all that. The meeting hasn't even occurred yet, she thought, realizing she would cause herself an aneurysm thinking about all that. She would meet the person tomorrow and then decide whether she wanted to move forward. To prevent herself from going crazy, she would do this step by step.

"Mom?"

"Yeah?"

"Why were you speaking outside on the phone?"

"It was work stuff," she replied dismissively.

And then it occurred to her. Should she bring Benny to the meeting? So the client could see she was capable of having a strong and healthy child?

She immediately dismissed such a crazy notion. She was spiraling again, thinking of nonsense. Of course, she would go alone. She didn't want to insert Benny into this. She would tell her son all he needed to know if and when the time came. Once again, she was ten steps ahead of herself. Carrie hadn't accepted the job. *Yet.*

"Mom?"

"Hmm?"

"Will you read to me now?"

"Sure. Go get your book."

"Already have it." He waved it.

Carrie settled on the couch next to him.

"Where were we?"

He pointed.

Carrie read as though on autopilot, her thoughts miles away. She couldn't stop thinking about this mysterious client. Who was she? Or he? Why would the client need a surrogate in the first place? Was the problem medical or cosmetic? This was L.A., so all options were possible.

Carrie had heard of actresses who didn't want to get pregnant and ruin their figures, so they hired surrogates to carry babies instead. A famous designer who didn't have a partner at the time and wanted a child also hired a surrogate to carry it for him.

She was dying to discover who hid behind a middleman named Maggie Courtland. It had to be someone big if she was required to sign an NDA. In this town, the possibilities were endless.

After she carried Benny to bed—he'd fallen asleep on the couch— she put on her uniform, still pondering on the opportunity presented to her.

I should do it if the people are kind and the money is reasonable. She debated whether to call Veronica and see what she thought about all of this but ruled against it.

Carrie hadn't even met this mystery client yet, so there was no point in getting hopes up. Besides, thanks to the NDA, she wouldn't be able to say anything to Veronica in the first place.

Miraculously, her car started, and she was able to drive to work.

The shift was busy and never-ending, but thoughts about the meeting she was about to have constantly occupied her mind. The nice thing was that the clientele had tipped well, so she made enough to at least purchase a few groceries.

True to her word, Maggie Courtland sent her the address of the meeting and Carrie gulped. She'd never visited such a fancy place before.

Finishing her shift in the morning, Carrie came home just in time to send Benny off to school. She fixed him pancakes for breakfast, and he ran off to catch his bus as Carrie yelled after him to be careful.

She called in sick to her other job before she went to bed to crash. There were still a couple of hours before her meeting, and she hoped not to show up with dark circles under her eyes. Fat chance: Those bags had become a permanent fixture. Luckily, she had mad skills with concealer.

Such silly thoughts, and even all the ones about the mystery couple she was about to meet vanished from her head as she finally managed to fall asleep.

Buy The Perfect Surrogate on Amazon today!

ABOUT COLE BAXTER

Cole Baxter loves writing psychological suspense thrillers. It's all about that last reveal that he loves shocking readers with.

He grew up in New York, where there was crime was all around. He decided to turn that into something positive with his fiction.

His stories will have you reading through the night—they are very addictive!

Sign up for Cole's VIP Reader Club and find out about his latest releases, giveaways, and more. Click here!

For more information, be sure to check out the links below!
colebaxterauthor@gmail.com

ALSO BY COLE BAXTER

The Hollow Husband

The Patient

I Won't Let You Go

The Betrayal

The Perfect Surrogate

The Perfect Surrogate

The Perfect Suitor

What She Witnessed

Finding The Other Woman

Going Insane

Prime Suspect

Trust A Stranger

Did He Do It

Follow You

The Perfect Nanny

What Happened Last Night

Perfect Obsession

She's Missing

What She Forgot

Before She's Gone

Stolen Son

Detective Carrie Blake Series

Deadly Truth - Book 1

Deadly Justice - Book 2

Box Sets:

Psychological Thriller Box Set Volume 1

Psychological Thriller Box Set

Printed in Great Britain
by Amazon

36463277R00219